Krampus

Copyright ©2024 by Patti Petrone Miller

All rights reserved.

No part of this publication may be reproduced, distributed, or transmitted in any form or by any means, including photocopying, recording, or other electronic or mechanical methods, without the prior written permission of the publisher, except as permitted by U.S. copyright law.

The story, all names, characters, and incidents portrayed in this production are fictitious. No identification with actual persons (living or deceased), places, buildings, and products is intended or should be inferred.

Book Cover by Grady Earls, GHOST WRITER BOOK DESIGNS

Edition 1

Patti Petrone Miller

Authors Book List

Accidental Vows
A Krampus Christmas
Sin Takes A Holiday
Barking Up The Wrong Bakery, Thankgiving
Barking Up The Wrong Bakery, Christmas
Best Served Dead
Bewitching Charms
Christmas at Hollybrook Inn
Christmas on Peppermit Lane
Krampus
Hex and the City
Love in Stitches
Pies and Perps
Spectres and Souffles
Mamma Mia It's Murder
Once Upon A Christmas
The Fatman
The Frosted Felony
The Purr-fect Suspect
The Boogeyman
The Gingerdead Men
Vikings Enchantress
Welcome to Scarecrow Hollow
The Pendleton Witches
The Cabinet of Curiosities
Christmas In Pine Haven
Love in the Stacks
Once Upon A Christmas

For Tessa...I miss you every single day

Patti Petrone Miller

KRAMPUS

Winter Kingdoms Saga

Krampus

CHAPTER ONE

A bruise-colored twilight brooded over the Winterspine Mountains, painting the ragged peaks in charcoaled hues as if the world had taken a collective, fearful breath and dared not exhale. Snow piled high upon ancient pines that leaned in close, whispering conspiratorially with their heavy-laden boughs. Their needles, oddly reluctant to drop, seemed to listen for secrets carried by the wind—secrets that might explain why these mountains, once balanced by old holiday rites, now felt so eerily hushed. The air, bitter as crushed bone, carried no cheerful cries of festivity or even the familiar crack of distant axes felling winter wood; instead, it was taut and soundless, as if nature herself had stepped behind a thick veil, holding her breath in anticipation of something dreadful.

High above any human warmth, where the wind's shriek grew thin and mean, Krampus stood in the mouth of his cavern. The entrance was a dark wound carved into a cliff of ice-blackened rock, iced over in places so that it resembled a gnarled mouth rimed with frozen spittle. His chains rattled faintly at his hips as he shifted from hoof to hoof, the iron links singing their quiet, metallic note. In the half-light, he was a silhouette of horn and sinew, of bristled fur and ancient purpose, the stench of iron and pine sap clinging to him like a warning. He watched the world below with narrowed, feral eyes—amber irises brightening and dimming as clouds scudded across a faint and miserly moon.

He stood perfectly still, save for the subtle twitch of his tufted ears. Down there, past the slopes and the treelines, the villages usually offered a distant hum of life: lamplight glowing warm in the windows, muffled laughter drifting upwards on ribbons of rising heat, the faint ring of bells or the clatter of hooves on cobblestone streets. Tonight, he caught only the dull hush of places sealed tight against the cold and something intangible that replaced joy—fear, perhaps, or uncertainty. His breath steamed, and he could smell on the breeze not the rich aroma of roasted chestnuts or fir boughs and mulled wine but something stale, something like old parchment and distant rot, the hint of ruin seeping into the cracks of a centuries-old arrangement.

The old ways were simple once. The Fatman—his brother in spirit if not in flesh—brought gifts, kindness, and hope. Krampus balanced that scale with the threat of punishment, ensuring that not all children were lulled into complacent indulgence. It wasn't cruelty for cruelty's sake. It was necessary: without the counterweight of fear, the notion of "nice" grew soft and meaningless. He had often considered himself a grim necessity, not evil incarnate but a living cautionary tale. Yet now, as the midwinter darkness stretched longer than ever, he wondered if he had become obsolete, or worse—irrelevant.

In the valley below, three villages—Sleetwood, Tallfir, and Icegrove—huddled like shy animals beneath blankets of snow. Sleetwood, the largest of the three, normally twinkled with lanterns by this time of evening, as villagers shared stories, sipped spiced drinks, and exchanged small homemade trinkets. Tonight, it lay mostly dark, save for a few sparse glimmers that struggled to burn steadily against the encroaching gloom. Krampus strained his keen vision to pick out movement: a solitary figure with a lantern, trudging through the snow, leaving anxious footprints that ended at shuttered doors. He recognized the gait of Jarlan Forgerook, the village's chronicler, a lean scholar who often roamed late with ink-stained fingers and a satchel of parchment. Jarlan had always been curious, sometimes nervously so, about Krampus and The Fatman and the deep tapestry of lore surrounding them. Tonight, that curiosity no doubt had shifted to alarm. Rumors had reached even Krampus's ears, borne on the wind: children vanishing without explanation, footprints leading nowhere, muffled cries in the night that neither rose nor fell but simply stopped.

Not far from Jarlan's path lay the stout workshop of Helgrid Stonestream, the dwarven blacksmith who served more than one village with her careful craft. Normally, at this hour, Helgrid might be polishing sled runners or forging decorative ironwork for the holiday season. Instead, Krampus imagined her stooped over her anvil in silence, hammer in hand, forging something else entirely—something less festive and more desperate, like iron rods that might serve as weapons, or protective charms etched with old runes. He could almost taste her fear and determination in the air. Her grandfather once told tales of Krampus's winter rounds, praising the horned figure's role in keeping children honest and families vigilant. Yet that legacy now hung in question. Krampus had not claimed a single child this season—no need, for the mischief had been subdued. Or had it simply been overtaken by something far worse?

Near a ruined chapel—little more than crumbling masonry and hollow arches—Branwynn Spellshiver, the wandering hedge-witch, was likely busy. She gathered herbs that still sprouted beneath evergreen shrubs, lit small bundles of sage and juniper, and whispered half-forgotten incantations meant to keep malevolent forces at bay. A tall, slender figure with runic stitching on her robes, Branwynn knew how to listen to the mountains. Tonight, she would hear unsettling murmurs, echoes of an imbalance creeping through the old magic that once ensured a proper order to things. There were spells older than any hymn sung in The Fatman's workshops of cheer, older even than Krampus's first chain. Those spells hummed in the roots of the pines and the veins of the stone, and when something threatened the balance, they stirred restlessly.

Krampus inhaled deeply, letting the biting air scrape his throat. He'd expected, as always, to find the occasional naughty child sneaking into cellars, stealing pastries, or pushing smaller siblings face-first into snowbanks. Those trifling sins formed the tapestry of his existence. He appeared at the edges of hearthlight to rattle chains, leave bundles of birch rods, and at times—though rarely—carry off the truly wicked into the dark. It was less about cruelty than maintaining boundaries: children needed to know that their actions had consequences, that their choices shaped their fate. The Fatman's jollity encouraged goodness and generosity, but Krampus's vigilance ensured that kindness never became complacent. Without him, how many children would grow into selfish adults who took The Fatman's gifts for granted?

Yet this year, something about the hush unsettled him. The stillness was not the calm of a well-ordered winter's night. It felt more like the silence of a predator waiting in the shadows. There were no playful shrieks or even frightened gasps at the sight of monstrous horns in the moonlight. Instead, there was absence—a void where human mischief should have been. Disappearances of children. Vanishings. Rumors that evil had grown bold enough to stalk the villages without leaving the telltale signs of a wayward youngster gone astray. Even The Fatman's elven helpers, known for their silly songs and tinkling laughter, had grown quiet. He could almost sense their nervous muttering behind closed doors. Where once they might have journeyed into the mountains to deliver cheer, now they likely hesitated, uncertain what dark force had slipped its leash.

Krampus stepped forward, iron-shod hooves scraping loose stones from the cavern's lip. The sound echoed faintly. The world felt larger somehow, emptier. He swept his gaze across the deep valleys and stunted forests below. He tried to recall the last time he'd ventured down to the villages. It had been a year ago—last midwinter—just before The Fatman made his rounds. That time he left a few tokens of warning, perhaps even took one exceptionally cruel older child for a midnight lesson among the pines (the boy returned home in tears but wiser, gentler). Such minor interventions were common, expected. The villagers never thanked Krampus—his role was not meant to be thanked—but they understood the necessity of it. At least, they used to.

Now he wondered if he should descend again without having identified a target. He felt in his bones that this crisis was different, that it would not yield to a simple show of force. Something was tampering with the old order, with the unspoken contract between himself, The Fatman, and the mortal world that they served in their peculiar, mythic dance. Could it be that the children were not simply misbehaving or wandering into forbidden places, but being lured away by some entity that mocked their understanding of naughty and nice?

He closed his eyes, ears twitching, trying to hear beyond the wind. A faint murmur came to him—a memory of The Fatman's laughter, distant and muffled, as if carried from another age. His brother, though beloved by mortals, often took for granted the delicate equilibrium of their existence. The Fatman brought joy, yes, but joy untempered by caution was a shaky foundation. Krampus provided that caution. Both roles were needed. Was The Fatman aware of what was happening? Did he sense the shift in the currents of magic and fear?

Another gust of wind blew up the cliff face, carrying scents from below: a hint of old smoke from the Sleetwood chimneys, tangy pine resin oozing from a wounded tree trunk, and something metallic, like iron filings or blood. The smell made Krampus's nostrils flare. He imagined Helgrid in her forge, sparks leaping as she hammered desperately at something that might protect her people. He wondered if Jarlan had discovered any hint of what old legends might explain these vanishings. And Branwynn—she would be weaving charms, layering protective wards around the chapel's ruins, perhaps hoping the residual holiness or old druidic forces that once sanctified the ground would lend her strength.

A sense of urgency gripped him. Krampus knew that standing idle in his cavern, brooding, would achieve nothing. Yet he hesitated. The moment he stepped down into the world of mortals, he would admit to himself that he needed information, maybe even their help. Pride whispered that he ought to remain aloof. In centuries past, he never stooped to ask mortals for guidance. He was the silent enforcer, the winter's judge, feared and necessary. But centuries past were not this night. Times changed, even in the timeless hush of eternal snows.

He recalled snatches of old stories, half-remembered from when the mountains were younger. Tales of spirits that resented the midwinter accord between The Fatman and Krampus, spirits who believed that children should be devoured rather than disciplined, or that humans should remain ignorant and terrified. Could one of those ancient grumblers have awakened, sensing discord between the brothers? Perhaps the subtle rivalry and imbalance—Krampus's bitterness at being overshadowed, The Fatman's negligence in acknowledging Krampus's importance—had created a crack in the grand design. Through that crack, a vile presence might have slithered, coiling around the roots of pines and the foundation stones of village cottages, snatching children away for its own dark feast.

The thought provoked a rumble in his chest, a low growl that steamed the air. Krampus would not allow his role to be twisted and scapegoated. If children were missing, some villagers might suspect him, which would only deepen the chaos. He remembered a time, generations ago, when a frantic mother accused him of stealing her babe. He had had nothing to do with it—that child had merely wandered off after a red fox and returned unharmed by morning. Still, the accusation stung. Now, with multiple disappearances, even the less superstitious among them might point their trembling fingers at him. He would need to show himself not as the culprit, but as a protector—or at least as someone who cared about restoring the rightful order.

He let his gaze drift to the distant lights. In Sleetwood, Jarlan Forgerook moved again, lamp bobbing as he searched for clues. He might be examining footprints, or odd symbols scratched into doorframes. Jarlan kept records of everything: weather patterns, births and deaths, unusual sightings. If anyone knew what might be emerging from the shadows, it could be he. Krampus considered how best to approach the chronicler. He could appear at Jarlan's window, rattling a chain for attention, or leave a birch branch on his doorstep to signal a desire to communicate. The idea of talking directly to a mortal felt strange, almost taboo. But desperate times called for new tactics.

Then there was Helgrid. Her family's name once echoed through dwarven songs as staunch allies of winter spirits. Her grandfather had negotiated a calm truce after a harsh season centuries ago, forging the very chains Krampus now carried. If Helgrid knew her family's heritage, she might already suspect that Krampus was not responsible for these horrors. He could rely on her to keep a level head—dwarves were practical folk. If he showed himself to her, would she strike him first or listen to what he had to say?

Branwynn Spellshiver was the real wildcard. Hedge-witches were adept at reading the invisible threads that bound the worlds of spirits and mortals. She might even sense his approach before he announced it. A cautious ally, perhaps. If the witch had discovered something lurking behind the veil, Krampus needed that knowledge. He envisioned her standing in her hut, mixing herbs in a mortar, her eyes glowing faintly as she chanted, the runes on her sleeves shimmering. She would know what to do. Or at least, she would know how to begin unraveling the mystery.

His chains rattled softly as he turned away from the ledge, retreating momentarily into the cavern's darkness. The space inside was spare, holding only a few crude furnishings: a stone bench worn smooth by centuries of his pacing, a heap of furs to rest upon, and shelves carved directly into the rock where he kept old tokens—carvings left by frightened children, small notes of apology or confession abandoned at the forest's edge. He traced a clawed finger over a wooden doll, once left out as a bribe by a particularly frightened girl. He did not accept bribes, but he had kept the doll as a reminder that children, for all their flaws and fears, were precious and deserving of redemption. The thought that something out there might be scooping them up without rhyme or reason filled him with a cold rage that surpassed even the wind's chill.

Closing his eyes again, he listened. Outside, the night stretched on. The hush deepened, or perhaps he simply became more attuned to its texture. The hush was not empty—it trembled with suppressed tension. He could almost imagine dark silhouettes creeping between the trees, sniffing out lonely cottages, searching for the unwary. If he did nothing, what would be left of these villages by dawn? Would The Fatman arrive in a few weeks to find silence where laughter once bloomed? Would the old traditions rot under the weight of fear and ignorance?

No, he would not let that happen. Grim necessity or not, Krampus had a duty to preserve the pattern. If the balance broke completely, there would be nothing left for either him or The Fatman to guard. Humanity would slide into chaos, forgetting why they ever cared about goodness, kindness, or consequence. The mountain would become just another haunted ruin, a blot on the face of the world.

He stepped out again to the cave's edge, curling his toes over the lip. Far below, a wolf howled—a jagged, lonely sound that echoed oddly, as if bouncing off more than just stone. It sounded distorted, as though some mocking voice tried to imitate a wolf. Krampus tensed, tail flicking. The mountains had always known predators, but this was something different. Perhaps a spirit or a mimic, testing its voice, seeing if it could rattle the villages' courage further.

Amidst all this uncertainty, he thought of The Fatman more keenly now. They rarely spoke; their roles were understood rather than negotiated. But perhaps this time he would need to confront his brother and demand answers. If The Fatman had grown too complacent, too sure that gifts and sweetness could keep the world on track, then Krampus would need to shake him into awareness. The Fatman's power was not in punishing or scaring, but in inspiring hope. If something were preying on children's souls, then that hope would be the most potent weapon against despair. Without it, Krampus's chains and rods were just tools of suffering, meaningless in the long run.

Krampus

He sighed—an odd, husky sound. The silence swallowed it easily. Below, Jarlan's lantern flickered and disappeared behind a cottage, leaving Krampus with nothing but speculation. In Tallfir, a quiet village to the east, he knew families huddled around sparse fires. In Icegrove, to the west, there might be parents weeping for a missing daughter or son, unsure whether to blame the horned figure on the mountain or curse the gods in silence. Krampus's presence in these legends made him an easy target for blame. He must act before that suspicion hardened into hatred. Hatred could become a powerful agent of chaos.

The wind changed direction. Now it carried a faint scent of resin and fungus, like the underside of a rotting log. He imagined damp hollows beneath twisted roots, where malicious entities might lurk, waiting for a chance to reshape old stories in their image. A lump formed in his throat, an unfamiliar sensation. He had never feared the darkness before—he was the darkness, the judge lurking in the corner of a merry room. But tonight, the darkness held dimensions beyond his ken, and he did not like being in ignorance.

What if he descended tonight, quietly, and observed the villagers more closely, gleaning what he could before making contact? He could slip through alleyways, peer through shutters, listen to hushed conversations. If he found Jarlan, he might reveal himself just enough to start a guarded dialogue. A dropped birch rod at a doorstep, a faint scraping at a windowpane, a whispered name carried on the wind—these were ways he had communicated indirectly before. But time might be too short for subtlety.

Krampus reviewed what he knew of the old accords: The Fatman and he were two sides of a cosmic joke, a reminder that kindness and cruelty, generosity and justice, coexisted. Tamper with one side, and the other faltered. If these vanishings were orchestrated by some malign force that understood the accord's intricacies, it could be attempting to break their ancient contract. Without children to guide and correct, without families to protect and cherish those children, what would be left? Krampus could not punish where there was no one to sin, and The Fatman could not gift where there was no one to delight.

A soft scraping behind him made him turn, ears pricked. Probably just a loose stone tumbling from an icy ledge, but for a moment, he thought he saw a flicker of movement deeper in the cavern's shadows. He hissed softly, and the noise ceased. Even in his own domain, paranoia began to sprout like poisonous mushrooms. He shook his head, annoyed at his own jumpiness. He must not let fear unman him. If something dared to enter his domain, it would learn swiftly that he was no mere legend to be trifled with.

The night grew colder, a deep chill sinking into rock and marrow. His fur, thick and coarse, protected him from the worst of it, but the temperature was a sign: it would be a hard season, harsher than most. The Fatman might struggle to navigate the snowdrifts when his time came. If the legends said true, The Fatman had once braved impossible blizzards and emerged smiling, but Krampus wondered if even he could keep up the old ways under such conditions. Without cooperation and understanding between them, the world might tilt further into confusion.

A distant door slammed—he could hear it echo faintly, a human sound of fear and frustration. Perhaps Jarlan had visited another empty bed and found no clues. Perhaps Helgrid had decided to bar her workshop door against unwelcome intruders. Perhaps Branwynn had cast her runes and found only ominous signs. The tension rolled down the slopes like invisible avalanches, piling fear upon fear.

Krampus let out a long breath, steam curling before his face. He would go down. He would do it tonight. With careful steps, he began to descend the winding path from his cavern, each hooffall leaving a deep print in the snow. He moved deliberately, neither hiding nor announcing himself. If someone saw him, let them tremble—but let them also know he was here, awake and aware. He would search the fringes of Sleetwood, look for any sign of struggle or clue as to what stalked the children. If fortune smiled, he might cross paths with Branwynn or Jarlan in secret. If he was unlucky, he might encounter that which he feared lurking in the pines.

His chains jingled softly in the silence, a lonely music. The forest below awaited him with needled branches and quiet drifts, the valleys beyond sleeping fitfully under the moon. Each step he took felt like a small surrender of the old ways, a concession that he could not simply follow his timeless script of scaring naughty children into good behavior. This was a new kind of darkness—one he might not banish alone.

A quarter of the way down, he paused at a ledge overlooking a frozen stream. He could see that the ice had cracked in places, long dark seams running through it. Just as cracks now ran through their traditions, through the unspoken compacts that knitted their world together. He flexed his claws and hunched lower, pressing on. The soft crunch of snow beneath his hooves felt unsettlingly loud to him. He must remain calm, deliberate, attentive.

With each cautious step, he sought signs: a tuft of strange fur caught on a branch, a crushed patch of snow where someone—or something—had crouched in wait, footprints that did not match child or adult. His senses honed in on the faintest of disturbances. The silence, so omnipresent, now buzzed in his ears, as if trying to block out any subtle clue. His breath came slow and steady. He would not panic. He would not fail.

Somewhere out there, children cried softly, or perhaps they didn't cry at all—their voices muffled by enchantments or wicked hands. He imagined small faces contorted in confusion, their last sight not the horned enforcer of naughty deeds but something else entirely, something with no right to touch this fragile balance. His chains rustled, and he gripped them tightly, anger burning cold in his chest.

If The Fatman could see him now, would he understand the gravity of the situation? Or would he chortle uncertainly, offering platitudes and trying to smooth things over? The Fatman's power was formidable, yet kind. But kindness alone would not restore stolen children. For that, Krampus would need cunning, strength, and the alliance of those who walked the line between fear and hope.

Another gust of wind rattled brittle branches. He stood still a moment, scanning the darkness. In the near distance, a dim glow—perhaps Jarlan's lantern—flickered between tree trunks. That might be his first stop, a vantage point to glean what the mortal scholar knew. Yes, that was wise. Krampus licked his lips, tasting the cold metal tang of the night. He would learn what he must. He would root out this threat. And if necessary, he would break the mold of his role, becoming not just a punisher of naughty children but a guardian of the innocent, a defender against whatever monstrous force dared to mock their ancient accord.

Steeling himself, Krampus descended further, vanishing into the darkness of pines and snow, taking with him the weight of centuries and the sharp edge of tonight's dread. The Winterspine Mountains held their breath. The silence deepened, as though expecting a confrontation far more profound than any solitary jingle of chains could herald.

CHAPTER TWO

A cramped darkness lay upon Sleetwood's narrow lanes, coiling through crooked alleys and pressing its weight against every shuttered window. The moon hung low, a bleary half-disc behind swaths of restless cloud, granting only a timid glow to the roofs and stoops beneath. Jarlan Forgerook, his oil lantern held high, picked his way carefully along a snow-choked path that cut through the heart of the village. The hush was so profound that each step—his boots crunching over packed snow—sounded treacherously loud, as if announcing his progress to whatever unseen watchers might be lurking in the gloom.

He paused outside the cottage of Hendor and Mirella Quinshale. Earlier that evening, a rumor had spread: the Quinshales' daughter, Elsbet, failed to return from a brief errand. The girl was only nine summers old, a slight thing with a penchant for singing silly rhymes on her way home from the baker's shop. Jarlan frowned, pressing his gloved palm against the cottage's rough-hewn door. No lamp burned inside. A silence radiated outward from this home, a silence that thickened the air and made his scalp prickle. He inhaled, forcing courage to lace his lungs. The chronicler had spent decades recording seasonal rhythms, minor scandals, births, deaths, and marriages—but nothing like this. These vanishings gnawed at the edges of his reason.

Carefully, he tried the latch. It lifted easily, and he slipped inside, lantern thrust forward. The interior smelled faintly of rye bread and old wool, reminding him that life here had been ordinary just days ago. Now, he observed chairs overturned, a curtain half-torn from its rail, and a scattered handful of dried cranberries on the floor, as if someone had dropped a snack in haste. The hearth's embers glowed faintly, barely illuminating the cramped space. "Hendor?" Jarlan whispered, his voice muffled by the low rafters. No reply. He crept deeper, lifting the lantern to reveal a small sleeping nook and shelves lined with simple crockery.

When he stepped into the bedroom, he found the bedclothes rumpled, flung aside in panic. A pair of small boots lay neatly by the door —Elsbet's boots, he assumed—yet there was no child to wear them. He knelt to examine the footprints in the half-melted snow that had blown in beneath the doorframe. They led out into the night, into nowhere. Jarlan's heart sank. Another disappearance. Another child wrenched from her family, leaving behind only the mute evidence of sudden absence.

Jarlan rose, mind racing. He wanted to call out, to alert someone, but who would listen? Everyone had barricaded themselves indoors, terrified. The village elders insisted that children remain inside after dusk, but that had not stopped whatever force stalked these streets. He blew out a trembling breath and stepped back outside, the night air feeling heavier than before.

He proceeded through the alley, lantern bobbing, casting warped shadows onto timber walls. After a few minutes of trudging through knee-deep drifts, he emerged into Sleetwood's central square. This modest gathering place, usually cheerful with a few lanterns, quiet conversations, and maybe a snippet of song, was now deserted. Snow had drifted against the steps of the meeting hall, and the old statue of a long-dead founder stared sightlessly across empty benches. Jarlan paused there, contemplating the hush. Once, he would have heard distant laughter or the crack of Helgrid's hammer from her forge. Now, Helgrid Stonestream worked behind shuttered doors, her forge's glow barely visible through the chinks in the plank walls.

A gust of wind made the lantern flame waver, casting jittery light over the square. He remembered the stories he'd recorded of Krampus and The Fatman: how they balanced each other's powers, how one frightened children into better behavior while the other rewarded kindness and generosity. Yet, this felt different. These disappearances were not the work of Krampus—at least not in the familiar sense. Jarlan could not imagine Krampus leaving homes in disarray, scattering dried fruit, and snatching children without a lesson or a warning. That creature, for all his ferocity, followed a pattern, a role understood if not welcomed. There was no pattern here, only dread and confusion.

In the distance, he heard a faint clank—metal against metal. He stiffened. Could it be Krampus's chains? The idea rattled him. If the horned one was near, what was he doing? Observing? Searching? Or had Jarlan's nerves conjured that sound from memory and fear? The chronicler squared his shoulders. He had to be methodical. Facts, not whispers, would guide him.

He strode toward the forge, leaving the square behind. Helgrid Stonestream's workshop was a squat structure of stone and timber, its roof pitched low to prevent heavy snow from caving it in. As he approached, he saw a strip of light escaping from a gap in the shutters. He tapped softly on the door. Within, silence stretched painfully. He tried again, a bit louder, and finally heard shuffling footsteps.

"Who's there?" came Helgrid's gruff voice. It was pitched low, as if she feared being overheard.

"It's Jarlan," he replied, voice quavering slightly. "I've news."

A pause, then the door cracked open. Helgrid's face, lit from behind by the forge's glow, was tense. She looked prepared to slam the door at the first sign of threat, her calloused hand gripping a hammer. The heat from her forge rushed out to meet Jarlan's face.

"Come in, then," she said tersely, standing aside.

He ducked into the workshop and shut the door behind him. Inside, it was warmer, though the tension lingered. The forge still glowed with half-bank coals, casting Helgrid's stocky silhouette across the floor. Tools hung neatly along the wall: tongs, chisels, hammers, all gleaming with meticulous care. She had been working on something—a thin rod of iron etched with runes—lying atop the anvil. It resembled neither a common tool nor a decoration. It looked like a ward, a protective charm hammered into iron.

"Another one?" she asked without preamble. Her voice was as steady as a mountain's root, but her eyes betrayed unease. Helgrid had never been one to flinch at trouble, yet tonight her jaw tightened with each breath.

Jarlan nodded grimly. "Elsbet Quinshale's gone. The cottage is empty. Doors forced open, footprints leading out into the snow. No sign of her parents either."

Helgrid cursed softly, then lifted the iron rod and examined it. "That makes five disappearances this week. Too many. Far too many." She traced a rune with her thumb. "What manner of creature does this?"

"Not Krampus," Jarlan ventured quietly. "It doesn't fit his pattern. He punishes, yes, but he leaves a lesson behind. He might drag away a wrongdoer, but he does not leave chaos for its own sake."

Helgrid nodded, half agreeing. "Krampus is cruel, but purposefully so. This… this is different. It reeks of malice without logic."

Jarlan hovered near the anvil, rubbing his fingers together anxiously. "We need help. Perhaps Branwynn Spellshiver could tell us something. She has a sense for these… energies."

Helgrid's gaze shifted to the shutters, as if expecting the hedge-witch to appear from the night air. "Branwynn said she'd be at the old chapel ruins tonight," she said at last. "Placing wards and trying to glimpse what's stirring. Maybe we should join her."

"Yes," said Jarlan. "We must gather what knowledge we can. The villagers are terrified. Some might flee by morning, if this continues."

Helgrid grunted. "Flee? To where? The Winterspine is vast and cruel, and who knows what lurks in the passes? No, we must solve this here." She pulled a wool cloak from a peg and wrapped it around her broad shoulders, tucking the iron rod inside. "Come. Keep that lantern steady."

They left the forge and stepped once more into the shrouded village lanes. The hush grew heavier, as if offended by their purpose. Jarlan struggled to keep pace, his boots crunching loudly. Helgrid moved with a grim determination, her dwarf-bred stamina evident in the way she pushed through drifts of snow without complaint.

As they approached the old chapel, Jarlan noted that even the wind had died down, giving the night a claustrophobic stillness. The chapel stood at the village's edge, half-buried by centuries of decay. Its roof had collapsed decades ago, leaving only broken arches and worn pillars standing sentinel against the starless sky. By the time they arrived, the moon had retreated behind thick clouds, reducing their world to shades of ink and ash.

A faint glow shimmered inside the chapel, not firelight, but something else. Helgrid raised a hand to silence Jarlan's approach. They listened, hearts hammering, as soft murmurs drifted outward. It was a voice chanting—a voice they recognized as Branwynn's. They crept closer, lantern dimmed, and peered around a crumbled wall.

Branwynn Spellshiver stood at the center of the ruined nave. She wore a cloak embroidered with runic patterns that glimmered faintly, as though infused with stardust. Her hair hung loose, catching sparks of eerie luminescence from a circle of carved stones arranged at her feet. She sprinkled a handful of dried herbs into the circle, causing the air to smell sharply of resin and decay. The hedge-witch's voice trembled as she recited words older than the village, older than the traditions of Krampus and The Fatman. This was old mountain magic, a language of wind and root.

Helgrid cleared her throat softly to announce their presence. Branwynn's chant faltered. She turned, eyes gleaming strangely, and let out a tired sigh.

"I was wondering when you would come," she said, her voice subdued. "We face something old and hungry, friends. Something that does not belong in our seasonal tapestry."

Jarlan approached slowly, holding the lantern low so as not to disrupt whatever delicate magic Branwynn had woven. He could feel a subtle pressure in the air, as if stepping into a sphere of influence that did not welcome him. The stone arches overhead seemed to lean inward, straining to hear their conversation.

"What do you know?" Helgrid asked, crossing her arms. The dwarf's breath steamed in the cold. "We've more disappearances tonight."

Branwynn nodded wearily. "I suspected as much. The magic grows heavier, more rancid. I've tried to scry the source, but it's elusive, like a serpent slipping through tangled roots. It feeds on fear and uncertainty, twisting the old accord between The Fatman and Krampus."

Jarlan swallowed. "Twisting how?"

The hedge-witch's eyes flickered with unease. "Our world relies on a balance. Generosity and joy on one side, punishment and caution on the other. We think of The Fatman as the kindly one, Krampus as the dark enforcer. But both are necessary. If one side weakens or falters, the equilibrium cracks. I fear something has reached into that crack and is prying it wider."

Krampus

Helgrid clenched her jaw. "So this entity, whatever it is, is trying to break the ancient pact? Why? To what end?"

Branwynn shook her head. "I cannot say for certain. But think of it this way: The Fatman and Krampus's roles ensure that children learn morality through both kindness and consequence. If those children vanish—if their innocence is snuffed out—then what remains of those traditions? Just hollow gestures, empty rites. Without future generations to believe and partake in these cycles, the old magics fade, leaving a vacuum for darker forces."

Jarlan closed his eyes, his heart pounding. He had recorded countless tales, but none like this. "Then we must alert The Fatman," he said softly. "Or seek out Krampus. Perhaps they themselves don't know what's happening."

Branwynn's gaze grew distant. "Krampus is aware, I think. His presence lingers in these mountains, restless. I sensed him earlier, high above in his cavern. He watches, uncertain how to proceed. As for The Fatman… he is distant, his season of generosity not yet at its height. But he will feel this unrest soon, if he has not already."

Helgrid gripped the iron rod she carried and held it up to the faint light. "So what do we do here and now? We cannot simply wait for legends to sort this out. We have children missing. Families in terror."

The hedge-witch sighed. "I've placed protective wards around the chapel. I will craft more for homes that shelter frightened families. But these are small measures. To truly combat this threat, we must restore the balance. That likely means convincing Krampus and The Fatman to set aside any differences and act together—swiftly and decisively."

A nervous silence followed. Each knew the difficulty of such a task. Speaking to Krampus was no small feat. He appeared when he wished, not at mortal summons. The Fatman was notoriously hard to locate until his season truly began. And with each passing night, more children might be lost to the invisible predator.

Jarlan cleared his throat. "I have old records in the meeting hall archives. Perhaps I can find references to similar occurrences—moments in history when something tested the accord. If we understand its nature, we might predict its moves."

Branwynn nodded approvingly. "Knowledge will help. Go. Search while you can. I will remain here, anchoring the wards and trying to glean more clues through scrying."

Helgrid set a hand on Jarlan's shoulder. "I'll accompany you. If something lurks in those archives, better we face it together." She glanced at Branwynn. "Be careful, witch. The night grows stranger by the hour."

With a final glance at the hedge-witch's glowing circle, they departed, leaving Branwynn alone among the ruined arches. Behind them, her chanting resumed softly, weaving through ancient syllables of protection and inquiry. The smell of herbs lingered as they trudged back toward the heart of the village.

They passed again through silent streets. Jarlan's lantern cast lurching shadows that stretched grotesquely across shuttered walls. Once, he'd have waved to neighbors peering curiously from windows. Now, no faces watched them. The people hid in dark rooms, clutching loved ones tight, afraid to even light a candle that might attract unwanted attention. The hush was absolute—until they heard something new: a faint rustling, as if cloth against stone, somewhere behind them.

Both turned, Helgrid's hammer raised, Jarlan's lantern held high. The alley behind them was empty, but the atmosphere quivered. Jarlan's skin crawled. They hurried on, refusing to linger. If something followed them, let it do so in the open square rather than a cramped alley.

Soon, they reached the meeting hall. It was a modest, two-story building with timber beams and a slate roof. Normally, it served as the hub of village governance and community events. Tonight, it loomed solemn and unwelcoming. Helgrid pushed the door open, revealing a hall lined with benches and a raised platform where the mayor often addressed the villagers. Beyond a side door lay the archives: a cramped room stuffed with shelves and stacks of parchment scrolls, bound ledgers, and clay tablets.

Jarlan stepped inside first, nostrils flaring at the familiar scent of old ink and dust. Helgrid followed, shutting the door behind them and dropping a heavy wooden bar into place. They worked by lantern-light. Jarlan knelt by a shelf laden with thick ledgers, flipping through pages by trembling fingers. He sought anomalies—records of winters past when children disappeared, or unnatural hushes settled on the village.

Minutes stretched into an hour, and the silence pressed on their ears. Helgrid stood guard near the door, occasionally glancing over her shoulder as if expecting some pale hand to slip through the cracks. Jarlan pored over texts, his breath steaming with concentration. He found mentions of Krampus's visits, The Fatman's generosity, and rare disputes with neighboring villages, but nothing like this scourge of vanishings. Until, at last, he stumbled upon a fragile parchment pressed between ledger pages. It was older than the rest, written in a shaky hand he did not recognize.

He squinted at the faded ink:

"In the year of the Black Frost, when the accord was still young, a nameless hunger rose in the valley. Children vanished from their beds, lured by whispers no living soul could name. Krampus and The Fatman stood apart, suspicious of each other's intent. Only when they met beneath the Iron Pines and renewed their oath did the hunger retreat, howling back into the void. Thus was forged the second pact, sealed with blood and birch, ensuring that fear and kindness would forever entwine."

Jarlan's blood ran cold. He showed the parchment to Helgrid, who frowned deeply. "This has happened before," he said, voice barely above a whisper. "Long ago, when their accord was still new. Some force tried to drive a wedge between them, to break their unity and devour innocence unopposed."

Helgrid's voice was grim. "Then the solution lies with them, doesn't it? Krampus and The Fatman must meet, must reaffirm their bond. But how do we arrange such a thing?" She tapped the iron rod she carried. "We are but mortals. How can we summon beings who walk between the worlds?"

Jarlan thought of the old paths leading up into the Winterspine, the secret glades where ancient runes were carved. "We must send a sign. Krampus can be found if we are brave enough to seek him. The Fatman may be harder to reach, but perhaps Branwynn can help with that, or perhaps Krampus himself can. But time is short. More children vanish by the night."

Helgrid nodded, her expression stone-set. "Then let's go. The night is not yet spent. We can at least try to find Krampus. If he has been spotted—or if he chooses to reveal himself—we might persuade him."

Jarlan wasn't sure if they could persuade the horned spirit of judgment to listen, but they had no alternative. He carefully tucked the old parchment into his satchel. This scrap of history might be their key to convincing the dark one. They had to show him that the danger was real, that the world needed him and The Fatman aligned, not at odds.

They slipped out of the hall, nerves frayed. A brittle wind had picked up, moaning softly between houses. Helgrid gestured northward, where the mountains rose. A faint glow there—maybe moonlight on a distant peak—flickered uncertainly. Krampus's lair was somewhere high above. Jarlan's stomach clenched at the thought of climbing the winter trails in darkness. But what choice did they have?

They hadn't taken more than a few steps from the meeting hall when a whisper skimmed Jarlan's ears. He jerked to a halt. Helgrid sensed it too, her hammer raised, eyes searching the gloom. The night had grown restless, the hush splintering into subtle murmurs. Jarlan glanced behind them and saw nothing, but the skin on his neck prickled.

"Maybe we should check on Branwynn first," he said, voice tight. "She might have seen something, or we can at least gain her help before we head into the mountains."

Helgrid nodded. "Agreed. I don't like how the darkness moves behind us. If we vanish, who will be left to solve this?"

They retraced their steps toward the chapel. The wind picked up, flinging stinging crystals of snow against their faces. Jarlan tried to shield the lantern flame with his hand, but the light guttered, threatening to go out. As they approached the chapel's broken walls, a queer hush fell again. No chanting greeted them this time. Jarlan's heart sank. They slipped inside the ruins, lantern searching the gloom.

Branwynn was gone. The circle of stones remained, but they had toppled, the runic patterns scuffed as if by hurried footsteps or a struggle. No sign of blood, no obvious violence, but the absence of the hedge-witch struck them both like a hammer blow. She would not have left willingly without informing them. Something had intervened.

Helgrid cursed quietly. "We are too late. Something took her. Gods help us."

Jarlan knelt, examining the ground with a trembling hand. He found a scrap of fabric—part of Branwynn's embroidered sleeve, torn free. He held it up, stunned. Without Branwynn's guidance and magical insight, their path grew even darker.

They stood in the broken chapel, snow drifting through the missing roof, silence pressing on their ears. Helgrid's knuckles whitened around her hammer. Jarlan felt despair nibble at his resolve. How could they hope to restore the balance when the village's only magic-worker had been snatched from under their noses?

Yet the parchment in his satchel weighed heavily, reminding him that all was not lost. There was a precedent. The ancient text hinted that this crisis could be resolved if the two legendary brothers stood united. Without Branwynn, they would have to rely on courage and cunning. Perhaps, in the process of searching for Krampus, they would find clues to Branwynn's whereabouts. Or maybe Krampus himself would sense the witch's disappearance and be stirred to action.

Jarlan stood, teeth clenched. "We must go on," he said, voice steadier than he felt. "We must try to find Krampus."

Helgrid nodded, though worry pinched her features. "Then we go now. But we must be wary. Whatever hunts these mountains grows bolder. Taking children is vile enough, but stealing our only hedge-witch... it mocks us."

They left the chapel behind, hearts heavy, and marched toward the village's edge. The path that led into the foothills was barely visible, choked with fresh snow. Jarlan wished for daylight, but dawn was hours away. The clouds denied them moon or star. He gritted his teeth, following Helgrid's broad back as she forged a path through the drifts.

Time stretched as they climbed. They passed silent cottages at the outskirts, each shuttered and sealed, each family huddled in darkness. A dog barked once, then fell silent, as if chastised by the very air. Jarlan's lantern flame flickered, and he feared it would fail. He recalled reading that Krampus moved like a shadow among pines, unseen unless he chose to be seen. How to attract his attention without provoking an attack?

They pressed on, the village falling behind. The forest rose around them, tall pines sagging under snow, branches drooping like mourners in a funeral procession. The silence here was profound, broken only by their labored breathing. Helgrid turned and whispered, "If Krampus roams these woods, he might have already noticed us. Keep your eyes open."

Jarlan nodded, squinting into the gloom. The lantern's radius of light felt pitifully small. Trees and shadows merged into a tapestry of black and grey. He half-expected something to leap out—a gaunt figure, a hungry wraith—but the forest remained still.

As they trudged uphill, the wind hissed, and Jarlan heard again the faint clank of chain. This time, Helgrid heard it too. She halted, raising her hammer high, eyes sweeping the darkness.

"Krampus?" she called, voice firm. "If you are here, show yourself. We seek counsel, not conflict."

Only silence answered. Then, a rustle—branches swaying overhead. Jarlan spun, holding the lantern up. He saw nothing but swaying pine boughs and drifting snow. His chest tightened. They were vulnerable out here, two mortals in a realm that belonged more to myth than man.

Minutes passed, each feeling longer than the last. They advanced a few more steps, then Helgrid hissed softly, pointing to the ground. A birch rod lay half-buried in snow—a traditional calling card of Krampus. Jarlan swallowed hard. The rod was unbroken, its bark pale in the lantern light.

"Is this an invitation?" Helgrid wondered aloud. "Or a warning?"

Jarlan bent down, carefully lifting the rod. It was slender and flexible, as though newly cut. He held it out, unsure what to do. Suddenly, a shape loomed from behind a cluster of pines—tall, horned, hunched. The lantern's glow caught a glint of amber eyes and the black gleam of matted fur. Jarlan's heart lurched into his throat. Krampus stood before them, silent, immense, chains rattling softly in the hush.

They did not run. Fear hammered at Jarlan's ribcage, but he forced himself to stand firm. Helgrid tightened her grip on the hammer and slowly lowered it, showing no aggression. Krampus watched them, head cocked, as if deciding their worth. He was an unsettling sight: horns curling back, eyes reflecting faint light, muscles coiled under thick fur, and a posture neither fully bestial nor human. When he spoke, his voice rumbled like distant thunder.

"Why do you seek me, mortals?" His tone was heavy, not cruel, but bearing centuries of austere purpose. His chains clinked as he shifted, towering over them.

Helgrid straightened. "We come on behalf of Sleetwood—and all the villages below. Children vanish nightly. Fear chokes our streets. We suspect something interferes with the ancient balance you share with The Fatman."

Jarlan, summoning his courage, held out the old parchment. "We found a record… it happened once before, long ago. A nameless hunger tested your accord with The Fatman. Only by renewing your oath, by standing together, did you banish the evil. We believe the same thing is happening now."

Krampus's eyes narrowed, amber sparks flickering. He took a step closer, sniffing the air near the parchment. Jarlan struggled not to flinch away.

"I have sensed it," Krampus said at last, voice quieter. "A distortion in our pattern. I have felt children vanish, not by my hand. The

Fatman's laughter is absent, his warmth distant." His chains rattled softly, a troubled sound. "You wish me to find him? To renew the bond?"

Helgrid nodded. "We must save the children. We must stop this horror. We need your help."

Krampus said nothing for a long moment, his silence pressing heavily on their hearts. The forest seemed to hold its breath.

Finally, he sighed, a low, mournful sound. "Mortals, you ask much. The Fatman and I have grown distant over the years. I resent his ease, his admiration. He forgets the necessity of my stern watch. Yet… I have seen the emptiness creeping into these nights. I cannot ignore it. If I do nothing, both our roles become meaningless."

Jarlan felt a flicker of hope. "Then you will help?"

Krampus's gaze drifted beyond them, toward the lower slopes and the sleeping village. "I will seek The Fatman. But heed this: finding him in these conditions may be difficult. The wind shifts strangely, and old wards fail. The Fatman's domain drifts beyond mortal roads. You must hold fast. Protect what you can. Arm yourselves. I cannot promise swift success."

Helgrid nodded solemnly. "We'll do our part. We'll warn the village, strengthen our defenses. If you find The Fatman, tell him we stand with you both."

Krampus dipped his head fractionally, an acknowledgment rather than agreement. Then he turned, his hulking form blending into the shadows between trees. Before he vanished, he paused, amber eyes fixing on them one last time. "Beware," he said, voice low, "the thing that stirs here is cunning. It will try to divide you, to seed distrust. Stand together, or you will stand no chance at all."

With that, he was gone. The forest swallowed him as if he had never been there, leaving only the faint memory of rattling chains.

Jarlan and Helgrid stared at each other, hearts pounding. They had done it—they had found Krampus and gained a promise of sorts. But Branwynn was missing, and the village lay defenseless. A long, treacherous night still stretched before them.

They began the descent, lantern flickering, fatigue tugging at their limbs. They would not rest. Not yet. The fate of their children, their traditions, perhaps their entire way of life, hinged on what happened next. All they could do was trust that Krampus would find The Fatman, that they would reconcile and push back this nameless hunger threatening to devour the innocence of Winterspine's future.

As they approached the village outskirts, Jarlan thought he heard a distant wail. He could not tell if it was the wind, an animal cry, or a stolen child's distant sob. He clenched his jaw and pressed on, Helgrid at his side. They had no room for fear now—only determination. In the bleak darkness, armed with ancient knowledge and fragile alliances, they would make their stand.

CHAPTER THREE

The darkness before dawn settled thickly over Sleetwood, pressing into every gap of the timbered houses, stretching its chill fingers through keyholes and under eaves. It was the hour when the world balanced on a knife-edge—no longer fully night, not yet morning. A time of indecision and frayed nerves. Jarlan Forgerook and Helgrid Stonestream trudged back down the rutted path from the foothills, their breath pluming in hard-won silence. Although they carried within them a tiny ember of hope after meeting Krampus, the air around them felt charged with the awareness that the world was slipping from its old certainties.

As they approached the first squat cottages at the village outskirts, Jarlan raised his lantern. Its glow seemed paltry against the swallowing dark. No welcoming lamplight shone from windows, and no one stirred outside. It felt as though Sleetwood were huddled beneath a quilt of silence, pretending that if it lay still enough, the horrors would pass by without noticing. Jarlan's heart ached at the thought that many families inside were awake, staring into gloom, trying to protect what innocence remained under their roofs.

Helgrid's boots scuffed against a plank bridging a ditch, making her wince at the noise. "We need to act quickly," she said under her breath. "By sunrise, we must have a plan. The villagers… they won't hold together if we show them nothing but uncertainty."

Jarlan nodded, pressing a trembling hand against the pouch in which he stored the old parchment. "We must reassure them that Krampus is on our side, that he's seeking The Fatman. But will they believe it without proof? And what of Branwynn?" His voice hitched on the hedge-witch's name. They had found no sign of her but a torn scrap of fabric and the disturbance of her protective circle.

Helgrid's jaw tightened. "We cannot lie. The truth is grim, but it's better than letting panic breed wild rumors. If we say Krampus is working to restore the accord, at least they'll know we're not alone in this. As for Branwynn…" She trailed off, shoulders slumping. Without Branwynn's runic wards and magical insight, they felt half-blind. "We must trust that she still lives. If these vanishings serve a purpose for our enemy, they might keep her alive—at least for now."

The words offered cold comfort, but Jarlan clung to them. As they passed into the central lanes of Sleetwood, he resolved to gather the villagers at first light in the old meeting hall. It would be risky—what if the entity struck while everyone was in one place? But they could not let fear atomize them into helpless solitude. Unity was their best shield.

Helgrid tugged at his sleeve. "Look," she said, nodding at a pair of tracks in the snow. Footprints smaller than an adult's, leading from a side alley toward a boarded-up carpenter's shop. Jarlan inhaled sharply, heart pounding. He followed them with his lantern. The prints ended abruptly at the corner, as though the child who made them had vanished into thin air.

"Fresh," murmured Helgrid, kneeling to examine them. "The edges haven't softened. This happened recently."

Jarlan's mind conjured the image of a child, perhaps awake due to nightmares, venturing outdoors foolishly in search of comfort, only to be snatched away by whatever lurked in the shadows. He clenched his fists. "We must hurry. At first light, we gather everyone. If children are still slipping out unguarded, we must organize patrols. Something has to be done."

Helgrid stood, her face grave. "We'll speak plainly. Better they know the enemy is cunning than remain ignorant." She gestured toward the silent houses. "Go home, Jarlan. Get whatever you need for record-keeping. I'll call at a few trusted neighbors' doors, tell them to spread the word quietly that all should meet in the hall at dawn. We must show them we have a plan."

Jarlan started to protest—he was reluctant to separate—but her logic was sound. They had only a few hours before sunrise. He nodded. "Be careful. If you sense anything strange, call out."

Helgrid's grim smile flickered. "I have my hammer. And I'm not afraid to use it."

With that, they parted ways. Jarlan hurried down a narrow lane toward his small cottage. Inside, he lit a candle, warmed his numb fingers, and rifled through his notes and supplies. He was no warrior, no enchanter, just a chronicler. Yet knowledge could be a weapon. He took ink, parchment, a quill, and the precious old page detailing the second pact. Clutching these to his chest, he muttered a desperate prayer to any benevolent force still listening in these dark times.

Helgrid Stonestream moved like a shadow between dark houses. She chose carefully whose doors to knock on: dependable neighbors known for their courage or wisdom, families who once helped organize seasonal gatherings. At each threshold, she rapped quietly and whispered instructions: "At dawn, the meeting hall. Bring lanterns, dress warmly, stay together." Faces blurred by darkness nodded, fearful but grateful for direction. Helgrid did not mention Krampus or The Fatman yet; such revelations required a stable platform—no one would believe her in hushed exchanges at their doorsteps.

After rousing a half-dozen families, she turned toward the blacksmith's forge—her domain—and slipped inside. The coals were low, but still warm. She knelt and stirred them, feeding kindling and a few lumps of charcoal until embers glowed red. The forge's warmth steadied her. This place had always been a refuge where metal and will combined to create something purposeful. Now, she would forge not sled runners or decorative hinges, but symbols of resilience.

Helgrid rummaged through her materials: iron rods, scraps of copper, bits of etched steel that she had prepared earlier. She recalled old tales passed down in her family, stories of forging chains that once bound unruly spirits at Krampus's behest. Perhaps she could craft something similar—amulets or tokens infused with the intent to repel whatever dark presence prowled the village. Without Branwynn's magical prowess, she couldn't enchant metals with arcane power, but she could rely on dwarven runes of protection, tapping into the primal language of the earth itself.

Painstakingly, she shaped small iron disks, hammered flat and smooth, then etched simple protective glyphs. Each glyph invoked the steadfastness of stone and the purity of unspoiled snow. She murmured in her ancestral tongue, calling on the old dwarven gods to lend a whisper of strength. It was a long shot—these were not true magical artifacts—but symbolism and belief could wield subtle power. If nothing else, these tokens would reassure people that they were not defenseless.

The hours crawled by as she worked, sweat beading on her brow despite the cold outside. Her arms ached, and the hammer rang dully in the silence. She made a dozen tokens, then two dozen, pushing herself, knowing dawn approached. When she finally stopped, placing the cooling charms in a cloth pouch, she felt weary but resolved. Let the villagers hold these tokens close. Let them believe they were protected. Belief might help close the cracks that the nameless hunger was prying open.

In the meeting hall, first light filtered through the small, iced-over windows. The hall's wooden beams groaned softly as the temperature shifted, and Jarlan Forgerook arranged benches to form a rough semicircle. He lit two lanterns and set them by the raised platform. The hall smelled of old varnish and candle wax, comforting in its familiarity.

One by one, villagers trickled in—some in grim silence, others whispering anxiously to neighbors. They looked haggard: red-rimmed eyes from sleepless nights, shoulders hunched as if expecting a blow. Many clutched blankets or scarves. A few carried stout cudgels or walking sticks. Jarlan saw fear in their eyes, but also a flicker of determination. At least they were here, together.

Helgrid arrived soon after, holding her pouch of tokens. She nodded at Jarlan and took a seat near the front. The hall grew crowded: parents holding frightened children close, older folk muttering that they had never seen the like. Jarlan waited until he could sense a collective hush, then stepped onto the platform.

He cleared his throat, heart pounding. "Thank you for coming," he began. His voice sounded thin in the large space, but people leaned forward, eager to listen. "I know these are terrible times. Children vanish. Our hedge-witch is missing. No one knows what moves in the darkness. But we cannot face this threat alone, hidden in our homes. We must stand together."

A murmur passed through the crowd. Eyes flicked nervously toward shuttered windows. Jarlan raised a hand for silence. "I have spent my life recording our village's lore. I found an old parchment that speaks of a time, long ago, when a similar menace threatened these lands. Back then, Krampus and The Fatman—yes, the very figures of our winter traditions—were forced to reforge their ancient bond to drive out a nameless hunger. It is happening again."

This statement provoked gasps. Some scoffed, as if unwilling to believe that their holiday legends lived as tangible beings. But others looked thoughtful. Jarlan pressed on. "We encountered Krampus last night." His voice almost broke at the admission, and the hall erupted in uneasy whispers. "He knows what is happening and has agreed to seek The Fatman. Together, they can restore the balance and end these vanishings."

Near the back, a stout baker named Orlan stood, red-faced. "You expect us to trust a monster that punishes children?" he demanded. "How do we know Krampus isn't behind this?"

Helgrid rose, fists clenched. "Krampus is harsh, yes," she said, voice steady. "But he follows a code—he doesn't snatch children without reason, leaving chaos in his wake. Those who vanish now are lost without a trace, without the moral lesson Krampus would impart. We must trust Jarlan's scholarship. Krampus and The Fatman's partnership is what keeps our world in check."

Another voice, quieter, spoke up: "What of Branwynn Spellshiver? Did Krampus take her, too?" A woman near the front, tears shining in her eyes, clutched a scrap of embroidered fabric—a hint that she might have known Branwynn well.

Jarlan shook his head sadly. "We do not believe so. Branwynn was working to protect us when she was taken. The entity responsible for these vanishings aims to weaken us by removing our sources of strength. But we must not give in. We must hold on until Krampus returns with The Fatman, or until we find another way to free the captives."

The crowd quieted, absorbing this grim message. Helgrid stepped forward, holding up the pouch of iron tokens. "I cannot offer magic," she said, "but I have forged these charms of iron and rune, small tokens of protection. Keep them in your homes, near your doors and windows. They may not be powerful sorcery, but they represent our resolve. We do not lie down and yield."

A line formed as people came up to receive tokens. Some wept softly, some gripped Helgrid's hand in gratitude. Others simply bowed their heads. In that moment, it seemed the villagers rediscovered their communal spirit. They might be afraid, but they would not scatter like frightened mice. They would stand shoulder to shoulder against the encroaching dark.

Jarlan noticed a figure slipping through the crowd: a gangly fellow named Edric, known for his keen hearing and skill in hunting. Edric approached the platform and spoke quietly: "If we organize patrols, I can help. The enemy thrives in silence and isolation. With careful rotations, we might keep watch and sound alarms at the first hint of trouble."

Encouraged, Jarlan nodded. "Yes, form patrols. Move in pairs or trios. Never go alone." He glanced at Helgrid. "We must ensure these people know what to look for. Any strange footprints, any half-heard whispers… report them immediately."

Helgrid agreed. "I will oversee the forging of simple weapons—mostly iron-tipped poles or weighted cudgels. We must show we are not helpless prey."

Though fear lingered, a quiet determination settled over the villagers. They had a role to play: to survive, to resist, to await the return of their legendary protectors. The seeds of resilience took root under the wooden beams of the meeting hall.

Hours crept by. The sun rose, weak and pale, casting uncertain light over Sleetwood. Patrols began to circle the lanes. One trio moved around the village's perimeter, stamping through snow, scanning the edges of forest for unusual tracks. Another pair stood near the old chapel ruins, gazing at the broken stone arches and wondering what Branwynn had seen before she vanished. Inside homes, parents hung Helgrid's iron tokens over lintels, whispering prayers that these humble charms would ward off evil.

Jarlan and Helgrid reconvened in the meeting hall with Edric and a few others who volunteered as coordinators: Marta Greshill, a widowed midwife known for her calm head, and Takrin Fellbow, a retired trapper with sharp instincts and a limp from an old injury. They spread out a crude map of Sleetwood and its environs on a bench, marking where disappearances occurred, where footprints were found, and where patrols would concentrate.

They spoke quietly, voices subdued but purposeful. Jarlan's lantern flickered as a draft slipped under the hall's door. "If Krampus succeeds in finding The Fatman, how soon can we expect them?" Marta asked, brushing a lock of gray hair from her face.

Jarlan bit his lip. "I cannot say. Legends suggest The Fatman wanders beyond ordinary realms, only appearing fully during his season of gift-giving. Krampus might have to traverse hidden paths or use ancient signs to reach him. It could be days—or longer."

A heavy silence followed. Days of this tension, this fear? Could they endure?

Helgrid gripped the edge of the bench. "We must. There is no other choice. In the meantime, we search for clues. Maybe we can find where Branwynn and the children were taken. If we can rescue even one child, imagine the hope that would bring."

Takrin spoke up: "In my trapping days, I learned to follow subtle signs. I'll comb the forest edge. If this enemy leaves any hint—a broken twig, a tuft of strange fur—I'll find it. Edric can listen for unnatural sounds. Maybe we can track the direction of these vanishings."

Jarlan nodded, heartened by their resolve. "Do it. But be cautious. This is no ordinary predator."

That afternoon, the wind changed. It blew in from the north, colder and sharper, carrying a distant keening sound. The villagers, busying themselves with meager chores and nervous conversations, glanced upward at the snow-laden clouds. Several patrols reported strange echoes in the forest—like laughter, but stretched thin and distorted. Others found footprints that began and ended abruptly, as if something leapt through shadows. Yet, no immediate attacks occurred, and no new disappearances were reported that day. It was as if the entity toyed with them, savoring their fear.

In the twilight, a group gathered at the old chapel ruins to place fresh wards. Without Branwynn, they had only mundane means: lines of salt, carvings of runes Helgrid recalled from old dwarven tales, and small mirrors set on stumps to catch any unseen shapes. Marta led a quiet prayer, not to any specific god, but to the spirit of life and continuity. The villagers hunched together in the cold, each breath a vow to endure.

Meanwhile, inside Jarlan's cottage, the chronicler spread his notes on the rickety table. He wanted to understand the pattern of past events. The parchment he found spoke of a "nameless hunger" that had once tested the accord. Could this be the same entity—or another of its kind?

His candle guttered as he read. He noted how the old text mentioned the entity's delight in unraveling trust. By sowing suspicion and fear, it undermined the moral lessons The Fatman and Krampus taught. Without children learning from these beings—either through kindness or caution—humanity would drift away from the values that shaped their world. The entity seemed to feed on that drifting, growing stronger as moral certainties crumbled.

Jarlan thought about Krampus's words: "Stand together, or you will stand no chance at all." This enemy wanted them divided. They must do the opposite. He would share this insight at tomorrow's meeting. Perhaps understanding the creature's motive might help them resist its manipulations.

A tap at his door startled him. He rose, heart in his throat, and unlatched it. Takrin stood there, breathing hard. Snow clung to his hood and beard. "Jarlan," he gasped, "come with me. I've found something in the woods—footprints not human or animal. You must see."

Grabbing his cloak and lantern, Jarlan followed Takrin out into the bitter night. The village seemed asleep, but he knew patrols watched from shadowed corners. They slipped between houses and into a narrow deer trail leading into the forest. The lantern's light flickered over snow-laden branches. Takrin moved with surprising silence for a man with a limp, and Jarlan struggled to keep pace without slipping.

They reached a small clearing surrounded by twisted firs. Under the lantern's glow, Jarlan saw tracks—thin, elongated prints with clawed tips. They formed a looping pattern, as if something danced or skittered in circles. The hair on Jarlan's neck rose. He knelt, examining them closely. The edges were crisp, likely recent. No known creature left such tracks. They tapered like a malformed hand pressed into snow.

Takrin pointed silently to a tree trunk. Jarlan moved the lantern and froze. A symbol had been scratched into the bark—a crude spiral with jagged lines radiating outward. It seemed to writhe in the lantern's unsteady light.

Jarlan touched the bark carefully. The scratches were fresh, no older than a day. His mind raced. The entity must have a physical form to leave these marks, or it employed servants. Perhaps twisted goblins or spirits coerced into service. Or maybe it was manifesting partially in their world.

He and Takrin backed away, careful not to disturb the tracks further. The trapper's eyes were grim. "We must tell the others. It's marking territory, or leaving messages."

Jarlan nodded, heart sinking. So the enemy toyed with them, leaving clues or warnings. "We'll bring Helgrid and Edric at dawn. We must study these signs further."

They returned to the village under a silent sky. Not even the wind dared to whisper now, as if expecting a confrontation soon.

Morning brought no comfort. The villagers gathered in the meeting hall again, huddling for warmth and reassurance. Jarlan explained what he and Takrin found. Gasps rippled through the crowd. Some wept quietly, clutching their children, who looked pale and silent. Others blanched at the idea of a creature carving ominous sigils in their forest.

Marta stepped onto the platform and raised her voice. "We must not surrender to despair. We have found signs—this means the creature can be tracked, understood. It reveals itself, in part, because it wants to frighten us. We can use that against it. Let us set traps near that clearing. If it returns, we might wound it or at least learn more about its nature."

The suggestion brought a murmur of agreement. Helgrid nodded firmly. "I'll craft snares with iron teeth. Even if we can't kill it, we might slow it down. And if we capture a minion of this entity, we could force it to reveal where our children and Branwynn are held."

Edric rubbed his chin. "We must be careful. This foe is cunning. But we have skills too. I can climb a tree and keep watch overhead, alerting the others at the first sign of movement. With coordinated patrols, we can force it into a confrontation on our terms."

They drew up plans, simple and desperate. Jarlan felt a strange calm settle over him. Two nights ago, Sleetwood was paralyzed by fear, scattered and unsure. Now, although still terrified, they were acting—taking steps, however small, to fight back. Perhaps the nameless hunger would realize that these people were not so easily broken.

By midday, the villagers worked quietly but efficiently. Groups trudged into the forest near the clearing, placing hidden traps, covering them with pine needles and snow. Edric climbed a thick-limbed spruce, testing vantage points that overlooked the clearing. Helgrid hammered sharpened stakes into the ground, arms trembling with exertion. Marta and Takrin scouted around the perimeter, ensuring escape routes were clear. Jarlan hovered near the center, trying to memorize every detail of the tracks and the sigil on the tree, hoping to glean a pattern or meaning.

He noticed subtle things: the spiraling symbol had six radiating lines, each angled slightly differently, as though representing discordant forces. Could it stand for corruption of the six core virtues taught through The Fatman and Krampus's lessons—generosity, gratitude, responsibility, honesty, courage, and humility—turning them into twisted inversions? Jarlan could only guess. But thinking along these lines reminded him that the entity thrived on moral confusion. Sleetwood's unity, its moral spine, would be the best defense.

They worked until dusk, then withdrew, leaving a few brave souls hidden behind snowbanks to watch if anything approached the traps. The hours ticked by, slow and tense. Jarlan and Helgrid waited in the meeting hall with a handful of others, sharpening tools and sipping thin broth to keep warm. The silence weighed heavily, broken only by coughs or the creak of wooden benches.

Close to midnight, a runner burst into the hall, breath steaming. "We heard something!" he panted. "In the clearing. A laugh like grinding ice. Something triggered a trap—chains rattled."

Everyone leapt up. Helgrid seized her hammer, face grim. Jarlan's stomach knotted. They must act swiftly and quietly, lest they lose this opportunity.

A dozen villagers—armed with makeshift weapons, iron tokens, and lanterns carefully hooded—followed the runner back into the darkness. They moved in cautious silence, guided only by starlight and memory. The wind had died again, leaving the forest unnaturally quiet.

When they reached the edge of the clearing, Edric slithered down from the spruce, eyes wide. "The trap near the spiral tree snapped on something," he whispered. "I saw movement—a shape hunched low, struggling. But it melted into the shadows before I could get a clear look. Still, blood—there's blood in the snow."

Helgrid nodded, jaw set. "We've wounded it. That's a start." She looked at Jarlan. "If we can track blood drops, maybe we can follow it back to its lair."

Marta and Takrin joined them, lanterns shielded. Carefully, they advanced into the clearing. True to Edric's words, the trap—a pair of iron jaws Helgrid had fashioned—sat askew, its spring triggered. Dark stains spattered the surrounding snow. Takrin knelt and touched a finger to the blood. It was oddly thick, with a faint, foul smell like stagnant water.

Jarlan's pulse hammered. "This proves it can be hurt," he murmured. "It's not invincible."

Marta set her lantern low, examining the tracks leading away. The footprints were smeared, as if the creature limped off at speed. They led deeper into the forest, toward a dense patch of firs. Edric volunteered to scout ahead, and Helgrid insisted on coming too.

Jarlan and the others waited, breath held, as Edric and Helgrid slipped into darkness. Time stretched. An owl hooted, startling them. Jarlan's heart thumped painfully. He imagined Helgrid holding her hammer, Edric gripping a shortbow, creeping between trunks, following a ribbon of dark droplets. If they found the creature's lair, could they rescue the children and Branwynn? Or would they stumble into a trap?

After what felt like an eternity, Helgrid returned alone. Her eyes shone with fierce triumph and terror combined. She spoke softly but urgently. "The blood trail leads to a rocky outcrop. We didn't get too close, but I smelled decay—like a den of rot. Edric saw movement: small shapes creeping around, maybe goblins twisted by this dark magic. We dare not go in without more force."

Jarlan nodded, mind racing. They had a lead, a direction. "We should return with more villagers, better armed," he said. "But if we strike too soon, we risk scattering them or endangering the captives."

Marta frowned. "If the creature is wounded, it may be more desperate. It could harm the children or Branwynn."

Helgrid's knuckles whitened on her hammer handle. "We must prepare carefully. Traps, torches, a planned assault. If Krampus and The Fatman return soon, that would be ideal—but we cannot rely on it. We must be ready to act on our own."

Her words hung in the cold air. The villagers exchanged grim looks. They were no warriors. Most had never fought anything more fearsome than a hungry wolf near their goat pens. Yet now they were challenged by a cunning, supernatural enemy.

Jarlan straightened. "We must hold firm. Our courage, our unity—these are the virtues this creature seeks to destroy. By standing together and helping each other, we deny it that victory." He swallowed hard, feeling the weight of his own words. "Let's organize a proper expedition.

By dawn, we'll assemble volunteers and supplies. We know where to strike."

Helgrid nodded. Marta and Takrin agreed. The villagers around them, though frightened, affirmed their support. Edric, reappearing from the gloom, added, "I'll guide us. I know those woods. If we move quietly, we might catch it by surprise."

So they retreated to Sleetwood again, hearts pounding with resolve and fear. They lit no bonfires—no need to announce their plans—but each home's window now held a faint glow of lamplight. No one wanted to sleep while the enemy prowled wounded and enraged.

In a quiet corner of his cottage, Jarlan unrolled the old parchment and read the words of ancient resolve once more. He imagined Krampus trudging through hidden realms to find The Fatman, perhaps facing his own tests of pride and doubt. As he read, he tried to steady his trembling hand. Their fate might still rest on that legendary reunion, but the villagers would not wait passively. They would fight for their children, for Branwynn, for their tradition and future.

Outside, the night deepened. Snow fell softly, muffling sound and thought. Somewhere in that darkness, a wounded foe hissed and bled. Somewhere else, old magic stirred, and the memory of ancient pacts lingered. Sleetwood's people, though small and fearful, had found their backbone. They would defy the hunger nipping at their heels until Krampus and The Fatman returned to restore the world's balance—or until, by their own courage, they carved a path back to the light.

CHAPTER FOUR

The darkness before dawn settled thickly over Sleetwood, pressing into every gap of the timbered houses, stretching its chill fingers through keyholes and under eaves. It was the hour when the world balanced on a knife-edge—no longer fully night, not yet morning. A time of indecision and frayed nerves. Jarlan Forgerook and Helgrid Stonestream trudged back down the rutted path from the foothills, their breath pluming in hard-won silence. Although they carried within them a tiny ember of hope after meeting Krampus, the air around them felt charged with the awareness that the world was slipping from its old certainties.

As they approached the first squat cottages at the village outskirts, Jarlan raised his lantern. Its glow seemed paltry against the swallowing dark. No welcoming lamplight shone from windows, and no one stirred outside. It felt as though Sleetwood were huddled beneath a quilt of silence, pretending that if it lay still enough, the horrors would pass by without noticing. Jarlan's heart ached at the thought that many families inside were awake, staring into gloom, trying to protect what innocence remained under their roofs.

Helgrid's boots scuffed against a plank bridging a ditch, making her wince at the noise. "We need to act quickly," she said under her breath. "By sunrise, we must have a plan. The villagers… they won't hold together if we show them nothing but uncertainty."

Jarlan nodded, pressing a trembling hand against the pouch in which he stored the old parchment. "We must reassure them that Krampus is on our side, that he's seeking The Fatman. But will they believe it without proof? And what of Branwynn?" His voice hitched on the hedge-witch's name. They had found no sign of her but a torn scrap of fabric and the disturbance of her protective circle.

Helgrid's jaw tightened. "We cannot lie. The truth is grim, but it's better than letting panic breed wild rumors. If we say Krampus is working to restore the accord, at least they'll know we're not alone in this. As for Branwynn…" She trailed off, shoulders slumping. Without Branwynn's runic wards and magical insight, they felt half-blind. "We must trust that she still lives. If these vanishings serve a purpose for our enemy, they might keep her alive—at least for now."

The words offered cold comfort, but Jarlan clung to them. As they passed into the central lanes of Sleetwood, he resolved to gather the villagers at first light in the old meeting hall. It would be risky—what if the entity struck while everyone was in one place? But they could not let fear atomize them into helpless solitude. Unity was their best shield.

Helgrid tugged at his sleeve. "Look," she said, nodding at a pair of tracks in the snow. Footprints smaller than an adult's, leading from a side alley toward a boarded-up carpenter's shop. Jarlan inhaled sharply, heart pounding. He followed them with his lantern. The prints ended abruptly at the corner, as though the child who made them had vanished into thin air.

"Fresh," murmured Helgrid, kneeling to examine them. "The edges haven't softened. This happened recently."

Jarlan's mind conjured the image of a child, perhaps awake due to nightmares, venturing outdoors foolishly in search of comfort, only to be snatched away by whatever lurked in the shadows. He clenched his fists. "We must hurry. At first light, we gather everyone. If children are still slipping out unguarded, we must organize patrols. Something has to be done."

Helgrid stood, her face grave. "We'll speak plainly. Better they know the enemy is cunning than remain ignorant." She gestured toward the silent houses. "Go home, Jarlan. Get whatever you need for record-keeping. I'll call at a few trusted neighbors' doors, tell them to spread the word quietly that all should meet in the hall at dawn. We must show them we have a plan."

Jarlan started to protest—he was reluctant to separate—but her logic was sound. They had only a few hours before sunrise. He nodded. "Be careful. If you sense anything strange, call out."

Helgrid's grim smile flickered. "I have my hammer. And I'm not afraid to use it."

With that, they parted ways. Jarlan hurried down a narrow lane toward his small cottage. Inside, he lit a candle, warmed his numb fingers, and rifled through his notes and supplies. He was no warrior, no enchanter, just a chronicler. Yet knowledge could be a weapon. He took ink, parchment, a quill, and the precious old page detailing the second pact. Clutching these to his chest, he muttered a desperate prayer to any benevolent force still listening in these dark times.

Helgrid Stonestream moved like a shadow between dark houses. She chose carefully whose doors to knock on: dependable neighbors known for their courage or wisdom, families who once helped organize seasonal gatherings. At each threshold, she rapped quietly and whispered instructions: "At dawn, the meeting hall. Bring lanterns, dress warmly, stay together." Faces blurred by darkness nodded, fearful but grateful for direction. Helgrid did not mention Krampus or The Fatman yet; such revelations required a stable platform—no one would believe her in hushed exchanges at their doorsteps.

After rousing a half-dozen families, she turned toward the blacksmith's forge—her domain—and slipped inside. The coals were low, but still warm. She knelt and stirred them, feeding kindling and a few lumps of charcoal until embers glowed red. The forge's warmth steadied her. This place had always been a refuge where metal and will combined to create something purposeful. Now, she would forge not sled runners or decorative hinges, but symbols of resilience.

Helgrid rummaged through her materials: iron rods, scraps of copper, bits of etched steel that she had prepared earlier. She recalled old tales passed down in her family, stories of forging chains that once bound unruly spirits at Krampus's behest. Perhaps she could craft something similar—amulets or tokens infused with the intent to repel whatever dark presence prowled the village. Without Branwynn's magical prowess, she couldn't enchant metals with arcane power, but she could rely on dwarven runes of protection, tapping into the primal language of the earth itself.

Painstakingly, she shaped small iron disks, hammered flat and smooth, then etched simple protective glyphs. Each glyph invoked the steadfastness of stone and the purity of unspoiled snow. She murmured in her ancestral tongue, calling on the old dwarven gods to lend a whisper of strength. It was a long shot—these were not true magical artifacts—but symbolism and belief could wield subtle power. If nothing else, these tokens would reassure people that they were not defenseless.

The hours crawled by as she worked, sweat beading on her brow despite the cold outside. Her arms ached, and the hammer rang dully in the silence. She made a dozen tokens, then two dozen, pushing herself, knowing dawn approached. When she finally stopped, placing the cooling charms in a cloth pouch, she felt weary but resolved. Let the villagers hold these tokens close. Let them believe they were protected. Belief might help close the cracks that the nameless hunger was prying open.

In the meeting hall, first light filtered through the small, iced-over windows. The hall's wooden beams groaned softly as the temperature shifted, and Jarlan Forgerook arranged benches to form a rough semicircle. He lit two lanterns and set them by the raised platform. The hall smelled of old varnish and candle wax, comforting in its familiarity.

One by one, villagers trickled in—some in grim silence, others whispering anxiously to neighbors. They looked haggard: red-rimmed eyes from sleepless nights, shoulders hunched as if expecting a blow. Many clutched blankets or scarves. A few carried stout cudgels or walking sticks. Jarlan saw fear in their eyes, but also a flicker of determination. At least they were here, together.

Helgrid arrived soon after, holding her pouch of tokens. She nodded at Jarlan and took a seat near the front. The hall grew crowded: parents holding frightened children close, older folk muttering that they had never seen the like. Jarlan waited until he could sense a collective hush, then stepped onto the platform.

He cleared his throat, heart pounding. "Thank you for coming," he began. His voice sounded thin in the large space, but people leaned forward, eager to listen. "I know these are terrible times. Children vanish. Our hedge-witch is missing. No one knows what moves in the darkness. But we cannot face this threat alone, hidden in our homes. We must stand together."

A murmur passed through the crowd. Eyes flicked nervously toward shuttered windows. Jarlan raised a hand for silence. "I have spent my life recording our village's lore. I found an old parchment that speaks of a time, long ago, when a similar menace threatened these lands. Back then, Krampus and The Fatman—yes, the very figures of our winter traditions—were forced to reforge their ancient bond to drive out a nameless hunger. It is happening again."

This statement provoked gasps. Some scoffed, as if unwilling to believe that their holiday legends lived as tangible beings. But others looked thoughtful. Jarlan pressed on. "We encountered Krampus last night." His voice almost broke at the admission, and the hall erupted in uneasy whispers. "He knows what is happening and has agreed to seek The Fatman. Together, they can restore the balance and end these vanishings."

Near the back, a stout baker named Orlan stood, red-faced. "You expect us to trust a monster that punishes children?" he demanded. "How do we know Krampus isn't behind this?"

Helgrid rose, fists clenched. "Krampus is harsh, yes," she said, voice steady. "But he follows a code—he doesn't snatch children without reason, leaving chaos in his wake. Those who vanish now are lost without a trace, without the moral lesson Krampus would impart. We must trust Jarlan's scholarship. Krampus and The Fatman's partnership is what keeps our world in check."

Another voice, quieter, spoke up: "What of Branwynn Spellshiver? Did Krampus take her, too?" A woman near the front, tears shining in her eyes, clutched a scrap of embroidered fabric—a hint that she might have known Branwynn well.

Jarlan shook his head sadly. "We do not believe so. Branwynn was working to protect us when she was taken. The entity responsible for these vanishings aims to weaken us by removing our sources of strength. But we must not give in. We must hold on until Krampus returns with The Fatman, or until we find another way to free the captives."

The crowd quieted, absorbing this grim message. Helgrid stepped forward, holding up the pouch of iron tokens. "I cannot offer magic," she said, "but I have forged these charms of iron and rune, small tokens of protection. Keep them in your homes, near your doors and windows. They may not be powerful sorcery, but they represent our resolve. We do not lie down and yield."

A line formed as people came up to receive tokens. Some wept softly, some gripped Helgrid's hand in gratitude. Others simply bowed their heads. In that moment, it seemed the villagers rediscovered their communal spirit. They might be afraid, but they would not scatter like frightened mice. They would stand shoulder to shoulder against the encroaching dark.

Jarlan noticed a figure slipping through the crowd: a gangly fellow named Edric, known for his keen hearing and skill in hunting. Edric approached the platform and spoke quietly: "If we organize patrols, I can help. The enemy thrives in silence and isolation. With careful rotations, we might keep watch and sound alarms at the first hint of trouble."

Encouraged, Jarlan nodded. "Yes, form patrols. Move in pairs or trios. Never go alone." He glanced at Helgrid. "We must ensure these people know what to look for. Any strange footprints, any half-heard whispers… report them immediately."

Helgrid agreed. "I will oversee the forging of simple weapons—mostly iron-tipped poles or weighted cudgels. We must show we are not helpless prey."

Though fear lingered, a quiet determination settled over the villagers. They had a role to play: to survive, to resist, to await the return of their legendary protectors. The seeds of resilience took root under the wooden beams of the meeting hall.

Hours crept by. The sun rose, weak and pale, casting uncertain light over Sleetwood. Patrols began to circle the lanes. One trio moved around the village's perimeter, stamping through snow, scanning the edges of forest for unusual tracks. Another pair stood near the old chapel ruins, gazing at the broken stone arches and wondering what Branwynn had seen before she vanished. Inside homes, parents hung Helgrid's iron tokens over lintels, whispering prayers that these humble charms would ward off evil.

Jarlan and Helgrid reconvened in the meeting hall with Edric and a few others who volunteered as coordinators: Marta Greshill, a widowed midwife known for her calm head, and Takrin Fellbow, a retired trapper with sharp instincts and a limp from an old injury. They spread out a crude map of Sleetwood and its environs on a bench, marking where disappearances occurred, where footprints were found, and where patrols would concentrate.

Krampus

They spoke quietly, voices subdued but purposeful. Jarlan's lantern flickered as a draft slipped under the hall's door. "If Krampus succeeds in finding The Fatman, how soon can we expect them?" Marta asked, brushing a lock of gray hair from her face.

Jarlan bit his lip. "I cannot say. Legends suggest The Fatman wanders beyond ordinary realms, only appearing fully during his season of gift-giving. Krampus might have to traverse hidden paths or use ancient signs to reach him. It could be days—or longer."

A heavy silence followed. Days of this tension, this fear? Could they endure?

Helgrid gripped the edge of the bench. "We must. There is no other choice. In the meantime, we search for clues. Maybe we can find where Branwynn and the children were taken. If we can rescue even one child, imagine the hope that would bring."

Takrin spoke up: "In my trapping days, I learned to follow subtle signs. I'll comb the forest edge. If this enemy leaves any hint—a broken twig, a tuft of strange fur—I'll find it. Edric can listen for unnatural sounds. Maybe we can track the direction of these vanishings."

Jarlan nodded, heartened by their resolve. "Do it. But be cautious. This is no ordinary predator."

That afternoon, the wind changed. It blew in from the north, colder and sharper, carrying a distant keening sound. The villagers, busying themselves with meager chores and nervous conversations, glanced upward at the snow-laden clouds. Several patrols reported strange echoes in the forest—like laughter, but stretched thin and distorted. Others found footprints that began and ended abruptly, as if something leapt through shadows. Yet, no immediate attacks occurred, and no new disappearances were reported that day. It was as if the entity toyed with them, savoring their fear.

In the twilight, a group gathered at the old chapel ruins to place fresh wards. Without Branwynn, they had only mundane means: lines of salt, carvings of runes Helgrid recalled from old dwarven tales, and small mirrors set on stumps to catch any unseen shapes. Marta led a quiet prayer, not to any specific god, but to the spirit of life and continuity. The villagers hunched together in the cold, each breath a vow to endure.

Meanwhile, inside Jarlan's cottage, the chronicler spread his notes on the rickety table. He wanted to understand the pattern of past events.

The parchment he found spoke of a "nameless hunger" that had once tested the accord. Could this be the same entity—or another of its kind?

His candle guttered as he read. He noted how the old text mentioned the entity's delight in unraveling trust. By sowing suspicion and fear, it undermined the moral lessons The Fatman and Krampus taught. Without children learning from these beings—either through kindness or caution—humanity would drift away from the values that shaped their world. The entity seemed to feed on that drifting, growing stronger as moral certainties crumbled.

Jarlan thought about Krampus's words: "Stand together, or you will stand no chance at all." This enemy wanted them divided. They must do the opposite. He would share this insight at tomorrow's meeting. Perhaps understanding the creature's motive might help them resist its manipulations.

A tap at his door startled him. He rose, heart in his throat, and unlatched it. Takrin stood there, breathing hard. Snow clung to his hood and beard. "Jarlan," he gasped, "come with me. I've found something in the woods—footprints not human or animal. You must see."

Grabbing his cloak and lantern, Jarlan followed Takrin out into the bitter night. The village seemed asleep, but he knew patrols watched from shadowed corners. They slipped between houses and into a narrow deer trail leading into the forest. The lantern's light flickered over snow-laden branches. Takrin moved with surprising silence for a man with a limp, and Jarlan struggled to keep pace without slipping.

They reached a small clearing surrounded by twisted firs. Under the lantern's glow, Jarlan saw tracks—thin, elongated prints with clawed tips. They formed a looping pattern, as if something danced or skittered in circles. The hair on Jarlan's neck rose. He knelt, examining them closely. The edges were crisp, likely recent. No known creature left such tracks. They tapered like a malformed hand pressed into snow.

Takrin pointed silently to a tree trunk. Jarlan moved the lantern and froze. A symbol had been scratched into the bark—a crude spiral with jagged lines radiating outward. It seemed to writhe in the lantern's unsteady light.

Jarlan touched the bark carefully. The scratches were fresh, no older than a day. His mind raced. The entity must have a physical form to leave these marks, or it employed servants. Perhaps twisted goblins or spirits coerced into service. Or maybe it was manifesting partially in their world.

He and Takrin backed away, careful not to disturb the tracks further. The trapper's eyes were grim. "We must tell the others. It's marking territory, or leaving messages."

Jarlan nodded, heart sinking. So the enemy toyed with them, leaving clues or warnings. "We'll bring Helgrid and Edric at dawn. We must study these signs further."

They returned to the village under a silent sky. Not even the wind dared to whisper now, as if expecting a confrontation soon.

Morning brought no comfort. The villagers gathered in the meeting hall again, huddling for warmth and reassurance. Jarlan explained what he and Takrin found. Gasps rippled through the crowd. Some wept quietly, clutching their children, who looked pale and silent. Others blanched at the idea of a creature carving ominous sigils in their forest.

Marta stepped onto the platform and raised her voice. "We must not surrender to despair. We have found signs—this means the creature can be tracked, understood. It reveals itself, in part, because it wants to frighten us. We can use that against it. Let us set traps near that clearing. If it returns, we might wound it or at least learn more about its nature."

The suggestion brought a murmur of agreement. Helgrid nodded firmly. "I'll craft snares with iron teeth. Even if we can't kill it, we might slow it down. And if we capture a minion of this entity, we could force it to reveal where our children and Branwynn are held."

Edric rubbed his chin. "We must be careful. This foe is cunning. But we have skills too. I can climb a tree and keep watch overhead, alerting the others at the first sign of movement. With coordinated patrols, we can force it into a confrontation on our terms."

They drew up plans, simple and desperate. Jarlan felt a strange calm settle over him. Two nights ago, Sleetwood was paralyzed by fear, scattered and unsure. Now, although still terrified, they were acting—taking steps, however small, to fight back. Perhaps the nameless hunger would realize that these people were not so easily broken.

By midday, the villagers worked quietly but efficiently. Groups trudged into the forest near the clearing, placing hidden traps, covering them with pine needles and snow. Edric climbed a thick-limbed spruce, testing vantage points that overlooked the clearing. Helgrid hammered sharpened stakes into the ground, arms trembling with exertion. Marta and Takrin scouted around the perimeter, ensuring escape routes were clear. Jarlan hovered near the center, trying to memorize every detail of the tracks and the sigil on the tree, hoping to glean a pattern or meaning.

He noticed subtle things: the spiraling symbol had six radiating lines, each angled slightly differently, as though representing discordant forces. Could it stand for corruption of the six core virtues taught through The Fatman and Krampus's lessons—generosity, gratitude, responsibility, honesty, courage, and humility—turning them into twisted inversions? Jarlan could only guess. But thinking along these lines reminded him that the entity thrived on moral confusion. Sleetwood's unity, its moral spine, would be the best defense.

They worked until dusk, then withdrew, leaving a few brave souls hidden behind snowbanks to watch if anything approached the traps. The hours ticked by, slow and tense. Jarlan and Helgrid waited in the meeting hall with a handful of others, sharpening tools and sipping thin broth to keep warm. The silence weighed heavily, broken only by coughs or the creak of wooden benches.

Close to midnight, a runner burst into the hall, breath steaming. "We heard something!" he panted. "In the clearing. A laugh like grinding ice. Something triggered a trap—chains rattled."

Everyone leapt up. Helgrid seized her hammer, face grim. Jarlan's stomach knotted. They must act swiftly and quietly, lest they lose this opportunity.

A dozen villagers—armed with makeshift weapons, iron tokens, and lanterns carefully hooded—followed the runner back into the darkness. They moved in cautious silence, guided only by starlight and memory. The wind had died again, leaving the forest unnaturally quiet.

When they reached the edge of the clearing, Edric slithered down from the spruce, eyes wide. "The trap near the spiral tree snapped on something," he whispered. "I saw movement—a shape hunched low, struggling. But it melted into the shadows before I could get a clear look. Still, blood—there's blood in the snow."

Helgrid nodded, jaw set. "We've wounded it. That's a start." She looked at Jarlan. "If we can track blood drops, maybe we can follow it back to its lair."

Marta and Takrin joined them, lanterns shielded. Carefully, they advanced into the clearing. True to Edric's words, the trap—a pair of iron jaws Helgrid had fashioned—sat askew, its spring triggered. Dark stains spattered the surrounding snow. Takrin knelt and touched a finger to the blood. It was oddly thick, with a faint, foul smell like stagnant water.

Jarlan's pulse hammered. "This proves it can be hurt," he murmured. "It's not invincible."

Marta set her lantern low, examining the tracks leading away. The footprints were smeared, as if the creature limped off at speed. They led deeper into the forest, toward a dense patch of firs. Edric volunteered to scout ahead, and Helgrid insisted on coming too.

Jarlan and the others waited, breath held, as Edric and Helgrid slipped into darkness. Time stretched. An owl hooted, startling them. Jarlan's heart thumped painfully. He imagined Helgrid holding her hammer, Edric gripping a shortbow, creeping between trunks, following a ribbon of dark droplets. If they found the creature's lair, could they rescue the children and Branwynn? Or would they stumble into a trap?

After what felt like an eternity, Helgrid returned alone. Her eyes shone with fierce triumph and terror combined. She spoke softly but urgently. "The blood trail leads to a rocky outcrop. We didn't get too close, but I smelled decay—like a den of rot. Edric saw movement: small shapes creeping around, maybe goblins twisted by this dark magic. We dare not go in without more force."

Jarlan nodded, mind racing. They had a lead, a direction. "We should return with more villagers, better armed," he said. "But if we strike too soon, we risk scattering them or endangering the captives."

Marta frowned. "If the creature is wounded, it may be more desperate. It could harm the children or Branwynn."

Helgrid's knuckles whitened on her hammer handle. "We must prepare carefully. Traps, torches, a planned assault. If Krampus and The Fatman return soon, that would be ideal—but we cannot rely on it. We must be ready to act on our own."

Her words hung in the cold air. The villagers exchanged grim looks. They were no warriors. Most had never fought anything more fearsome than a hungry wolf near their goat pens. Yet now they were challenged by a cunning, supernatural enemy.

Jarlan straightened. "We must hold firm. Our courage, our unity—these are the virtues this creature seeks to destroy. By standing together and helping each other, we deny it that victory." He swallowed hard, feeling the weight of his own words. "Let's organize a proper expedition.

By dawn, we'll assemble volunteers and supplies. We know where to strike."

Helgrid nodded. Marta and Takrin agreed. The villagers around them, though frightened, affirmed their support. Edric, reappearing from the gloom, added, "I'll guide us. I know those woods. If we move quietly, we might catch it by surprise."

So they retreated to Sleetwood again, hearts pounding with resolve and fear. They lit no bonfires—no need to announce their plans—but each home's window now held a faint glow of lamplight. No one wanted to sleep while the enemy prowled wounded and enraged.

In a quiet corner of his cottage, Jarlan unrolled the old parchment and read the words of ancient resolve once more. He imagined Krampus trudging through hidden realms to find The Fatman, perhaps facing his own tests of pride and doubt. As he read, he tried to steady his trembling hand. Their fate might still rest on that legendary reunion, but the villagers would not wait passively. They would fight for their children, for Branwynn, for their tradition and future.

Outside, the night deepened. Snow fell softly, muffling sound and thought. Somewhere in that darkness, a wounded foe hissed and bled. Somewhere else, old magic stirred, and the memory of ancient pacts lingered. Sleetwood's people, though small and fearful, had found their backbone. They would defy the hunger nipping at their heels until Krampus and The Fatman returned to restore the world's balance—or until, by their own courage, they carved a path back to the light.

CHAPTER FIVE

A bitter dawn mist curled through the pines, blurring the stark outlines of trunks and branches into wavering shapes. The first hints of pale light seeped through the forest canopy, making the snow glow faintly in shades of lavender and ghostly white. Sleetwood stirred from its uneasy vigil, doors creaking open, hooded heads peering out. No one had slept soundly—if at all. Instead, they'd listened to the night breathe around them, waiting for another cry, another sign of terror. Yet the hours had passed in tense quiet, and now the villagers gathered in the meeting hall once more, determined and grim.

Jarlan Forgerook stood on the raised platform, unrolling a rough sketch of the forest's northeastern quadrant where Takrin and Edric had found the blood trail and the strange sigils. Before him, about two dozen villagers—those who had volunteered to join the expedition—milled with nervous energy. Helgrid Stonestream and Edric stood at his sides, forming a small, resolute triangle of leadership. Marta, the midwife, hovered at the edge of the group, her face set, ready to tend to wounds if the expedition returned battered. Takrin's keen eyes scanned the room, ensuring that the volunteers were well equipped and sober-minded.

Jarlan cleared his throat, and all eyes turned to him. "We have found a lead," he said softly, his voice carrying in the hush. "Last night, our trap wounded the creature, leaving a trail of blood leading to a rocky outcrop deeper in the forest. Edric and Helgrid saw signs of movement there—small shapes lurking in the shadows, a stench of decay. It may be the lair of our enemy."

A ripple of anxiety passed through the crowd. They had heard these tidings already, but hearing them again in the pale dawn heightened the reality. None wanted to imagine what dwelt in that hidden place—captured children, Branwynn Spellshiver, or worse, a hunger waiting to devour their last shreds of hope.

Edric raised a hand and stepped forward. "We plan to move as a coordinated party. No more than a dozen will approach the lair's perimeter. The rest will form a second line, some distance back, ready to offer support if needed. We must be quiet, careful. We will bring torches, ropes, and Helgrid's iron-tipped spears. We don't know what we'll face inside."

Helgrid nodded, arms folded over her broad chest. "We have no magic to rely on. Our advantage is preparation, courage, and the iron runes I've crafted. Keep them close," she urged, patting the pouch at her belt where she'd stored additional tokens overnight. "They may not be spells, but they stand for our unity and resolve. If fear and disunity fuel this enemy, we must deny it those weapons."

At this, a villager named Garren, a thin man with hollow cheeks and darting eyes, spoke up anxiously. "What if we fail? What if this thing is too strong, too cunning? We can't match Krampus or The Fatman in power."

Jarlan met Garren's eyes steadily. "Our role is not to defeat it alone—our role is to hold the line, to try and rescue those taken, to learn more, to survive until Krampus and The Fatman return to restore balance. Krampus promised to find his brother. We must trust that he is working even now, beyond our sight. Meanwhile, we do what we can to protect what remains of our community."

The words settled over them like a fragile net of reassurance. They were not heroes from legends, but ordinary folk struggling in extraordinary darkness. Yet ordinary folk could rise to meet challenges when all else failed. They could refuse despair; they could fight for their children and their future.

Takrin stepped forward, limping slightly, and tapped the map. "We'll leave within the hour. Edric and I know the route. We'll move in silence. The forest is thick, and the entity might have scouts—or worse. If any of you see or hear something strange, alert the group quietly. We must not let panic scatter us."

A hush followed as the volunteers nodded. Among them, Jarlan recognized faces he'd known for years—neighbors who once laughed over cider, now grim and pale. He recognized the baker Orlan, who had previously doubted Krampus's innocence, standing with shoulders squared, gripping a stout club. He saw Annet, the tailor's daughter, trembling but resolute beside her older brother, who carried one of Helgrid's spears. He saw Colreth, a former woodcutter turned reluctant guard, strapping on old leather bracers as if heading to a battlefield rather than a forest trail.

"Let's prepare," said Helgrid quietly. "Gather your cloaks and weapons. We meet at the village's north edge at sunrise."

The crowd began to disperse. Marta stayed behind, holding Jarlan's gaze. "I'll remain here to tend any who return injured. But be careful, Jarlan. If you find Branwynn or the children, send runners back so we can prepare safe refuge."

Jarlan nodded and touched her arm. "We will do our best. Thank you."

Outside the meeting hall, a watery sunlight tried to pierce the haze, rendering the snow-crusted roofs in dull pewter tones. Villagers whispered farewells to loved ones. Some pressed small gifts into the volunteers' hands—warm mittens, a strip of dried meat for strength, a wooden token carved with the likeness of a friendly sprite. These gestures reminded everyone that their fight was not just against an unknown horror, but for the simple comforts of home and family.

Jarlan ducked into his cottage briefly to take a final look at the old parchment. The words were burned into his memory: how the ancient crisis had ended when Krampus and The Fatman renewed their bond. He prayed silently that their legendary allies would hurry, for time felt short. Before leaving, he tucked the parchment inside his coat, as if carrying a piece of that old hope with him.

At the northern edge of Sleetwood, about a dozen volunteers assembled. Helgrid distributed iron tokens and spears. Edric inspected his bowstring one last time. Jarlan stood near Helgrid and Takrin, lantern unlit in his hand—light would come later, if needed. For now, they would trust their eyes and ears and the faint guidance of memory.

They marched out, boots crunching softly. Behind them, a few villagers stood watch, silent silhouettes against the snow. It felt like embarking on a quest out of old tales, only without the comfort of a hero's blessing. Just fear, love, and necessity.

The forest greeted them with hush and shadow. Snow-laden branches arched overhead, forming a ribcage of white and black. Edric led, scanning for signs of tracks. Jarlan followed near the middle, heart thudding, keeping a vigilant watch on his companions' faces. No one spoke. They communicated with nods and gestures, learning the language of stealth on the fly.

As they ventured deeper, the air turned colder, and an eerie quiet settled in. Not even birdsong broke the silence. Jarlan recalled how, in friendlier winters, chickadees would flit among the pines, and distant crows would caw at midday. Now, nature itself seemed to hold its breath. The entity's influence stretched beyond vanishings and twisted sigils; it hollowed out the world's normal rhythms, leaving a stage set only for dread.

After nearly an hour of trudging through snow and weaving between pines, Edric raised a hand, halting them. He crouched and pointed at a faint streak of brownish-red staining the snow. Blood. The trail picked up here, confirming they were on the right path. Takrin tested the scent. It still carried that fetid, stagnant odor. The creature bled, and it was not healing quickly—this was good news for their cause, though grim in its implications.

They pressed on, following the blood spatter as it led them through a thick stand of firs. The trees here were twisted, their trunks bent at odd angles, as if the land itself suffered from some invisible blight. Jarlan's boots slipped on patches of ice beneath a thin crust of snow. He steadied himself against a trunk, feeling its bark crumble strangely under his glove. Rot, in midwinter? Unnatural.

A low whistle from Helgrid brought them to another halt. She pointed ahead, and Jarlan saw the rocky outcrop looming through the mist —a jagged protrusion of dark stone, half-veiled by dead vines. At its base, there was a depression, like the maw of a shallow cave. This must be the lair.

The volunteers clustered behind a fallen log to plan. Edric's eyes narrowed as he studied the site. He had seen movement here last night, small shapes lurking. Now, the place looked deserted. No tracks visible from their vantage point, no obvious guards. But that was suspicious. The enemy would not leave its lair unguarded.

Takrin lifted his hand, showing two fingers, then gestured in a circle. He proposed that he and two others circle around to check the perimeter. Helgrid agreed. They selected Orlan and Colreth, men steady and quiet, for the scouting task. The three of them slipped away into the brush, leaving Jarlan and the others hunkered down, waiting, breath steaming in the cold.

Time stretched, minutes feeling like hours. Jarlan gripped an iron token so tightly it left an imprint on his palm. He replayed Krampus's words in his mind—"Stand together, or you will stand no chance at all." In this moment of stillness and fear, he understood the wisdom. Any panic, any rash action, could doom them.

At last, Takrin and the others returned, crawling on hands and knees to avoid silhouette against the stone. Takrin shook his head once: no guards spotted. But Orlan tapped the ground with his finger, then mimed something small scurrying. Edric nodded—likely goblin-like creatures just out of sight, maybe lurking inside the cave. If these minions were influenced or controlled by the entity, they would be cunning and cruel, even if physically weak.

Helgrid pointed to two volunteers holding ropes and nodded toward the outcrop's western flank. If they could secure lines, they might descend from above into the cave's mouth, surprising whatever lay within. Jarlan watched these preparations, heart pounding. This was it—the edge of the known. Would they find the children inside? Branwynn Spellshiver? Or only horror?

Before they moved in, Jarlan placed a hand on Helgrid's shoulder. They locked eyes, sharing unspoken resolve. She nodded and raised her hammer slightly—a silent vow. Behind them, the others tightened grips on weapons. Each knew they might not return unscathed.

Edric led again, creeping forward with exaggerated slowness, boots barely whispering on snow. The rest followed in pairs, some taking the flank, others staying behind Edric. Jarlan ended up near the center, straining his ears. He heard faint dripping—a trickle of water inside the cave. No voices, no sobbing children, no chanted spells. Just emptiness, or the illusion of it.

They reached the cave entrance, a shallow maw in the outcrop. It sloped downward, just high enough for a man to stand hunched. The smell that greeted them was rank—damp rot and old blood, a stench that tugged at the stomach. Helgrid grimaced but pressed on, knuckles white around her hammer.

They entered in pairs. Edric first, lantern hooded to reduce light but provide enough glow to see a few steps ahead. Behind him, a spearman with one of Helgrid's iron-tipped weapons. Then Jarlan and Helgrid, followed by others in careful sequence. The cave walls were slick, the floor uneven. Loose stones shifted underfoot, threatening to send echoes of their intrusion deeper inside.

Deeper they went, step by step, until the gloom swallowed the daylight entirely. Edric opened the lantern's shutter a hair wider, revealing cramped stone passageways. The cave split in two directions. One path slanted right, the other left. Without words, Edric chose the right path, guided by the faint odor of decay growing stronger.

They advanced, hearts hammering, until they reached a hollowed chamber. Inside, the lantern revealed a ghastly sight: scattered bones—not human, but animal, perhaps deer or foxes—gnawed and broken. A crude arrangement of stones formed a makeshift altar in the center, daubed with a dark, sticky substance. Jarlan's stomach twisted. The shapes scrawled on the altar resembled the sigil carved in the forest tree—spirals and radiating lines. This was a place of foul rites.

But no children. No Branwynn. Just silence and bone.

Edric gestured for them to remain still. He knelt and touched a patch of blood-stained earth. Still tacky. The wounded creature must have come here recently. Then why was it gone now?

A hiss echoed from somewhere deeper in the cave. Everyone froze. The sound did not repeat, but now their hearts raced faster. Helgrid inched toward a narrow passage that branched off the chamber. She held her hammer high, while a spearman took her flank.

They followed the hiss to a smaller alcove. The light revealed a lump of fur and flesh—some twisted beast that lay dying, one leg caught in a length of chain. It resembled a goblin, but with elongated limbs and patchy fur, eyes milky and unfocused. The iron jaws of last night's trap had caught and torn it. Blood pooled beneath it, seeping into the dirt. At their approach, it bared needle-sharp teeth and rasped out a series of clicks and growls.

Orlan recoiled, but Helgrid stood firm. "What are you?" she whispered, as if expecting an answer. The creature only hissed again, swiping feebly at the air. Then, shocking them all, it gurgled a few distorted words.

They were not in a language Jarlan recognized, but the tone was mocking, pain-laced yet triumphant. As if even dying, it took pleasure in their horror. Helgrid raised her hammer, uncertain whether to strike the creature down.

Jarlan knelt, bracing himself, and tried to speak calmly: "Where are the children? Where is Branwynn?" Of course, it might not understand, but desperation spurred him.

The creature coughed, spattering blood. Then it croaked a single recognizable word amid its guttural nonsense: "Deep...er..."

The volunteers exchanged looks. Deeper. Another chamber, perhaps, another part of this warren. They must go further. Before they could question it more, the creature spasmed and lay still, a final wheeze escaping its throat. Dead. Its blood steamed faintly in the cold cave air.

They moved on, carefully, leaving the corpse behind. Jarlan's heart tightened. They had confirmation that something lay deeper within. He imagined a nest of horrors, or a prison cell carved into rock. The path sloped downward again. The stones felt slicker, and once Jarlan nearly slipped, saved only by Helgrid's steady arm.

After a few more twists and turns, the tunnel opened into a larger cavern. The smell was overwhelming now: old fur, damp earth, and something like burned metal. Edric shuttered the lantern even more, worried that too much light would give them away. But in the dim glow, Jarlan glimpsed shapes that made his blood run cold: cages made of twisted branches and bone lashed together with sinew. Inside one cage—he dared not cry out—he saw a child's foot poking out.

He gestured wildly to Helgrid, who brought the lantern closer. Indeed, a cluster of cages stood along the far wall, half-submerged in a shallow pool of dark water. Huddled within, small forms—children, possibly alive but unmoving. Jarlan's throat constricted. They had found them. The missing children. Yet they were silent, too silent. Enchanted, or drugged?

Helgrid's jaw clenched. She turned to Jarlan and mouthed, "We must free them." He nodded, tears burning at the corners of his eyes. He counted at least five small shapes. Could Branwynn be here too?

They stepped carefully, aware that at any moment the enemy could strike. One by one, volunteers fanned out, checking corners, looking for guards. The cavern floor was muddy, their boots squelching softly. The silence pressed in. Where was the creature itself, or its minions?

Edric reached a cage and tested the bars with his dagger. They were surprisingly tough, bound with resin or tar. He signaled for Helgrid, who brought her hammer. With careful, muffled strikes, she tried to crack the lashings.

Meanwhile, Jarlan moved to another cage, heart pounding so loudly he feared it would echo. Inside were two children, eyes half-lidded, chests rising and falling slowly, as if in a trance. He recognized one: Elsbet Quinshale, her pale face smudged with grime. Relief and rage warred in him. They were alive, but stolen and caged like animals. He whispered softly, "Elsbet?" No response. The girl breathed, but did not stir.

Across the cavern, a volunteer stifled a gasp. Jarlan looked over and saw them kneeling by a shape on the ground, draped in tattered robes. Branwynn Spellshiver. The hedge-witch lay unconscious, hands bound with twisted vines, her face slack. A hush of gratitude and dread fell over them. They had found her too. Now they had to get out before the entity returned.

Helgrid's hammer cracked a branch-bar with a muffled snap. They began cutting children free, passing them gently to others. The youngsters weighed almost nothing, limp and cold. They wrapped them in cloaks and whispered soothing words. Across the chamber, another pair of volunteers worked to free Branwynn, sawing at the vines with a knife. The hedge-witch moaned softly, eyelids fluttering. Good—she was alive.

Just as they managed to free the last child, a sound like distant laughter echoed through the cavern. Everyone froze, hearts jolting. The laughter rose, then faded, then rose again. It sounded like multiple voices overlapping, high and low, a distorted chorus. Edric motioned for silence, pulling everyone back toward the tunnel with urgent gestures. They had their precious cargo—five children, Branwynn, all unconscious or barely conscious. They must retreat.

They moved quietly, two volunteers carrying Branwynn between them, others carrying children bundled in cloaks. Jarlan took Elsbet in his arms, her head lolling on his shoulder. Helgrid led the way back, hammer ready. If something leapt from the shadows, she would strike first.

The laughter continued, mocking and alien. It reverberated through the stone, making it impossible to discern direction. The volunteers stuck close, weapons up. Edric brought the lantern higher now, sacrificing stealth for speed. They could not navigate in darkness with wounded and children in their arms.

They passed the dead goblin-like creature, still lying limp where it had fallen. Its blood had congealed into a tar-like puddle. The corridor felt different now—colder, narrower. Jarlan's breath came in sharp gasps. He imagined the entity's presence closing in on them like invisible jaws. Had they just robbed it of its prizes?

At the first chamber, where bones littered the floor, they heard a shuffle at the edge of the lantern light. A twisted silhouette darted across their path—another minion, perhaps. Helgrid growled low in her throat. "Faster!" she hissed, and they hurried on, stumbling over stones.

A screech rang out, followed by skittering sounds. Something launched from a crevice—a gaunt figure with hollow eyes and too-long arms. It landed near Orlan, who swung his club desperately, connecting with a damp thud. The creature shrieked and retreated, leaving dark slime on the club's end. More sounds scuttled behind them. A pack, perhaps?

Takrin pressed them onward, forging ahead. They could not stand and fight; they must escape. Jarlan's chest tightened with panic. The narrow tunnel forced them into single file. Behind him, he heard volunteers grunting, striking blindly at shapes that appeared and vanished in the gloom. The children remained eerily silent, as if locked in unnatural sleep. Branwynn moaned again, but did not wake.

They reached the main entrance passage at last. Faint daylight glimmered ahead. Relief surged in Jarlan's chest. Almost out. Helgrid took the lead, raising her hammer to ward off any ambush near the exit. Edric brought up the rear, loosing an arrow at a flicker of movement, eliciting a pained hiss.

Bursting into the open air felt like a rebirth. The daylight—dim though it was—blinded them momentarily. They stumbled out onto snow and ice, lungs gulping fresh cold air. Behind them, screeches and chittering laughter sounded from the cave mouth. None of the creatures dared follow into the full light, or perhaps they feared the villagers' iron weapons. The volunteers formed a defensive circle, spears bristling. For a tense minute, they waited, but nothing emerged. Only mocking laughter that gradually faded.

They had escaped with their captives.

Jarlan almost sobbed in relief. He glanced down at Elsbet's pale face, smoothing a strand of hair from her forehead. She was alive, rescued. The others murmured softly to their freed children, wrapping them warmly.

But it wasn't over. They stood in the open forest, still deep in enemy territory. They must return to Sleetwood without delay. Helgrid nodded curtly, leading them away from the cave, following their old tracks. They would move quickly, if carefully, and get these victims into warm beds and protective arms.

As they hurried through the forest, Jarlan's mind raced. They had found the children and Branwynn, but they had not confronted the entity itself. They'd seen only its lair, its minions, and signs of dark rituals. The creature behind this horror remained at large, wounded but not defeated.

He thought of Krampus and The Fatman again, praying they would come soon. Surely the brothers' renewed bond would drive back this nameless hunger. Until then, the villagers had proven they could act to save their own. They had braved darkness and rescued their loved ones, proving that unity and courage mattered.

Halfway back to Sleetwood, Branwynn stirred more strongly. Jarlan, who had taken a turn carrying her, paused as her eyes fluttered open. They were unfocused, frightened. He hushed her gently, "You're safe now. We've got you." She shuddered and tried to speak, voice raw: "The children… I tried to protect them. Magic… failing…"

"Shh," Helgrid said, stepping close. "They're safe, we have them." Branwynn's gaze slid to the children, carried by the volunteers. She seemed to relax a fraction, tears glistening. Then her expression hardened with remembered terror.

"Entity… wants to break the accord," she managed, voice rasping. "Tried to twist their innocence. Feed on it… must stop it soon…" She coughed, and Jarlan held her closer, feeling her shiver. "Krampus… The Fatman… must hurry."

Jarlan nodded. "We know. We're holding on."

Despite the grim news, hope flickered. Branwynn was alive, and when she recovered, perhaps she could help restore protective wards. With her guidance, they could better resist the entity's influence. The children might be traumatized, but alive and home where they belonged. Sleetwood had scored a small victory this day.

As they approached the village's edge, lookouts shouted in surprise and joy. Word spread quickly. Villagers poured from cottages, gasping at the sight of their missing children returned. Mothers wept openly, hugging volunteers as they carried the small, unconscious forms inside. Fathers bowed their heads in silent gratitude. Marta rushed to Branwynn's side, guiding them to a warm bed in the meeting hall's back room. Jarlan handed Elsbet over to her parents, who clutched their daughter as if never letting go again.

Within minutes, Sleetwood's atmosphere transformed. Relief warred with lingering fear, but relief held firm. They had done the impossible: entered the lair and returned. Though they had not slain the monster, they had reclaimed what it had stolen. This was a statement of defiance that would echo in every whispered conversation that night.

Helgrid, exhausted, sank onto a bench in the meeting hall. Jarlan joined her, shoulders slumped. Edric paced the room's perimeter, uneasy. Takrin leaned against a wall, breathing deeply. Outside, snow drifted lazily, as if the world itself were exhaling after a long gasp.

Marta emerged from the back room where Branwynn and the children were settled. She smiled faintly. "They're stable. The children sleep as if drugged, but they show no sign of injury. Branwynn is weak but conscious. She needs rest and broth." She touched Jarlan's arm. "You did well. All of you."

Jarlan swallowed hard, remembering the horror in that cavern, the dead creature's milky eyes, and the laughter that had chased them. "We must not be complacent," he said softly. "We wounded the beast's servants and robbed it of its prizes. It will be angry."

Helgrid nodded. "But we've shown we are not helpless. Let it think twice before striking again." She glanced around at the exhausted volunteers now receiving thanks and warm food from relieved neighbors. "We must reinforce our defenses. Add more traps, more patrols. And now that Branwynn is safe, perhaps she can restore wards around the village."

Edric approached, running a hand through his hair. "We still need Krampus and The Fatman, don't we? Even if we hold the line, the root of this evil remains. The children's innocence was its target. Without that innocence nourished by their traditions, our future dims."

Jarlan sighed, closing his eyes. "Yes, we need them. But we've given ourselves time. We've proven that even without legends at our side, we can resist. Maybe that strength will make it easier for Krampus and The Fatman to do what they must."

Takrin grunted in agreement. "Meanwhile, we study those sigils, that altar in the cave. Maybe we can learn its nature. Knowledge is our weapon now."

Night fell slowly over Sleetwood as they tended their wounded and sleeping. Though fear still throbbed under the surface, a sense of solidarity had settled in. Villagers lit small lamps in windows, not to lure danger, but to show one another they were not alone. Quiet songs were hummed, lullabies to calm frayed nerves. The iron tokens Helgrid had forged took on deeper meaning—emblems of resistance. Everyone in Sleetwood understood now: courage and unity were their shield.

In a quiet corner of the meeting hall, Jarlan unrolled the old parchment once more. By lamplight, he read it carefully, noting each line about the ancient accord and how it was tested before. History, it seemed, was repeating itself. Then, Krampus and The Fatman had reunited, forging a second pact that banished the nameless hunger. Now, the same hunger—or one like it—had returned, trying to unmake their traditions and values.

Jarlan whispered softly to himself, "Come back soon, Krampus. Hurry, Fatman. We're holding on, but we need you." He dared imagine them somewhere far away: Krampus trudging across icy ravines, chains rattling as he followed some faint sign of his brother's presence; The Fatman perhaps journeying through half-real realms of snow and starlight, feeling in his bones that something was terribly wrong in the mortal world. Would they sense the villagers' resilience, their refusal to give in?

Meanwhile, Marta tended Branwynn. The hedge-witch stirred, muttering fragments of spells and warnings. Helgrid checked the doors and windows, assigning a pair of volunteers to guard the hall through the night. Edric sharpened arrows, each scrape of stone on metal a promise of defiance. Takrin whispered plans with a few others, discussing how best to seal off the cave or lay more traps near the outcrop. Everyone had a role, a purpose.

Outside, the wind picked up, but it no longer howled despair. It felt more like a restless guardian, circling the village. A few stars dared to shine through ragged clouds, as if curious about the mortal drama unfolding below.

As the evening deepened, Jarlan joined Helgrid at a window. Together, they looked out over the lamplit lanes of Sleetwood. Families huddled together, relieved but still tense. The children and Branwynn were back, yet the enemy lived on. Jarlan imagined dark eyes watching from the forest's edge, enraged, plotting vengeance. Let it come. Now they knew they could strike back.

Helgrid broke the silence: "We've done something good today, Jarlan. We showed we won't break easily. When Krampus and The Fatman return, they'll find a village that still believes in what they represent."

Jarlan nodded. "Yes. Belief and action. We won't let this hunger have our future. We'll guard it fiercely."

She placed a heavy, reassuring hand on his shoulder. "We must rest in shifts. Tomorrow, we strengthen the perimeter, and I'll see if Branwynn can help restore wards. We must give Krampus and The Fatman as much time as possible."

Jarlan agreed, suddenly feeling the weight of exhaustion. He'd carried Elsbet, faced horrors underground, and organized desperate plans with no rest. Yet he also felt a strange calm. They had not won the war, but they'd won a battle that mattered.

"Helgrid, thank you," he said quietly. "For your strength. Without you, I—"

She shook her head. "We all did this together. Your knowledge, Edric's eyes, Takrin's cunning, Marta's care... everyone played a part. That's what's saving us. Not one hero, but many hearts."

He managed a tired smile. "A lesson fitting for a world balanced by two brothers—one kind, one stern—both necessary. Perhaps we've learned their lesson well."

The dwarf nodded thoughtfully, and together they turned from the window, ready to face whatever came next. Outside, the wind hummed over snow and timber, and deep in distant forests, unseen eyes smoldered. But Sleetwood stood firm, a beacon of stubborn light against the encroaching dark.

They would endure. They had to. And with each passing hour, they forged a strength that no nameless hunger could easily devour.

CHAPTER SIX

A pale hush settled over Sleetwood as the next dawn broke, neither cheerful nor warm, but not entirely despairing either. The villagers had spent the night on edge, taking turns sleeping in fitful snatches, always with one ear tuned to creaking timbers or rustling branches outside. After the daring rescue in the cave, hearts pulsed with a strange blend of relief and anxiety. Yes, they had reclaimed the children and Branwynn Spellshiver, but the enemy that prowled beyond the treeline was still at large. There would be no easy peace until the ancient accord was restored—until Krampus and The Fatman stood once again shoulder to shoulder.

Inside the meeting hall, a soft murmur of activity drifted through the air. Branwynn lay propped up on a makeshift cot near the back room, where Marta and Jarlan hovered. The hedge-witch's cheeks had a bit more color now that she'd sipped broth and warm tea. Though still weak, her eyes no longer held that distant, vacant look. Every so often, she would try to speak, voice raspy with disuse and shock, as if sifting through fractured memories of captivity to find something useful.

"Branwynn," said Jarlan quietly, kneeling by her cot. He placed a gentle hand on her wrist, feeling the slight tremor of her pulse. "We need your guidance. You were taken by this entity—do you remember anything that can help us defend against it?"

Marta hovered close, exchanging a worried glance with Jarlan. The children, still recovering, slept in a separate quiet room under watchful eyes. Their breathing was steady, but they had yet to fully wake from their strange torpor. If the village was to understand the enemy's methods—how it ensnared its victims—the hedge-witch was their best hope.

Branwynn frowned, closing her eyes as if searching the darkness behind them for words. "It... it felt old," she said, voice thin but determined. "A force beneath the skin of the world, feeding on fear, on doubt. While I was trapped, it spoke through dreams, twisting shapes. It thrives when trust erodes, when belief falters. I tried to shield the children, but my wards cracked. I had no proper materials, no time."

Jarlan nodded, heart sinking. He remembered reading that the nameless hunger tested faith and moral order—just as it had done centuries ago. "We've regained the children," he said gently, "and we have you back now. We're reinforcing our defenses. The villagers have set traps, formed patrols. But we need stronger wards—something that can keep it at bay. And perhaps a way to shield minds from its illusions."

At that, Branwynn's eyes fluttered open more fully, focusing on Jarlan. "Wards," she repeated, coughing softly. Marta offered her a sip of water. "Yes... I can craft wards if I have the right components: herbs, certain runes carved into iron or wood. I'll need help. My strength isn't what it was."

Jarlan smiled, relief touching his face. "We have Helgrid," he said. "She's a skilled blacksmith and has been forging protective tokens. She'll help with metal runes. We have gatherers who can find herbs. Whatever you need, we'll gather it."

Branwynn nodded, though her brow furrowed in worry. "Hurry. The entity won't remain idle. It lost its captives, and that must have enraged it. It will try subtler methods now—illusion, infiltration, whispers that turn neighbor against neighbor. We must reinforce not just the village's perimeter but its spirit."

Those words settled heavily on Jarlan. He remembered how easily fear had spread when the vanishings began. Suspicion had stirred at every corner. If the entity thrived on such discord, they must remain vigilant and united. "We'll be careful," he said. "Rest now. I'll fetch Helgrid and the others."

Marta laid a cool cloth on Branwynn's forehead as Jarlan rose to carry out his task.

Outside, the sky pressed low and gray, as if unsure whether to weep snow or simply brood over the winter landscape. Helgrid Stonestream stood near her forge, fanning coals until they glowed hot. She had slept only a few hours, yet her resolve was unwavering. Around her, a handful of villagers waited to be assigned tasks—some carried armfuls of dried branches for fuel, others brought metal scraps and old nails that might be reforged into warding runes.

When Jarlan approached, Helgrid glanced up, soot smudging her cheek. "How's Branwynn?"

"Better," said Jarlan. "She can help us create wards. She needs special herbs and runes. Can you craft metal charms that hold runes of protection?"

Helgrid nodded, stoking the coals thoughtfully. "I've been working on tokens before, but now we must get more specific. Tell me which runes and what shapes. I can handle the forging." She paused, brow knitting. "We must hurry. I can sense the villagers' relief waning, turning into tense anticipation. They know another blow may come."

Jarlan admired Helgrid's calm steadiness. "We'll bring Branwynn here once she's stable. She'll guide you. In the meantime, we should send gatherers into the forest's safer fringes to find the herbs she needs. She mentioned needing certain plants—rowan bark, maybe witch-hazel twigs, and ironweeds. The forest is dangerous, but we must risk small expeditions."

At that, Helgrid frowned, hammering a red-hot piece of iron on her anvil. Sparks flew, lighting her determined face. "We'll send a small group with guards. Edric can lead them—he's good at spotting trouble. The rest of us will stay close to the village. The traps we set around the perimeter should help, but we must remain on guard. The entity may send scouts or illusions."

"Agreed," said Jarlan. "I'll organize it now."

Leaving Helgrid to her work, Jarlan returned to the meeting hall to share the plan. In a short time, a small party formed: Edric, Takrin, and two gatherers—Annet and Ralden—both known for their knowledge of local flora. They would scout the forest, careful to avoid deep penetration into enemy territory, and harvest what they needed.

Before they departed, Jarlan addressed them quietly. "Be cautious. If you see anything strange, anything at all, return immediately. And watch each other closely. The entity likes illusions. Confirm signals and words—agree on a code so you know you are who you say you are. We cannot allow it to trick us."

Edric met Jarlan's gaze firmly. "We'll be careful," he said. Takrin patted a hunting knife strapped to his belt, and Annet and Ralden nodded nervously. Together, they vanished into the treeline, their figures swallowed by the pale mist.

Back in Sleetwood, the villagers reorganized their defenses. Under Branwynn's quiet instructions (delivered in hushed tones from her cot), they started sketching runes on doorframes with charcoal and placing small bowls of salt and dried juniper near thresholds. It was makeshift magic, barely enough to ward off a determined foe, but every measure counted. The children who had been rescued still slept, their slumber heavy and dreamless. Marta and a few mothers watched over them, singing soft lullabies in strained voices, hoping the familiarity of a mother's tune might coax them back to wakefulness.

As the sun edged higher, a strange tension settled over the village. People worked with grim purpose, rarely smiling. Though they had achieved a small victory, no one mistook this lull for peace. Rather, it felt like the calm before a gale. Every snap of a twig outside, every distant creak of wood, drew nervous glances.

Late morning turned to midday. Helgrid hammered away at the forge, shaping thin iron bands inscribed with symbols Branwynn had recalled from old lore—circles for unity, jagged lines for deflection, spirals reversed to reject the entity's influence. Jarlan hovered nearby, assisting by bringing her cooled iron scraps or dabbing sweat from her brow. They worked in efficient silence until Helgrid stepped back, holding up a half-finished warding charm.

"Will it work?" Jarlan asked softly, eyes reflecting the faint glow of the forge.

Helgrid shrugged. "I know metal and runes. Branwynn's knowledge of magic is deeper than mine. Together, maybe we can make something that holds. If nothing else, these charms might steady the villagers' hearts. Confidence is a weapon against fear."

Jarlan nodded. Confidence could help. Belief could stiffen spines, strengthen unity, push back the enemy's attempts to divide them. He thought of Krampus and The Fatman again, hoping that somewhere beyond mortal ken, their reunion was drawing closer.

As the afternoon waned, Edric's party returned. They emerged from the mist carrying bundles of stripped bark, handfuls of thin twigs, and clumps of wiry roots. Their faces were drawn, and Edric's eyes flicked nervously at every shadow. Takrin reported that they had heard strange laughter echo through the pines, but had seen no enemies. They'd found rowan bark and ironweed, though the witch-hazel was scarce.

"Something followed us," said Edric quietly, depositing his load of herbs on a makeshift worktable outside the meeting hall. "We never saw it clearly. We used the code words as planned. None of us turned on each other. Still, it felt like eyes on the back of our necks." He brushed a broken pine needle from his cloak. "We must reinforce patrols tonight."

Jarlan thanked them and hurried inside to deliver the herbs. Branwynn managed a wan smile when she saw the gathered materials. "Good," she breathed. "We can brew a protective wash to paint on your doorframes and weapons. Let's not waste time."

With Marta's help, Branwynn prepared a steaming cauldron over a small brazier. She crushed roots with a mortar and pestle, stirring them into hot water with a sprig of pine. A pungent aroma filled the hall, making eyes water. Over this concoction, Branwynn chanted softly—fragmented verses in an old tongue. Jarlan couldn't catch all the words, but he recognized the cadence of invocation, calling on ancient benign forces, the quiet spirits in the mountain roots, and the primal integrity of the Winterspine.

Once the brew cooled, they dipped cloth strips into it, handing them to volunteers who wrapped them around spear shafts or tied them onto door latches. Branwynn insisted these talismans would heighten awareness, helping the villagers resist illusions. "If it tries to cloud your sight," she explained, voice steadier now, "the smell of these herbs and the touch of iron runes will sharpen your mind. It's not a perfect defense, but it may buy you precious moments."

Jarlan nodded solemnly. Moments could mean the difference between life and death out here.

As dusk began to seep into the sky, Helgrid and Jarlan organized a council of the villagers' informal leaders in the meeting hall. Branwynn was propped up on pillows, pale but alert. Edric, Takrin, Marta, Orlan (the baker turned reluctant guard), and a few others gathered around a table lit by lanterns.

"We face a subtle enemy now," Branwynn began, her voice still hoarse but resolute. "It will not storm our gates with brute force, not yet. It knows we stand united. Instead, it may send illusions—false faces of friends, deceptive sounds, half-seen shapes—to lure us into traps. It may try to turn us against each other, sow rumors and mistrust."

Jarlan leaned forward. "We must have a system of verification. Agreed-upon code words, signals, times to check in. If anyone disappears for too long, we send patrols. No one wanders alone after dark."

Marta folded her arms. "We must also tend to the children. They remain asleep. Can we wake them safely?"

Branwynn frowned. "They're ensnared in a dream state, likely induced by the entity's influence. It might be draining them even now—lessons of fear etched into their sleep. But I think we can help them awaken by bathing their brows with the herb wash and speaking their names, reminding them of who they are. It may take time, but we must do it. We need their laughter and innocence, not as victims but as participants in our community's spirit."

Edric nodded. "We'll do that. One by one if need be."

Helgrid tapped the table with a thick finger. "What about the perimeter? We set traps, but we should double-check them. Also, light torches tonight. Fire might disrupt illusions—at least, it gives us a point of reference. If something tries to mimic a friend, we can ask them to approach the light and show their face plainly."

Takrin added, "We can rotate watchers every hour. Keep everyone fresh. The moment someone feels strange or hears voices that don't belong, raise the alarm."

They agreed on these measures, speaking quietly but firmly, like soldiers planning a siege. If the enemy craved discord, they would starve it by working together, trusting each other, and acknowledging that fear must not drive them apart.

Night fell gently over Sleetwood, the sky a tapestry of dull clouds and a few brave stars. Torches flared at the village's edges, and watchers stood wrapped in cloaks, weapons ready, strips of herb-scented cloth tied around wrists or ankles. The scent was sharp, medicinal, cutting through the chill air.

Inside, mothers and fathers took turns at the children's bedside, dabbing their foreheads with the herbal wash, whispering soft encouragement. Jarlan knelt by Elsbet Quinshale, whose disappearance had spurred much of the village's alarm. Her eyelashes fluttered, her small hand twitched. Jarlan smiled weakly, whispering, "Come back, Elsbet. We're waiting. Your parents miss you."

A faint murmur escaped Elsbet's lips—nonsense, or perhaps a half-formed word. Nearby, another child stirred, eyes flickering beneath lids. Progress, however slight, offered hope.

As the hours crawled past, the silence weighed heavily. Occasionally, a distant giggle or sobbing sound would drift across the rooftops, causing watchers to stiffen. But no source could be found, and no attack came. Perhaps these were illusions cast at a distance, testing their resolve. Each time, villagers muttered the agreed-upon code words to each other—"Iron pine"—before proceeding, ensuring no one had been replaced or led astray.

Near midnight, Branwynn managed to stand with Marta's help, leaning on a staff carved with runic patterns. She hobbled to the door of the meeting hall, gazing out at the torchlit streets. "They hold fast," she said softly. "No panic, no cries of betrayal. We might be winning the war of nerves tonight."

Marta nodded, relief softening her features. "We'll keep it up. The enemy can't feed on fear if we deny it."

Branwynn's grip tightened on her staff. "Still, we mustn't grow complacent. It may try more daring tricks."

Past midnight, a patrol reported that they found strange footprints near the western perimeter—prints that ended abruptly, as if the creature vanished into thin air. Helgrid inspected them and noted they resembled the clawed marks from before. She ordered more traps set, despite the danger of working in darkness. Volunteers carefully placed iron-jawed snares and arranged sharpened stakes, whispering the code words to keep their courage firm.

Jarlan, making rounds with a lantern, paused by a group of villagers huddled at a corner where two cottages met. They whispered anxiously, claiming they heard a familiar voice calling from behind the barn, someone who died last winter. Jarlan closed his eyes. The entity was indeed testing them with personal illusions.

"Remember our rules," he said softly. "Don't follow strange calls. Stay together. Check faces, code words. If a dead voice calls, it's a lie."

The villagers nodded, clinging to their iron tokens. With that gentle reminder, they held their ground, refusing to chase ghosts into the dark.

Toward the deepest hours of the night, when exhaustion gnawed at everyone's nerves, something new happened: Elsbet Quinshale opened her eyes and spoke a name. Not her parents, not Jarlan, but "Krampus." Her voice was quiet, trembling, as if caught between nightmare and wakefulness.

Jarlan, who had been resting nearby, rushed to her side. "Elsbet, can you hear me? It's Jarlan. You're safe."

The girl's eyes were glassy, still heavy with sleep. "Krampus…" she repeated, voice quivering. "He… he was in my dreams, sort of. Someone tried to turn him into a monster, to make me afraid. But he whispered back. He said not to listen. He said… he said help is coming."

Jarlan's heart pounded. Could Krampus have reached the children's minds somehow, countering the entity's illusions from afar? Or was this Elsbet's subconscious clinging to a comforting figure from legend? Either way, it was a sign that not all influence in their dreams belonged to the enemy.

"Stay calm," he told Elsbet, stroking her hair. "We're all working together. Rest now. We'll keep you safe."

Elsbet managed a nod, then drifted into a more natural sleep, breathing softly. Jarlan's mind whirled. If Krampus was fighting on a spiritual plane, countering the entity's whispers, that meant he was working to uphold his role. Maybe The Fatman was near too, lending subtle warmth to their courage. The thought sparked hope.

He hurried to tell Branwynn and Helgrid. The hedge-witch listened quietly, brow knitted. "This might mean Krampus is close to finding The Fatman," she said. "Or that he's strengthening his own resolve. If he reaches the children's dreams, he's battling the entity's illusions on their own ground. That's a good sign."

Helgrid grunted. "Good sign indeed. Let's keep holding firm. If Krampus is fighting in dreams, we can fight here in the real. Together, we'll squeeze this enemy until it slinks away."

Dawn approached, gray light creeping over the rooftops. The villagers maintained their vigilance all through the night. A few illusions had probed their defenses—whispers, phantom silhouettes, impossible voices—but no one had panicked. No one had turned on their neighbors. The entity's attempts fell flat against the wall of trust and preparation.

As the morning brightened, more children began to stir. One by one, the sleeping captives awoke groggy but aware, confused but relieved to be home. Parents wept tears of joy, holding their children close, thanking the gods, Krampus, The Fatman, and each other. The heart of Sleetwood beat stronger for every child's return to wakeful life.

With this emotional surge came a deepening resolve. If they could save their children from the enemy's clutches and deny its illusions, they could hold out until their legendary protectors arrived.

Branwynn managed to shuffle outside with Marta's support, standing in the crisp morning air. She inhaled, tasting iron in the breeze—residual magic from their wards and tokens. The village hummed with weary relief. She looked to Jarlan, who stood nearby, eyes rimmed with fatigue but shining with pride.

"We did it," she whispered. "Not won the war yet, but we've repelled its assault on our minds."

Jarlan nodded. "We must keep going. But this night proves we can stand as a shield until Krampus and The Fatman restore the ancient accord."

Edric and Takrin returned from a final patrol of the perimeter. "No sign of fresh attacks," Takrin reported. "The traps are untouched. Either it retreated or is planning something else."

Helgrid, stepping out from the forge after stoking a morning fire, crossed her arms. "If it wants to break us, it will have to try harder. We've shown we won't break easily."

Branwynn smiled faintly. "We must remain cautious. Last night was a test. The entity may now try a different approach—corruption from within. We must continue reinforcing our wards, restoring normalcy for the children, and strengthening our moral bonds."

At that, Marta joined them, leaning on the doorframe of the meeting hall. "We should also restore our traditions. Gather the villagers for a small ceremony, perhaps. Light a communal fire, share warm bread. Remind everyone what we stand for—the joys of life that The Fatman celebrates and the responsibility that Krampus enforces. The enemy wants to strip meaning away, leave us hollow. Let's fill ourselves with meaning."

Jarlan's eyes lit up. A ceremony might indeed bolster spirits. "Yes. We can share stories, sing old songs. Even if we do it quietly and carefully, it might strengthen our collective courage."

Helgrid nodded. "I'll forge a new batch of tokens in the shape of the old festival ornaments. Symbols that remind us of better times. We must show this foe that we will not forget who we are."

Branwynn lifted her chin. "I can help bless them, once I regain a bit more strength. Iron and herb, ward and memory—these things combined can form a bulwark against fear."

By midday, after a brief rest and shared meal, the villagers convened in the center of Sleetwood's main square. The sky remained gray, but the air felt crisper, cleaner. A few torches and lanterns formed a ring of light. In their center stood a makeshift altar—just a simple table draped with a cloth embroidered with pine boughs. On it, Helgrid placed a handful of new tokens she had forged: small iron shapes representing pine cones, snowflakes, and stags. Each bore runes etched along their edges.

Jarlan, as chronicler, cleared his throat and addressed the gathering. "We have endured much. Children taken and returned, a hedge-witch rescued, illusions resisted. The enemy tries to sever us from our traditions, from the balance that Krampus and The Fatman represent. But we remember who we are."

Murmurs of agreement rippled through the crowd. Parents held children close, and the awakened youngsters looked around with wide eyes. Some remembered dream-fragments of horrors, others had hazy recollections of comforting voices urging them to stay strong.

"Today," Jarlan continued, "we reaffirm our unity. We will share stories—remind ourselves of the old tales that gave us these traditions in the first place. The Fatman brings gifts and warmth, teaching us generosity and joy. Krampus guards the boundary, teaching us consequences and moral strength. Together, they ensure that kindness and caution balance our world."

Branwynn stepped forward, leaning on her staff. Her voice carried a gentle resonance: "I remember an old blessing once sung during midwinter festivals—words that praise the turning of seasons and the endurance of hope." She began to hum, and the villagers listened, some quietly joining in when she shaped old syllables.

The melody was simple but ancient, a tune that tasted of pine resin and hearth smoke. As they sang, Helgrid distributed the tokens—one per family. Their iron gleam was modest, not flashy, but in the lamplight they shone like small promises. Marta passed round a basket of warm bread rolls, freshly baked by Orlan the baker, who had rediscovered his purpose beyond fear.

Children nibbled the bread, blinking in the mild glow. Adults exchanged relieved smiles. Edric and Takrin stood guard at the perimeter, but even they hummed along softly, their hands resting on weapons that now felt less ominous and more protective.

This communal act was not magic in the strict sense, but it might as well have been. The enemy wanted them divided, terrified, stripped of identity. Here, they stood arm in arm, singing and sharing warmth, weaving a tapestry of belief and belonging that no illusion could easily unravel.

As dusk approached again, Branwynn mustered enough strength to help carve new runes onto doorframes and fences. She and Jarlan recited old incantations under their breath, reinforcing the protective wash that still clung to wood and iron. The villagers established a routine: patrols at set intervals, code words updated nightly, a central fire lit at sundown to gather around.

Elsbet and a few other children began to talk quietly about their dreams. They spoke of strange voices that tried to frighten them, showing them monstrous images of Krampus as a devourer rather than a teacher. But they also mentioned flickers of resistance—soft laughter that countered the menace, silhouettes that stood guard in their dreamscapes. It seemed the children's innocence, once weaponized against them, now served as a bastion of imagination that could reject terror.

Branwynn listened to these accounts closely. "The entity tries to rewrite our stories," she said to Jarlan, "turning Krampus into a horror and The Fatman into a distant, false hope. But the children's minds, if supported by real care and love, refuse this rewriting. They know in their hearts these beings stand for something more nuanced and kind."

Jarlan nodded. "We must hold onto that understanding. Tradition is more than just tales; it's a moral compass. The entity's greatest threat is moral confusion—if we recall what Krampus and The Fatman truly mean, no lie can shake us for long."

Night fell once again, and the routine of vigilance continued. Outside the village's ring of torches, darkness pooled and waited. The enemy was silent tonight—no illusions drifted across their thresholds, no whispered mockeries coiled in the eaves. Perhaps it watched and seethed, searching for a new angle. But inside Sleetwood, a quiet confidence had taken root.

In the meeting hall, Branwynn guided Helgrid's hand as they etched more refined runes into a set of iron amulets. These would be placed at key points around the perimeter—fence posts, gate hinges, the corners of the meeting hall itself. Each rune invoked stability, memory, and moral clarity. The smell of herbs from the cauldron still lingered, reminding everyone of the steps they had taken to safeguard their minds.

Marta checked the children again. Many were awake now, weak but recovering, eating broth and sipping warm drinks. They spoke softly with their parents, pressing close, seeking comfort. The scars of their ordeal would not vanish overnight, but the love that surrounded them offered a healing balm.

Edric reported that the traps remained undisturbed, and Takrin noted no new footprints. A lull before a storm? Possibly. But the villagers no longer trembled at every shift of wind.

Jarlan scribbled notes by lantern light, recording what had transpired since the vanishings began. He documented their strategies, the wards, the code words, the tokens—knowledge that future generations might need if this nameless hunger ever returned. He wrote of the unity forged in adversity, of how fear had nearly consumed them but was pushed back by mutual care and courage.

He ended his current entry with a quiet prayer: "Krampus, Fatman, if you see these words or sense our plight, know that we hold fast. We guard what is good and true, resisting the illusions that would break us. Come soon, if you can. But know that until you do, we carry your lessons in our hearts."

In the hours past midnight, a gentle snowfall began. Flakes drifted down, covering rooftops and lanes in a hush of white. Usually, snowfall might bring worry—muffling sounds, hiding footprints—but tonight it felt cleansing, as if the world tried to bury old fears. Patrols adjusted their rounds, leaving fresh boot prints that would be easy to track come morning.

Branwynn, leaning on her staff at the threshold of the meeting hall, watched the snow with half-lidded eyes. She sensed changes in the magical currents around the village. The herbs, iron runes, and collective spirit had created a resonance that resisted the entity's influence. The creature still lurked, of that she had no doubt, but it seemed hesitant now, uncertain how to proceed.

Marta joined her, offering a fur-lined cloak. "You should rest. You've done so much already."

Branwynn smiled weakly and accepted the cloak. "I will, soon. Just want to feel this moment—the calm after so much terror. The villagers stand strong. The children are safe. The entity finds no easy prey here."

Marta nodded, gratitude shining in her eyes. "We owe much to you, to Jarlan, Helgrid, Edric… everyone worked together. It's a lesson we won't forget."

Branwynn closed her eyes, listening to distant murmurs of guards checking in, neighbors whispering goodnight. The entity had tried isolation, terror, confusion. They answered with unity, clarity, and faith. It was a victory, albeit incomplete.

In her mind's eye, Branwynn imagined Krampus trudging through icy wilderness and The Fatman stirring from distant halls of starlit snowdrifts. She dared to believe that, carried on subtle winds of magic and morality, they might sense the village's steadfastness. If so, perhaps they would hasten their return, bringing with them the final restoration needed.

By early morning, the snowfall thickened, muffling the world in white silence. Sleetwood awoke to a soft landscape, torches guttering in the gentle drift. Villagers emerged from their homes, blinking at the brightness. Children, though still weak, looked out windows with curiosity. Parents prepared simple breakfasts, passing bread and salted fish around. A humble feast in a time of trial.

Jarlan and Helgrid inspected the perimeter. The traps were half-buried in snow, but untouched. No sign of intruders. They exchanged a nod, trudging back to the meeting hall. Inside, Branwynn rested, but her sleep was peaceful, not the fitful doze of the injured. Marta offered hot tea, and the children quietly played with carved wooden toys, rediscovering normalcy one step at a time.

Krampus

The enemy had not vanished—the villagers knew it was out there, licking its wounds and brooding. But now they had a blueprint for resistance. They understood how to counter illusions with fact-checking and code words, how to shore up courage with rituals and tokens. They had discovered that fear could be tempered by solidarity and that moral clarity could repel corruption.

As midday approached, Jarlan took a moment to step outside and gaze at the Winterspine Mountains towering in the distance. Their snow-laden slopes glistened under a hesitant sun. He thought of Krampus and The Fatman again, hoping that each passing day brought them closer. He felt an odd certainty that the legendary brothers would return—not out of mere duty, but because Sleetwood had proven worthy of their efforts. The village now embodied the principles they upheld: generosity without naïveté, caution without cruelty, a moral backbone that refused to buckle under pressure.

Stepping back into the hall, Jarlan found Branwynn awake, sipping tea. She caught his eye and gave a slight nod, as if sharing a silent understanding. The nameless hunger had not given up, but it no longer had easy footholds. The villagers would remain vigilant, weaving new layers of defense—stories retold, songs sung softly, tokens passed hand to hand.

In that quiet resolve lay a power stronger than any rune: the collective will of ordinary folk who refused to surrender their world to despair. And if that power shone brightly enough, it would surely help guide Krampus and The Fatman back home, where they belonged.

For now, they waited, forging strength from hardship, ever ready to face what lay beyond the snowy treeline.

CHAPTER SEVEN

A soft drizzle of sleet hissed against the rooftops of Sleetwood, sliding down wooden shingles and gathering in half-frozen puddles along the lanes. The sky had turned the color of dirty wool, and the few pale sunbeams that ventured down were feeble and short-lived. Yet, despite the gloomy weather, the village felt sturdier than it had in weeks. The children, once lost in dreamless captivity, were awake and recovering, their curious voices once more threading through doorways. Branwynn Spellshiver regained a fraction of her old vigor, enough to advise on wards and herbal brews. Iron runes gleamed faintly from lintels, fence posts, and doorframes. Bundles of protective herbs dangled at every threshold. The villagers had settled into a steady rhythm of patrols, code words, and daily rituals meant to hold the darkness at bay.

Within the meeting hall, a cluster of villagers gathered around a table: Jarlan Forgerook, Helgrid Stonestream, Branwynn Spellshiver, Edric, Takrin, Marta, and a few others who had risen to the occasion as leaders and problem-solvers. By now, their council felt natural. They had weathered illusions, reclaimed their children, and proven that mere mortals could resist the nameless hunger lurking beyond the treeline.

Branwynn studied a fresh set of carved runes on iron tokens. She traced them with a fingertip, muttering softly. "These are better balanced now," she said to Helgrid, who stood close by. "The shapes are correct, and the iron has taken the incantations well. Each token should help ward off not only illusions but subtle influences—whispers in the mind, suggestions of despair."

Helgrid grunted approvingly. "Glad to hear it. The forging took hours, but if it strengthens our defenses, it's worth every spark."

Jarlan stepped closer, arms folded over a thick woolen shawl. "We should distribute these tokens to the perimeter watchers first," he said. "They're our first line of defense. If the entity tries to slip in unseen or send a new trick, our watchers must remain clear-headed."

Marta nodded. "Agreed. I'll see that everyone on duty gets one, and we'll cycle through so that everyone inside the village has one by tomorrow. Now that we've mastered these runes and wards, can we think of a way to track the entity itself?"

That question hung in the air. So far, their success lay in defense—foiling illusions, preserving unity—but the enemy remained elusive, a presence felt rather than seen. Jarlan rubbed his chin. "We've found footprints, heard laughter, fought off twisted goblins and wraith-like shapes. But these were servants, not the creature's true form. We must consider that it may hide in places we have not dared to explore. The old scrolls mentioned that long ago, the entity retreated only when Krampus and The Fatman renewed their pact. Without them, we may never fully banish it."

Branwynn's eyes flickered with a quiet intensity. "Still, we can try to weaken its influence, force it into making mistakes. Our unity is a weapon. If we remain calm and vigilant, it may be compelled to show itself or risk losing all advantage. And if it shows itself, perhaps we can bind or wound it enough to hold it at bay until Krampus and The Fatman arrive."

Edric tapped the hilt of his dagger. "I'm willing to lead a scouting party deeper into the forest again. Not too far—just enough to see if the blood trail or those strange sigils reappear. Maybe we can find clues."

Helgrid's jaw tightened. "Be careful. Last time we ventured deep, we risked ambush. Let's send a small party, heavily warded. We'll choose a clear day so we can track footprints easily."

Jarlan sighed. "These storms of sleet and snow aren't helping. Everything is blurred." He paused, thinking. "Maybe we should try something else first—like strengthening our tether to the legends that protect us. The children spoke of Krampus's presence in their dreams. If we enact a ceremony, calling upon the ancient accord—both the merciful generosity of The Fatman and the stern lesson of Krampus—maybe we can draw their attention more directly."

Marta's eyes lit with interest. "A ceremony could rally the villagers' spirits further. We have songs, stories, and symbols of the midwinter traditions. If we align these with the runes and wards, and Branwynn weaves her magic into it, could that send a kind of beacon?"

Branwynn nodded slowly. "It might, at least on a spiritual level. Magic is often about resonance. If we fill the air with honest devotion to the balance they represent, Krampus and The Fatman might sense it. Or the entity might become nervous and attempt to disrupt us, revealing itself in the process."

Takrin, silent until now, stroked his beard. "If we perform such a ceremony, we must be prepared for interference. The entity will not remain idle if it feels threatened."

Helgrid bared her teeth in a humorless grin. "Good. Let it come. We're ready this time."

They spent the next day preparing. Word spread through the village: at dusk, they would hold a grand invocation—a careful blend of old festival rites, moral affirmations, and newly forged wards. Parents explained to their children that this was a special night, a time to honor the stories that underpinned their world. Some children were frightened, remembering captivity and nightmares, but their parents reassured them: "We stand together now, and we do this to call our guardians home."

Jarlan delved into his archives to find the oldest midwinter hymns and chants. He selected lines praising kindness and responsibility, weaving them into a simple refrain that all could sing. Marta organized the baking of round loaves of bread studded with nuts and dried fruit—foods traditionally offered during midwinter feasts. Helgrid added finishing touches to the tokens, ensuring they were evenly distributed so every household had at least one. Branwynn spent long hours meditating, gathering her strength for the coming ceremony. If the entity tried illusions again, her focused mind would help anchor everyone's resolve.

Late afternoon brought a thin shaft of sunlight that pierced the clouds, lighting the village square with a gentle, golden glow. It felt like a sign. Villagers emerged from their homes carrying lanterns, bread, and small carved trinkets—old ornaments once used to celebrate The

Fatman's gift-giving. Children clutched wooden figures of stags or carved pinecones, shy but determined to participate.

At the center of the square, they arranged a small altar with symbols of both Krampus and The Fatman: a birch branch for Krampus's discipline, a red cap trimmed with white fur to represent The Fatman's warmth. Amid them lay the iron tokens and bowls of herb-infused water. Branwynn placed a wreath of evergreen at the top, binding their intentions together.

As dusk fell, Jarlan stood before the gathered crowd, voice steady but soft: "We come together tonight to remind ourselves of who we are and what we believe. The world balances on kind generosity and measured justice, on hope and consequence. The Fatman and Krampus, two brothers in spirit, ensure this balance. We have faced a force that would tear us from these truths, make us doubt, make us fear, but we have not yielded."

A chorus of murmured agreement rose from the crowd. Parents and children pressed closer. Torches crackled. The scent of pine and ironweed drifted through the air.

Jarlan continued, "Tonight, we call out to those who guide our moral compass. We sing, we share food, we show that our community stands firm. May Krampus and The Fatman hear us and know that we hold the line until they return."

Marta lifted a basket of bread. "These loaves represent our willingness to share and care for each other. Even in hardship, we give what we can. Take a piece and pass it along."

As villagers broke bread, Branwynn raised her staff. She chanted softly, words from an old dialect that hummed with subtle power. Her voice wove through the crowd, calming anxious hearts, imbuing them with a sense of connectedness. Helgrid stood at the circle's edge, hammer resting on her shoulder, scanning the darkening streets for any sign of intrusion.

Then the singing began—low and uncertain at first, but growing stronger with each repetition. A simple melody, carried by memory and longing, praising a world where lessons were learned gently and gifts were earned and cherished. Children joined in, their thin voices bright sparks in the twilight. The old lines Jarlan found fit perfectly: "In winter's hush, we stand as one, / The stern and kind beneath one sun."

Midway through the singing, a chill wind swept across the square, dimming a few lanterns. The villagers tensed, but no one screamed. They simply relit the lanterns and continued singing. No illusions would stop them now.

Branwynn closed her eyes, feeling the magical currents swirl. She sensed something watching, pressing at the edges of their warded space, testing for weaknesses. The entity was near, drawn by their display of unity. She whispered to Jarlan, "It's here, I can feel it. Hold steady."

Jarlan nodded and addressed the crowd. "Do not fear. If something lurks, it has no power over those who trust each other. Remember the code words, remember the tokens. Stand firm."

They continued the ceremony. Helgrid moved quietly around the perimeter, distributing additional charms to nervous onlookers. Edric and Takrin took up positions at key intersections, bows and spears ready. No one would wander off alone tonight.

A faint laugh echoed through the alleys—thin, mocking. Villagers stiffened, but kept singing. In the flicker of torchlight, a shape skittered on a rooftop—gone too quickly to identify. Another laugh, this time from the opposite end of the square. The enemy was trying to rattle them, to make them break formation.

Branwynn struck the ground with her staff, sending a light tremor through the circle. Her voice rose, calm but firm: "Nameless hunger, we know you watch. We name you a coward, feeding on fears you cannot earn. Look upon this village and see no prey, but a shield of unity you cannot pierce."

The laughter paused. For a moment, the air thickened, and a hush deeper than silence fell. Everyone held their breath. Then, a howling shriek erupted from the darkness behind the old chapel ruins. Shapes emerged—three twisted goblin-like creatures, limbs too long, eyes glinting with hate. They rushed forward, claws scraping the ground. In past nights, this sudden attack might have triggered panic. Now, the villagers stood ready.

"Form up!" Helgrid's voice rang out, hammer raised. A line of armed villagers stepped before the unarmed, spears leveled. Jarlan positioned himself near the children, chanting a code word repeatedly to reassure them. "Iron pine, iron pine," he muttered, and neighbors responded in kind.

The goblins closed in, but as they neared the ring of runes and herbs, they flinched. One hissed, trying to leap over a fence post etched with Branwynn's runes. Sparks of greenish light crackled, and the goblin yelped, forced to the ground. Another tried to dart around, only to meet Edric's arrow—a clean shot to the shoulder. The creature screamed and stumbled back, black ichor dripping.

The third goblin slunk into a shadowed alley, perhaps seeking a flank. Takrin called out, "Check the alley to the east!" Two villagers, holding torches, advanced. The goblin hissed and retreated, unwilling to face fire and iron together.

In the midst of this chaos, the singing never stopped. The tune wavered, but the villagers kept humming, holding onto that thread of hope. Branwynn murmured a protective charm, and Marta scattered handfuls of dried juniper into the air, creating a pungent haze that seemed to deter the attackers.

The goblins retreated, snarling, but did not flee far. They circled at the edge of torchlight, waiting. Branwynn knew they were testing defenses before the main strike—if it came.

Then came a voice—a deep, hollow whisper that seemed to emanate from every shadow. It spoke in broken phrases, scraping at their ears: "Foolish… mortals… clinging to old tales… no saviors… only hunger…"

The villagers shuddered but maintained their circle. Jarlan shouted back, "We know your lies! We've seen your illusions. We know Krampus and The Fatman are real and vital. Your emptiness cannot break us."

A furious snarl answered. The goblins snarled in unison, and a shape coalesced at the far end of the square—a tall, crooked figure cloaked in shifting darkness. Its form refused to settle: at one moment a gaunt man with hollow eyes, next a horned silhouette mocking Krampus's outline, then a rotund parody of The Fatman twisted into a leer. The villagers gasped but did not scatter. They recognized the illusion for what it was: a hollow puppet of fear.

Branwynn gritted her teeth, focusing on the staff's runes. She raised it high, and Helgrid stepped beside her, hammer at the ready. Edric and Takrin flanked them, weapons drawn. Jarlan stood behind, ensuring children and parents remained calm.

The entity's voice raked across their ears again: "They... will not... come. You are alone. Give in... surrender your faith, and I will spare your... minds."

But no one moved. Instead, Marta lifted her chin and spoke softly, "We are never alone. We have each other. And we have them—Krampus and The Fatman—bound to these lands by old promises. They will come."

Her words, so simple yet fierce, struck a chord. Villagers murmured agreement. Some children even shook their heads at the entity's threat, holding their carved ornaments tighter.

The figure's shape flickered, struggling to maintain a coherent form. It leaned forward, as if pressed by an invisible wind. The singing swelled, stronger now, and the iron tokens at the altar glowed faintly. Branwynn whispered an incantation, and a gentle warmth spread through the crowd, knitting their courage together.

The entity screeched—a sound like ice cracking underfoot. The goblins howled and lunged again, desperate. But this time, they found the villagers braced and ready. A spearman stabbed at one, driving it back. Helgrid swung her hammer, catching another in mid-leap, sending it crumpling to the ground. Fire and iron, voice and unity—tools that mortals wielded expertly now.

Cornered, outmatched, the goblins retreated once more, disappearing into the gloom. The entity's flickering silhouette snarled, then stretched unnaturally tall. Its form tried another tactic—showing faces of villagers' loved ones, mimicking children's cries. But now they knew to check words and tokens. They whispered code phrases, looked to each other's eyes, and found no one missing or replaced. The illusions had no purchase.

At last, the entity's mocking grin twisted into a grimace. It realized this village would not break. A feral hiss escaped its shapeless maw. "You rely on old myths... They abandoned you centuries ago!" it spat.

Jarlan's voice rose clear and unwavering: "They never abandoned us. They guide us through legends and balance. If they are delayed, we hold their place until they return. We know what is right and true."

A wind gusted through the square, rattling shutters and snuffing a few torches. For a heartbeat, darkness surged, and in that darkness, the entity tried one final trick. It conjured a sudden vision: a swirl of snow and ice as if a blizzard had descended. Villagers coughed and shielded their faces, feeling icy needles prick their skin. But through the swirling white, they continued humming their hymn, refusing to panic.

When the vision cleared, the entity was gone. Only the soft hiss of sleet remained, and footprints in the snow where goblins had fled. The village stood intact, their circle unbroken.

A hush followed, broken by Edric's relieved exhale. Takrin surveyed the ground, confirming no one was harmed beyond minor scratches. Branwynn sagged against her staff, sweat beading her brow. Jarlan helped a trembling child hold onto an iron token.

Marta's gentle voice rose: "We have repelled it again. It tried everything—fear, illusion, violence—and still we stand."

Helgrid nodded grimly. "We're not rid of it, but we've shown it we won't bow. This must force it to reconsider."

Branwynn managed a tired smile. "It knows we won't crumble easily. Perhaps now it realizes it must deal with Krampus and The Fatman after all—unless it flees entirely."

Jarlan looked to the horizon, where faint stars winked behind thinning clouds. "We must keep faith. That performance of illusions and rage felt desperate. Maybe Krampus and The Fatman draw near, unsettling it."

The villagers dispersed slowly, returning to their homes to rest. The altar remained in the square, bread crumbs and tokens scattered, symbols of resilience. Patrols resumed their quiet circuits, more confident than ever. The children settled into sleep with fewer nightmares. And the adults, though exhausted, breathed easier. They had confronted the enemy in the open and held fast.

In the following days, the village continued to fortify its spirit. Branwynn and Helgrid refined more tokens, placing them at strategic points. Jarlan and Marta encouraged small gatherings to retell stories of old times, reminding everyone why The Fatman's generosity and Krampus's stern lessons mattered. They honored both aspects of moral order: kindness tempered by accountability, freedom bounded by responsibility.

Edric and Takrin led a careful expedition into the forest on a crisp morning. They found old tracks of the goblins, now vanished, and a few scattered bones—leftovers from past horrors. But no fresh footprints from the entity, no new sigils carved into bark. The woods felt quieter, as if the presence had withdrawn to plot anew or nurse its wounds.

Back in Sleetwood, the children gradually recovered their normal chatter. They asked questions about Krampus and The Fatman—why they weren't here yet, when they would return. Parents explained patiently: "They have their own journeys. Our job is to keep their spirit alive until they arrive. We trust them, and they trust us."

Branwynn tested the magical resonance each evening, scrying quietly in a bowl of melted snow. She sensed subtle tremors in the world's weave, hints that old balances were stirring. She told Jarlan, "I cannot say when they'll come, but I feel the veil thinning. We must remain patient."

Jarlan nodded. "We have time. The entity tried and failed to break us. It must know that when Krampus and The Fatman return, its chance will be gone. We've proved ourselves as worthy guardians of this tradition."

Helgrid overheard this and smirked. "If that thing shows its face again, we'll remind it who's in charge here. Mortal courage is not so easily crushed."

As more days slipped by, the village settled into a routine that balanced vigilance with careful optimism. They no longer jumped at every creak of wood or distant whistle of wind. The runes at each door, the herb bundles, and the iron tokens had become as familiar as family heirlooms. Each villager carried a piece of their community's resolve.

One afternoon, while clearing snowdrifts near the chapel ruins, Marta found something curious: a twisted birch branch stuck upright in a snowbank. At first glance, it seemed ordinary, but as she drew closer, she noticed a faint carving along its length—runes that resembled those used by Krampus. She called Jarlan over.

Jarlan examined it, heart thumping. "This might be a sign," he whispered. "Krampus often leaves birch rods as warnings or messages. Perhaps he's letting us know he's near, or that he acknowledges our stand."

Marta's eyes shone. "If that's so, it means he's watching. Maybe The Fatman is not far behind. Our ceremony, our resilience—it must have drawn their attention."

They carried the branch back to the meeting hall, showing Branwynn and Helgrid. Branwynn ran her fingertips over the carvings and nodded. "These are old symbols of moral accounting—Krampus's language, reminding us that deeds have weight. It's no threat to us; it feels more like approval. He sees we've upheld the balance in their absence."

Edric grinned at this news. "If Krampus left a sign, maybe The Fatman will leave one too. Or maybe we'll wake one morning to find them both among us, laughing at how we surprised their enemy with mortal bravery."

Takrin chuckled softly. "We can hope. In the meantime, let's keep doing what we've done—holding the line. If Krampus respects us, perhaps the entity now fears us as well."

That night, the villagers gathered again in the square, not for a desperate ceremony, but for a quiet moment of gratitude. They built a small bonfire, roasting chestnuts and sharing stories under the pale moonlight. The tension that once gripped their throats had eased. Though they remained watchful—patrols still circled, code words still passed between neighbors—they could smile again, find comfort in each other's presence.

Branwynn watched from a bench near the meeting hall. The children played in the snow, forging tiny snow-figures of Krampus and The Fatman, imitating their voices in good humor. Parents sipped hot broth and reminisced about past midwinters when gifts and lessons were delivered without terror.

Jarlan sat beside Branwynn. "We did what seemed impossible," he said softly. "We held back an ancient terror with nothing but faith, iron, and unity."

Branwynn nodded. "This village has grown stronger. Even if the entity returns, we know how to handle it. We've proven that tradition is not just a story, but a living flame we carry in ourselves."

Helgrid approached, plopping down on a stump, hammer across her lap. "I'd never have guessed we'd become warriors of spirit and song," she said with a wry grin. "But here we are, forging not just metal, but hope."

Marta joined them, hands clasped around a steaming cup. "The Fatman and Krampus would be proud, I think. We've shown that their lessons took root, that we don't collapse at the first sign of darkness. When they come—if they come—we can greet them as partners, not supplicants."

Edric and Takrin strolled by, patrolling lazily around the square, exchanging a nod with the group. No alarms tonight, just a peaceful vigilance.

They watched the bonfire crackle, sparks dancing up to the stars. Far above, the sky had cleared, revealing constellations shimmering in the icy air. Branwynn's eyes unfocused slightly, sensing magical currents. She felt a gentle stirring, as if old patterns were aligning.

Jarlan leaned closer, voice hushed. "Do you feel that? Like a distant warmth?"

Branwynn smiled faintly. "Yes. Something shifts. Perhaps Krampus and The Fatman draw nearer through unseen paths. Or maybe it's just the weight of our fear lifting, making the night seem kinder."

Helgrid shrugged. "Either way, we've earned this calm."

Two mornings later, a young boy ran into the square, breathless with excitement. He'd been helping his father gather firewood near the edge of the forest when he spotted something unusual: large footprints in fresh snow. Not the twisted goblin prints, nor the entity's clawed marks, but something heavy, round, and distinct—like boot prints far too large for any human in Sleetwood.

The villagers hurried to see for themselves. They found a line of massive footprints leading from the forest's edge toward a rocky overlook. Alongside them, strange elongated hoof prints—no ordinary animal could have made them. Jarlan's heart soared. These matched the old descriptions: The Fatman's heavy boots and Krampus's cloven hooves, walking side by side, leaving a trail in the snow.

Marta nearly wept. "They're here—or close, at least. Look at the stride. They came together!"

Branwynn pressed a hand over her mouth, relief washing over her features. "So soon after we strengthened our stand… they must have felt it. Our call, our refusal to break."

Helgrid knelt, running a finger along a print. "Still fresh. Hours old at most. They might be watching us from a distance, ensuring we're ready."

Edric scanned the treeline. "Should we follow the prints?"

Jarlan shook his head. "No need. We must respect their ways. They'll approach us when the time is right. Let's return to the village and make ready. We've shown our worth; now we can offer them welcome."

Back in Sleetwood, excitement rippled through the population. Children bounced on their toes, parents exchanged stunned smiles. After so much struggle, now a sign that their legendary guardians had arrived together was almost too good to believe.

Branwynn guided villagers in freshening the wards and setting a modest feast in the meeting hall. They had little to offer beyond bread, dried fruits, cheese, and tea, but they prepared it with reverence. Jarlan retrieved the old parchment from his archives—the one that spoke of how, centuries ago, Krampus and The Fatman restored balance. He laid it on a table so they could acknowledge their shared history.

Helgrid arranged a few iron tokens carved with the runes that had protected them, placing them near the parchment. Marta and Edric lit lanterns along the main lane, a gentle glow to guide any visitors arriving from the forest's edge.

As dusk approached, a hush fell over Sleetwood. Everyone waited, hearts pounding. They had endured nightmares, illusions, monstrous raids. They had stood firm. Now came the moment that might confirm their faith.

A distant jingle of chains reached their ears—faint, but unmistakable. Children gasped, recognizing Krampus's signature sound. Moments later, a soft "ho-ho" drifted through the snowy air, gentle and kind, sending waves of relief through all who heard it.

Two figures emerged from the dim outskirts of the village: one tall and dark-furred, horned and carrying chains and birch rods; the other stout and jolly, clad in red robes trimmed with white, a warm glow about him. They walked calmly, side by side, as equals returning to a place they never truly left.

The villagers gathered in the square, breath held in awe. No one spoke at first, fearing to break the spell. Krampus inclined his horned head, amber eyes studying them with pride. The Fatman smiled broadly, cheeks rosy as if lit from within, his eyes twinkling with gratitude.

Jarlan stepped forward, heart in his throat. He bowed slightly, voice steady but reverent. "Welcome. We have waited long and held strong. We know you have your own paths, but we never lost faith."

The Fatman chuckled kindly. "We felt your courage through the snow and silence, my friends. You reminded us that good folk can uphold the spirit of balance even in our absence."

Krampus nodded, voice low and resonant. "You faced illusions without flinching, honored the old ways, and guarded innocence fiercely. We owe you recognition. Your steadfastness helped us find our way back."

Tears welled in some villagers' eyes. Children pressed forward, wide-eyed, relieved that the figures from their tales were real and benevolent. Branwynn dipped her head, respectful. Helgrid grinned, pleased her hammer never had to strike these honored guests. Marta, smiling through her tears, offered the simple feast. "It's humble fare, but made with thanks," she said.

The Fatman accepted a piece of bread, savoring it as if it were a grand delicacy. Krampus held an iron token between his claws, studying the runes. "Clever work," he said approvingly to Helgrid. "You forged strength from hardship."

Jarlan exhaled, feeling a weight lift from his soul. "We learned that your presence isn't just a story we tell children—it's a pattern woven into the world. Without you, we discovered we could still uphold that pattern. We did our best, hoping you would return."

The Fatman's eyes shone. "We return because you proved worthy. Fear not—we do not blame you for struggling, nor do we expect perfection. The world is tested now and then to remind all creatures that goodness, kindness, and moral clarity are alive in their hearts."

Krampus added, "The entity that plagued you fed on doubt. You starved it by trusting one another. It may still lurk, but with us here and your resolve strong, it shall find no foothold."

Villagers murmured, relief and joy mingling. Some knelt briefly, others simply stood in respectful awe. The children circled closer, drawn to The Fatman's kindly aura and to Krampus's quiet strength. The tall figure offered a rare, gentle smile to a young girl who once dreamed of him as a terror. In that moment, all the twisted illusions the entity conjured seemed laughably thin.

Branwynn raised her staff, voice clear. "We welcome you both, guardians of balance. We pledge to keep your lessons alive, to cherish kindness and remember consequences. Stay as long as you wish—your presence warms these cold nights."

The Fatman laughed softly. "Oh, I think we'll linger awhile, enjoy your company, ensure the old ways settle back into place. The gifts of faith and courage you've shown us are more precious than any toy or trinket."

Krampus dipped his head to Jarlan and the others. "You remind me that even stern lessons mean nothing if no one heeds them. You heeded them well."

Under starry skies, the villagers and their legendary guests shared a simple meal and stories. They spoke quietly of the trials endured, the illusions defied, and the runes that glowed with determination. The children found their nightmares replaced by wonder. The adults understood that the accord they once took for granted was something they had upheld themselves.

Outside the meeting hall, beyond the ring of lanterns, the forest loomed silent. The entity, if it still lurked, had lost its chance to break them. Now that Krampus and The Fatman were united and returned, their presence would restore the world's moral axis. Fear would recede, and the old cycle of rewards and lessons would resume with renewed purpose.

As the night deepened, laughter and gentle conversation drifted through the lanes. A peace unlike any they'd known in weeks settled over Sleetwood—hard-earned, cherished. Tomorrow, life would go on: chores done, bread baked, lessons taught. But now these daily acts carried a deeper meaning, woven into a tapestry of myth and reality, hardship and triumph.

In the glow of torches and starlight, the villagers saw clearly what they had accomplished. They had faced the nameless hunger, refused to yield to despair, and signaled across worlds that they were worthy heirs of old traditions. Krampus and The Fatman, their distant guardians, had heard their call and come home.

If winter nights in the Winterspine Mountains still stretched long and cold, the villagers no longer feared them. They had learned how to kindle an inner warmth, bright and unyielding. And as they shared smiles with their legendary guests, they knew that this warmth would guide them through countless seasons to come.

CHAPTER EIGHT

A raw wind clawed at the thatched roofs of Sleetwood, rattling shutters and howling through the narrow gaps between cottages as though searching for something—some chink in the villagers' newfound armor of hope. It had been mere days since Krampus and The Fatman's return, days that should have been a time of healing. Yet, a heavy tension settled over the village like a choking fog. Shadows lengthened at odd hours. The iron runes and herb-charms that once hummed quietly with reassurance now seemed dull and strained. Some children woke from dreams clammy with fear again, whispering of strange shapes lurking just beyond the lamp-light.

Those who ventured beyond the perimeter to gather firewood or check traps returned uneasy, reporting that the forest was too silent, as if some greater presence lurked within the boles of the pines. The entity had not vanished. It had retreated, yes—but now it seethed. An ember of malice smoldered at the very edge of the villagers' senses.

Inside the meeting hall, the lanternlight flickered low. Krampus stood in a corner, half in shadow, arms folded over his bristled chest. His horns scraped the rafters when he shifted. The Fatman sat heavily upon a bench, stroking his white beard, worry deepening the crinkles at the corners of his warm eyes. Branwynn Spellshiver, pale and drawn, hovered near the old parchment Jarlan Forgerook had retrieved. Helgrid stood guard at the door, hammer in hand, her gaze flicking at every creak of timber. Marta, Edric, Takrin, and a few others formed a tight circle, grim-faced.

"It's changed tactics," Branwynn said softly, voice hollowed by anxiety. "We reclaimed unity, weathered illusions, summoned your return. Yet it lingers. Stronger. Bolder. Perhaps it is feeding on something deeper now."

The Fatman's eyes, usually kind, burned with quiet wrath. "I sense it too—an old hunger, slithering below reason. It knows that our presence threatens it. We stand for balance, and it thrives in imbalance. Perhaps it seeks to wrench that balance apart once and for all."

Krampus stirred, chains rattling faintly. "It wants to strike at the core. The illusions and skirmishes failed. Now it gathers darkness to test not just the villagers, but us. It may attempt a direct confrontation, or worse, twist the villagers' minds more violently than before."

A silence settled. Jarlan swallowed hard, remembering the terror that had once choked them. They had come so far. He glanced at Helgrid, who set her jaw. "We're ready," she said gruffly. "Let it try. We beat it back before, and we'll do so again."

But The Fatman lifted a gloved hand, shaking his head. "This is no mere test. I fear we face something older than the pacts we forged, a rancid wound in the world's moral fabric. When it first rose centuries ago, Krampus and I were forced to reaffirm our accord. We succeeded, and it fled. This time, it may seek to sever our bond—or devour it."

Marta's voice trembled, "Devour it? You mean it could... if it destroys the connection between you, wouldn't that unravel everything we've protected?"

Krampus nodded slowly. "Yes. The Fatman and I embody a delicate balance. If it tears us apart, turns us against each other, or drains our essence, the world's moral gravity could collapse. Kindness without caution becomes empty indulgence; discipline without compassion becomes cruelty. Children would never learn genuine morality—only fear or hollow greed."

Branwynn hissed, "We cannot let that happen." She closed her eyes, straining to recall half-forgotten wards that might reinforce the mythical bond. "We must strengthen your accord, anchor it not just in old vows, but in the living faith of these villagers."

Jarlan nodded eagerly. "Yes. We can help. Our belief gave us strength before. Perhaps if we stand by you, openly reaffirming your roles in our world, we can deny the entity the leverage it needs."

The Fatman smiled wanly. "Your faith is precious. But be warned: the entity will lash out harder than ever. Expect nightmares, violence, corruption. It knows we prepare a stand. Tonight—or soon— it may strike in full force, trying to weaken us before we anchor our accord."

Krampus's eyes glowed amber in the half-light. "Let it come. I tire of its games. This time, we face it openly, break its spine of malice."

Helgrid thumped her hammer's haft on the floor. "Then we must prepare at once."

The rest of that day, Sleetwood bustled with grim determination. Branwynn directed the forging of new wards. This time, they carved runes not just into iron tokens, but into the very beams of the meeting hall and the thresholds of every home. Marta mixed stronger herb concoctions to burn in censers, their acrid smoke meant to keep vile influences at bay. Jarlan led villagers in reciting the old hymns and tales, embedding them in memory so deep no illusion could unravel them.

Edric and Takrin checked the perimeter snares, setting crueler traps and sharpening stakes. They raised torches that would burn through the night, and positioned watchers in high lofts. The children were gathered in the chapel ruins—now warded and sealed with charms—where parents and elders sang lullabies that doubled as protective chants. Children clung to wooden carvings of Krampus and The Fatman, no longer frightened by their presence, but comforted.

As dusk crawled over the mountains, a tension crackled in the air. Snow began to fall, heavy and wet, muffling sound. Light fled from the sky, and in its absence, the village lanterns glowed like fragile stars. Inside the meeting hall, Krampus and The Fatman stood opposite each other before a makeshift altar, atop which lay old symbols of their pact: a birch rod entwined with red ribbon, a piece of iron etched with balancing runes, and a circle of evergreen branches symbolizing renewal.

Jarlan, Branwynn, Helgrid, and Marta formed a circle around them. The villagers pressed in behind, silent, watchful. The Fatman began to speak in a low, resonant tone, telling again the story of how he and Krampus emerged in ancient times to guide moral understanding. Krampus added a few words, curt and solemn, describing how fear and kindness must dance together to shape true virtue.

The air thickened. Branwynn felt magic stir. The villagers felt their hearts tighten with emotion. It was beautiful—and dangerous, for such a surge of meaning would surely draw the entity like blood in water.

A sudden scream cut through the stillness.

Everyone turned, hearts lurching. The cry came from outside, near the chapel. Helgrid and Edric rushed out, weapons ready. Jarlan and Marta followed, lanterns bobbing in the dark.

They found a villager stumbling toward them, eyes wide with terror. It was Ralden, one of the gatherers. He clutched his arm, bleeding from deep scratches. "It came from the forest," he gasped, voice shaking. "A shape... it looked like my mother—dead these ten years—but twisted, calling my name. I... I couldn't stop myself, I got too close. It attacked."

Marta pressed a cloth to Ralden's wound. Jarlan scanned the darkness beyond the torches. He saw nothing, but heard distant rustling. "Back inside," Helgrid ordered. "We knew it would try something. Let's not break formation."

They retreated, Ralden limping, heart hammering. More cries rose from the opposite side of the village. A watcher shouted alarm, then fell silent with a strangled choke. Panic nipped at the villagers' heels.

"Stay together!" Branwynn's voice carried over the chaos. "Hold to the plan. Don't chase phantoms alone."

Families clustered closer to the meeting hall, pressed under the protective gaze of Krampus and The Fatman. The legendary beings scanned the darkness outside, faces grim. The Fatman clenched his mittens, knuckles turning white. Krampus's chains rattled softly as he shifted stance.

From the gloom, silhouettes formed—at first a handful, then dozens. The entity had summoned a horde of horrors: goblins twisted into new grotesque shapes, phantomlike figures with too-long limbs, and worst of all, imitations of dead loved ones. They stood at the edge of torchlight, whispering vile enticements. Some wept, some laughed, all trying to lure the villagers into confusion and despair.

A child sobbed, recognizing a phantom wearing the face of a lost grandfather. A mother clenched her jaw, recalling the code words, repeating them under her breath, refusing to believe the lie. The illusions pressed closer, rattling fences, hissing foul curses.

Within the meeting hall, The Fatman and Krampus stepped forward. The villagers parted for them like wheat before a farmer's scythe. They emerged onto the steps, lit by lantern glow.

"Enough!" Krampus's voice boomed, rattling windows. "You dare mock the dead, feed on sorrow? Come forth and face us openly."

A shudder passed through the horde. The nearest phantoms flickered as if uncertain. The Fatman spoke next, his voice rich with sorrow and anger. "We know your hunger. It ends now. This village stands with us, and we with them."

Branwynn slipped outside, staff in hand, chanting softly. The runes carved into doorframes glowed faintly, as if awakened by her words. Marta followed, bearing a censer smoking with bitter incense. Jarlan clutched a birch rod, feeling its weight symbolic of the moral order they protected. Helgrid prowled near the flank, hammer raised, meeting the eyes of any villager who wavered and offering a steady nod.

The illusions pressed inward, trying a new tactic—voices overlapped, screaming nonsense, laughing cruelly. Some creatures rushed forward, claws scraping earth. Villagers shouted, forming ranks behind The Fatman and Krampus. They brandished spears and iron-tipped staves, chanting code words, ignoring the pleas of false loved ones. Children, secured in the chapel ruins, cried quietly but did not break into panic. They remembered their lessons, trusted their parents.

A fierce melee erupted. Helgrid crushed a goblin's skull with a single strike. Edric loosed arrows into the shimmering forms, each arrowhead dipped in Branwynn's herbal wash. Where they struck, illusions fizzled into sparks of black ash. Takrin led a flanking maneuver, tripping lurching beasts into traps that snapped with cruel finality.

But for every monster that fell, two more emerged. The entity was expending its reserves, hurling nightmares at them. The Fatman pushed forward, surprisingly nimble, swinging a great oak staff he had conjured from nowhere. He struck illusions and beasts alike, each blow cracking the air with righteous force. Krampus leapt into the fray, chains whirling, birch rods snapping bones and splintering illusions.

Still, the enemy pressed harder. The snow-shrouded lanes turned into a battlefield lit by torch and lantern. Screams and snarls intermingled. Black ichor stained the snow where goblins fell, and the bitter smell of Branwynn's herbs fought against the stench of decay.

Krampus

As the fight raged, the entity's voice slithered through minds, whispering doubts: *They will fail you. Krampus cares only for punishment, The Fatman for indulgence. They cannot truly unite. You know this. Give in.*

Jarlan felt a throb of despair lodge in his throat. What if the entity was right? For centuries, these legends existed in tension—Krampus's severity and The Fatman's kindness. Could they truly stand as one when tested to this extreme?

He forced himself to recall the villagers' resilience, the children's awakening, the ceremony that drew the brothers back. He remembered how they had faced illusions before and won. "Iron pine," he whispered. Others echoed him, code words passing like sparks through the crowd. They would trust each other, trust their guardians.

A colossal shape emerged from behind a cottage, towering over the battlefield. Antlers twisted like molten metal, eyes hollow pits of darkness. Its form warped, draped in tattered shadows that dripped with oily residue. This must be the entity itself, incarnating at last. It stooped low, reaching with elongated arms tipped in claw-like protrusions. Where it moved, illusions intensified—screaming faces sprouted from its torso, wailing children's cries and mocking laughter.

The villagers recoiled. Even Krampus and The Fatman hesitated, feeling the creature's raw malevolence radiate like heat from a forge. Branwynn gasped, staff trembling. Helgrid cursed under her breath, knuckles white on her hammer.

The entity spoke, its voice a chorus of agony: *I am older than your stories. I do not fear your tokens. Yield your balance, break your accord, and I shall spare your minds the torment of endless doubt.*

Krampus snarled, stepping forward. The Fatman moved beside him, shoulders squared. "We forged our bond to withstand such threats," The Fatman said quietly, voice firm. "We will not break it now."

The entity's laughter crackled like ice. *Your bond is fragile. Krampus, can you truly abide The Fatman's endless mercy? The spoiled children, the indulgence without consequence? And you, Fatman, can you truly respect Krampus's harsh methods, his heavy hand in disciplining innocents? Is your alliance not a convenient lie?*

Krampus growled. The Fatman's eyes tightened. For a moment, tension sizzled between them—old resentments, unspoken jealousies. The villagers felt it like a knife twisting in the gut. If they faltered here, all would be lost.

Jarlan stepped into the fray, voice cracking. "Remember us!" he shouted, drawing both guardians' eyes. "We learned to cherish both your lessons. We upheld kindness and caution while you were away. We proved these values can coexist, must coexist! Don't listen to its poison."

Marta raised the censer higher, smoke curling into shapes of protective runes. Branwynn began chanting louder, summoning old magic etched into memory by long nights of study. Helgrid bellowed, "We stand with both of you! We need your balance, not one or the other!"

Villagers took up the cry, shouting encouragement. Children's voices rose from the chapel, thin but determined, chanting code words and hymns. They reminded Krampus and The Fatman that neither could hold the world alone. Their synergy, forged over centuries, was not a flimsy convenience. It was the axis upon which moral order spun.

Krampus's amber eyes darted to The Fatman's twinkling gaze. The Fatman nodded curtly. "We differ in approach, brother, but we share purpose. The children need both of us—fear and comfort, justice and mercy. Let no foul creature rend us apart."

Krampus exhaled, muscles loosening. "Agreed. Let's silence this parasite once and for all."

The entity hissed, losing its grip. Illusions flickered, some fading as the guardians' resolve solidified. It lashed out physically, arms sweeping down to crush them. Krampus leapt onto a roof, chains clanking, and hurled his birch rods like spears. The Fatman swung his oak staff, striking the entity's limb and sending a spray of black ichor into the snow.

Villagers joined in, hurling torches and iron-tipped spears at the monstrosity. Edric's arrows bit deep. Takrin's traps snapped at its twisted legs. Branwynn focused her magic into a single glyph, etched into the ground with her staff's tip. As she chanted, the glyph glowed white-hot, searing through the darkness, creating a zone where illusions could not form.

The entity screeched, retreating from the glyph's light, dragging its shattered limbs behind. It tried to muster new horrors, but the villagers pressed their advantage. They had no fear left to feed it, no hidden resentments to exploit. The circle of trust held strong.

Krampus

The Fatman and Krampus struck in tandem: The Fatman to the right, staff crunching through shadowy hide, Krampus to the left, chains whipping like iron snakes. Each blow weakened it. The entity howled, its many voices devolving into guttural snarls. It lashed out with a barbed limb, catching The Fatman's shoulder, tearing cloth and drawing bright blood. A gasp rippled through the villagers. The Fatman winced but did not fall.

"Stand firm," The Fatman said through clenched teeth, comforting a weeping child just out of the monster's reach with a gentle glance. "I'm still here." His resilience rekindled the villagers' fury. They would not let this creature take their guardian.

Krampus roared, fury incarnate, raking his horns along the entity's flank. Sparks flew where horn met ephemeral flesh. The Fatman braced and struck upward, staff connecting with an eye-like hollow. The entity reared back, screeching as greenish fire erupted from the wound. Branwynn's glyph flared brighter, feeding on the villagers' collective will.

The entity tottered, limbs shaking. It shrank, its monstrous antlers curling inward, collapsing under the weight of their assault. Illusions died by the dozen, leaving only a scattering of twitching goblins and wisps of shadow that dissipated into the night.

Seeing its doom, the entity tried one last desperate gambit. It hissed a whisper so thick with venom that it felt like cold slime on the villagers' minds: *If I cannot break your bond, I shall poison what you protect. I shall linger in nightmares, forever haunting children's sleep. They will never rest peacefully again...*

But the children in the chapel, guided by their elders, began to sing a simple lullaby—a song of gentle snowfall and safe hearths. Their voices, though trembling, were pure and insistent. The lullaby drifted into the battlefield, and the entity flinched at the sound, as if burned by innocence it could not corrupt.

Jarlan added his voice, recalling verses of kindness and responsibility from old scrolls. Marta and Helgrid joined, followed by Edric, Takrin, and every villager who still drew breath. Even wounded Ralden managed a soft hum. The chorus rose, blending with Branwynn's magic and the steady presence of Krampus and The Fatman.

Cornered by hope, the entity's last threat unraveled. Its form sputtered, collapsing into a heap of oily shadows that hissed and boiled upon the snow. Krampus hurled a final birch rod into its center, and The

Fatman slammed his staff down with thunderous finality. The ground shuddered, and the entity's remains dispersed like ash on the wind.

A hush fell. Smoke curled in lazy patterns. Villagers stood amid scorched earth and broken illusions, panting. The monstrous presence was gone. Truly gone. They felt it in their bones: a suffocating weight lifted. The world seemed to sigh with relief.

Krampus and The Fatman lowered their weapons, backs straightening. Blood darkened The Fatman's torn robe, and Krampus's fur was matted with soot, but they stood strong. Branwynn leaned on her staff, tears of exhaustion glistening. Helgrid dropped to one knee, murmuring thanks. Jarlan's legs wobbled, and he sank onto a fallen crate, heart pounding with weary triumph.

The children's lullaby ended softly, replaced by muffled sobs of relief and ragged laughter from parents. The chapel's doors creaked as elders led the children out, showing them a battlefield empty of horrors.

Marta knelt beside The Fatman, carefully bandaging his wound. He smiled down at her, a gentle sadness in his eyes. "You all fought bravely," he said softly. "I knew mortals could be strong, but this… you surpassed all expectation."

Krampus nodded, amber eyes reflecting torchlight. "Without your unity, we might have faltered. The entity's words nearly found purchase in old grudges and doubts. But you reminded us why we must stand together, why our roles exist."

Jarlan swallowed a knot in his throat. "We needed you both. You needed each other. And you needed us. This is how the world should be, isn't it? Each playing their part, no single force overshadowing the other."

The Fatman placed a warm hand on Jarlan's shoulder. "Exactly. Balance is not a static thing—it's a dance. Sometimes mortals support us, sometimes we guide mortals. Tonight, we danced together."

Krampus retrieved a charred fragment of the entity's remains from the snow, watching it crumble into dust between his claws. "It will not plague this village again. There may be others like it in distant lands, but here and now, we have restored harmony."

Branwynn mustered a tired smile. "We learned that old gods and legends aren't distant. They live in our choices, in the stories we keep alive. The entity tried to tear our narrative apart, but we stitched it stronger than ever."

Helgrid stood, leaning on her hammer. "We lost some innocence, though. The children saw horrors. We tasted fear. That can't be undone."

The Fatman sighed, voice heavy with compassion. "True. But hardship can refine understanding. They will grow with a clearer sense of right and wrong. They know now that kindness and discipline are not hollow words but shields against real darkness."

Krampus agreed. "Lessons learned in fire last long. They'll remember this struggle and pass wisdom on, ensuring future generations walk a steadier moral path."

The villagers began to gather, forming a circle around their protectors. Wounded were tended, shaken souls comforted. Candles were lit, illuminating the scene not as a place of horror, but as hallowed ground where they overcame the unimaginable.

A gentle snowfall resumed, covering bloodstains and scorch marks with a soft white blanket. The wind that once howled with hunger now carried a lullaby of stillness. Edric and Takrin salvaged arrows and reset traps, though it seemed unnecessary now. Marta distributed warm drinks, sweetened with honey, to steady rattled nerves. Children clung to parents, and parents clung to each other, forging bonds that would outlast winter's chill.

Near the altar in the meeting hall, Jarlan, Branwynn, Helgrid, and Marta prepared to complete the ritual that had been interrupted. Krampus and The Fatman stood before them, and this time, the villagers encircled them more tightly, no foe at the edges to threaten.

Jarlan's voice rose, cracked but earnest: "We reaffirm the accord that balances our world. We honor both the warm gift and the stern lesson, the compassion and the consequence. We have seen what happens when one tries to sever this bond. We will not forget."

Branwynn chanted softly, drawing patterns in the air with her staff. Helgrid pounded her hammer lightly on the floor, a rhythmic heartbeat. Marta sprinkled dried herbs over the birch rod and red ribbon. The villagers hummed a lullaby tuned now to hope rather than fear. The Fatman and Krampus clasped forearms, sealing their unity before all eyes.

A subtle warmth filled the hall, not a blaze but a comforting glow, easing aches and quieting sobs. The rift the entity tried to exploit was now sealed tighter than ever. The presence of both guardians felt solid, as if anchored by countless mortal hearts.

Outside, the forest murmured softly, pine needles brushing in gentle breezes. If any lingering malicious spirit dared watch, it would find no scraps of doubt or fear to feed on here. The village had learned to stand on its own two feet, fortified by legends who had become living allies.

As night wore on, the villagers tended the wounded, consoled the grieving—some had lost friends in the melee—and cleaned their shattered lanes. Krampus and The Fatman offered quiet encouragement, helping to stack broken planks or whispering gentle words to a traumatized child.

Eventually, the survivors drifted to their homes, guided by moonlight and the quiet confidence that no shadow loomed, no whisper of despair hovered beyond their thresholds. The chapel's doors closed softly behind elders and children, now safe and sound. The meeting hall grew quiet, lanterns dimming as exhaustion claimed even the bravest souls.

Before dawn, as the sky hinted at pale light behind the Winterspine peaks, Krampus and The Fatman stood alone in the village square. Snow muffled their steps. They surveyed Sleetwood's sleeping rooftops, each house holding a family that had faced nightmares and emerged stronger.

The Fatman sighed, contentment and sorrow mingled in his eyes. "They will mend, in time. And they will remember the lesson: that balance is precious and must be guarded."

Krampus nodded, tail flicking softly over trampled snow. "We should remain a while, help them rebuild confidence, ensure no bitter seed remains."

"Agreed," said The Fatman. "They earned our presence and our gratitude."

In a distant window, Jarlan watched their silhouettes. He smiled faintly, knowing that even if they departed someday—following cosmic paths unknown to mortals—the imprint of their bond would remain. The village would continue to tell tales of this winter, of how they stood beside legendary guardians and stared down ancient horror.

As dawn's first glimmer broke over the peaks, Sleetwood lay quiet and secure. The darkest trials had passed. The entity's threat had been met with steel, song, and unbreakable unity. A new day promised healing and memory, lessons etched in frost and fire. No matter what challenges the future might hold, villagers, Krampus, and The Fatman knew they would face them together, guided by the balance they had fought so hard to preserve.

And somewhere, beyond mortal sight, the world's moral axis spun smoothly again, the old accord shining brighter for the darkness it had survived.

CHAPTER NINE

In the days following the entity's downfall, Sleetwood appeared at first glance like a village waking from a nightmare. The snow that had been trampled into dirty slush by frantic battles was gently covered by fresh, delicate flakes. The crude fortifications—spears of iron and sharpened stakes—still rimmed the perimeter, but now children ventured near them with hesitant curiosity rather than terror. Adults moved with tired purpose, patching roofs, setting broken beams, clearing debris. Lanterns flickered in quiet windows, and simple meals were shared in an atmosphere of weary relief.

Yet the peace that settled was not a cheerful one. A pall lingered over every street. The villagers had seen horrors beyond normal winter hardship—shifting nightmares, familiar faces twisted by malevolence. They knew too well that darkness, though beaten back, remained part of their world. More than ever, they understood that goodness required constant vigilance, and that The Fatman and Krampus, though protectors in their own way, were not gentle guardians who shielded mortals from all pain. Instead, they were forces that required mortals to stand on their own feet, braced against moral storms. The scars, both physical and spiritual, were slow to fade.

Krampus

That recognition seeped into their daily rhythms. Parents watched their children more closely. Not with fear the entity would return—it had truly been driven out—but with an understanding that innocence could be tainted if not guided properly. The Fatman still lingered, offering quiet comfort and mild cheer when possible. His presence warmed hearths and set children giggling shyly when he passed by. He left small tokens—carved wooden toys, neatly wrapped treats—on doorsteps for those still recovering.

In contrast, Krampus's presence in these days of rebuilding was more subtle and far darker. He did not dote on children, nor spread sweetness. Instead, he moved at the edges of sight, hooves crunching softly on icy ground late at night. Sometimes, villagers glimpsed him standing under a crooked pine, amber eyes glowing, chains rattling softly as if he measured their resolve. If The Fatman reminded them of hope and generosity, Krampus now stood as a silent reminder that complacency had no place here. Anyone who thought to exploit the fragile calm for cruelty or selfishness might feel his presence looming.

Some nights, uneasy murmurs spread through back alleys: Did you hear Krampus rattling chains near the old grain shed? Or did you see two yellow eyes peering from the barn loft as you tried to sneak an extra loaf of bread not meant for you? The children who had seen him fight the entity's horrors now shivered with another kind of awe: they realized Krampus was no fairy-tale monster, but something far more real and necessary. He was a shadow cast by The Fatman's gentle glow, ensuring moral lines remained sharp and meaningful.

As the village mended fences and carried on, one particular evening stood out like a bruise on fresh skin. A boy named Tollen, perhaps ten winters old, decided to test the boundaries newly drawn. He had survived terror, yes, but fear had hardened into a reckless bravado. He sneered at other children's caution, stole extra sweets left by The Fatman's helpers, and poked fun at smaller kids for trembling when they thought of the recent horrors. When his mother scolded him, Tollen shrugged and rolled his eyes. He'd seen worse than any punishment she might give—what was a birch rod compared to monsters with hollow eyes?

In the week after the great battle, Tollen grew bolder in his mischief. He taunted another child into tears, snatched a small wooden stag carved as a comfort toy from a younger girl, and hid it in the snow.

When confronted, he grinned and lied without shame. Rumors spread among the villagers—Tollen's mother wept, unsure how to curb his cruelty. Others whispered that the boy was testing lines, daring Krampus to appear. Some said quietly: perhaps Krampus's dark presence is exactly what's needed, that a reminder must be given. But none dared say it too loudly, fearing to invite that grim visitation.

As dusk bled into night, a hush pressed down on the village. The Fatman passed through the square, distributing a few kind words and sweets. He paused at Tollen's doorstep, sensing discord within. He debated leaving a gentle gift—perhaps a small wooden toy that might teach empathy—but shook his head, deciding that kindness alone would not right this tilt. He moved on, his footsteps soft in the snow, and vanished into darkness. Later, as torches sputtered low, Tollen slipped out of his family's cottage, smirking. He intended to pilfer a neighbor's honey jar, just to prove no one could stop him.

The night was still. No wind stirred. Tollen crept between cottages, breath steaming. He found the jar hidden under a cloth on a windowsill, easy pickings. He licked his lips, reached out—and froze. Chains rattled, faint but distinct. He spun, heart thumping. No one stood behind him, only empty air and drifting snowflakes. He swallowed, dismissing it as nerves, and snatched the jar. As he turned to flee, he caught a flicker of movement at the alley's end.

Two amber eyes reflected moonlight. A tall silhouette, horned and furred, stood statue-like beneath a sagging rooftop. Tollen felt a surge of defiance and fear swirl together, making his stomach clench. He remembered the stories: how Krampus punished naughty children, how he carried rods and chains. Tollen had seen Krampus from a distance in the daylight—a presence helping drive back horrors—but now, alone and with stolen honey in hand, the boy saw no ally. He saw judgment incarnate.

The boy mustered a sneer. "Go away," he hissed. "You're just a story to scare children. I'm not afraid." His voice wavered slightly, betraying him.

Krampus did not move. His silence was heavier than any scolding. Tollen's bravado cracked. The boy took a step back, clutching the honey jar. The clink of metal broke the hush—Krampus shifted his chains, sending a thin, scraping sound down the alley. Tollen's heart hammered.

He imagined the entity's nightmares, the horrors, and he realized this was not some phantom. Krampus was very real.

Panic flared. Tollen dashed away, slipping between houses, forging a frantic path toward the chapel ruins. He'd hide there, wait out the night. No one would follow him into that eerie place, surely. Behind him, he heard slow, deliberate hoof-steps. Not running, just following, as if Krampus knew exactly how to corner a frightened soul.

In the chapel yard, the old wards had faded since the battle. Only mild charms remained, to keep curious children safe. The moonlight cast long shadows of broken arches and tilting gravestones. Tollen cowered behind a fallen pillar, trembling. He dared peek out—no sign of those amber eyes. Perhaps he'd lost the monster. A moment passed, two, three—nothing. He sighed relief, steadying his breath.

Then a birch rod cracked against the pillar, inches from his face. Tollen yelped and scrambled backward, dropping the honey jar. Sticky sweetness oozed into the snow. Krampus stepped from behind the crumbling stone, impossibly quiet for something so large. His horns grazed a broken arch, his chains glinted in faint light, and his breath steamed around pointed teeth. He did not speak—he rarely did when delivering lessons—but his gaze spoke volumes: I see what you do. I judge your deeds, not your excuses.

Tollen stammered, "I-I didn't mean—" He choked on his own lie. He had meant it. He had enjoyed bullying and stealing. The village's suffering had not tempered him. Instead, he tried to exploit the lull in fear to elevate himself. Now he realized that in a world where Krampus existed, cruelty did not go unchecked.

Krampus raised a birch rod, the thin branches bound with twine. It crackled in the silence. The boy's courage dissolved into whimpers. He thought of pleading, but words failed him. Fear rooted him to the spot.

At that moment, another presence approached. A soft glow—subtle warmth that made Tollen's eyes sting with relief—emerged from the darkness. The Fatman stepped into the ruined chapel yard, boots crunching softly. Tollen gazed at him with tearful eyes, hoping for rescue.

The Fatman's face was grave. He met Krampus's gaze without flinching. There was no surprise in him, only understanding. For centuries, they had balanced each other's roles. He knew why Krampus was here. Sometimes, mercy alone faltered if it never found correction.

This boy was a symptom of what happened if moral lessons failed to take root.

Krampus lowered the rod slightly, acknowledging The Fatman's presence. The Fatman nodded, stepping closer. He knelt beside Tollen, who cowered, expecting a scolding or perhaps a kind excuse. Instead, the old man's voice was gentle but sad. "You tested boundaries for no reason but to harm. You learned nothing from your village's ordeal. You revel in petty cruelty as if it makes you strong. It does not."

Tollen sobbed, confusion and guilt twisting inside him. Why was The Fatman not comforting him? Why no gentle words of forgiveness? He realized too late that kindness required a foundation of respect and goodness. Without that, mercy became hollow. The Fatman's sorrowful gaze pierced him more than anger would have.

The Fatman stood again, turning to Krampus. The silence hummed with tension. A choice had to be made. How severe a lesson would they teach?

Krampus exhaled, nostrils flaring. He lifted the rod, tapping it lightly against his palm. For a moment, Tollen saw a flicker of something in those amber eyes—disappointment, not just in the boy, but in the fragile nature of morality itself. The entity's evil had been grand and monstrous. This was pettier—the weakness of a child who should know better. Yet Krampus's role did not diminish before petty sins. On the contrary, such sins were the seeds from which worse evils might grow if left unpunished.

Tollen wailed, "I'm sorry! Please, I'm sorry!" He reached out as if to grab The Fatman's robe, to hide behind him.

The Fatman stepped aside, gentle but firm, offering no shield. "Your sorrow must be true," he said softly. "You must feel it honestly, not only because you're caught." He glanced at Krampus. The two guardians understood each other well—now more than ever. The Fatman's generosity would mean nothing if it protected cruelty from consequences. Krampus's punishment would mean nothing if it came without the chance for redemption. They would not sever compassion from retribution.

Krampus knelt, chains rustling. He tilted the boy's chin up with the rod's blunt end. Tollen trembled, meeting those inhuman eyes. He saw no blind rage there, only stern expectation: confess your wrongdoing, understand it, and pay the price.

Krampus

In a voice rough as bark, Krampus finally spoke, words rarely heard by mortal ears. "Kindness, child, is not weakness. Compassion is not foolishness. You sneered at it, twisted it, and for what? To feel powerful? Your village fought horrors beyond measure and learned unity. You would discard that lesson so easily?"

Tollen choked back sobs, shaking his head. "N-no. I-I was wrong, I swear. I just… I just wanted to feel bigger than my fear."

Krampus narrowed his eyes. "To feel bigger, you trampled others. There are other ways to be strong. Facing fear, helping friends, building trust—these make you strong. Not stealing honey or making children cry."

Tollen nodded frantically, tears carving hot paths down his cheeks. He felt The Fatman's presence behind him, warm and sad. He felt Krampus's rod beneath his chin, not striking yet, but promising consequence. He realized something crucial: the world would never be free of darkness, temptation, or malice. Strength must come from moral choice. He had chosen wrongly.

"I'm s-sorry," Tollen stuttered again, voice softer, "Not because I'm caught… but because I see now what I did. I made the world colder. After we all fought so hard to keep it warm, I made it worse. I don't want to be that person."

Krampus studied him a long moment. The wind picked up, rattling loose stones in the chapel ruins. The Fatman waited silently, trusting his brother's judgment.

At last, Krampus lowered the rod. Not without a lesson—he did not let the boy escape unscathed. He gripped Tollen's arm with surprising gentleness, hauling him upright. With careful deliberation, he struck once, a swift lash across Tollen's backside. Pain blossomed, sharp and sudden. The boy cried out, more in shock than agony. One blow—not enough to harm permanently, but enough to brand the memory of this night into Tollen's soul.

Tollen sobbed openly now, clutching his smarting backside, tears dripping. Krampus nodded, satisfied. Sometimes a single lash was enough if guilt and truth had found a foothold. He did not relish this role, but it was necessary. Better a stinging reminder now than a descent into greater cruelty later.

The Fatman stepped forward, laying a warm hand on the boy's shoulder. Not to comfort him prematurely, but to help him stand. "Return home," he said quietly. "Apologize to those you wronged. Return what you stole, or if you cannot, make amends through honest labor. Earn forgiveness by deeds, not words."

Tollen sniffled, nodding. He tasted honey still lingering on his lips, now bitter. This memory would guide him in days to come. He understood now that kindness and fear walked hand in hand, and if he tried to twist kindness into weakness, he would face fear at its most righteous.

Krampus stood aside, letting Tollen stagger from the chapel ruins. The boy stumbled home, leaving two sets of footprints behind him: one light and hesitant, another heavier, a reminder that justice had a name.

After Tollen vanished into the darkness, The Fatman and Krampus lingered a moment, both gazing at the ruined chapel's stone arches and fallen pillars. This place had once sheltered desperate rituals, frantic wards, and terrified children. Now it had witnessed a smaller, quieter confrontation—a child's moral reckoning.

"That was well done," The Fatman said softly, voice heavy with understanding. "I cannot always forgive without consequence. Nor can you punish without hope. We have found our balance again."

Krampus inclined his horned head. "The entity tried to break our accord by magnifying doubts. But this village, these mortals, show that our roles endure because they understand we are both needed. Tonight proved it again."

The Fatman sighed, sadness lingering. "It will not be the last time a child or adult challenges that balance. Humans are flawed, always testing limits. But we remain."

Krampus smirked faintly, the closest he came to a smile. "If they never erred, what need for us?" His voice held no mockery, just calm realism. They existed precisely because humans wrestled with right and wrong. Without that struggle, no legends would be needed.

They parted ways, walking through silent streets. The Fatman headed toward a corner where a widow lived alone, leaving a small parcel of tea and dried fruit at her door—kindness for no reason but to ease her burden. Krampus slipped into a dark alley, checking for any sign of late-night mischief. Finding none, he vanished into shadows.

By dawn's first pale glow, Sleetwood roused to another cold morning. The villagers discovered small signs that their guardians had moved in the night: a new token carved into a lintel, a missing honey jar returned with a note of apology scrawled by Tollen's trembling hand. Word spread that Tollen had confessed his misdeeds to his mother, sobbing as he promised to do chores for those he wronged. Some villagers nodded, understanding that this was not random coincidence.

Jarlan, Branwynn, Helgrid, and Marta met in the meeting hall that morning, savoring hot broth. News of Tollen's reckoning had reached their ears. Jarlan's eyes were thoughtful. "Darkness lingers even after great evils are banished. The child's cruelty was small, but dangerous. Krampus reminded us that no evil is too small to matter."

Helgrid sipped her broth, nodding. "A painful lesson, but necessary. We cannot rely on The Fatman's kindness alone. Without Krampus's discipline, we'd slide into comfortable selfishness."

Branwynn looked at the runes etched into the meeting hall's beams. They had served well against the entity, and now they served as a reminder that moral order was never guaranteed. "I'll strengthen these runes," she said. "Not because another great evil lurks, but because maintaining balance is an ongoing work. We must keep ourselves honest."

Marta's gaze drifted to a window where children played quietly in the snow. "They'll grow with these stories shaping them," she murmured. "They'll know that if they hurt others, Krampus watches. If they despair, The Fatman comforts. They must choose their path wisely."

That evening, The Fatman shared quiet smiles with parents who taught kindness at the dinner table. Krampus, unseen, listened outside windows where children repeated lessons learned, a faint clink of his chains suggesting approval.

In the following days, Tollen mended his ways. He returned stolen items when possible, chopped wood for the family he had wronged, helped shovel snow from a neighbor's path. He did not suddenly become a saint, but he tried harder, flinching whenever he recalled that night in the chapel. He understood now that mercy and judgment were not distant forces—he had touched them, and they had touched him. That knowledge would guide him through future temptations.

The villagers rebuilt their lives with deeper reverence. They held small ceremonies around the old altar, singing hymns that praised The Fatman's generosity and thanked Krampus for ensuring their kindness meant something. Children placed carved figures of both guardians side by side, no longer fearing contradiction: a kind elder brother and a stern, goat-legged watcher, both essential parts of the story.

Some nights, a few villagers whispered they saw Krampus's silhouette on a distant hill, outlined against moonlit pines. Others said they heard The Fatman chuckling softly behind a shutter before leaving a doll carved with intricate runes as a gift. There were no grand pronouncements—both guardians preferred their subtle, timeless roles. The entity had been a rare overt war. Daily life was a quieter battleground, one fought in hearts and actions.

In this delicate calm, darkness never fully vanished. Winter nights were still long, and cold winds still moaned through rafters. People still felt envy, anger, fear—these were human conditions. But now they understood that legends were not just tales told to children; they were living principles that demanded renewal in each generation's choices.

Sleetwood became something of a living parable: a village that had confronted grand terror and petty malice, guided by two old beings who embodied moral polarity. The Fatman and Krampus lingered as long as necessary, until they sensed that the lesson truly stuck. Perhaps in another season, they would move on, returning to their timeless pattern—The Fatman delivering joy, Krampus ensuring it never became empty indulgence. But for now, they watched, satisfied that the villagers would not soon forget what they had endured.

On one of these nights, a thin crescent moon hung low. A woman, nursing a restless infant, paused in her lullaby as she thought she saw Krampus's horned shape slip past her window. Instead of fear, she felt grateful. With him here, no cruel soul would go unchecked. With The Fatman in the village, no despair would go unsoothed. In this balance, life persisted.

Another family, grieving a grandparent lost in the earlier chaos, found a small gift of spiced biscuits at their door. They understood at once who had left it, and the sweetness in their mouths mingled with tears. Compassion and consequence, side by side, made their grief bearable. The Fatman's offering helped them remember kindness, while Krampus's presence reminded them not to let grief twist into anger or negligence.

And so the dark element of Krampus settled into daily life like a necessary shadow cast by a warm fire. A child caught lying might hear distant chains at night. A teen considering petty theft remembered Tollen's sobs echoing in the chapel ruins. An adult tempted to cheat a neighbor recalled how easily fear could return if moral lines were blurred. This was

Krampus's gift: fear in service of moral clarity, darkness that defined the edges of light.

As days stretched into weeks, the villagers integrated these lessons into their routines. They started each morning not with dread, but with awareness. They ended each night whispering code words or saying a brief prayer, acknowledging that good and bad impulses lived within them, tempered by the lessons of these strange guardians.

Branwynn refined her wards not to guard against monstrous foes now vanquished, but to remind everyone that they must guard against the monsters within. Jarlan recorded the events in his ledgers: the great battle, the quiet punishments, the subtle gifts. He wrote of Krampus and The Fatman not as distant gods, but as partners reflecting human nature back at them.

Helgrid forged a new set of iron tokens and hung them from eaves. Not for war this time, but as symbols of the village's promise to remain vigilant, honest, and kind. Marta brewed soothing teas, distributing them freely, knowing that kindness must flow like warm water through their community, and that Krampus watched to ensure it never ran stale.

In this tapestry of small acts, the dark element of Krampus remained a constant undercurrent. His silence was eerie yet comforting, a guarantee that cruelty would never rule unchallenged. And each time the villagers felt tempted to stray, they recalled that horned silhouette in moonlight, the rattle of chains, and the single lash that had set one boy's course straight.

Eventually, the seasons would shift, snow would melt, and life would return to planting and harvest cycles. The Fatman would slip away to other corners of the world, delivering kindness where needed. Krampus might fade from common sight, content that fear of wrongdoing simmered in just the right measure. But Sleetwood's people knew that, come next winter or whenever moral confusion swelled, these figures could return. Their story was etched into the village's bones now.

On a final twilight before The Fatman and Krampus planned to recede into quieter patterns, Tollen approached the meeting hall. He carried a small carving—a clumsy attempt at shaping wood into something meaningful. He left it on the doorstep and hurried away, heart thumping. Anyone finding it the next day would see a roughly carved figure: half gentle, half fearsome, two faces sharing one body, entwined in evergreen boughs. It was an homage to the accord that saved them from grand evil and petty malice alike.

When Krampus passed by that night, unseen, he paused and considered the carving. A low rumble of approval, almost a purr, escaped him. The Fatman, from a distant rooftop, smiled into his beard. They needed no thanks, but knowing the lesson had taken root pleased them both.

Thus, darkness remained woven through Sleetwood's tapestry, not as a curse, but as a defining thread that gave shape and meaning to the light. The villagers would never forget what they had learned: that kindness flourished best when it stood beside caution, that mercy gained strength when balanced by consequence. In acknowledging their own frailties, they embraced the roles of their legendary guardians—and found that even the dark element of Krampus, so feared at first, was essential to their moral world.

Dusk pressed down early that day, as if the mountains themselves conspired to shorten the villagers' light. The Winterspine peaks loomed black and immovable, and thin clouds drifted like grey ghosts over their ridges. Within the village of Sleetwood, still bearing wounds of battle and terror, people moved quietly, as though reluctant to raise their voices above a whisper. Though the monstrous entity had been defeated, its defeat had come at a terrible cost—innocence was tarnished, and fear, once purged, had settled into a wary acceptance that darkness would always have a claim on the world.

The Fatman and Krampus lingered in the village, their presence a living reminder of how quickly chaos could descend. Their roles had shifted subtly since the night they united to overcome the entity. The Fatman still wore kindness on his face, offered small comforts and gentle words when he encountered villagers fretting over repairs or grieving their losses. Yet even he seemed wearier now, as though the night's horrors had tempered his natural warmth with a sober understanding that sweetness without vigilance risked collapse.

Krampus, by contrast, had always embodied darkness and consequence. His arrival had first sparked terror, his standing presence—horned, furred, and equipped with chains and birch rods—once signified the grim lessons lurking at the edges of comfort. Before, he was feared mainly in stories and whispers, a distant figure of moral checks and balances. Now, after facing an evil force beyond mortal comprehension, the villagers knew Krampus as a real and ancient power, as old as the first midwinter frost. They had seen him fight with feral intensity, had watched him lash out at horrors spawned by a greater darkness. And they had known relief then, to have a monster on their side against a monstrosity. But now that the entity was gone, Krampus's presence unsettled them once more. He was no gentle protector, no kindly uncle—they knew better. He was a necessary shadow, a presence that demanded moral clarity and did not hesitate to punish those who strayed.

No one dared openly defy him, of course. Not now. Yet, the villagers felt a certain heaviness whenever they glimpsed him at the edge of a clearing, or heard the faint rattle of his chains near the chapel ruins. His darkness was not banished—it lived here now, stitched into the daily routines. If The Fatman gave them hope and mercy, Krampus gave them fear and consequence, ensuring that the hard-won moral order did not fray.

As the last sliver of daylight waned, Branwynn Spellshiver sat outside her makeshift hut near the old chapel. She had set a small iron brazier on the ground, feeding it scraps of dried birch bark that crackled and smoked. Its scented smoke curled into patterns reminiscent of ancient runes. She watched them closely, lips moving in silent incantations. Without the entity's looming dread, her magic now served as a subtle compass, guiding the village back into something resembling balance. But the smoke showed troubled patterns. The villagers were restless. There were mutterings among them—complaints that while The Fatman offered sweets and kind words, Krampus hovered as a menacing shape in the periphery. People wondered how long this uneasy truce would last, how long both brothers would remain in Sleetwood.

Helgrid Stonestream approached, her hammer slung over one shoulder, breath fogging in the chill. She paused to watch Branwynn's smoke. "It's not clearing, is it?" she asked, voice kept low. "You've been at it for hours."

Branwynn shook her head. "The patterns are... conflicted. I see guilt and remorse tangled with resentment. The villagers lived through horrors and learned unity, yes. But now that the immediate threat is gone, old habits threaten to resurface. Fear alone won't hold them forever."

Helgrid let out a slow breath. She recalled how a child, Tollen, had been corrected harshly by Krampus days earlier. That event lingered as a cautionary tale. "We have The Fatman's kindness and Krampus's severity in equal measure now. If the villagers become complacent—" She did not finish her thought. She did not need to. They both understood that as soon as complacency took root, cruelty and indifference could bloom, and Krampus would have cause to assert his ancient role with iron certainty.

Over the next few days, tension seeped into ordinary events. Marta, the midwife, noticed neighbors snapping at each other over minor disagreements—missing tools, rationed flour, rumored pilfering of supplies. Edric and Takrin, still leading patrols though no enemy lingered, found themselves breaking up arguments that should have been solved with a handshake and a kind word. Sometimes at night, people heard faint laughter—The Fatman's gentle chuckle as he tried to soothe wounded pride, and occasionally a low rumble from somewhere unseen, perhaps Krampus clearing his throat as a subtle reminder that wickedness would be met with punishment.

Jarlan Forgerook documented these subtle changes in his ledger by lantern light. He noted that after the initial victory and moral enlightenment, humans seemed to slip, as humans always do, back into patterns that required constant maintenance. He wrote: *We stand between mercy and menace. The Fatman and Krampus watch us, shaping our conduct by their presence. Without the entity's threat, we are left with ourselves—our petty sins and stubborn pride. How long can we hold true?*

The next evening, a small incident flared into a public scandal: a villager named Rofeld accused his neighbor Drena of hoarding salted fish. Rofeld shouted in the square, demanding The Fatman intervene to restore fairness. Drena spat back that Rofeld lied. A handful of onlookers formed a circle, hushed. The Fatman stepped forward, arms folded over his ample belly, face grave. He spoke softly to them, asking for calm, suggesting they share what they had and keep honest records. His words dripped with understanding. Rofeld's anger cooled, Drena's indignation softened. It seemed resolved—until a grating of chains sounded behind them.

Krampus emerged from behind a storage shed. He did not speak. He simply stood, horns scraping the gloom, amber eyes fixed upon the pair. Instantly, Rofeld and Drena blanched. Was one of them guilty of deception? Had Krampus come to mete out punishment?

The Fatman laid a gloved hand on Krampus's arm and gave a slight shake of his head, as if to say: *Not yet, brother.* Krampus snorted, chains rustling. His gaze lingered on Rofeld, then Drena, as if peeling away their pretenses. Finally, he stepped back into the shadows, hooves crunching on ice. The villagers breathed again. But they all knew what this meant: The Fatman might forgive easily, but Krampus was watching closely. If they lied or harmed each other under cover of night, Krampus would return with no gentle hand to still him.

Branwynn, witnessing this from afar, worried that the village's moral fabric would be tested again and again. Without a great evil to unite them, would they rely too heavily on fear of Krampus's lash? The Fatman tried to nurture genuine goodness, but would people choose goodness on their own, or only because they dreaded punishment? She understood that both guardians wanted more than compliance. They wanted the villagers to embrace moral order freely. But Krampus's legacy was older than written law—he was the dark figure who haunted the edges of winter's longest night, punishing evil without appeal.

As the next midnight approached, a heavy snowfall descended, muffling the village in layers of silence. Snowdrifts hugged the walls, and roofs sagged with white burdens. In the gloom, a small figure trudged through alleyways: a teenage boy named Aflen, known for his quiet nature. He carried a basket of bread loaves, intending to share them with the widow Donella, who had fallen ill. This was a kind deed, something The Fatman would smile upon. Yet Aflen trembled, not from the cold but from the weight of what lurked in Sleetwood's shadows. He feared to run into Krampus, not because he'd done wrong, but because the silence magnified the sense of constant judgment.

Halfway there, he stumbled on something half-buried in snow—a small wooden toy stag, carved and left behind. Perhaps one of The Fatman's gifts. He picked it up gingerly, smiling at its craftsmanship. At that moment, a silhouette moved at the alley's far end. Fear pricked his heart. Was it Krampus? The figure passed by a lantern's glow—a villager, nothing more. But the anxiety coiled inside Aflen's chest. Even doing good things felt fraught when darkness and judgment pressed close.

What none of them knew was that Krampus remembered a much older time, when mortals did not rely solely on fear. In the earliest days of winter traditions, people understood that Krampus was no simple brute—he was a primal force reminding humans that without moral backbone, kindness would rot into weakness. The Fatman, or beings like him in other lands, offered joy and generosity, but these gifts were meaningless if recipients never learned to cherish them properly. Krampus's darkness came from ancient forests, from nights when wolves circled villages and people clung together for survival. Back then, a single act of cruelty could doom a whole family in winter's harsh grasp. Krampus enforced a code that preceded parchment laws—a code written in frost and blood and hunger, teaching that selfishness was death.

Now, centuries later, that primal lesson returned. The entity's attack had exposed how thin the veneer of civilization could be. Sleetwood had survived by banding together, supported by The Fatman's gifts and Krampus's grim resolve. With the immediate threat gone, would they maintain that harmony or slip into petty evils that required Krampus to bare his teeth again?

A few nights later, a child dared whisper to her father as they huddled over a candle: "Papa, will Krampus leave when we learn to be good?" The father smiled wanly, stroking her hair. "Krampus doesn't leave so easily, child. He stays as long as we need him. Perhaps if we all do what's right—genuinely right—he'll fade back into legend. But that's not easy."

The Fatman listened outside their shuttered window, nodding softly to himself. He yearned for that day when fear of Krampus would not be necessary, when people chose virtue for virtue's sake. But reality seldom matched such ideals. That was why he and his darker counterpart existed—eternal poles ensuring the world did not tip into madness.

Another incident flared two days later. A man named Sten was found cheating his neighbors on a trade of smoked herring. Minor, trivial perhaps, but in these fragile times, even small deceits rippled through the collective psyche. The Fatman confronted him in the square, eyes stern, reminding him that trust was hard-won and easily lost. Sten shrugged, offering half-hearted excuses. Some villagers grumbled. Others looked around nervously, wondering if Krampus lurked in a nearby alley, waiting to punish deceit with his birch rods. The tension built.

That night, as Sten tried to sleep, the wind moaned under the eaves. He woke to a scraping sound at his window. Fear gripped him. Had he truly believed he could weasel out of this moral order so easily? He peered out and saw only swirling snow. But then a shape resolved—tall, horned, draped in shadows. Sten's heart hammered. He scrambled from bed, heart in his throat. He tried to shout for forgiveness, but his voice croaked uselessly.

Krampus

He did not see Krampus enter—he never even heard the door creak. Yet suddenly, Krampus stood inside, towering over the modest bed. Sten choked on terror. The Fatman was nowhere to be found this time. This was Krampus's domain—the hush of a winter's night, no witnesses, no pleas. Krampus's chains jingled softly, a cruel lullaby to Sten's trembling knees.

No words were exchanged. Sten knew his sin: petty cheating, a small cruelty that eroded trust. He also knew Krampus never needed a lengthy trial. The old spirit could sniff out wrongdoing as a wolf scents blood. Sten thought he saw pity flicker in those amber eyes—pity for a mortal too foolish to learn. Krampus did not linger. He raised the birch rods and delivered two swift strokes across Sten's back, each blow a crack like bone snapping. Pain blossomed, hot and immediate, but it was not lethal. Krampus would not kill. He was not a murderer, but a teacher whose lessons carved themselves in flesh and memory.

Sten gasped, tears streaming. He stammered apologies, swore he'd set things right. But Krampus had already turned, vanishing as silently as he'd come. The wind howled once more, and Sten found himself alone, panting, pressing a hand to his burning skin. He understood that the moral order here was not optional. The villagers would hear rumors by morning—Sten's stammered confession, his promise to repay what he stole. No one would question how he came to his senses. The sight of his fearful eyes and stiff posture would be enough: Krampus had reminded them what was at stake.

As dawn came, The Fatman approached Sten's house. He knocked gently and found the man awake, restless, eyes haunted. He offered a mug of spiced milk, silently conveying a hint of mercy. Sten accepted with trembling hands. There was no condemnation from The Fatman, no lecture. Just a shared understanding: You've been corrected. Now choose better.

The village, though unsettled, began to settle into a pattern. They saw that The Fatman and Krampus did not contradict each other. Rather, their interplay defined the boundaries of moral life. The Fatman forgave, nourished hope, and encouraged second chances. Krampus made sure that second chances did not become hollow pardons, that forgiveness came with the expectation of better behavior. Those who tried to twist kindness into a shield against consequence found themselves facing horns and chains in the quiet hour before dawn.

Branwynn sensed this equilibrium as she studied her smoke patterns again. They were no longer conflicted lines but a complex tapestry—swirls of compassion entwined with dark threads of fear. It reminded her of ancient tales she had read: before laws and kings, there were spirits of winter who demanded that humans keep faith with moral principles or face dire warnings. Krampus was no demon plucked from imagination—he was the old forest's whisper that every kindness must have teeth lurking nearby to prevent decay.

In hushed gatherings, the villagers told stories to their children about the recent events. They spoke of The Fatman's quiet gifts, of Krampus's relentless vigilance. They did not soften Krampus's image—if anything, they sharpened it. Let the children know the truth: that comfort without consequence leads to rot. Let them know that the creature who lurked in darkness, rattling chains and wielding rods, was not cruel for cruelty's sake but cruel because humans needed that edge to remain honest.

A few children woke from nightmares calling for their parents, sobbing that they had glimpsed Krampus's horns. Their parents held them close, gently explaining that Krampus would not harm them if they strove to be good. "He's part of winter, like the biting cold," a mother told her daughter. "The cold is harsh, but it keeps us alert and grateful for warmth."

As days blended into nights, The Fatman and Krampus maintained their presence. They rarely appeared together in public now. The Fatman roamed during daylight or early evening, smiling at those working hard to repair roofs or sharing loaves of bread. He whispered encouragements, reminded them of the kindness they were capable of. Krampus preferred late nights and early mornings, drifting at the periphery, ensuring that no one forgot his lesson. Sometimes he simply stood outside a window where a dishonest whisper passed between two neighbors, letting his silhouette fall across the lamp's glow, scattering their conspiracies.

Jarlan recorded these quiet deterrences, marveling at how crime and cruelty all but vanished. Not from love alone, nor from fear alone, but from the balance of both. He wrote that Sleetwood had achieved a rare moral poise—though tenuous, it shone all the brighter against the long shadows of winter.

Helgrid marveled at how effectively this dark element worked. The entity, a colossal evil, had required both guardians' direct intervention. Now, petty evils cowered under Krampus's watchful stare and The Fatman's gentle disappointment. In some ways, these small interventions felt more personal, more immediate, than battling a great monster. This was the real work of moral order—tending the garden of daily life, plucking weeds before they strangled the flowers.

Branwynn's magic supported this equilibrium by maintaining mild wards, not to fight monsters now, but to keep everyone's mind clear and honest. She carved runes on doorframes reminding folk of the pledges they made: to care for each other, to share burdens, to resist greed. The runes did not enslave anyone's will—they merely nudged memories of the recent horror, letting everyone recall that unity saved them once and would again.

Marta, caring for families, noticed that mothers and fathers taught their children differently now. They spoke more openly of moral stakes, not sugarcoating the darkness. The children learned that the world held wonders—The Fatman's gifts, shared laughter, cozy fires—and that it also held deep shadows, represented by Krampus. To live well, one must navigate both. This did not produce paralyzing fear; instead, it nurtured a careful respect. The children would grow into adults who understood that generosity was precious only if guarded by conscience.

The Fatman observed these changes from quiet corners. He missed the days when he could simply bring joy and see it spread without complication. But he understood that his role had matured here. The villagers knew him now not as a jolly giver in isolation, but as one half of a cosmic arrangement. They no longer took his gifts for granted. They knew each sweet treat, each kind word, carried the expectation of moral effort, lest Krampus step from the shadows to remind them otherwise.

Krampus took no joy in watching humans squirm, no pride in the fear he caused. He existed as he always had: a primal necessity. If he felt satisfaction, it was in the stillness of a quiet night when no screams rang out, no cruelty festered. He did not disappear immediately. He would remain as long as these lessons needed reinforcing. In some distant future, perhaps, the villagers might act with unwavering kindness and honesty of their own accord, and he could recede into distant myth once more. But Krampus was old and knew human nature well—he suspected they would always need him.

One late night, as snow fell softly, Krampus stood behind the chapel ruins again. He remembered how recently desperate prayers and frantic wards were woven here to repel the entity. Now, only a mild tension hovered. He watched a young woman kneel by a broken pillar, leaving a small carved birch token—perhaps a gift to honor both guardians. She whispered: "We remember you, Krampus. We will not stray." Her voice trembled, but with respect rather than terror. Krampus inclined his head behind her back. She never knew he stood there. That was enough.

Beyond the village, frostbitten trees stood as silent witnesses. The Fatman occasionally roamed to the outskirts, leaving small caches of dried fruits or nuts for passing travelers—if any dared traverse these harsh lands. He hoped that news of Sleetwood's moral awakening might spread quietly. Not all places had both of them present to enforce balance. Many lands knew only stories of a kindly gift-bringer or a monstrous punisher, never realizing these were two halves of one truth. Perhaps, in time, this village's experience would birth new legends and sharpen old ones, teaching others that kindness must be earned and guarded, not assumed.

As the moon waxed and waned, the villagers adapted. They realized they could not rid themselves of Krampus's darkness without losing the structure that held their moral world upright. They learned to treasure The Fatman's warmth more deeply, recognizing that comfort meant nothing if never tested. Some nights they sang quiet songs that praised both the joy of giving and the sternness of justice, weaving The Fatman's name and Krampus's horns into the same verses. These were no lullabies for children alone—adults participated too, forging a collective memory that would last beyond this winter.

Branwynn watched these developments with cautious optimism. Her smoke readings now showed more stable patterns—fewer jagged lines of conflict, more complex spirals indicating that the villagers internalized the lessons. She noted that the darkness in the story was not gone—nor should it be. Darkness defined where light ended and began. Krampus embodied that darkness, ensuring the flames of goodwill never dimmed into complacency.

Helgrid continued forging iron tokens, distributing them as symbols of moral commitment. Each token bore a balanced motif: on one side a smiling face reminiscent of The Fatman's cheer, on the other a horned silhouette of Krampus's stern profile. Villagers hung these tokens in their homes, not as idols, but as reminders. At night, when candles guttered, the faint shape of horns on iron reminded them that any wrongdoing might call forth a silent visitor in the shadows.

Jarlan updated his ledger again: *We have reached an accord that surpasses the original pact these guardians forged. Now the villagers themselves engage in the discipline of maintaining virtue. They know Krampus is real, The Fatman is real, and that their presence is not to be taken lightly. Our fear of Krampus is no longer blind terror but informed respect. Our gratitude to The Fatman is no longer greedy comfort but earnest appreciation.*

The winter dragged on. The howling storms diminished, leaving crisp nights of star-glittered silence. Snow blanketed fields and rooftops, muffling the world's sounds. In this hush, moral order found steady ground. By the end of the month, no new incidents of cruelty surfaced. Villagers helped each other repair a collapsed shed without haggling over payment. A child who found a fallen trinket returned it without waiting to be asked. Another who caught himself lying stopped midway, corrected his words, and apologized.

Each time these small acts of honesty or kindness played out, they reaffirmed the balance. The Fatman's silent approval warmed their hearts, while Krampus's unspoken vigilance kept them honest. This did not mean perfection—only a stalemate where virtues and vices wrestled openly, with the villagers aware that their choices had weight. They lived in a world where The Fatman and Krampus had become guiding stars: one bright and comforting, the other dark and warning. Together, these stars defined the map of morality.

And so, under the long nights and brief days, Sleetwood adapted to a permanent twilight of moral tension. The people accepted that darkness would never vanish—Krampus would not sweeten. He would remain the old, horned figure born of primal fears, a teacher who lashed out when words failed. The Fatman could not save them from their own failings if they refused to learn. True salvation lay in embracing the lessons both brothers offered.

This was, in a way, closer to the original myth of Krampus: he was never meant to be an inexplicable terror, but a companion to generosity. Ancient villagers had understood that winter's gifts—warmth, food, safety—were precious precisely because they were never guaranteed. Krampus's darkness reminded them to treasure what The Fatman gave and to remain vigilant. Over centuries, these lessons dulled in kinder times, but recent horrors and close calls had restored the old understanding.

In the final week of winter's deepest cold, a quiet gathering took place in the chapel ruins. Families brought lanterns, placing them around the old stones. Branwynn recited old verses, Helgrid presented newly forged tokens, Marta offered herbal tea, and Jarlan read excerpts from his ledger. They spoke openly of the entity's defeat, of The Fatman's kindness and Krampus's stern lessons. Children listened wide-eyed, absorbing this moral tapestry not as a fable but as a living truth they had witnessed.

At the edge of the clearing, The Fatman stood, cloak dusted with snow, eyes reflecting lanternlight. Krampus loomed beside him, half in shadow, as if belonging more to the ruin than to the crowd. No one screamed or cowered. Instead, they bowed their heads in respect. They did not ask Krampus to leave, nor did they beg The Fatman to shield them from all pain. They thanked them both, acknowledging each one's necessity.

"Stay as long as needed," an elder said softly. "We know now: your presence is no curse. It is part of life's hard truth."

Krampus inclined his head, silent. He knew humans well—they would falter again, perhaps less dramatically but still requiring nudges back in line. The Fatman smiled gently, heartened that these mortals saw beyond gifts and punishments to the meaning behind them.

As torches sputtered out and lanterns dimmed, the villagers dispersed. The Fatman and Krampus remained a moment longer, two figures against ancient stones. Neither spoke, yet an unbreakable accord thrummed between them. Then The Fatman turned, walking toward a row of cottages where he would leave small treats of dried fruit, subtle affirmations of faith. Krampus slipped into the deeper darkness between trees, ensuring that if anyone dared exploit The Fatman's kindness, they would find no refuge.

In the quiet hours before dawn, a bitter wind blew over Sleetwood's roofs. Inside their homes, people slept peacefully, dreams touched by both comfort and caution. They would wake to another day of hard work and shared burdens, knowing that kindness and terror were braided together in their understanding of the world. In that braid lay their strength, and in that strength lay their future.

And so the village continued, bound by an ancient logic older than any empire: to cherish generosity, one must fear its absence. To revel in mercy, one must respect the presence of judgment. Krampus's darkness was not their enemy—it was their reminder, their bulwark against moral decay. In that darkness, they found a strange solace. For in winter's longest night, a candle burns brightest when guarded by the certainty that, left untended, it could gutter and fail. The villagers would never let it fail again, not with Krampus's watchful eyes and The Fatman's gentle smile guiding their hearts through the cold.

CHAPTER TEN

The Winterspine Mountains had never truly embraced mercy, but now, in deep midwinter, their indifference felt almost personal. Clouds crouched low over the jagged peaks, and the smell of ice permeated every breath. Nights stretched so long that the day felt like a fleeting hint of forgiveness. Yet Sleetwood carried on. Its people had forged an uneasy peace, standing between The Fatman's soft lamplight and the dark edge of Krampus's shadow.

Days passed into a pattern that some found comforting, others strained: petty wrongs curbed by the mere rumor of Krampus's presence, small kindnesses fostered by The Fatman's quiet encouragement. The villagers whispered that they had found a stable balance. But even as a thin veneer of moral order settled, deeper currents stirred. People were still human—capable of noble acts and sly betrayals. Some wondered how long the guardians would remain. Could the village thrive without them? Or had these legends become as fundamental as the cold wind itself?

On one particular afternoon, a brittle sun managed to break through heavy clouds, igniting the snow in diamond-sparkle brilliance. Helgrid Stonestream, her beard rimed with frost, stood atop a small rise overlooking the village's western edge. She watched a figure trudge through the distant pines—Branwynn Spellshiver, collecting rare bark for her wards. Helgrid admired the hedge-witch's dedication. The world felt safer with Branwynn's runes humming softly over doorframes, gently reminding everyone to keep their promises. Behind Helgrid, two children laughed as they helped mend a broken fence, carefully supervised by their parents—proof that moral lessons had taken root in small, tangible ways.

Yet Helgrid's mood soured at a distant shape on the horizon. A column of smoke rose beyond the foothills, faint but distinct. It was not from Sleetwood's chimneys. Could it be travelers? A distant cabin's hearth? She had heard rumors that as the main roads to distant towns iced over, some desperate souls ventured new routes, seeking shelter or trade. Sleetwood had grown insular since the horror with the entity; outside contact was rare. How would strangers respond to The Fatman's gentle smile and Krampus's dark silhouette?

Helgrid descended the slope, boots crunching, mind uneasy. The village thrived on its newly affirmed moral code, nurtured by these twin legends. Outsiders might challenge that delicate equilibrium. Would The Fatman offer them kindness untested? Would Krampus enforce rules they never agreed to? The thought gnawed at her as she returned to the center of Sleetwood, where Jarlan Forgerook and Marta awaited an update.

Jarlan was perched on a crate near the old meeting hall, re-checking his ledgers. Marta stood beside him, arms folded in her cloak. When Helgrid relayed what she saw—smoke to the west, possibly strangers—Jarlan frowned. "We're barely stable now," he murmured. "If newcomers arrive without understanding our ways, they might stir old temptations. Or they might bring good trade. Hard to say."

Marta considered this, her breath steaming. "We should prepare. If they come as merchants or wanderers, we must greet them fairly. But we must not hide what we are now. If they flout our rules, Krampus won't overlook it simply because they are strangers."

Helgrid nodded grimly. At mention of Krampus, both women felt a chill that had nothing to do with the wind. The old guardian's darkness pervaded their morals like ink in water—impossible to remove, essential to the texture of their current peace.

Within an hour, The Fatman appeared, strolling through the lane with a quiet grace. He had taken to wearing a fur-lined cloak, blending more with mortal customs, though the warmth in his eyes never waned. He listened patiently as Jarlan explained the possibility of outsiders. His gaze drifted toward the western horizon, thoughtful.

"Strangers might test your resolve," he said softly. "Will you uphold what you've learned or revert to suspicion and greed?" His tone carried no accusation, only a gentle challenge.

Helgrid cleared her throat. "We will try our best. But what if they cheat us or provoke violence? We know Krampus…" She trailed off, not sure how to phrase it delicately.

The Fatman inclined his head. "Krampus remains. He will not allow cruelty to pass unremarked. But remember, fear alone cannot guide you forever. I urge you to show strangers kindness without foolishness, generosity with caution. If they come, treat them honestly and await their response."

He left them with that advice, heading toward a cottage where a widow struggled to light her hearth. They watched him go, comforted and uneasy at once. His words highlighted their responsibilities, reminding them that the guardians did not absolve them of moral labor. They must choose right action, not hide behind myths.

Two days later, the travelers arrived.

A small band—seven figures trudging through the snow-laden forest—emerged from the pines near midday. Sleetwood's watchers spotted them first: Edric and Takrin exchanged a look, gripped their spears a bit tighter. The newcomers wore heavy wool cloaks and battered boots. Their leader, a tall woman with scarred cheeks, carried a long staff wrapped in oiled cloth. They looked tired, hungry, perhaps desperate. No wagon, no pack animals—just a cluster of humans seeking shelter.

The village formed a cautious reception. No one brandished weapons openly, but Helgrid, Jarlan, Marta, and Branwynn stood in front, flanked by a half-dozen villagers holding tools that could double as weapons. The Fatman observed from a distance, leaning on a post, while Krampus was nowhere to be seen—yet everyone felt him lurking just beyond sight.

The tall woman halted a few strides from the villagers, raising a hand in greeting. Her companions huddled behind her, eyes wary. "We mean no harm," she said, voice raspy. "We come from Ashwell, a settlement beyond the western ridge. Our village suffered a landslide—our stores buried, our homes lost. We seek refuge, trade, anything you can spare."

Her tone was neither pleading nor commanding, more a statement of fact. The villagers hesitated. Ashwell was a name some recalled vaguely from old travel routes. Once, traders passed that way, but not recently. Jarlan stepped forward. "We are sorry for your loss. We have limited supplies. We survived a harsh ordeal ourselves not long ago." He glanced at Helgrid, who nodded, urging honesty. "But we won't turn you away without hearing more."

The woman inclined her head. "I am Kirsa. My people are weary. We have little to offer—only a few salvaged tools and smoked roots we carried. If we could stay a while, perhaps we can repay you with labor. We are not beggars by choice."

Marta's eyes softened. "We understand hardship," she said, stepping forward. "We can offer hot broth and shelter in the old meeting hall for a start."

Branwynn watched carefully, sensing undercurrents. She did not detect immediate malice, but hunger and desperation could breed deceit. Still, denying these travelers aid would contradict everything The Fatman and Krampus had taught them: kindness must have a place at the table.

They led the newcomers into Sleetwood. Villagers murmured as they passed, curious and cautious. Children peeked from behind fences. The travelers hunched under scrutinizing gazes. Inside the meeting hall, Marta served broth, Helgrid lit lanterns, and Jarlan asked careful questions. Kirsa explained their ordeal: torrential rains loosened the slopes near Ashwell, burying food caches and forcing them to flee. They traveled for weeks, guided only by rumor that a village survived deep in the Winterspine. Their supplies ran thin. Without shelter, they might have died in the snow.

The Fatman entered quietly, bringing a small basket of dried berries and nuts. He offered it to Kirsa without a word. She thanked him, startled by his generosity and odd aura of warmth. She did not know him, but sensed something unusual—his presence comforted her people. One of them, a younger man named Elric, relaxed his tense shoulders, nibbling on the berries.

Outside, as dusk gathered, the torches flickered. Through a gap in the meeting hall's shutters, someone glimpsed two amber eyes reflecting firelight. Krampus observed from afar, chains barely audible. He neither approached nor retreated. The travelers were on notice—just as the villagers were. Everyone understood that this new dynamic would test moral codes.

For a week, the travelers recuperated. They helped mend fences, hauled water, shoveled snow—small tasks to prove their worth. Sleetwood's people watched them closely, hoping goodwill would be returned in honesty. The Fatman occasionally dropped by with simple treats or encouraging words. Branwynn scoured them with a subtle magical gaze, finding no trace of sorcery or hidden malice. Just humans, broken by misfortune.

But as stores ran low, tensions simmered. Sleetwood was not prosperous. Every mouthful given to strangers meant less for the lean months ahead. Whispers arose: *Should we send them away? They give too little in return. The Fatman might encourage kindness, but can we afford it? What if they take advantage?*

In the chilly evenings, a few villagers murmured these doubts, hoping Krampus wouldn't appear at their window. Fear did not erase self-interest. People struggled to reconcile compassion with practicality. If The Fatman offered kindness, could they refuse? If they refused, would Krampus punish them for cruelty? Yet was it truly cruelty to guard their scarce resources?

Kirsa sensed this hesitation. She gathered her people—Elric, a stoic man named Ravn, two women called Haldi and Stena, and two older men, Brenn and Joval—and discussed their next steps. "We cannot linger without offering more," she said. "They have their own trials. We must prove our usefulness." So they ventured to help more concretely, repairing the chapel's roof, assisting Helgrid at the forge when she hammered out new nails, accompanying Branwynn on herb-gathering trips to replenish medicinal supplies. They even taught a few new skills—Ravn knew how to lash sled runners from twisted birch, improving villagers' transports.

This eased some suspicions, but not all. Some locals remained wary. They remembered how easy it was to slip into sin if no one watched. These strangers were untested by Krampus's presence. Would they comply with moral order once they realized the cost of disobedience?

One evening, as the travelers and villagers shared a meal of thin stew and stale bread in the meeting hall, The Fatman visited. He listened to quiet chatter, saw how each tried to appear gracious. Outside, wind rattled shutters. After a moment, The Fatman raised his voice gently: "Kindness that endures hardship is true kindness. Do not resent sharing what little you have, lest your hearts harden and rot." His tone was calm but carried a warning undercurrent. He reminded them that their moral code meant nothing if abandoned at the first strain.

Kirsa, feeling the tension, stood. "We are grateful, more than words can say. We do not intend to be a burden. Once we are strong enough, we'll move on, or find a fair exchange. We understand this village has a… presence." She hesitated, choosing words carefully. "Some of us saw something at night. Horned, tall. Is it… an animal?"

The villagers exchanged glances. They had not explained Krampus to these strangers yet. How could they describe him without sounding mad?

Jarlan cleared his throat. "That is Krampus," he said plainly. "He is as real as the cold wind, and as old. We live under his watch, and also under The Fatman's kindness. They are…" He searched for the right phrase, "Two sides of our moral compass. One encourages generosity, the other enforces accountability."

The travelers stared, uncertain if this was a ruse. Kirsa frowned. "A living legend?" she asked. "You mean to say this horned figure punishes wrongdoing?"

Marta nodded. "We have seen it. Petty theft, deceit, cruelty—Krampus does not overlook them. We suffered a great evil once, and these two guardians helped us survive. Now we try to keep our moral balance, knowing they watch."

Elric scoffed softly. "Sounds like stories to scare children. We are adults, and we know hunger and cold. Tales of a horned punisher mean little to an empty belly."

A hush fell. The Fatman watched Elric with sad eyes, Krampus unseen but surely listening. Helgrid tensed, waiting. Would this stranger's skepticism provoke a demonstration?

Kirsa hushed Elric with a gesture. She considered the villagers' serious faces. They did not seem like liars conjuring bedtime stories. After all, they had fought off a monstrous entity. Perhaps these legends were truths of this place.

"Even if it's true," Kirsa said slowly, "We have no desire to test such a presence. We know hardship. We will conduct ourselves fairly."

The villagers relaxed slightly. This was enough for now. But The Fatman's gaze lingered on Elric, who muttered to himself about superstitions. A seed of doubt was planted. Would the strangers abide by this code, or would they probe its boundaries when desperation rose again?

As days passed, a quiet routine emerged. The travelers integrated partially, trading labor for food. They learned the code words the villagers sometimes used as subtle reminders of trust. They heard stories of the entity's defeat, of how Krampus and The Fatman saved the village from utter darkness. They remained skeptical but cautious. When children mentioned seeing Krampus's silhouette at dusk, the travelers shivered. Fear, even if doubted, had a way of settling in the gut.

One crisp morning, Branwynn and Haldi ventured into the forest to gather willow bark for medicine. With them went Ravn, skilled in woodcraft, and a local boy named Detrin to carry baskets. The forest was hushed under a recent snowfall. Branwynn explained that honesty guided their community now—that they must trust each other. Haldi listened, impressed by the witch's conviction. She confessed that in Ashwell, when times grew tough, neighbors sometimes cheated or hoarded. No Krampus hovered to punish them. They relied on flimsy promises and soon fell into bickering. Branwynn replied that they too once knew such troubles, until horrors forced them to adopt stricter moral lines.

As they worked, Ravn drifted away, attracted by footprints in the snow—perhaps a hare to snare. Time passed, and he did not return. Detrin fretted. Branwynn, concerned, followed Ravn's trail. She found him kneeling behind a thicket, holding something in his hand. As she approached, he startled, hiding the object. Branwynn felt a prickle of suspicion but said nothing, only asked if he found game. Ravn shrugged. On their return, Branwynn noticed Ravn's gaze flicking nervously at shadows. Had he taken something not his? The forest offered little wealth besides herbs and sticks. Why hide it?

That night, Branwynn shared her unease with Helgrid and Jarlan. They debated: should they confront Ravn? Without proof of wrongdoing, they risked appearing paranoid. The code they lived by required fairness. Yet ignoring suspicion might allow a problem to fester. Jarlan suggested a quiet watch on the travelers' behavior. If Ravn had stolen something or lied, Krampus would sense it eventually. That thought chilled them but also reassured them—no crime would remain hidden long.

Two nights later, trouble surfaced. Detrin, the boy who helped gather willow bark, discovered his family's meager store of dried apples missing. Only a small bag, but precious at this season. The boy insisted he saw Ravn lingering near their shed earlier. Accusations flared silently in the meeting hall after dusk: Ravn was stealing to supplement the travelers' diet. Kirsa protested, claiming Ravn was no thief. Elric growled that these were baseless accusations. Tension mounted.

The Fatman arrived, drawn by raised voices. He listened quietly. Marta pleaded for calm—maybe there was a misunderstanding. But the villagers remembered old sins. Had they invited wolves into their midst? They glanced anxiously at dark corners, expecting Krampus's chains to rattle. The Fatman said, "Truth will surface. If anyone is guilty, let them confess. Honesty will spare worse outcomes."

Ravn lowered his head but said nothing. Kirsa eyed him sharply. If he lied, he risked their fragile alliance. If he admitted theft, how would the villagers react? Pride and hunger wrestled in his mind.

At that fraught moment, a distant scraping drew all eyes to the window. Two amber pinpoints of light hovered outside in darkness. The villagers tensed. Elric's face went pale. Kirsa shuddered—so it was true. The horned watcher was real. The Fatman nodded gravely, as if acknowledging his brother's presence. No one dared open the door, but everyone felt Krampus's judgment pressing on them like a hand on their throats.

Ravn cracked first. "I took them," he confessed, voice shaking. "I was hungry. We all were. I thought just a few apples wouldn't matter. I'm sorry."

Silence rang like a bell. The Fatman's eyes held sorrow, not anger, but he stepped aside, as if ceding the next step to Krampus's domain. Outside, chains rattled. The villagers parted, uncertain whether Krampus would enter. Kirsa tried to speak up for her companion: "He did wrong, yes, but we traveled so far—have mercy."

Ravn trembled, recalling stories of dreadful punishments. He looked to The Fatman for help, but the old gift-bringer only shook his head slowly, indicating that the resolution lay elsewhere. Mercy without consequence would unravel the trust they built.

The door creaked. Cold air gusted in, snuffing a lantern. In that sudden dimness, Krampus stood in the threshold, horns nearly scraping the lintel. Villagers shrank back, travelers gasped. Krampus's eyes locked on Ravn, who cowered behind Kirsa. The horned figure stepped forward, chains hissing over the floor. He lifted a birch rod.

No one dared move. Even The Fatman remained still, face pained but resolved. In one swift motion, Krampus delivered a single lash to Ravn's shoulder. It was not crippling, but stung fiercely. Ravn yelped, clutching his arm. The lesson was administered. Krampus regarded him a moment longer, ensuring no doubt remained about the moral order here. Then, as silently as he came, he withdrew into the night, the door swinging shut behind him.

The travelers stood stunned. The villagers—though shaken—understood: this was justice as it existed now, swift and inescapable. Ravn panted, tears in his eyes, but there was also relief. He knew exactly where he stood. Steal again, and worse might follow.

Kirsa found her voice. "You… you allow this?" she asked the villagers, equal parts horrified and amazed.

Marta stepped forward, voice trembling slightly. "We do not 'allow' it. It simply is. After what we faced—monstrous entities, moral collapse—this order keeps us alive and honest. Without Krampus, kindness could rot into exploitation. Without The Fatman, fear would crush all hope. This balance saved us."

The Fatman placed a gentle hand on Kirsa's shoulder. "Stay if you will, learn this balance. If not, once you are strong enough, you may depart. But know that here, generosity and consequence walk hand in hand."

Kirsa, struggling to calm her racing heart, nodded grimly. She understood now that this was no ordinary village. It had transcended old compromises. In Sleetwood, morality had teeth.

In the following days, the travelers became quieter, more respectful. They worked harder, asked permission before taking anything. Their skepticism about Krampus's reality evaporated. Elric, who once scoffed at superstitions, now looked over his shoulder at twilight, careful with every word. Kirsa reflected that maybe this was what was needed in a broken world—some force to ensure decency. Ashwell had lacked such a presence, and look what befell them.

Meanwhile, the villagers learned about their guests more intimately. The travelers softened under stable shelter. Haldi showed children how to twist reeds into sturdy mats. Stena, once guarded, sang old lullabies that lightened weary hearts. Brenn and Joval, the older men, helped strengthen roof beams. Through these exchanges, genuine trust began to bloom—not from fear alone, but from honest cooperation. The

Fatman smiled to see it, encouraging small acts of shared culture. People laughed together around firesides, telling stories that mixed traditions. The dark memory of Ravn's punishment lingered as a caution, not a wedge.

Branwynn watched all this with cautious optimism. She sensed the village evolving: fear of Krampus still hovered, but now it underpinned a larger tapestry of genuine goodwill. The strangers, once a threat to equilibrium, were integrating, forging bonds that might survive even without constant watchfulness—though she doubted Krampus would vanish soon. Humans needed reminders of consequence, especially in hard winters.

The Fatman noted that people now approached him less to beg for gifts and more to ask guidance. They understood that his kindness must be deserved. Helgrid observed that theft and deceit vanished entirely. Even the children embraced their chores cheerfully, proud to live in a place that had reshaped moral law itself.

Krampus's sightings grew rarer, yet his reputation deepened. Even a rumor of his approach made dishonest thoughts shrivel. This fascinated Kirsa, who confided in Jarlan one afternoon: "In Ashwell, we tried to solve moral dilemmas with council meetings and arguments. We had laws, but people bent them. Here, you have something primal. Is it not tyrannical?" Jarlan paused before answering, "Tyranny would be cruelty without purpose. Krampus acts only when kindness fails, when lies and harm appear. His presence is harsh, but it ensures The Fatman's kindness remains meaningful. We learned that without this darkness, light is cheap."

Kirsa sighed, thoughtful. She began to understand why The Fatman and Krampus stayed in Sleetwood. Perhaps they feared a relapse into selfish chaos. Maybe they wanted to witness humans learning to balance mercy and justice on their own. Or maybe their roles were eternal—destined to roam from place to place, maintaining moral order where it wavered.

One twilight, Elric approached the Fatman privately near a shed. Elric's voice trembled with humility. "I doubted you and your... brother," he said, hesitating on the word. "I thought these people were fools, believing childish fables. Now I see they are stronger for it. How can we learn this strength without always looking over our shoulder for Krampus?"

The Fatman smiled sadly. "You must internalize his lesson. If fear alone guides you, it is not true morality. You must choose kindness and honesty because they are right, not because you dread punishment. Krampus ensures that even if you fail, you cannot hide your wrongdoing. But to transcend fear, you must do good for its own sake. That is how true virtue grows."

Elric nodded, eyes damp. He understood now that these legends offered more than threats—they offered a path to moral maturity. A path where kindness stands firm even if no one watches, and darkness exists only as a last resort, not a constant whip.

As the winter deepened, the bond between villagers and travelers solidified. They planned for future trade routes, forging sled runners so that when the thaw came, the travelers might return to Ashwell's remnants or find a new home. Sleetwood, once isolated by terror, now considered cautious interaction with the outside world. If others learned of this moral order, would they embrace it or mock it?

Jarlan recorded these developments meticulously. He wrote: *We host strangers who tested our system. They learned our ways. Though fear played a role, genuine understanding followed. Perhaps this is how we spread true moral equilibrium—one lesson at a time, tempered by darkness and kindness together.*

Branwynn's wards hummed softly in each home, reinforcing memory rather than compelling behavior. People no longer required constant scrying for hidden sins. They policed themselves, mindful of Krampus's silent watch. The Fatman continued small acts of mercy: leaving a warm blanket for a cough-ridden child, whispering encouragement to a distraught mother. Neither guardian demanded worship or tribute. They simply existed, frames of reference for a fragile species grappling with right and wrong.

Helgrid, in her forge, shaped new iron charms with motifs that combined The Fatman's gentle symbols—bells, holly sprigs—with Krampus's darker signs—birch rods, horned silhouettes. These tokens adorned doorframes as if to say: *We accept both sides of this moral coin.* The villagers and travelers took comfort in these symbols, understanding that life's brightness required a contrastive edge.

One evening, Kirsa stood at the edge of the forest with Marta, watching shadows stretch long and thin. Kirsa mentioned leaving in spring, once paths cleared. Marta nodded. "We will miss you, but we understand you must rebuild your lives. Carry our lessons with you. Spread them, if you can. Let others know that morality can be anchored by stories made flesh."

Kirsa smiled wryly. "They will think us mad if we speak of horned figures punishing thieves. But perhaps we can at least teach them the principle: that kindness must be guarded by consequence, and fear shaped into caution, not cruelty."

Marta placed a hand on Kirsa's arm. "That would be a start. We once doubted too, until reality forced our eyes open."

And so the village settled into a peaceful tension—no paradise, but a place where the threat of Krampus's lash and the gift of The Fatman's comfort held humans accountable to their better selves. Winter's darkness did not end, but the people learned to live with it, to find meaning in the interplay of light and shadow.

Each night, when clouds parted, villagers and travelers glimpsed stars glinting coldly overhead. They knew that beyond their roofs, the world remained harsh, indifferent. But here in Sleetwood, they had carved a moral foothold against that indifference. They did not pretend to be perfect—fear remained a factor, after all. Yet fear now served a higher purpose, reinforcing The Fatman's gentle lessons, ensuring no gift was squandered and no cruelty left unchecked.

If Krampus prowled less frequently, it was because he sensed the people's sincerity. If The Fatman's smile grew more genuine, it was because he saw them choosing kindness more often without waiting for his nod.

Ravn, nursing his still-tender shoulder, learned humility. He repaid the stolen apples by hunting small game and sharing the meat. The villagers accepted his efforts, seeing he had learned. Even Elric, once scornful, offered to help restore a half-collapsed storage hut. The day they finished that hut, children clapped and The Fatman left a small tin of honeyed nuts—no words, just a subtle reward. The children giggled, and Ravn managed a grateful smile despite recalling his painful lesson.

From time to time, late at night, a passing villager or traveler glimpsed Krampus on a distant ridge, outlined by moonlight, chains glinting. He never approached without reason. It felt as though he simply watched, ensuring the moral tapestry remained taut. His ancient origin, older than their memories, resonated in each creak of snow under hoof.

He was not a friend nor an enemy—he was necessity, a darkness that gave shape to their moral dawn.

As winter's heart reached its apex, The Fatman and Krampus both sensed a subtle shift. The villagers and guests had absorbed the lessons deeply. Mistakes would be made again, of course, but now they possessed a blueprint for correction. They had tools to resist sliding into corruption: empathy from The Fatman, fear of Krampus, and a growing instinct for honest virtue. Perhaps, in time, the guardians might step back, letting humans navigate with the memory of horned silhouettes and kind smiles.

But not yet. For now, the world remained dark, the future uncertain. Sleetwood stood as a beacon—not of purity or perfection, but of willing struggle against moral decay. The Fatman and Krampus anchored it, ensuring that each gift of comfort bore the weight of responsibility, that each temptation to sin faced a reckoning.

In the last weeks of deepest winter, as icy winds knifed through alleys and pines groaned under snow, the villagers and travelers shared long evenings around communal fires. They swapped stories of old homes lost and new hopes forming. They ate sparingly, but with gratitude. They joked quietly, learned each other's songs, mended clothes together, and taught children small crafts. Differences of origin and belief melted under the shared moral code.

Branwynn watched these scenes, heart brimming with cautious pride. Marta whispered that the village had never felt so oddly at peace, even with fear still lingering like a distant thundercloud. Jarlan added new entries to his ledger, recording how strangers became neighbors under the dual guidance of mercy and judgment. Helgrid smoothed iron charms, satisfied her forge's labor had symbolic meaning.

If someone asked The Fatman about the future, he would gently shrug and say humans must guide themselves, eventually. If they asked Krampus, they would get no words—just silence, a warning that humans must never forget their capacity for cruelty, and the need to confront it.

In the stillness of a midnight, Kirsa walked alone beneath the chapel ruins. She carried a small carving she had made: a figure of The Fatman and Krampus back-to-back, each holding a symbol of their role. She placed it on a broken stone ledge inside the ruin, a quiet offering. Not worship, but acknowledgment. She whispered, "We will remember this place and what we learned. We will tell others there is a village that survived horror by embracing both kindness and darkness."

Krampus

Unheard, The Fatman smiled softly in his distant watch, and Krampus stood still as stone behind a pine, listening. Perhaps this village would become a tale carried beyond the Winterspine. Perhaps other communities would learn from their delicate equilibrium. Krampus and The Fatman did not control such fate—they only ensured that where they dwelled, moral order had teeth and warmth in equal measure.

Thus ended the harshest phase of winter, not in grand miracles but in steady, humble growth of understanding. Sleetwood no longer trembled under threat alone; it breathed with a new rhythm, each inhale balanced by caution, each exhale warmed by compassion. The travelers would move on come spring, carrying the story of a place where legends walked and shaped men's hearts. The villagers would remain, forging their destiny with iron runes and whispered code words, forever mindful that in the darkness outside their doors, a horned figure and a kindly giver watched and waited.

In this quiet twilight, neither The Fatman nor Krampus spoke. Words were unnecessary. Their presence was etched into the village's bones. The old ways—fear and mercy, darkness and gift—merged into a single truth: that humans, left alone, teeter between nobility and depravity, and sometimes need gods made flesh to show them the path.

The world beyond remained indifferent, but here, in Sleetwood, a fragile moral flame flickered strong and steady, fed by the memory of horrors survived, the blessings of kindness, and the eternal vigilance of ancient powers who demanded that kindness mean something real.

CHAPTER ELEVEN

Winter's grip had begun to loosen. Not that the Winterspine Mountains ever truly softened, but subtle signs of change touched Sleetwood. Snow drifts, once towering, now lay packed and slowly crusting with ice. The daylight lingered a few heartbeats longer each evening. A distant drip of meltwater teased the high eaves of cottages, a tiny promise that spring would eventually come. The villagers still hunched in their cloaks and trudged over frozen ground, but their faces were less pinched. They had survived so much: monstrous entities, moral upheaval, and the delicate negotiations of welcoming strangers. They had emerged more unified, tethered to a moral code that felt both ancient and painfully earned.

In the weeks since the travelers' arrival and subsequent moral lessons, a quiet routine settled. Villagers and travelers labored side-by-side, each contributing to repairs and preparations for spring. The Fatman still drifted through lanes at dusk, offering small comforts—a whispered reassurance here, a handful of dried cranberries there—while Krampus remained a distant, horned silhouette at the edge of vision. His absence from immediate punishment was not complacency, but observation: watching if these humans had internalized the balance. The villagers knew he was still there; any hint of cruelty or theft would summon him like a storm cloud. That knowledge had seeped into their bones.

One late afternoon, Helgrid Stonestream and Jarlan Forgerook stood atop a gentle rise north of the village, surveying what they hoped would be a cleared path once the snows receded. With help from Kirsa's group, they'd marked potential routes for trade or travel. This place was no longer a sealed enclave. They envisioned a cautious future where Sleetwood might exchange goods or knowledge with distant communities. But the question lingered: could this moral equilibrium survive contact with the wider world?

Jarlan lowered his hood, letting the chill nip his ears. "We've grown so used to The Fatman and Krampus guiding us. What if outsiders scoff at these tales? Will we lose our resolve if they doubt us?"

Helgrid flexed her shoulders. "We managed to impart the lesson to Kirsa's people. They didn't believe at first, but they learned. Others might too, if we remain steadfast. Besides, Krampus and The Fatman are not here to entertain skeptics. They exist to ensure we keep our promises."

Jarlan nodded. "True. Perhaps this is our next test: can we hold to these truths even if the world outside mocks us or tempts us back into old sins?"

Helgrid's gaze drifted to the village below, where lamplight began to shimmer in windows. "We must try. If our morality depends solely on fear of punishment, then we have learned nothing. We must stand by goodness for its own sake."

As darkness fell, villagers gathered in the meeting hall. The travelers, now healthier and more confident, joined them. Over thin porridge and stale bread, they discussed plans. Kirsa announced that when the passes cleared, her group intended to depart. This was met with mixed feelings: sadness at losing new friends, relief that resources would stretch further, pride that they had helped others, and curiosity about how these lessons might spread beyond the valley.

Marta stepped forward, addressing both villagers and travelers. "We have lived through dark times. We owe our survival and moral clarity to the balance maintained here: The Fatman's kindness and Krampus's vigilance. You, travelers, have witnessed it. If you carry this story outward—carefully, truthfully—others may learn from it. We hope you do."

Kirsa bowed her head. "We will. Though many may doubt, we won't forget. We saw Krampus with our own eyes, felt The Fatman's warmth. More importantly, we learned to respect honesty and generosity. Our future community, wherever we settle, will remember your lessons."

Elric, once skeptical, now nodded earnestly. Stena and Haldi exchanged looks of agreement. Even Ravn, the one who had tasted Krampus's rod, managed a rueful smile—painful but instructive. Brenn and Joval, the older men, hummed quietly. They would take this strange gospel of moral equilibrium with them. Perhaps, in scattered conversations around future campfires, the seeds of these lessons would sprout elsewhere.

Outside, The Fatman listened by a window. He did not enter. He was content to know that understanding had taken root. From a distant stand of pines, Krampus watched too. He had no interest in spreading doctrines—he simply existed as a law of nature. Yet knowing that humans carried his lesson forward might amuse him. Ancient as he was, he recognized that mortals would never fully transcend their flaws, but every step toward genuine virtue lightened the burden he carried.

In the following days, villagers and travelers worked feverishly to prepare sleds and packs for the upcoming journey. The season had not truly broken yet, but signs hinted that within weeks, paths might open. They repaired harnesses and stitched fur cloaks. Kirsa's group wanted to be ready when the chance came. Between these labors, they shared meals, stories, even laughter. Suspicion no longer thickened the air as it once had.

And yet, beneath this harmony, tension coiled, waiting. Nature and humans rarely allowed perfect peace to settle long. If morality was truly internalized, fate would not hesitate to test it again.

The test came as a quiet calamity: the smoked fish stores, carefully rationed all winter, showed signs of spoilage. A subtle rot had crept into a portion of the stock. The discovery caused gasps of alarm—food was scarce, and losing even a portion was a blow. Frustration sparked. Some villagers muttered that sharing with travelers had strained them too far. The travelers bristled at such insinuations. Was goodwill so fragile that a bit of spoiled fish could unravel it?

Branwynn tested the remaining supplies with herbal concoctions, hoping to salvage what she could. Marta tried to soothe tempers, but the mood soured. If moral principles faltered over a few lost meals, what good was all their learning?

The Fatman arrived amid the rising tension, offering words of caution: "Do not let hardship erase compassion. You have overcome worse trials. Remember that unity saved you before." His plea carried weight, but worry gnawed at him. If fear of Krampus's punishment was still their main deterrent, would they regress now?

Krampus lingered unseen, perhaps to gauge if another lash was needed. The villagers sensed his presence, becoming tight-lipped, careful not to hurl accusations too freely. Kirsa's people offered to reduce their share further, even skip a meal. This magnanimity shamed the suspicious villagers. Helgrid scolded them: "They show generosity despite hunger. Have we learned nothing? Let's solve this fairly."

Jarlan proposed a solution: everyone would tighten belts for a week, dividing what remained equally. If spring allowed hunting and foraging soon, they'd survive. The travelers agreed without hesitation. The villagers, remembering old lessons, nodded. Grudges simmered but did not boil over. Ravn cast nervous glances at shadows, mindful of Krampus's vigilance.

That night, a hush fell over Sleetwood. No screams, no stolen goods—just hungry bellies and determined hearts. The crisis had tested their resolve and found it intact. Even The Fatman, passing through lamplit snow, seemed relieved. Perhaps they did not need Krampus's direct intervention every time a conflict arose.

Another week passed, each day feeling like an inch gained toward warmer weather. Snow melted imperceptibly, ice along creek edges loosened. Branwynn reported finding tender shoots of green beneath a rotten log—tiny harbingers of spring. Children played carefully, aware of scarce rations, but still able to laugh. The travelers sharpened tools, planning their route. They hoped to leave once they were certain the passes would not trap them.

As they prepared to depart, Kirsa sought a private audience with Helgrid, Jarlan, Branwynn, and Marta. The Fatman arrived too, sensing the importance. They met inside the chapel ruins, now partially repaired, a place symbolic of moral rebirth. Without words, Krampus stood in the gloom near a fractured arch, listening. The group formed a circle in that sacred-seeming space.

Kirsa spoke, her voice echoing slightly in the old stones: "We will leave soon. We owe you a debt—not just for shelter and food, but for teaching us a moral order we never knew could be so tangible. We want your permission to carry this story beyond these mountains. We will tell others of The Fatman and Krampus, of your code, of how fear and kindness forged a better life."

Jarlan looked to The Fatman, who nodded, and to the dark silhouette of Krampus. Krampus did not object. If humans chose to carry these tales, it was their choice. Jarlan replied: "We cannot stop you. We trust you to speak honestly. But be warned: not everyone will believe. Some may mock. Others might try to twist these lessons for their gain."

Kirsa understood. "We'll be careful. We won't claim miracles lightly. We'll describe what we saw and learned. Maybe one in a hundred will listen, but that's enough. In desperate times, a hint of moral clarity can save lives."

Marta smiled tearfully. "Go with our blessing. Spread the word that there's a place where kindness and consequence live side by side, where mercy and fear create a just balance."

Branwynn added a final gift: a small iron token, forged by Helgrid, etched with runes. On one side, The Fatman's symbol—a simple circle representing generosity. On the other, Krampus's mark—a twisted branch. "Keep this as a reminder," Branwynn said. "Not a talisman of magic, but a memento that you carry these lessons in your heart."

Kirsa accepted the token, her companions looking on with solemn respect. The Fatman laid a gentle hand on Kirsa's shoulder. "I hope your new home finds strength in these truths," he said softly. She nodded, tears glistening in her eyes, moved by the simple sincerity of these guardians.

Krampus remained silent, but his presence was felt. Perhaps that was approval enough.

The next morning, as dawn painted the horizon in pale lavender, the travelers readied their sled. They had precious few supplies—some dried roots, a little smoked meat scavenged late in the season, gifts of warm cloaks from villagers. They hugged and clasped hands. Children wept softly, having grown fond of these guests. The travelers vowed to return someday if fate allowed, or at least send word if they found stable ground elsewhere.

The Fatman stood at the village's edge, quietly observing. Krampus lingered behind a half-collapsed fence. The departing group looked back one last time—at the stout cottages, the meeting hall where they learned to share meals without deceit, the chapel ruins where moral vows were reaffirmed. They saw in this village a living story they would carry forth. With determined steps, they headed into the thawing wilderness, their silhouettes shrinking until they vanished behind snow-laden firs.

In their wake, Sleetwood felt emptier, but also prouder. Marta led a short gathering in the meeting hall, where villagers acknowledged their mixed emotions. Jarlan recorded the departure in his ledger, writing: *We have shared our moral code with strangers. May they kindle it elsewhere. We remain here, guardians of a delicate truth.*

With the travelers gone, life returned to local concerns. Now the villagers must stand on their own. Without outsiders, would their moral resolve hold steady? The Fatman believed so. Krampus would not vanish; he was too old and integral to simply leave. But if humanity here truly internalized these lessons, perhaps his interventions would become rare as shooting stars, reserved for only the gravest sins.

Spring's approach brought other changes. The snow receded from fence posts, revealing mud and matted grass beneath. A few villagers ventured beyond the perimeter, checking if small game or early greens could be found. Others repaired the old trading paths. Children ran more freely, splashing in slush, giggling. The mood lightened, though they remained respectful of their code. Just because the entity was gone and the travelers departed did not mean they could relax their moral standards.

Yet fate tested them again, as fate does. A young man named Haren, a villager with restless ambitions, decided to push boundaries. He had chafed under the strict moral regime. He wondered: if The Fatman and Krampus had guided them for so long, would they let small clever tricks pass now that peace reigned? Haren reasoned that maybe Krampus and The Fatman had grown complacent. The travelers were gone, the entity defeated. Perhaps he could profit from subtle wrongdoing—no one would suspect him, a local boy with a disarming smile.

Haren attempted a quiet deception: he "forgot" to report a small sack of dried mushrooms he'd gathered. He sold them secretly to a neighbor in exchange for a promise of future favors. In isolation, this seemed minor. No violence, no overt cruelty. Just a hidden theft from the communal stock.

But Sleetwood's moral net had fine mesh now. The neighbor, anxious about deception, hesitated, then confessed to Marta, who informed Helgrid. The rumor spread in hushed tones. Fear rippled through the community: would Krampus appear? Did they need that threat, or could they handle this themselves?

The villagers decided to confront Haren openly, in daylight, at the meeting hall. They summoned him to answer the charge. The Fatman arrived, standing by quietly. Branwynn's wards glowed faintly in the corners, as if anticipating a showdown of principle. Helgrid crossed her arms. Jarlan held his ledger ready to record a just resolution. Marta waited with steady eyes.

Haren blanched at the accusation. He tried to lie at first, claiming ignorance. But the neighbor's testimony was clear. The Fatman frowned, disappointment etched in every line of his face. Haren felt a chill. Was Krampus lurking outside, ready to burst in with rods and chains?

Before panic could set in, Marta raised her hand. "We know what you did, Haren. You betrayed trust for petty gain. We could call on Krampus, and you know he'd answer. But have we not learned to uphold morality ourselves? Must we rely on punishment from shadows every time?"

Haren's heart hammered. He expected Krampus to appear any second. Yet The Fatman and Marta were suggesting something else: that the village handle this transgression. If they dealt with it honestly and fairly, would Krampus hold back?

Helgrid spoke, voice firm: "Haren, you know the code. Return what you owe, perform extra labor to compensate for the harm. Show genuine remorse. If you do so, we need not provoke Krampus's intervention. He will sense our resolve."

Haren glanced around, sweat on his brow. Everyone watched. Outside, perhaps Krampus listened. The Fatman said nothing, letting mortals decide. This was a critical moment: would they choose virtue freely, ensuring wrongdoing was addressed without needing supernatural terror?

Haren's shoulders slumped. Without an outside force, they still held him accountable. Not out of fear alone, but because they believed in what they'd built. Shamed, he admitted his fault, returned the mushrooms, and vowed to spend the next days helping reinforce the footbridge for spring's thaw. He apologized to his neighbor, to the villagers, to The Fatman. His voice cracked with genuine regret.

A hush fell. No chains rattled, no horns loomed. Krampus did not appear. The villagers breathed out relief. They had resolved a moral failing without the lash. The Fatman's eyes shone with quiet pride. By handling this themselves, they proved maturity. Fear of Krampus had started them on this path, but now they walked it by choice.

As dusk settled, people drifted back to their homes. Haren's lesson spread through whispers—good moral order could stand on its own legs now. The Fatman lingered in the meeting hall, running a hand over the old timbers. He recalled when despair and confusion filled these walls. Now confidence and moral agency replaced it. He stepped outside to find Branwynn leaning against a post, smiling faintly.

"You hoped we'd reach this point," she said softly. "Where we handle moral breaches without summoning fear."

He nodded. "You've grown strong. The memory of Krampus's darkness and my kindness guide you, but you do not rely on them blindly."

Branwynn laughed quietly. "We still need you both. Perhaps less dramatically now, but you embody truths we must never forget."

The Fatman's gaze drifted to a distant fence line, where a tall silhouette faded behind a shed. Krampus, present but distant, acknowledging their achievement by not intervening. He said, "Krampus will remain a presence. Humans are fallible. But you've taken a step beyond raw fear, and that matters."

In the following week, subtle signs of spring increased. Small rivulets of meltwater trickled near the village edges. Hunters found a few fresh game trails. The children squealed at the sight of a robin darting among pines, a bird rarely seen in deep winter. The villagers cleaned tools, repaired broken sleds into carts. They spoke quietly of the travelers' departure, wondering if their message would find fertile ground elsewhere.

Moral life continued at a steady hum. No major infractions occurred. Even small arguments resolved gently. The Fatman sometimes found himself becoming an observer rather than an active comforter—people needed his gifts less often, as their kindness toward one another had become more natural. It gladdened him to see baskets of bread shared without prompting, disputes settled over a handshake. He still left small tokens of encouragement, but now they were subtle acknowledgments rather than essential sparks.

Krampus's sightings diminished further. Occasionally, a latecomer returning from the forest at dusk claimed they saw two amber eyes in the gloom, but no punishments followed. Perhaps Krampus accepted that they had learned the lessons he existed to enforce. He was still there, of course, as enduring as old roots under snow, but willing to let them stand on their own two feet more often.

Jarlan wrote a new entry in his ledger: *We near a season of transitions. With no crises looming, our code solidifies. We rely less on dread and more on understanding. The Fatman and Krampus remain, but as guiding constellations rather than daily enforcers. Is this not what we always wanted? A moral order that outlives fear, held up by conviction.*

Helgrid forged new iron charms, not because anyone needed them desperately, but as symbols of their identity. She crafted delicate scenes: a birch tree and a round loaf of bread, representing Krampus's rod and The Fatman's gift, intertwined. Villagers hung them not just on doors, but on small stands inside their homes, tokens of pride in the moral story they had forged.

With each passing day, the sky brightened earlier. The snow in the central square turned slushy by midday. Children played more openly, singing tunes that mentioned both The Fatman and Krampus without terror, as if these legends were beloved elders watching from afar.

And so, gradually, Sleetwood settled into a stable new chapter. The horrific memories of the entity's attack faded into cautionary tales that strengthened their moral resolve. The recent travelers became a fond memory of how they shared these lessons beyond their valley. Even the minor crisis with spoiled fish and Haren's deception stood as milestones: tests passed, proving they could handle challenges without collapsing into chaos.

One evening, as stars pricked the purple sky, Branwynn and Marta climbed a small knoll outside the village. From there, they could see faint lights from distant ridges—maybe Kirsa's group had lit a campfire somewhere out there, forging their new destiny. Branwynn sighed contentedly. "We are not perfect," she said, "but we are better than we were. The Fatman and Krampus helped us grow up."

Marta nodded, pulling her cloak tighter. "We must never forget this winter, these lessons. Even if someday The Fatman and Krampus move on to other places that need them, we'll hold this code in our hearts."

Branwynn considered that possibility. Would these legends depart entirely? Maybe not soon. They might remain as guardians, less visible, a background presence. In any case, their imprint was permanent. The village had become a moral stronghold. That alone was miraculous.

In the silent woods behind them, a twig snapped. They tensed, then relaxed when a faint jingle of chains drifted on the breeze. Branwynn caught a glimpse of horns silhouetted against starlight, then nothing. A reminder: Krampus would never be far, just as The Fatman's gentle smile would always find a way through cracks of despair. Their existence was woven into the village's narrative now.

As dawn broke the next day, people rose to their chores cheerfully. The threat of starvation still lurked at the edges, but they faced it together, confident they'd share what they had. The Fatman, pausing at a cottage door, left a small jar of honey—one of the last from winter's stores—and smiled to himself, satisfied that they'd savor it responsibly. Krampus, if anyone dared look, might be found perched on a distant branch, just another shape among old pines, silent testament to boundaries that must not be crossed.

Children asked fewer fearful questions now. Instead, they integrated the guardians into playful stories: one told of The Fatman guiding lost travelers with a lantern of starlight, another of Krampus scaring away not just evil but also winter wolves, ensuring humans had a chance to learn. These tales, while simplified, carried essential truths: kindness tempered by caution, fear transmuted into respect.

Helgrid hammered a final set of iron tokens, distributing them to each household. Marta organized a small ceremony in the chapel ruins. All villagers attended, forming a circle under the patched roof. Jarlan read from his ledger a condensed history of their trials and triumphs. Branwynn sprinkled juniper and rosemary, scents of renewal. The Fatman appeared at the doorway, silent and smiling. Krampus's presence was felt as a shiver along their spines, even if he chose to remain unseen this time. They lit candles and pledged once more to uphold their code, not out of terror, but gratitude and responsibility.

After the ceremony, people lingered, hugging each other, whispering hopes for spring planting and future prosperity. Even without abundant food or warm summers, they had something priceless: moral resilience. This intangible wealth meant The Fatman's gifts would be cherished, not taken for granted. It meant Krampus's rod would gather dust, used rarely, because they now policed themselves sincerely.

Before the last candle guttered, The Fatman stepped forward. "You have done well," he said, voice echoing in the old stone arches. "I see a village that learned to stand tall. I remain because I care, but you need not depend on me for every kindness. You can create kindness yourselves." He glanced toward a shadowy corner, as if acknowledging Krampus's silent endorsement. "Likewise, my brother remains watchful, but less needed. Honor that by living rightly, even when no horned silhouette looms."

The villagers bowed their heads, tears shining in some eyes. This felt like a graduation of sorts. They thanked The Fatman and, indirectly, Krampus. No grand farewell, but a gentle shift: guardians stepping into the backdrop, humans moving center stage.

As the days passed, the weather finally broke. The snow softened, runnels of water trickled into ditches. A faint green haze appeared on south-facing slopes. With early spring, new tasks demanded attention—clearing fields, repairing ditches, sorting seeds. Their moral code guided them through these labors. When someone accidentally broke a tool, they compensated fairly. When a child cried over a lost toy, neighbors replaced it without expecting return. These kindnesses flowed naturally now, not forced by fear alone.

In quiet moments, a villager might spy The Fatman strolling under budding branches, humming softly, or hear a distant rattle of Krampus's chains at twilight. They took these signs not with dread, but respect: reminders that goodness was a choice they reaffirmed daily.

Jarlan updated his ledger once more: *We enter a gentler season. Our moral code, shaped by legends and trials, stands firm. Fear and mercy now co-exist in our hearts, not only in the shadows. We can face the world without shame, ready to share what we've learned.*

He closed the ledger, knowing the story continued beyond words. The village would grow, transform, and face new challenges. But one truth remained constant: The Fatman and Krampus had anchored them to a moral axis, and now they spun confidently on that axis, guiding themselves.

On a calm evening, the villagers gathered at the edge of the village to watch a last snowdrift collapse into a muddy rivulet. Children laughed, adults smiled, and The Fatman stood among them, blending in as if just another kind neighbor. In a distant treeline, two amber eyes flickered and then were gone. No alarm, no screams—just understanding. They did not need constant intervention. Krampus was content to watch from afar, a silent guarantor, while The Fatman's kindness merged seamlessly with their own hearts.

So ended a long, dark chapter of their history, ushering in a new era where the people of Sleetwood carried the essence of both legends within them. They would never be saints, but they would strive earnestly for goodness, using fear to sharpen their moral senses, using kindness to nurture their souls. In that delicate balance, they claimed their true strength, lighting a small but steady flame against winter's endless night.

CHAPTER TWELVE

The first rays of dawn cast pale streaks of light across the frosted peaks of the Winterspine Mountains. Below, the village of Tallfir huddled beneath its blanket of snow, eerily silent except for the mournful howl of the wind. Smoke no longer curled from chimneys; shutters were drawn tight, and footprints leading from doorways were covered by fresh snowfall, as though the land itself sought to erase the traces of the vanished.

In the shadows of the ruins of the old chapel, the villagers gathered with bated breath. The air inside was cold, colder than outside, and Branwynn could feel the weight of magic lingering in the stones. She adjusted her grip on her staff, her fingers trembling slightly. Helgrid stood beside her, her hammer resting on her shoulder, her expression as sharp and unyielding as the steel she forged.

And then, he appeared.

The Fatman emerged from the swirling snow with deliberate steps, his crimson robes striking against the white. He was not the jovial figure of song and legend; his presence carried a solemn weight, as if every step bore the burden of centuries. His usually twinkling eyes were grave, his smile absent.

The villagers stared at him, some in awe, others with suspicion. To them, The Fatman was an idea—comforting, warm, a figure who ensured balance by rewarding the good. But his expression today held none of that warmth. Instead, he seemed old, weary, and fraught with worry.

He stopped in the center of the ruins, his eyes scanning the crowd. When he spoke, his voice was low but carried easily through the still air. "This village has always known the balance—the giving and the taking, the light and the dark. But the balance is broken."

Murmurs rippled through the crowd like restless waves. Helgrid stepped forward, her hammer thudding against the snow-dusted stone. "You mean Krampus," she said, her tone more a challenge than a question. "He hasn't been seen. He hasn't taken anyone this season."

The Fatman nodded gravely. "He hasn't. And that is why you're all in danger."

Branwynn frowned, stepping closer. "Danger from what? You're here. You're the balance's light. Isn't that enough?"

The Fatman's gaze shifted to her, his eyes filled with something deeper than sorrow. "No," he said quietly. "Because I am only half of what keeps this world from unraveling. Without Krampus, the darkness grows wild."

Jarlan, the chronicler, cleared his throat nervously. His ink-stained fingers gripped a roll of parchment tightly. "Are you saying," he began hesitantly, "that Krampus keeps the darkness in check by... punishing us?"

The Fatman nodded. "His role is not cruelty for cruelty's sake. He teaches. He corrects. Without him, the dark forces we keep at bay grow bolder."

A low murmur of fear swept through the villagers, and Branwynn exchanged a glance with Helgrid. It was one thing to fear Krampus; it was another to fear what came in his absence.

"But there's something more, isn't there?" Helgrid asked, her voice hard. "This isn't just about him being gone."

The Fatman's jaw tightened. "The balance isn't simply broken. It's being unraveled—unbound by something old. Something I have not felt in centuries."

After the gathering dispersed, Branwynn lingered near the chapel ruins, her thoughts heavy. The villagers returned to their homes, most still reluctant to trust the weight of The Fatman's warnings. Helgrid joined Branwynn at the edge of the chapel, her breath puffing in the cold air.

"So what now?" Helgrid asked, her tone grim. "We sit and wait for Krampus to come back? Or hope the darkness doesn't swallow us before then?"

Branwynn tightened her grip on her staff. "Neither," she said firmly. "If there's something unraveling the balance, then we have to stop it. Waiting is a death sentence."

Helgrid nodded, her hand resting on the hilt of her hammer. "Agreed. But we need a place to start. And I think I know where."

Branwynn arched a brow. "Where?"

"The altar," Helgrid said simply.

Branwynn's eyes widened. The Forgotten Altar was little more than a whisper among the villagers, a place high in the mountains where ancient bargains were said to have been struck. The Fatman had mentioned something about bargains earlier, hadn't he? Her pulse quickened.

"You think it's still intact?" Branwynn asked.

Helgrid shrugged. "Intact or not, it's a place of old magic. If the balance is unraveling, we might find answers there."

The two women set out at dawn, their boots crunching through the snow as they climbed higher into the Winterspine Mountains. The air grew colder with every step, the wind biting at their faces and carrying whispers they couldn't quite decipher.

"This path hasn't been used in years," Branwynn muttered, glancing nervously at the jagged cliffs around them. "If the altar's even still here, who's to say it hasn't been destroyed by the elements?"

"Old magic tends to linger," Helgrid replied, her breath forming clouds. "Even in ruins, there's power. And if something is unraveling the balance, it might have started here."

They trudged on in silence, their unease growing with every step. The forest around them was unnervingly still, the trees standing like silent sentinels, their snow-laden branches barely moving despite the wind. Branwynn couldn't shake the feeling that they were being watched.

And then came the sound.

It was faint at first, a soft scratching noise like claws on stone. Branwynn froze, her staff held tightly in her hands. "Did you hear that?"

Helgrid stopped, her hammer raised. "I hear it."

The noise grew louder, circling them, coming from everywhere and nowhere at once. Branwynn's heart pounded as her eyes darted through the trees, searching for the source.

Then, without warning, something lunged from the shadows.

It was a twisted, half-formed creature, its body a grotesque amalgamation of fur and bone. Its eyes burned with an unnatural light, and its claws gleamed like freshly sharpened steel. Branwynn barely had time to react before it was on her, its claws slashing at her staff.

She raised a shield of light just in time, the creature's claws sparking against the barrier. "Helgrid!" she shouted, her voice high with panic.

Helgrid moved like lightning, her hammer striking the creature with a sickening crunch. It let out a screech, its body dissolving into ash as it collapsed. But the moment it was gone, more emerged from the trees.

"Run!" Helgrid shouted, swinging her hammer at another creature. "Get to the altar! Go!"

Branwynn hesitated, her instincts screaming at her to stay and fight, but she knew Helgrid was right. The creatures were multiplying, their numbers too great to hold back for long. She turned and ran, her staff lighting the way as she climbed the final stretch of the path.

The Forgotten Altar stood in the center of a clearing, its stones cracked and weathered but still pulsing faintly with magic. Branwynn slowed as she approached, her heart hammering in her chest. The air around the altar was heavy, charged with an energy that made her skin prickle.

She stepped closer, her eyes scanning the runes etched into the stone. They glowed faintly, flickering like dying embers. Whatever power had once bound this place was fading—and something else was taking its place.

Behind her, the sounds of battle grew louder. Helgrid's shouts mingled with the screeches of the creatures, each one sending a fresh wave of fear through Branwynn's veins. She turned back toward the altar, forcing herself to focus.

Her fingers brushed the surface of the stone, and a shock of cold shot through her body. Images flashed in her mind—visions of Krampus and The Fatman standing side by side at the altar, their voices rising in ancient chants. She saw chains, fire, and shadow, and then a third figure—one she didn't recognize.

The third figure was shrouded in darkness, its form shifting and indistinct. But its presence was undeniable. It had been here when the bargains were struck, its power woven into the fabric of the balance. And now, it was unbound.

"Branwynn!" Helgrid's voice cut through the vision, snapping her back to the present. She turned to see her friend staggering into the clearing, her hammer swinging wildly as the creatures closed in around her.

"I found something!" Branwynn shouted, raising her staff. She sent a burst of light toward the creatures, forcing them back. "The balance—there was a third force. Something older than either Krampus or The Fatman."

Helgrid's eyes widened, but before she could respond, the ground beneath the altar began to tremble. The runes on the stone flared, their light growing brighter and more erratic. The air filled with a low, rumbling growl.

And then the altar split open.

From the fissure rose a figure cloaked in shadow, its form towering and indistinct. Its eyes burned with cold fire, and its voice was a low, resonant growl. "You have broken the chain," it said, its tone filled with ancient malice. "And now, I will take what is mine."

Branwynn raised her staff, her heart pounding. "What are you?"

The figure's gaze fixed on her, its many eyes narrowing. "I am the darkness before balance. I am the void between the light and the shadow. I am the first."

Chapter Thirteen

The sky that morning was a bruised tapestry of purple and grey, as if the winter had not fully relinquished its grip. Though the valley had begun to thaw, a cold bitterness still clung to the air. Meltwater trickled in unseen gullies, ice cracked along creek beds, and trees shed their icy sheaths with soft sighs. The village of Sleetwood awoke to a world on the brink of transformation, yet no one assumed that change would come easily or gently. They understood by now that each new season brought its own moral trials.

In the weeks since their small delegation returned with modest success in trading beyond the valley, Sleetwood's people had felt a subtle shift in their hearts: a growing confidence that they could uphold their values even outside their sheltered community. The Fatman had become a quieter presence, weaving in and out of daily life with less fanfare, while Krampus remained mostly a memory, a distant shadow that still colored their choices. But balance, once found, must be guarded jealously. Even a minor slip could unravel so much hard-won moral order.

On a late afternoon, Helgrid Stonestream stood at the edge of the old chapel ruins, which now doubled as a kind of informal forum. The sky above glowed dully, and crows circled in the distance. She had come to inspect a new carving that Branwynn and Jarlan had planned to place in the chapel's arch—an emblem that combined The Fatman's symbol (a circle suggesting unity and kindness) and Krampus's mark (a twisted birch branch) into a single motif. The carving was nearly finished, chiseled into a sturdy plank of oak. Helgrid ran a calloused hand over the rough edges, pleased with how it represented their moral story. This emblem would greet anyone who entered, reminding them of their history and code.

As she examined the carving, footsteps approached: Jarlan, his ledger tucked under one arm, and Branwynn, carrying a small pouch of herbs that rattled softly. Both greeted Helgrid with weary smiles. The last days had seen a flurry of small disputes—a neighborly misunderstanding over borrowed tools, a minor quarrel about fishing rights in a half-frozen creek—but all resolved without summoning Krampus or requiring The Fatman's active intervention. They did it themselves now, using fairness, memory, and the gentle fear of backsliding.

"I think it's time we considered something more proactive," Jarlan said quietly, breaking the silence. His voice echoed slightly in the half-restored chapel. "We've shown we can uphold this code. But will it endure if a greater challenge comes?"

Branwynn nodded, her hair catching dull light. "We rely less on The Fatman's gifts now. Kindness flows more naturally. But I sense unrest in the wind, a tension that might not come from inside the village. The land beyond is still hard and unforgiving."

Helgrid frowned. "You feel something, Branwynn?" The hedge-witch often caught subtle hints in the wind's murmur, in the patterns of melted snow. Her runes no longer warded off monstrous threats, but they still read the moral currents of the world around them.

Branwynn hesitated. "Not something specific. Just a feeling. As if we stand in a clearing while wolves circle beyond the treeline. Our code is strong, but untested by true malice since the entity fell and the travelers left. Those travelers carried our story outward. Who knows what ears have heard it by now, and what envy or hatred might be stirred?"

Jarlan stroked his short beard thoughtfully. "If others learn that we have stability and moral wealth, some might see it as a resource to exploit. Bandits, desperate wanderers, or cunning traders might come not to learn but to take advantage."

Helgrid's hammer, slung over her shoulder, felt heavier as she considered this. The world outside did not share their peace. For months, they had nurtured a delicate bloom of decency in a soil of old fears. A

Krampus

truly dark force—maybe not as monstrous as the entity, but cruel and human—could shatter all they built.

They agreed to keep watchful. Not out of paranoia, but a readiness to defend their moral ground. The carving would be finished and hung at dusk, a symbolic act that might strengthen their resolve. Branwynn offered to sprinkle protective herbs at the chapel's threshold, not as magic against monsters, but as a reminder of their vows to remain honest and kind even under threat.

That night, as lanterns winked out one by one, a figure approached the village from the north, unseen by sleeping eyes. A lone traveler, cloaked in ragged furs, moved silently under a moonless sky. He paused at a rise, peering down at the dim silhouettes of cottages and rooftops. His breath steamed as he considered his approach. Rumors had reached him—rumors of a village spared from winter's worst horrors by strange legends and iron moral laws. He smiled thinly in the dark. He was not here to trade fairly or learn their ways. He was here to test their weakness, find cracks in their fabled code, and profit from them.

This stranger had a name—Lorad—but he would not share it easily. He considered himself a practical man, one who understood that kindness was often a mask for weakness. In places without strong external enforcement, cruelty thrived. The tales he'd heard of Sleetwood intrigued him: a place where theft was nearly extinct, where people spoke of The Fatman and Krampus as living presences. He scoffed at such superstitions. If they feared a horned shadow or relied on a fat old man's gifts, maybe he could manipulate them. Fear and faith could be turned into leverage if one was cunning enough.

At dawn, Lorad entered the village openly, posing as a weary traveler. He stumbled into the square, coughing theatrically. When a few villagers gathered, concerned, he spun a tale: he claimed to have escaped bandits in the far north, that he was starving and friendless. His eyes darted around, noting details—where people stored supplies, which houses had stronger doors, who carried weapons. He saw only a handful of iron-tipped staves and simple tools. No hardened soldiers. A soft place, he thought, ripe for schemes.

The villagers, true to their code, offered him a seat by the hearth in the meeting hall and a bowl of thin porridge. Marta approached him kindly, asking his name and story. Lorad gave a false name—Arlek—and made his voice tremble slightly. He praised their hospitality, pretending ignorance of their reputation. But he dropped hints that he had heard strange rumors, sowing curiosity. The villagers exchanged knowing smiles and explained that they had a special moral arrangement, guided by The Fatman and overseen by Krampus's stern presence. Lorad feigned awe, nodding politely.

Over the next days, Lorad observed everything. He marveled at how disputes ended quickly, how people shared resources without barter. He tested their patience by requesting small favors repeatedly—an extra blanket here, a handful of dried fruit there. No one refused him outright, though they politely reminded him that they had limited stores. Lorad noted their restraint. Despite scarcity, they did not show suspicion openly. Fools, he thought, they're too kind for their own good.

He also noticed subtle signs of unease. When he pushed too far—asking for more than was reasonable—a certain tension appeared. He saw some villagers glancing at dark corners, as if expecting a horned figure to emerge. This intrigued him. They truly believed in Krampus as a moral enforcer. Lorad considered how to exploit that fear. If he could commit a hidden crime and shift blame onto another, perhaps he could watch their system crack under pressure.

Meanwhile, the village leaders kept a careful eye on Lorad. They had learned not to trust blindly. Helgrid noticed he asked more than he offered. Branwynn sensed no magical evil but felt a strange dissonance in his presence. Marta tried gentle conversation to see if he'd slip up and reveal something inconsistent. Edric and Takrin, remembering their trade expedition, knew outsiders could be skeptical or cunning. Yet they had no proof of wrongdoing, and their code demanded they not condemn without cause.

Lorad's opportunity came a week after his arrival, when he discovered a small storeroom behind the meeting hall. It contained the last of the village's precious dried herbs and a barrel of salted fish—resources crucial to their slow recovery from winter. One evening, while most villagers attended a small communal supper at the chapel ruins (celebrating the hanging of the new carving), Lorad lingered behind, feigning a headache. He slipped into the storeroom, pocketing several handfuls of dried herbs and a chunk of salted fish. He planned to hide these outside the village, create scarcity, then resurface them later to sell back to them at a desperate moment. A small cruelty, but profitable.

Krampus

He moved silently, proud of his stealth. Yet as he pocketed his loot, a faint sound caught his ear—chains rattling softly, far away. He froze, heart pounding. Nonsense, he thought, it must be his imagination. Still, his spine prickled. He hurried to hide the stolen goods in a hollow under a loose board behind an abandoned cottage. Then he joined the villagers at the chapel, acting concerned when he arrived late.

At the chapel ruins, the villagers had just finished a short dedication to their carving. Branwynn's herbs scented the air, Jarlan recited a short verse from his ledger about the journey from fear to moral strength. The Fatman stood at the back, smiling. Krampus did not appear, but a hush fell as if all recognized his unspoken presence. Lorad entered, feigning respect. He marveled at their reverence—how quaint. Yet a sliver of anxiety gnawed at him. If their legends were true, would he face consequences?

A few days passed, and the villagers discovered the missing herbs and fish. Alarm spread quietly. Had someone stolen their supplies? They looked to Lorad—after all, he was new—but had no proof. They asked him if he'd seen anything suspicious, and he shook his head, offering help to search. His offer seemed genuine, but some noticed a gleam in his eye. Others wondered if a villager had faltered. After all, outsiders were not the only ones capable of sin. Doubt festered.

The Fatman sensed this unrest. He visited Marta and Helgrid in private, urging them to handle the situation with fairness, to seek truth without rash accusations. The villagers agreed. They had resolved a theft before without Krampus's lash. Maybe they could again. Yet fear crept in: what if this time the culprit was truly cunning? Fear of Krampus might return in force, fracturing their hard-earned trust.

Lorad watched all this, smugly pleased. The missing goods caused tension. He dropped subtle suggestions that maybe certain villagers envied the travelers who had left, or perhaps someone feared lean times and took a secret stash. He played innocent well, posing questions to sow doubt. Some villagers grew uneasy, suspecting that maybe Lorad was testing them, but they had no evidence. They found footprints near the storeroom, but melting snow made them indecipherable. The hollow where Lorad hid his loot remained secret.

One twilight, Branwynn dared to confront Lorad indirectly. She led him on a walk near the old forge, talking about the village's history. She stressed how they overcame lying and stealing, how Krampus's unseen eye ensured that injustice would surface. Lorad feigned admiration, but a bead of sweat formed at his temple. Her tone hinted that she suspected something. He wondered if he should cut his losses and slip away at night. But where was the profit in that? He wanted more—a bigger haul, maybe even leverage to make them trade valuable items for their own stolen goods.

That night, Lorad decided to escalate. He took more herbs, a larger chunk of salted fish, and this time he purposely left a half-footprint of a villager's boot near the scene—someone else's boot he had surreptitiously borrowed earlier. If he could frame a local for the crime, it would spark conflict. If they turned on each other, their precious moral code might shatter. Then he could exploit their panic and fear to negotiate a "solution" at a high cost. He chuckled softly to himself as he planted the clues, imagining The Fatman's disappointment and Krampus's absence. He still doubted any horned punisher would appear. After all, he'd seen no proof of these legends besides fearful glances.

When morning revealed more thefts and suspicious footprints, the village shuddered. Finger-pointing began quietly. Helgrid and Marta struggled to maintain calm. They gathered everyone in the meeting hall to discuss openly. The Fatman appeared, grave-faced, and urged restraint. Jarlan read past cases from his ledger, reminding them that hasty blame leads to injustice. Branwynn cast a subtle spell to sense truthfulness, but Lorad remained cautious, avoiding direct lies or confrontations. He only hinted at suspicions against a timid villager named Gresha, whose boots vaguely matched the partial print.

Gresha, horrified by the accusation, wept and denied it. She had no reason to steal. The Fatman placed a comforting hand on her shoulder, and The Fatman's kindness gave her courage to speak up. "I would never betray our code," Gresha sobbed. "Think, who gains from our strife?" Her words made some turn suspiciously toward Lorad. He noticed the shift and knew he had to sow more confusion or risk exposure.

That evening, Lorad prepared a final strike. He would steal enough supplies to cause real panic, then vanish, only to return later as a "rescuer" with hidden stocks he'd pretend to have "found." But as he crept toward the storeroom, something felt off. The air crackled with tension. The moon hung like a silver blade overhead. He moved silently, yet he felt eyes on him. The stables' shadows seemed deeper, the wind colder. He stepped into the storeroom and reached for the barrel of fish—then froze.

A soft rattle of chains, unmistakable now, brushed against the silence. His heart lurched. Was it just a loose chain on a tool rack? He spun around, holding his breath. Amber pinpoints gleamed in a dark corner, beyond the lantern's weak glow. He blinked hard. Impossible. That must be a trick of the light, some reflection. He stepped forward, squinting. The shadows seemed to congeal into a shape: tall, horned, furred. Panic clenched his gut.

He had scoffed at these legends, considered them manipulative stories. Yet here stood Krampus, or something that wore that shape. He wanted to run, scream, anything—but fear paralyzed him. He tried to rationalize: maybe a villager dressed up to scare him. He reached out timidly, expecting cloth or a mask. But his fingers touched coarse fur, iron-hard muscle beneath. The creature's breath steamed, reeking of pine and old winter nights. Lorad recoiled, terror loosening his bowels.

A low growl, not a word, vibrated in the silence. Lorad understood instantly—this was no mortal disguised in furs. This was the darkness given form, the enforcer he had disbelieved. Krampus raised an arm, chains clinking softly. Within those chains hung birch rods, rattling like bones. Lorad tried to speak, to beg, but his throat clamped shut. He had been caught mid-crime, in the act of undermining what these people cherished.

Krampus did not need accusations or words. His role was older than language: punish the wicked, preserve moral order. Lorad sensed no mercy in those amber eyes. He had planned to shatter their trust, prey on their kindness. Now he faced primal justice.

With a sudden, inhuman speed, Krampus seized Lorad's arm. The traveler gasped in pain as claws dug into his flesh. No blade, no chain lash yet—just a crushing grip that conveyed absolute dominance. Lorad whimpered, tears streaming, as he realized his cleverness meant nothing here. Fear spiked as he remembered stories: that Krampus punished not just children but anyone who mocked moral law. He had mocked it indeed.

In silence, Krampus dragged Lorad out of the storeroom and into the icy night. The village slept, unaware of this grim tableau. Under a crooked pine, Krampus released him momentarily. Lorad stumbled, struggling to stand. He wanted to shout for help, confess everything, promise to return what he stole. Would that save him?

He opened his mouth, and a birch rod cracked against his shoulder. He yelped, falling to his knees. Another lash caught his back. Pain exploded, harsh and unrelenting. Lorad sobbed, pleading now, "I'm sorry, I'm sorry!" But the horned figure did not speak. Another lash burned his flesh. Lorad understood the lesson: no trick would save him. He had chosen cruelty and deceit, and now he paid in pain and terror.

After three lashes, Krampus paused. Lorad curled into a ball, weeping. He dared to look up. Krampus stood like a statue, steam rising from his fur. The silence was complete except for Lorad's ragged sobs. He wanted to beg for mercy, but words failed him. All he managed was a faint, choked apology.

Perhaps that was enough. With a low snort, Krampus gripped Lorad's collar and dragged him toward the meeting hall. The villager's dwellings loomed around them. Lorad trembled, half-conscious. Krampus dumped him in the middle of the square, in plain sight. Then, with a final rattle of chains, vanished into darkness.

Moments later, a villager on night watch—Detrin, a young man—rounded a corner and gasped at the sight of Lorad curled on the ground, whimpering. Detrin raised an alarm softly, and soon a handful of villagers gathered, lanterns casting long shadows. The Fatman appeared too, eyes heavy with sorrow. Marta knelt beside Lorad, checking wounds. Not fatal, but painful enough to brand this lesson into his soul.

Lorad sobbed broken words: "I—stole… fish… herbs… I lied… I tried to turn you against each other…" He confessed everything, surrendering all illusions of cleverness. The villagers listened, stern but controlled. Some felt righteous anger, others pity. Even now, they chose not to become cruel. They understood Krampus had dealt the necessary punishment. Their role was to respond with fairness, ensuring no hatred festered.

Helgrid's hammer gleamed in lantern light as she spoke: "You thought to break us. You underestimated both The Fatman's mercy and Krampus's justice. Now you know we do not bluff."

Jarlan recorded this event in his ledger, heart heavy. Another moral test had arrived, more insidious than a hungry traveler—it was a cunning intruder who tried to corrode their trust. Yet they endured. They did not panic or accuse blindly. Krampus himself intervened this time, proof that their code still stood under divine scrutiny.

Branwynn offered Lorad a cup of bitter herb tea to ease shock. He drank, trembling. He expected them to cast him out immediately or lynch him. Instead, they stood in a silent circle. The Fatman placed a gentle hand on Lorad's shoulder. Lorad shuddered, expecting a rebuke, but found only calm sadness. "You have learned the hard way," The Fatman said softly, "that kindness is not weakness. Our fear of Krampus, our love of mercy, are balanced. You tried to exploit it and failed."

Marta's voice was firm but not cruel: "Return what you stole. Show us where you hid it. Then leave. We will not harm you further, but you must go. We have no place for deceivers who relish our downfall."

Lorad sobbed again, nodding violently. He would return everything. He had no strength left to argue. He crawled to his feet, leaning on Detrin's arm for support. They fetched the stolen goods from the hollow he had chosen outside the abandoned cottage. Villagers murmured as precious herbs and salted fish came back into their hands. Relief and vindication mixed with renewed respect for their code. Even under a cunning test, they stood firm.

At dawn, they led Lorad to the village edge. He limped, bruised and humiliated. No one hit him now; Krampus had delivered the only blows needed. The Fatman watched from a distance, arms folded, expression neutral. Helgrid pointed down the muddy trail: "Go. If you learn anything from this, let it be that moral law here is not a joke. We do not desire vengeance, only that you never return to test us again."

Lorad's tear-streaked face contorted with regret and pain. He could scarcely believe they let him live. He had expected savage retaliation. Instead, they dismissed him with stern dignity. Something in his heart twisted. Perhaps he had underestimated the power of genuine morality. He could not face their eyes any longer, turned, and staggered away, each step a reminder of his failure.

Branwynn whispered to Marta, "Will he tell tales of Krampus and The Fatman's vengeance?" Marta shrugged. "If he does, others may mock him. But we know the truth, and that is enough."

Jarlan added a new entry in his ledger: *We faced a cunning intruder, a human test of our code. Krampus intervened to show us that old darkness still stands guard. We cast the deceiver out without becoming monsters ourselves. Our moral code grows stronger.* He underlined that last sentence, satisfied that their story continued to affirm their hard-won principles.

The Fatman stepped forward, meeting the gaze of Helgrid, Branwynn, and Jarlan. "You handled this well. Krampus acted, yes, but you responded with justice, not cruelty. You maintain the balance, proving you don't rely solely on fear. I am proud of you." They bowed their heads, gratitude warming them. They had passed another test, more subtle and human than monstrous.

As spring deepened, the soil softened under gentle rains. The villagers turned to planting seeds, repairing wooden carts, and preparing for new ventures. The memory of Lorad's deception lingered not as a scar but as a reminder. Even as they engaged with the broader world, they must remain vigilant. Not everyone seeking entry would be like Kirsa's group, willing to learn and respect their code. Some would try to exploit it. Sleetwood must never grow complacent.

No new intruders arrived in the following weeks. The villagers sometimes discussed Lorad's attempt and Krampus's swift punishment, reassuring themselves that their moral guardians still watched. The Fatman made fewer appearances, content to let them rely on their own goodness. Krampus remained mostly unseen but ever-present, the dark edge to their moral blade.

Children now included Lorad's story in their play-acted lessons. One child pretended to steal imaginary herbs, another wore a crude mask of horns and rattled a chain to scare the "thief" straight. Adults smiled at this play. Even children understood that kindness must be protected, that wrongdoing bore painful consequences.

Branwynn noticed more travelers passing along distant ridges, not entering the village, just skirting its domain. Perhaps word had spread that Sleetwood was no easy mark. Rumors might have turned the village into a legend of fear and compassion, two forces no outsider could easily bend. This suited them fine—let the cruel fear their reputation. It might spare them more tests.

Helgrid and Jarlan took another trip to the chapel ruins, checking the carving. It remained sturdy, symbol of their accord. The runes Branwynn had sprinkled beneath its arch still whispered of trust. A crow perched on a beam, watching them with bright eyes. Helgrid laughed quietly. "We've become something rare, haven't we? A place where myths live in hearts and keep our feet on moral ground."

Jarlan nodded, "We have. And we must carry this forward, never forgetting that darkness is always near, pushing us to fail. We stand firm only because we choose to."

They left the chapel, lanterns swinging softly, content that their moral compass remained true. Outside, the village bustled with mild spring chores—nothing dramatic, just ordinary life stabilized by extraordinary principles. The Fatman observed from a distance, pleased that they did not need him at every turn. Krampus watched unseen, ready to strike if they faltered, but pleased they gave him little cause.

As the season grew milder, villagers planted small gardens. They sang while working, voices rising under a sky that no longer felt so oppressive. The memory of the entity's horrors had faded into cautionary lore told on cold nights, the moral confusion of old times now replaced by clarity. The trials after that—travelers, deceivers—had strengthened their identity. They were a community defined by their code, supported by legends proven real.

A subtle darkness still hovered, not from within but from the knowledge that the outside world teemed with potential threats. They would eventually trade more widely, invite more travelers, and each encounter would risk moral compromise. Yet they felt ready. They had The Fatman's gentle approval, Krampus's silent vigilance, and their own proven ability to resist temptation.

That evening, the village held a modest feast—root vegetables, the last of their dried berries, and even a bit of fresh greens found near a thawed spring. They toasted not to gods or legends alone, but to themselves and their guardians. The Fatman smiled among them, sharing their meal. No one toasted Krampus explicitly—they knew he preferred the shadows—but they honored him by leaving a token at the chapel door: a small birch rod wrapped in evergreen sprigs. A silent gesture of respect for the darkness that kept them honest.

Under starlight, children danced around a low fire, singing simple rhymes of kindness and caution. Adults reminisced about past winters, relieved that this year ended better than the last. Branwynn played a gentle tune on a reed flute, notes carrying through the mild night air. Helgrid carved new symbols into a plank of wood: a stylized horned silhouette beside a plump figure with a sack, both encircled by runes of unity.

In the deepest hours, when the feast wound down and people drifted to their beds, The Fatman lingered outside the meeting hall. He placed a hand on the doorframe, feeling the warmth within. He thought of The Fatman and Krampus as siblings in myth, different yet entwined. Their influence had guided humans through chaos. Now humans took their lessons forward, strengthening virtue with their own will.

A distant shape moved at the edge of a grove—Krampus, or just a deer? The Fatman smiled softly, whispering into the stillness, "We remain, brother, but they need us less as crutches and more as north stars. This is good."

No answer came, only a faint rustle as if a horned head nodded, acknowledging the truth.

Dawn found Sleetwood at peace. The villagers woke, fed livestock, planned their day without dread. If their code was forged in darkness and light, now it guided them through each moment. They knew their history of terror and temptation had not ended darkness forever—darkness was part of life. But they had learned to navigate it, to hold their moral line even when cunning intruders tried to break it.

In the coming days, Lorad's name barely surfaced except as a cautionary tale. The supplies he returned allowed them to plant and preserve some food. Children asked why Krampus had thrashed him. Parents explained gently: Krampus punished the wrongdoer who threatened their fragile trust, ensuring they would not be easy prey for cruelty. The lesson was that wrongdoing leads to pain, and honest living to harmony.

As the sun climbed higher over thawed fields, Helgrid and Jarlan met near the chapel, discussing plans to send another delegation once the main roads dried. This time they might carry their code more openly, explaining their system to skeptical traders. They knew not everyone would respect it, but they had proven they would not yield or break. If anyone tried what Lorad had done again, Krampus would ensure swift justice. More importantly, the villagers themselves would stand firm, punishing dishonesty by collective moral judgment without descending into cruelty.

Branwynn listened to their talk, nodding approval. She sensed a new maturity in their ambitions. No longer content to hide their light under a bushel, they would spread their example carefully. Not converting others by force, but leading by demonstration. The Fatman's presence, though quieter, still infused them with gentle optimism. Krampus's silent watch reminded them to never slacken their vigilance.

Marta passed by, carrying a basket of seedlings ready to plant. She smiled at the trio, glad they planned for a future interwoven with moral clarity and practical trade. The darkness and fear that once defined them had become tools of understanding. They knew darkness existed, within and without, but they faced it with balanced hearts.

At midday, a soft rain fell, pattering on half-repaired roofs, washing mud from the lanes. Villagers took shelter under eaves, chatting about the next steps. Some suggested teaching their children more about the entity and old evils, so they'd never take peace for granted. Others considered inviting a sympathetic traveler to stay longer, learn their code in depth, and carry it beyond these mountains. Debate was lively but respectful.

The Fatman appeared in the meeting hall's doorway, nodding approval at their lively exchange. He did not interrupt. They had learned to deliberate wisely. Even disagreements ended with handshake and mutual understanding. Krampus's rod did not hover over them now; they behaved not from terror, but from genuine belief.

Late that afternoon, a group of children approached the chapel, leaving small clay tokens they crafted—figures of animals and plants symbolizing life's renewal. They placed these tokens beside the birch rod left for Krampus and a small circle for The Fatman. This quiet ritual signaled that the new generation understood the village's moral tapestry. Legends had become part of their cultural identity, not oppressive force.

In the fading light, Branwynn gathered a few herbs near the forest edge. She thought about Lorad's cunning attempt. He had almost fractured their unity. Without Krampus's timely punishment, could he have succeeded in sowing long-term distrust? Probably not. She trusted her people, but his plot would have lingered, caused wounds that took longer to heal. Krampus's intervention confirmed that while they grew more independent, their guardians still cared enough to ensure no mortal cunning would topple them too easily.

The Fatman passed behind Branwynn, offering a nod of encouragement. She smiled. They understood each other without words now. Their relationship had evolved from desperate pleas to calm acknowledgement of each other's role. The guardians provided a moral scaffold, and the villagers stood firmly upon it.

That night, under a starry sky, the villagers gathered in small clusters to talk, laugh, and share modest hopes. Someone played a stringed instrument fashioned from old scraps, and a quiet lullaby drifted over the rooftops. They savored these moments of peace, knowing that darkness would come again in some form—another cunning stranger, a shortage of supplies, a conflict with distant settlements. But each challenge would be met with the balance they had nurtured.

The Fatman lingered near a lamplit window, listening. Inside, a family read bedtime stories to their child—tales of kindness rewarded, cruelty punished. The child asked, "Will Krampus watch over me forever?" The parent answered, "He watches over our village, yes, but we watch ourselves too. We choose to do right, so Krampus need not appear. That's how we grow strong." The Fatman smiled, pleased that they understood so well.

Across the square, near a shed, a shadow detached from the darkness—Krampus, silent and inscrutable. He surveyed the calm scene: no panic, no weeping victims, no petty theft. His intervention had restored moral clarity without undermining their autonomy. Satisfied, he slipped back into the night. If they continued on this path, they might truly become a beacon of balanced morality in a world often swayed by cruelty or naïveté.

Jarlan, watching from a window, thought he glimpsed Krampus's silhouette vanish behind a stand of birches. He wrote in his ledger by candlelight, describing Lorad's attempt and how swiftly it ended. He recorded The Fatman and Krampus's ongoing roles, pleased that he could document a living moral tradition. If future generations read these entries, they'd see a lineage of lessons learned from darkness and guided by compassion and consequence.

As the long chapter of late winter and early spring closed, the village settled into a confident rhythm. They understood that darkness and light were not enemies but partners shaping moral growth. Fear alone would have made them brittle; kindness alone would have made them gullible. Together, they formed a resilient culture, absorbing challenges and emerging stronger.

Morning came with a gentle mist over the fields, dew glinting on tender shoots. The villagers rose early, gathering tools to begin their day's work. No dread shadowed their hearts. They carried within them the memory of horrors past, of Krampus's lash and The Fatman's gifts, of cunning foes cast out, of travelers transformed by their example. Each memory a thread in the tapestry of their moral identity.

They did not claim perfection. They knew human nature: envy, pride, desperation—these weeds could sprout anytime. But now they tended their garden of values with vigilance. Krampus and The Fatman were ever-present reminders that no good deed lived in a vacuum, no sin went unnoticed. They had chosen this balance willingly, forging a destiny where legends walked invisibly by their side.

Spring's gentle warmth hinted at a better harvest. A visiting bird sang perched on a thatched roof. Children chased each other around the chapel ruins, weaving stories that mixed old terrors with new hopes. Adults paused to listen, smiling at how fear had become a tool of understanding rather than despair. Darkness was part of their world, but not its master.

In that equilibrium, The Fatman drifted toward a distant cottage, leaving a small wooden charm shaped like a leaf—a silent blessing for health and growth. A subtle rustle in the forest told of Krampus's presence, not angry now, but watchful. If new threats emerged, he would be ready, and so would they.

As the hours passed, villagers prepared a noon meal. They shared bread and honey (from a small store they protected carefully), reminiscing about the day Lorad arrived. They spoke not with bitterness, but gratitude. He tested them, and they prevailed. Even a cunning man who mocked their faith in legends could not shatter what they'd built. The Fatman and Krampus had not failed them, and they had not failed themselves.

By dusk, warm colors bled over the sky. The chapel's new carving caught the last sunlight, the combined symbols of birch rod and circle glowing softly. Branwynn, Helgrid, and Marta gathered there, lighting a small lantern as a nightly habit. They prayed silently, not to gods, but to the moral principles embodied by their guardians. Jarlan arrived late, adding a short note to his ledger by lantern glow, a habit that had become a ritual of reflection.

They stood together, these four representatives of the village's soul. The Fatman hovered at a respectful distance, pleased by their calm unity. Krampus watched from afar, satisfied that his presence no longer needed to be overt. If sin reared its head again, he would return, swift and silent. Until then, humans would guide their own moral ship.

In the quiet that followed, the village breathed as one. Darkness remained a fact of existence—lurking in human hearts, in strangers' schemes, in the memory of monstrous evils. But darkness was balanced by unbreakable kindness and vigilance. The Fatman and Krampus were integral parts of their story, and the villagers had learned to internalize their lessons, making each day a testimony to the power of moral equilibrium.

The villagers lined the main square, shoulders touching, faces illuminated by torchlight. Through gaps between their legs, children peeked out at the retreating shadows of those who'd tried to deceive them. Old Thomas kept his weathered hand on the church bell rope, ready to sound another warning if needed. Up on the hill, the ancient oak trees still stood sentinel, their branches swaying in the night wind just as they had through a hundred winters. In cottage windows, candles burned steadily against the dark, each flame a testament to Sleetwood's unwavering heart. Come spring thaw or autumn storm, the village would endure, just as it always had.

CHAPTER FOURTEEN

Morning filtered through the sparse pines in delicate shards, painting the muddy lanes of Sleetwood with pale gold. The village was awake early, as it often was now in this gentler season. Snowmelt trickled quietly into streams, and tender shoots of green hinted that spring was finally taking hold. If one listened closely, one could hear the dull hum of distant industry: hammers tapping on iron, the shuffle of feet as villagers prepared for daily tasks, the rustle of homespun cloth in doorways.

In these softer days, The Fatman drifted through the village with a calm, almost paternal aura. He seldom had to leave treats or intervene in disputes now—people resolved their conflicts with patience and memory. They had learned from their trials that kindness and caution must stand shoulder to shoulder. The Fatman watched them like a gardener admiring sturdy plants grown from seeds he had nurtured. He took pride in how rarely he needed to remind them of their code.

Krampus's presence lingered on the periphery. He was rarely seen, but never forgotten. His horned silhouette and rattling chains had become part of the village's moral landscape. They knew he stood ready to punish grave wrongs. Yet in recent weeks, he had not needed to lift a birch rod. Even petty temptations were snuffed out by the villagers' own conscience and the faint whisper that Krampus's yellow eyes might be watching. This allowed the village to mature beyond fear into voluntary uprightness.

And yet, no system could remain untested for long. Outside their valley, the world churned with other agendas. Rumors had spread. Months ago, travelers had carried stories of a peculiar place surviving behind moral guardians both kind and fearsome. Some scoffed at these legends. Others were intrigued. A few were drawn like vultures to light, hoping to pick at whatever advantage they could find. The village's name, Sleetwood, whispered among merchants and rogues alike, had begun to provoke curiosity.

On a chilly afternoon, as a faint drizzle draped the horizon in grey veils, a caravan of four wagons appeared. They rolled slowly over the softening ground, skirting the ridges and approaching from the southwest. The watchers on the outskirts—Edric and Takrin—first spotted them. The wagons were covered in patched canvas, led by sturdy ponies. The procession moved without haste, yet deliberately, as if certain of their destination.

Edric and Takrin exchanged a glance. Another group of outsiders, so soon after the last deception they thwarted. They did not panic. Their code demanded courtesy. But they would not be naïve. They would greet these newcomers with open eyes, remembering Lorad's cunning attempt to fracture their unity. Edric signaled to a messenger, who slipped back to the meeting hall and informed Helgrid, Marta, Branwynn, and Jarlan.

As the wagons neared the village's edge, the drizzle intensified to a soft hiss. A handful of villagers assembled, tools in hand—not raised as weapons, but kept visible as a reminder that they were not defenseless. The Fatman stood under a small overhang, observing quietly. There was tension in the air, but not fear. They had faced challenges before.

When the caravan halted, a woman climbed down from the lead wagon. She wore a wool cloak pinned with a copper brooch, and her hair was braided with ribbons. Behind her, two men and another woman peered out, measuring the villagers with curious eyes. The lead woman smiled broadly, raising empty hands in a gesture of peace.

"Good day," she said, voice carrying through the drizzle. "I am Lirina, a merchant of sorts, traveling with my companions. We've heard faint tales of a village that overcame terrible odds and now stands as a moral stronghold. Are we in Sleetwood?"

Marta stepped forward. "You are. What brings you here, Lirina?" Her tone was cordial but not effusive. They had learned to keep a careful balance with strangers.

Lirina's eyes sparkled as she surveyed Sleetwood's modest lanes, the repaired chapel arch, the iron tokens that hung from doorways. "We trade in rare goods—textiles, spices, odd trinkets. We also pay well for unusual items. Rumor has it your village embraces a unique moral code, guided by legends both kind and stern. We thought to see for ourselves, perhaps engage in respectful trade. We mean no harm."

Edric studied the wagons. They bore no obvious weapons, but that proved little. Merchants could hide knives or ill intent behind smiles. Still, no reason to refuse them outright. "We welcome fair traders," he said. "But understand, we do not tolerate deceit. If you come in good faith, we will treat you accordingly."

Lirina nodded, smiling. "Excellent. May we camp near the village for a few days? We can show our wares, learn about your customs."

Jarlan, arriving with his ledger, exchanged a glance with Helgrid. They nodded. "You may camp in the clearing near the chapel ruins," Helgrid said. "But keep in mind, we have a strict code. The Fatman and Krampus stand behind it. If you doubt our sincerity, ask the last intruder who tried to cheat us—though he can tell no tale since we sent him away rather bruised."

A flicker of curiosity crossed Lirina's face at the mention of Krampus and punishment. So the rumors had substance. She bowed gracefully. "Understood. We respect your ways."

The villagers guided the caravan to a suitable spot. The Fatman observed from a distance, rubbing his chin thoughtfully. Krampus, unseen, no doubt watched as well. Another test, perhaps. How would these merchants behave?

Over the next day, Lirina's crew set up camp. They hung bolts of dyed cloth from their wagon sides, displayed polished stones, small carved figures, and pouches of aromatic spices. The villagers examined these with mild interest. They had little surplus to trade, but they were open to honest exchange. Marta tried a pinch of spice, delighting at its warmth. Branwynn admired a length of dark blue fabric that could make fine cloaks.

Lirina and her companions engaged in friendly chatter, asking about the village's history. The villagers explained their code: generosity balanced by the knowledge that cruelty would not go unpunished, courtesy supported by The Fatman's kindness and the silent threat of Krampus's rod. The merchants listened politely. Some seemed skeptical, others intrigued. None openly mocked.

By twilight, small deals were made—swaps of woolens for spices, iron tools for carved trinkets. Jarlan recorded each trade fairly. No arguments arose, no haggling beyond reason. The merchants played along with the village's honesty. In fact, they seemed eager to confirm the rumors. This cooperation felt too smooth, too easy. Helgrid remained cautious. She saw how Lirina's eyes lingered on the iron tokens shaped by Helgrid's forge—tokens symbolizing moral order that hung on every doorway. Why would a merchant be so interested in symbolic trinkets?

Late that night, while most slept, Lirina and her closest companion—a man named Carveth—huddled in their wagon, whispering. Carveth twirled a small iron token he'd acquired in a trade. Just a plain piece of iron with a birch branch and circle motif. Yet, something about these tokens fascinated Lirina. She believed them imbued with mystique. If people elsewhere craved uniqueness, these tokens could sell as exotic charms. She imagined spinning tales—claiming they came from a village guarded by mythical beings, a place where no theft occurred. Superstitious or curious buyers would pay handsomely.

Lirina wanted more than a few tokens. She desired a monopoly over whatever symbolic items Sleetwood produced. If she could coax the villagers into crafting tokens for export, branding them as "Krampus and Fatman Charms," she could profit immensely. But how to convince the villagers to commodify their moral symbols?

Carveth raised doubts, reminding her that these people took their code seriously. Turning their sacred symbols into merchandise might offend them. Lirina smirked. "That's why we must be subtle. We'll praise their code, claim we want to spread its goodness. If we can show them that forging more tokens and selling them outside will inspire other places to adopt their morals, they might agree. We'll pay well, of course."

Carveth nodded, impressed by her cunning. They would appeal to the villagers' desire to influence the outside world. Perhaps frame it as a noble mission: "Your tokens can remind others to be honest!" Lirina chuckled softly. These villagers might have integrity, but even good people like to think their values can spread. If money and flattery nudged them, they might transform their sacred emblems into trade goods.

At dawn, Lirina approached Helgrid, Branwynn, and Jarlan near the chapel ruins. She complimented their moral system, extolled how impressed she was by their stability. "I've traveled wide," she said, "and most places lack your clarity of values. I wonder, could we help spread your wisdom? Many out there are lost, craving guidance. If we carried these iron tokens—these symbols of your code—to distant lands, others might learn from them."

Jarlan's brow furrowed. "These tokens are not mere souvenirs. They represent our journey from terror to equilibrium. They're personal, meaningful. We share them with those who understand, not to profit."

Lirina raised her hands in a placating gesture. "I understand. But consider: if people elsewhere heard of Krampus and The Fatman, learned that balanced morality is possible, might it not inspire change? We could frame these tokens as lessons in metal, each one a reminder that kindness and consequence go hand in hand. We would pay generously, ensuring your village prospers. You could use the wealth to improve your lives, store supplies, trade more widely."

Branwynn narrowed her eyes. She sensed a delicate trap. The woman's words sounded noble, but the tone felt too eager. "We never intended to profit from our story," Branwynn said. "We share it with travelers who show sincerity. Turning our symbols into commodities could cheapen their meaning. Our code isn't a product."

Helgrid stepped closer, hammer resting on her belt. "Our tokens emerged from necessity. Each one forged when we needed a reminder. They're not fashion accessories for distant strangers who know nothing of our struggle."

Lirina feigned hurt. "I mean no disrespect. But think how many could benefit from your example if these tokens spread far and wide. Perhaps they'd ask about Krampus and The Fatman, learn to value honesty. Isn't spreading goodness part of your code?"

Jarlan considered carefully. He understood the temptation: spreading moral influence beyond their valley sounded good. But something felt wrong—Lirina's emphasis on profit, her quick assumption that moral lessons could be packaged and sold. The villagers knew their code was lived, not purchased. "We must discuss this as a community," he finally said. "We do nothing in haste."

Lirina nodded, smiling sweetly. "Of course. Take your time. We want only to help."

As she left, the three villagers exchanged concerned looks. Branwynn whispered, "I don't trust this. She's trying to commercialize our moral identity."

Helgrid grunted. "Agreed. Turning tokens into a commodity might invite corruption. People might start forging them just for coin, forgetting their meaning."

Jarlan sighed. "Yet some villagers might be tempted by new wealth or the idea of spreading their influence. We must tread carefully. Let's call a meeting tonight."

That evening, the villagers gathered in the meeting hall. The Fatman stood in a shadowed corner, arms folded, listening silently. Krampus, unseen but undoubtedly aware, hovered in their minds. Jarlan explained Lirina's proposal: to produce iron tokens for export, supposedly to teach others about their code. He stressed the risks: commodification of their sacred symbols, outsiders wearing tokens without understanding. Might that erode their sincerity?

Marta spoke up, voice steady. "If we turn our moral symbols into goods, what stops them from becoming mere trinkets? Next thing we know, people might pretend to follow our code just to sell more tokens. That invites hypocrisy."

Edric raised a hand. "But think: if these tokens reach distant lands, even a few people might ask about our story, learn from it. Could that not be good?" He sounded torn. He genuinely wanted their moral lessons to help others.

Takrin, more cautious, shook his head. "We share our code through example, not commerce. What if Lirina's buyers misunderstand and think the tokens themselves have magic power? They might treat them as lucky charms, ignoring the deeper meaning."

The debate turned lively. Some villagers, intrigued by new wealth and the chance to influence distant communities, argued that selling tokens could spread hope. Others insisted their moral code must remain pure, not corrupted by markets. The Fatman listened, eyes solemn, as they wrestled with the dilemma. This was a true moral test—no obvious villain, just a subtle temptation.

As arguments looped back and forth, a distant jingle of chains drifted through an open window. Many fell silent, hearts tightening. Krampus's distant reminder. They recalled that moral confusion often precedes wrongdoing. The presence of that sound—if real or imagined—

stirred them to think more deeply. What was Krampus's silent counsel here? That chasing profit over sincerity might invite dark consequences?

Jarlan raised his voice gently. "We must remain faithful to the spirit of our code. Profiting from its symbols feels like selling our soul. Didn't we learn that goodness must not be hollow? If we turn these tokens into mere merchandise, we hollow them out."

Helgrid nodded firmly. "I say we refuse Lirina's proposal. We can share our wisdom with travelers face-to-face, offering tokens as gifts to those who earn them, not selling them in bulk."

Marta agreed. "Yes. If others truly want to learn, let them come here and understand our code. We need no shortcuts or profits that risk diluting our moral truth."

The majority agreed. Even those who initially considered the idea saw the risks. They would not let their identity become a commodity. The Fatman's eyes shone with relief, proud they reached this conclusion without him having to speak.

The next morning, Jarlan and Helgrid informed Lirina of their decision. They tried to phrase it kindly: "We appreciate your admiration, but our tokens are not for sale. They are personal emblems of a code lived daily. We cannot mass-produce them for distant buyers."

Lirina's face tightened. This was not the answer she wanted. But she kept a pleasant mask. "I understand, though I regret your choice. There's real demand out there for symbols of hope and morality. You might miss an opportunity to spread your influence."

Branwynn, standing by, replied calmly: "If influence comes from sincerity, it must grow slowly and authentically, not through profits. Those who truly care will come here, learn our story, and leave changed. We do not seek easy fame or wealth."

Lirina forced a smile. Inside, frustration simmered. Without access to these tokens, what profit could she glean? Maybe she could try another angle. She decided not to give up so easily. "May we remain a bit longer?" she asked sweetly. "We have other goods to trade—no schemes, just fair commerce. We admire your village. Perhaps we can learn more by staying."

The villagers hesitated. They had no proof Lirina meant harm. Trading simple goods for a few days was not a threat. They nodded. "You may stay," Edric said, "but remember our boundaries." Lirina inclined her head.

Over the next few days, Lirina tried to ingratiate herself differently. She praised the villagers' crafts, offered better deals on spices, and even suggested teaching them weaving techniques. While doing so, she pried for more information about the village's past ordeals, how they interacted with The Fatman and Krampus, and which individuals were key influencers. Perhaps if she charmed key figures—like Helgrid the smith or Branwynn the hedge-witch—she could persuade a more private arrangement for token production. If she obtained just a small batch secretly, she could replicate them elsewhere, claiming authenticity.

But the villagers had grown skilled at reading outsiders. Branwynn noticed how Lirina lingered near the forge, flattering Helgrid's skill. Helgrid, no fool, accepted compliments politely but remained guarded. Jarlan watched Lirina's pattern of questioning—always circling back to tokens, moral symbols, how exactly the villagers decide who receives them. Marta found it odd that Lirina kept asking which families were closest to The Fatman's presence, as if looking for weak links.

Realizing subtle pressure wouldn't work, Lirina considered a bolder trick. Perhaps she could stage a scenario where villagers needed quick coin—maybe by secretly damaging some tool or quietly sabotaging a small stock of supplies—then offering them coin to help fix it, on the condition they produce a few dozen tokens. She planned carefully, choosing a night when few guards were posted.

However, The Fatman and Krampus had taught the villagers vigilance. Even at night, a rotation of quiet watch existed now. Takrin and a young woman named Alha patrolled softly, carrying lanterns with shutters half-closed. When Lirina crept toward a storage shed with a small blade, intending to slash some woven nets (a vital resource for fishing), she did not realize she was being observed.

Alha spotted a shape by the shed. She signaled Takrin, and they closed in silently, lantern shutters blocking direct light. When Lirina bent to cut the nets, Takrin stepped forward, illuminating her with sudden light. Lirina froze, caught red-handed with a blade near their supplies. Takrin's eyes narrowed. Alha gasped softly, heart pounding. Another attempt to undermine them?

Lirina tried to laugh it off. "I-I was just checking your nets, curious about their weave. I meant no harm." But her blade gleamed, and the villagers knew better. They called quietly for Helgrid and Marta, who arrived swiftly.

Helgrid's jaw tightened. "You think we're fools? We told you our code. Didn't you learn from Lorad's fate that deceit is punished here?"

Lirina blanched at the mention of punishment. She recalled whispered tales of a horned figure who enforced their law. She stammered, "I just—I wanted to understand your craftsmanship better. Maybe I was too curious."

Marta stepped closer, voice firm: "You lie poorly. You intended sabotage, perhaps to force us into a desperate bargain. If you think to blackmail us or profit from our code, you misjudge us."

Jarlan arrived last, ledger in hand, face grim. "We gave you a chance to trade fairly. You pressed for immoral shortcuts. We caught you before real damage was done. But attempted wrongdoing is still wrongdoing."

Lirina's heart hammered. She imagined Krampus emerging from a shadowy corner, chains rattling, delivering a savage punishment like Lorad endured. Panic flared in her eyes. She pleaded, "No, wait, I didn't actually cut anything. Let's just forget this. I'll leave quietly, no harm done."

The villagers exchanged glances. Should they call upon Krampus by name, or handle this themselves? They remembered that with Lorad, Krampus intervened directly. But now they had grown stronger. They might enforce their moral law without needing Krampus's lash every time. Yet this was a grievous attempt, a cynical plot to extort them.

Marta's voice trembled with controlled anger. "You came under false pretenses, tried to commercialize our sacred symbols, and now attempt sabotage to manipulate us. We cannot overlook this."

Branwynn emerged from the chapel ruins, having sensed trouble. She bore a small iron token in her hand and said softly, "These tokens represent honesty and balance. You tried to twist them into mere goods. Now you vandalize our livelihood. Do you expect mercy?"

The Fatman stood apart, watching. He would allow them to choose their response. Krampus remained unseen. Perhaps the villagers were ready to handle such moral crimes without waiting for supernatural intervention. This was a chance to prove their maturity.

Helgrid stepped forward, gripping her hammer. "Return to your wagons. Pack your things. You leave by dawn. We have no place for cunning thieves. If you resist, we will call Krampus's name aloud—and trust me, you do not want that."

Lirina's face contorted with fear at the mention of Krampus's name. The villagers seldom invoked him directly. He was a presence felt, not summoned. The threat carried weight. She nodded frantically, "I-I'll go, no argument."

Jarlan took a calm breath. "Also, to ensure you gained nothing, we will check your wagons for any stolen property before you depart. Understand that if we find anything missing from us, your fate will be harsher."

Lirina nodded, tears forming at the corners of her eyes. She had gambled and lost. These people were unyielding. She cursed her greed silently, realizing too late that moral codes backed by living legends were not to be trifled with.

At dawn, the villagers searched the caravans under watchful eyes. They found no stolen items—she had not yet succeeded. The merchants stood pale and silent, shocked that their leader had stooped so low. Some of them looked ashamed. Perhaps not all shared Lirina's cunning; some were just traders who followed her lead.

The Fatman observed from the lane, sadness in his eyes. Another attempt to exploit kindness had been thwarted. The villagers handled it decisively. They did not demand blood or cruel punishments, just banishment and a warning. The Fatman felt that was right—fear was part of their code, but mercy must shape their justice. They had evolved from needing Krampus's rod at every wrongdoing. They now wielded moral authority themselves.

Helgrid, Marta, and Jarlan escorted the caravan to the village's edge. Branwynn stayed behind, tending to a few who were shaken by the night's events. The merchants said little, embarrassed and subdued. Lirina tried once more to apologize, voice hollow, "I misjudged you. I am sorry. I will speak truthfully elsewhere of your integrity."

Marta gave a curt nod. "We care not what you say outside. Lie if you wish—but remember what happened here. Know that cruelty and deceit bring pain. If you carry any lesson away, let it be that you cannot twist moral order for profit without consequences."

The merchants departed, wagons creaking over muddy trails. The villagers watched them vanish into a hazy distance. No farewell words were shouted, just silence. Once they were sure the caravan was truly gone, Helgrid and Jarlan returned to the square. The Fatman waited there, arms folded, expression thoughtful.

Jarlan sighed. "Twice now outsiders tried to exploit us—Lorad and now Lirina. Both failed. But these attempts leave a bitter taste. Are we destined to repel trickery forever?"

The Fatman stepped forward, voice quiet. "The world beyond remains hard and cynical. Your moral code, shaped by myth and discipline, shines like a beacon. Moths will always come to a flame, some pure and curious, others hungry to extinguish or control that light. You cannot stop them from arriving. You can only maintain your integrity."

Marta placed a hand on Jarlan's shoulder. "We overcame these tests. We did not surrender to greed or vendetta. Each time, we reaffirm our code. Perhaps that is how we ensure its permanence."

Branwynn joined them, carrying a pouch of herbs. "True. We must accept that darkness comes in many forms—not just monstrous entities, but human cunning. The Fatman and Krampus guide us, but we do the work ourselves. That is our strength."

They stood in a loose circle, the drizzle gone now, sun breaking timidly through cloud layers. Children approached cautiously, having heard rumors of last night's drama. Helgrid reassured them: "We handled it. No one was harmed. The thieves are gone."

A child asked, "Did Krampus hurt them like he hurt Lorad?" Marta knelt down. "Not this time. We did not need to call him. We used his memory and The Fatman's lessons to enforce our code ourselves."

The child's eyes widened. "So Krampus and The Fatman trust us to do right?" The Fatman nodded gently from a step away. "Yes," he said softly, "they trust you to stand on your own feet."

The villagers felt a quiet pride bloom. They had grown from terrified survivors into moral custodians of their own fate. They respected The Fatman and Krampus as anchors, but no longer craved their constant intervention. Like children becoming adults, they had internalized the rules and enforced them without descending into cruelty or chaos.

That afternoon, Branwynn, Helgrid, and Jarlan went to the chapel ruins to check the carving and add a small rune at its base. The rune was simple, symbolizing resilience. After each test—Lorad's trickery, Lirina's cunning—they emerged stronger. Let these marks stand as historical notes that they resisted corruption and commodification of their morality.

Marta organized a small feast that evening. Nothing grand—just shared bread, a pot of herb-infused broth, some fresh greens scavenged from thawed patches. They ate together, laughter cautious but real. They spoke of distant futures, possible alliances with honest traders who might appear someday. The Fatman sat among them, a serene presence. Though The Fatman had less to say now—his lessons were understood—he enjoyed their company as one enjoys the fruits of long labor.

As dusk settled, someone asked: "If more challengers come, will we tire? Will we ever find lasting peace?" Edric answered, "Our peace lies not in absence of trials, but in our unwavering response. We do not seek a world without darkness. We have learned to navigate it, guided by these twin pillars: mercy and fear of wrongdoing."

A soft breeze stirred, carrying perhaps a distant rattle of chains, too faint to confirm. They did not panic. Krampus's presence had become a comforting threat—paradoxical but true. The villagers knew if they faltered, he would appear. And if they stood strong, he remained a distant guardian. The Fatman's quiet smile also lingered, encouraging them to remain compassionate.

Before turning in for the night, Branwynn paused near the chapel door, glancing skyward. Stars emerged faintly. She remembered the entity's horror, the travelers who learned from them, Lorad's punishment, Lirina's failure. Each chapter tested their code's durability. So far, no force had broken it. She prayed silently: *May we continue on this path, balancing dark and light, kindness and vigilance, never forgetting that we guard something precious.*

Helgrid joined her, whispering, "We should be proud." Branwynn nodded. "We are. Yet we must not grow arrogant. Arrogance invites complacency."

Jarlan, passing by, said gently, "Arrogance would make us think we no longer need The Fatman or Krampus. We do need them—maybe less actively, but as reminders that morality is not self-sustaining without memory and boundary."

Marta, last to leave, placed a small wildflower at the foot of the carving in the chapel. "For hope," she said softly. "Because even tested as we are, we grow more hopeful. We know we can face darkness without losing ourselves."

The Fatman watched them disperse, pride and melancholy mingling in his ancient heart. He was a guide, a figure of myth and flesh who witnessed human beings embrace true moral adulthood. Krampus, he knew, felt similarly from his silent vantage point. What began as fear-driven obedience had matured into chosen virtue.

Krampus

As the night spread its ink over the valley, the village settled into calm sleep. No restless terrors prowled the lanes. The memory of cunning intruders and thwarted schemes rested like old scars—visible reminders of what they overcame. The Fatman strolled along a fence line, leaving a single polished stone token on a post, a subtle gift of congratulations. If any villager found it in the morning, they'd understand it as a nod of approval.

Krampus, somewhere in the darkness, might have watched this small gesture and nodded. Their partnership, always strained and paradoxical, had born remarkable fruit in these humans. Perhaps that was always their purpose—to cultivate a community strong enough to handle evil without constant supernatural correction. They had not eliminated darkness—impossible—but balanced it. That was more than many human settlements achieved.

By morning, the drizzle had passed, leaving the ground damp but workable. Children found The Fatman's polished stone on the fence post and showed it to their parents, who smiled knowingly. Another quiet acknowledgment that they stayed true to their path. Work resumed: planting seeds, repairing roofs, weaving baskets. Ordinary tasks suffused with moral meaning. They knew each grain of kindness, each honest trade, each fair judgment was a stitch in the grand tapestry of their story.

They had refused to sell their symbols, refused to be tricked by sabotage, and dealt fairly with intruders. Their moral law, backed by The Fatman's gentle guidance and Krampus's dark vigilance, stood unshaken. Darkness still hovered at the edges of the world—an eternal fact—but here in Sleetwood, darkness found no easy prey.

As the day wore on, Jarlan recorded recent events in his ledger, carefully noting how they overcame Lirina's schemes. He underlined the phrase: *We did not need Krampus's direct intervention this time.* The whisper of chains was enough. Their internal moral compass had grown robust. He smiled at that thought, grateful that their growth allowed a gentler enforcement of the code, a sign of true maturity.

Branwynn visited the forest edge to gather fresh herbs. The scent of moist earth comforted her. She recalled the outsiders' attempts to profit from their virtue and concluded that moral strength must stand firm against not just brute evil but subtle corruption. Her basket filled with herbs, she returned with renewed conviction that their vigilance must never fade.

Helgrid hammered iron at her forge, making a new set of tokens. Not for sale, not for outsiders to flaunt meaninglessly, but for villagers who achieved something noteworthy or helped maintain balance. Each token would be earned, not bought. This custom ensured that their symbols retained authenticity. They were no mere trinkets but medals of moral accomplishment.

Marta taught children a new song—one that narrated their journey from terror to trust, from needing Krampus's rod to choosing honesty willingly. The children sang with bright voices, oblivious to the complexity of adult moral struggles, yet absorbing the lessons like sponges. In them lay the future of Sleetwood's moral legacy.

The Fatman passed by the singing children, smiling softly. He imagined them growing into adults who might never need Krampus's lash at all, who might carry the code into other lands through genuine example. That would be a triumph beyond measure. And if darkness rose again, as it inevitably would, they'd face it with the confidence and wisdom forged in these crucibles.

As dusk painted the sky in lavender and pink, the villagers gathered by the chapel ruins once more, lighting lanterns and sharing a simple meal. No one spoke of Lirina's caravan with bitterness. They treated it as another chapter closed. They had enforced their code with fairness, sending a clear message that moral authenticity could not be bought or twisted.

In a quiet moment, Helgrid asked Branwynn, "Do you think The Fatman and Krampus watch us more calmly now that we handle these threats ourselves?" Branwynn nodded. "I believe so. Their presence shaped us, but we stand on our own legs. That must please them."

Marta agreed. "We have become the guardians of our code, not mere subjects of fear or hope. We wield both kindness and vigilance like steady tools."

Jarlan sipped tea, reflecting on how far they had come. Once they cowered, now they engaged the world with measured trust. They said no to greedy merchants, tricksters, and thieves. They balanced mercy with firmness, love with discipline. This, he thought, is the heart of their covenant with The Fatman and Krampus.

The Fatman lingered at the edge of the lamplight, content. Krampus, unseen, surely approved from the shadows. Darkness pervaded the world, but here it was kept at bay by clear-eyed humans who would not sell their souls or symbols for profit. They had learned that moral purity was priceless, and cheapening it would only invite chaos.

As night deepened, the village returned to calm slumber. The sound of a distant owl hooting, the gentle clink of a wind chime made from old iron scraps, and the soft breathing of sleeping families filled the darkness. They would continue to face challenges—no code stands untested in a world rich with cunning—but each test strengthened their resolve. Guided by The Fatman's quiet encouragement and the latent threat of Krampus's wrath, they upheld a moral standard few communities could match.

Chapter Fifteen

A hush had settled over Sleetwood's lanes, the kind that follows adversity and lulls a place into cautious peace. After repelling cunning merchants, the villagers were more confident than ever that their moral code could withstand external manipulation. They carried on with daily life—hoeing small patches of newly thawed earth, repairing creaky doors, and cleaning gutters long choked by ice. Some spoke of future expansions, maybe even building a modest covered market for honest traders. The Fatman's presence hovered in gentle background notes, while Krampus's silent watchfulness gave their world an enduring edge.

Summer's promise lingered in the thickening green canopy and the milder breezes. A few villagers even risked short hunting trips beyond the valley's rim, returning with modest catches of hares or a basket of wild greens. They felt stronger, not just physically but morally. The panic, deceit, and treachery they had once known felt distant now. They had survived monstrous threats, cunning intruders, and temptations of commerce. Each trial had tempered their integrity like iron in Helgrid's forge.

But no place, however balanced, stands immune to the darkness that humans carry within them—or that drifts along the uncertain roads of distant lands.

It was on a warm, late afternoon—when dappled sunlight stretched through the chapel ruins and children laughed while playing with carved toys—that strange tidings reached Sleetwood. Edric, who had ventured beyond the valley's western edge on a cautious scouting trip, returned pale and breathing hard. He summoned Helgrid, Marta, Branwynn, and Jarlan to the meeting hall. The Fatman, perched at the edge of the green, tilted his head, concerned. Something in Edric's demeanor suggested unease not stirred by simple strangers or petty thieves.

Inside the meeting hall's wooden walls, Edric described what he found: footprints on a distant trail—heavy boots, too many for a small party. He saw broken branches, disturbed earth, and scraps of fabric snagged on thorns. Signs of a larger group passing too close for comfort. He followed carefully and from a distance. He overheard voices on the wind—hushed, gruff, unfamiliar. It might be a warband or a group of desperate men, rough sorts who might see Sleetwood as easy prey. He could not confirm their numbers or intent, but the undertone of what he heard—curses, mentions of raiding—uneased him.

At this, Marta pressed a hand to her heart. They had faced individual rogues and cunning merchants, but never a group possibly bent on violence. "We must not panic," she said softly. "But we must prepare. If they come with weapons, how do we uphold our code without descending into brutality? We have no standing warriors, just tools and moral convictions. The Fatman and Krampus have guided us, but can we deter armed raiders with fear of a legend?"

Helgrid's hammer glinted in a stray beam of sunlight. "We cannot surrender. If they attack, we must protect ourselves. But we must not abandon our moral laws. Violence must be measured, not gleeful. If forced to fight, we fight without cruelty."

Jarlan wrote notes in his ledger, recording the concern. "We can set watches, strengthen our perimeter. We must try to talk if they appear, to show we are not easy victims and that wrongdoing has dire consequences here."

Branwynn's brow furrowed. "If they come expecting to pillage, will words suffice? Or must we rely on Krampus's shadow to scare them off? That might work once, but what if they scoff at legends?"

Silence weighed heavily. The Fatman drifted in, arms folded, eyes grave. He understood the villagers' fear. They had progressed far in moral maturity, but standing against brute force tested more than honesty—it tested courage and the willingness to uphold morality even at physical risk. If Krampus intervened too blatantly, would that stunt their growth? And what if these outsiders were too many, too ruthless?

They decided on a measured response: increase night patrols, quietly shape a plan to warn intruders that Sleetwood is protected by formidable moral guardians. They would not boast or lie, but they might leave subtle signs—tokens, warnings scratched into bark—hinting that cruelty here brings swift punishment. If the raiders were superstitious or cautious, perhaps they'd avoid Sleetwood altogether.

Over the next days, Edric and Takrin scouted more, confirming that a band of nearly a dozen rough men lurked two valleys over, possibly testing paths to various settlements. Edric glimpsed them from afar: they wore mismatched leathers, carried axes and short swords, spoke in gruff tones about finding "rich pickings." He couldn't make out details, but he saw them send a small scouting party east—toward Sleetwood's direction.

When Edric reported this, the villagers grew tense. This was not a lone thief or a merchant caravan—this could be violence on a scale they never faced. The children sensed the adults' anxiety and quieted their play. The Fatman's reassuring nod helped, but everyone knew kindness and fear of Krampus might not deter hardened raiders who knew nothing of the village's legends.

That evening, Helgrid assembled a few villagers to forge simple defensive measures. Not traps that kill, but alarm lines, sharpened stakes, and hidden vantage points. They agreed that if talk failed, they must protect lives. Branwynn prepared herbal smoke pouches to confuse and disorient intruders without causing needless bloodshed. Marta organized quiet drills, teaching even the timid how to wield a staff if cornered, reminding them they must not relish violence, only use it to preserve moral order. Jarlan wrote instructions in his ledger, a grim chapter that he hoped would never be tested.

The Fatman watched with solemn pride. They did not rely on him or Krampus to solve everything. They took responsibility, adapting their code to practical defense without turning feral. This was moral adulthood—facing darkness without becoming it.

On the second night of heightened watch, as lanterns flickered in tense anticipation, a lone figure stumbled into the village from the west. Not the raiders—just one person, limping, clothes torn, face bruised. A woman, younger than middle age, trembling and exhausted. She collapsed near a fence, and Alha, on watch duty, rushed to her side.

The villagers gathered quickly. The woman managed a few words between ragged breaths: she had fled from the raiders' encampment. They captured her from a distant hamlet, used her as forced labor, then planned worse. She escaped when they argued among themselves. She begged for shelter, tears cutting through grime on her cheeks.

Marta knelt beside the woman, offering water and a warm cloak. The Fatman stood quietly nearby, approving of their immediate kindness. But as they comforted the stranger, she sobbed, "They are coming. They plan to raid villages, take what they want. They said they heard of a place with special tokens and beliefs—something about a horned punisher—and they want to test it. They think your fear is a myth they can exploit."

The villagers exchanged grim looks. The raiders knew about their moral code, saw it as weakness or a challenge. The stranger—her name was Teryn—insisted she wanted no part of them. She pleaded to stay, at least until she healed. "I have done no wrong," she promised, "I was their captive."

They believed her, but her words confirmed the threat. The band would come soon, drawn by rumor. The villagers would have to stand firm. They decided Teryn could stay in the meeting hall's back room, under watch, just to be safe. They trusted, but verified—lessons learned from earlier deceptions.

At dawn, Edric and Takrin reported more worrying signs: a trio of the raiders' scouts lurked on a hill west of the valley. Possibly they spied on Sleetwood, counting heads, noting defenses. The villagers must show strength or risk a swift attack.

Helgrid suggested a direct gesture: hang a large iron token at the valley's entrance—an unmistakable symbol of their code—and carve warnings around it, implying dire consequences for villains. Marta frowned, "But will that stop armed men?" Branwynn shrugged, "If they are superstitious or cautious, maybe. If not, at least we tried words first."

They forged a large iron token, bigger than usual, etched with Krampus's silhouette and The Fatman's circle, runes for justice and mercy surrounding them. They placed it at the narrow pass leading into Sleetwood, along with carved warnings: *Here no cruelty goes unpunished. Here kindness and vigilance rule. Enter if you dare.* Edric planted it with quiet determination, hoping to discourage at least some aggression.

Meanwhile, Teryn recovered slightly, telling them more about the raiders. Led by a man named Gorven, a brute who delighted in breaking moral codes. Gorven liked to "test" villages by performing small cruelties first, seeing if fear or confusion followed, then escalating. If a village showed no strong deterrent, Gorven's gang plundered freely. This was no random band; it was a group that thrived on moral breakdown.

The villagers steeled themselves. They must not break. They had never faced open violence on this scale, but they believed in their code. If forced, they would fight defensively, showing no cowardice, and if that failed, rely on Krampus's intervention. But they prayed it wouldn't come to that—Krampus's lash could stop criminals, but at what cost to their own moral growth?

As dusk settled on the third night of tension, watchers spotted movement near the iron token at the pass. Edric, hidden behind a shrub, saw three scouts approach it with torches. They read the warnings, scoffed loudly. He heard one say, "Look at this nonsense! Horned punisher? A fairy tale. They rely on fear and stories." Another laughed, "We'll show them fear. Let's see if their punisher appears when we burn their fancy symbol." They held torches close, intent on defacing or destroying it.

Edric's heart hammered. Should he reveal himself, attack, or wait? If he attacked alone, he might spark a preemptive battle. If he let them destroy the symbol, would that shatter the villagers' morale? No, their moral code was not tied to a single token. Still, allowing mockery might embolden the raiders. He waited, hoping they'd retreat.

The scouts tapped the iron token, realized they could not burn iron, only blacken it with soot. They cursed, hammered at it with a rock, denting it slightly. Then they spat and withdrew, laughing. Edric let them go, reasoning that a direct confrontation might be too risky. He returned to report what happened. The villagers, though upset, agreed they must not panic. A dented token did not break their code, it only tested their patience.

Krampus

Shortly before midnight, Teryn gasped awake from a nightmare, warning that Gorven himself might come soon. She recalled overhearing that if subtle intimidation fails, Gorven stages a cruel spectacle—killing an animal or harming a captive in plain view—to provoke fear. The villagers paled at the idea of such cruelty. They had no captives now, except Teryn, who was a victim seeking refuge. Would Gorven try to lure them out by cruelty to some innocent animal?

They tightened their patrols, prepared herb smokes and sturdy staffs. Branwynn prepared a mild sedative to calm nerves of frightened children. Marta whispered prayers, not to gods but to the moral principles that held them together. Helgrid's hammer was ready, Jarlan's ledger at hand to record whatever happened, The Fatman watched from a shadow, solemn. In a distant copse of trees, amber eyes might have gleamed—Krampus on alert.

At dawn's first blush, the raiders tested them. A lone figure—one of the scouts—approached the valley, dragging something behind him. The watchers tensed: it was a dead hare, strung up with twine, its belly cut open. A pointless cruelty, meant to shock. The scout hammered a post into the ground near the entrance and hung the mutilated hare there, then retreated, shouting insults about their "fancy morals" and "imaginary punisher."

Some villagers flinched, tears pricked their eyes. They cherished life, never killing except for food. This was raw brutality. The Fatman's face fell with sadness. Krampus's presence pressed on their minds. Would they rush out to avenge the animal, or remain calm?

Marta and Helgrid removed the gruesome display, burying the animal respectfully. They discussed how to respond. Attacking the raiders' camp seemed reckless. They must hold their ground. If the raiders intended to escalate, let them see that cruelty did not break their resolve.

Branwynn had an idea: "If they mock our legends, we show them a sign that might spook them. We can create silhouettes of Krampus and hang them in the trees, let them see shadows that confirm their fears." Jarlan considered this deception. Was it morally right to scare off raiders with illusions? It did not harm them. It might prevent bloodshed.

They agreed that preventing violence justified some intimidation. Helgrid and a few crafters carved rough wooden masks with horns, placing them in distant trees so that torchlight might reflect eerily at night. They arranged a few chains to rattle when pulled by hidden cords. If the raiders probed at night, they'd encounter unsettling sights and sounds, hopefully encouraging them to leave without forcing a direct confrontation.

Another day passed with no direct attack, just distant shapes moving on ridges, testing the edges. The villagers maintained iron discipline, rotating watches, keeping children safe indoors at night. The Fatman left small tokens of encouragement: a warm loaf of bread on a windowsill, a quiet hum near frightened watchers. Krampus remained invisible, but the villagers felt his tension in the air. Darkness pressed close, but they did not break into panic or cruelty. They remained poised and ready.

On the fourth night of tension, scouts returned to test the village again. This time, they tried to approach quietly from the east, away from the iron token. Edric and Takrin lay in wait. As the scouts neared, they triggered a cord, causing chains in a tree to clank and a carved horned mask to sway ominously. The scouts cursed, startled. Then the herb smokes Branwynn had placed earlier released a pungent haze. The scouts, coughing and confused, stumbled back. One shouted, "They trap the night with magic! Let's tell Gorven."

They fled. The villagers watched from hiding, relieved that their harmless illusions worked. Still, this dance couldn't last forever. Gorven would either escalate or back down. They prayed he would leave. Inside the meeting hall, they debated what if he attacked with force. Could they repel him without losing their moral stance?

Near midnight, Teryn emerged from the back room, trembling, and said she remembered more details: Gorven sometimes challenged villagers by demanding they hand over a victim or surrender something sacred. If refused, he'd burn a cottage or kill livestock. Sleetwood had minimal livestock, but their moral tokens and the chapel might be targeted. Would they trade away their principles to spare bloodshed?

Marta insisted no. "We must not yield moral ground to bullies. If he demands we abandon our code, that's the ultimate test. I trust we will stand firm, even if it costs us."

Helgrid nodded, though her eyes shone with worry. They were prepared to fight if cornered. They would not revel in violence, but they would not abandon their code. The Fatman listened silently, heart heavy that good people faced such trials. He recalled their promise: kindness and fear balanced, never losing sight of compassion, even in self-defense.

Could they preserve mercy if forced to swing a staff or hammer at a raider's skull?

Before dawn, a shout echoed from the valley entrance. The villagers sprang to alertness. Edric and Takrin reported that a raider came close, calling for parley. "Show yourselves, defenders of this moral code! Face me and let's talk!" he shouted.

The villagers agreed to meet this caller at sunrise, under watchful guard. Better to talk first. Perhaps words could deter bloodshed. They armed themselves with staffs, no lethal weapons brandished, just readiness.

At sunrise's edge, Jarlan, Marta, and Helgrid, flanked by Edric and Takrin, approached the valley entrance where the iron token stood. The Fatman watched from behind a hedge, unseen but ready. Krampus, invisible, surely hovered in their minds. On the ridge before them stood a stocky man with a scarred face and a cruel grin—likely Gorven himself. Behind him, several raiders loomed, weapons in hand, confidence in their eyes.

Gorven barked, "So you're the righteous village, hmm? We've heard tales. Horned punisher, fat gift-bearer, moral tokens. We think it's nonsense. Hand over supplies. Give us your valuables. If you comply, we might spare you. If not, we'll burn your pretty chapel."

The villagers' hearts thudded. Here it was: a direct threat demanding surrender. They remembered their code: never yield to cruelty, never let fear rule them. Marta stepped forward, voice steady, "We do not fear empty threats. Our code stands. Cruelty is punished here. If you harm us, you harm yourselves."

Gorven laughed, a harsh bark. "Punished by what? Your fancy stories?" He waved a sword, pointing at the iron token. "We dented your symbol. Nothing happened. We hanged a dead hare. No gods or demons struck us down."

Helgrid clenched her jaw. "We are no fools. You face a choice: leave us in peace or taste consequences that are real, not just legends. We stand together. We will not feed your greed."

Gorven sneered, "You think a handful of farmers and tokens can stop armed men? We've dealt with worse. Either give us what we want—food, metal tools, maybe a few hostages for good measure—or we'll raze this place. Let's see your punisher then."

Jarlan felt dread coil in his belly. They must hold firm. He tried reason. "If you attack, we will resist. We have methods to confuse and deter you. And if you commit atrocities, you invoke forces beyond our control. We have seen Krampus strike down wickedness."

Some raiders shifted uneasily at Jarlan's calm confidence. Gorven noticed and scowled. "Don't let their tall tales scare you. They rely on fear. We carry steel. Steel beats stories."

Silence stretched. The villagers realized words alone might not suffice. The raiders, smelling no immediate weakness, prepared to push harder. Gorven advanced a few steps, sword glinting in morning light. "Last chance," he snarled. "Give us supplies now. Or we pick one of you to hurt first. Show us if your punisher appears to save them."

At that horrifying ultimatum, The Fatman closed his eyes in sorrow from his hiding place. Marta's voice trembled but remained steady, "We will not yield an innocent victim to your cruelty. We'd rather fight and die with honor than betray our code."

Gorven grinned, anticipating compliance or panic, but got defiance. Edric, Takrin, and others behind the main trio tensed, ready if the raiders lunged. The villagers refused to cower. Branwynn, hidden among bushes, readied her herb smokes.

Gorven raised his sword, and the raiders shifted forward. The villagers braced, holding staffs, no turning back. This could spill blood. The Fatman clenched his fists, torn. Should he intervene more directly? That might shatter their independence. Krampus… would Krampus appear in full terror? Doing so might spare the village but cost them their moral growth. Or was this moment where they must stand alone?

Suddenly, a scream rose from behind the raiders. One of their number, posted as a lookout, stumbled down the slope, clutching his face. He gasped about a horned shape that emerged from shadows and rattled chains near him. The raiders twisted around, startled. Gorven snarled at the lookout, calling him a coward. Was Krampus striking first?

The villagers dared hope that maybe a subtle sign would scare the raiders off without bloodshed. But Gorven, furious, advanced again. "Tricks! Enough games. Surrender now!" His sword pointed at Marta's chest.

The Fatman's breath caught. If the villagers fought, some would die. If Krampus struck openly, it might save lives but reduce their moral autonomy. The tension hit a breaking point. The villagers raised their staffs, prepared to defend Marta. Edric whispered a prayer. Helgrid stepped in front of Marta, hammer ready, heart pounding.

A sudden gust of wind rushed down the valley, rustling trees and rattling the iron token. The raiders hesitated. Did they feel an unseen presence? The villagers sensed something profound: as if The Fatman and Krampus both hovered at the edges, waiting to see what choice humans made. Fight with honor, or try one last plea?

Jarlan, desperate, tried once more, "Leave now, and we let you go unharmed. We want no blood. But harm us, and you face consequences that no man should endure." His voice cracked with genuine passion. The raiders saw no trembling coward but a man defending his moral homeland.

Gorven spat, "Your bluff ends here." He stepped closer, raising his sword. The villagers tensed, muscles coiling. Helgrid tightened grip on her hammer. Edric notched a makeshift spear. Takrin prepared to block Gorven's swing. If steel clashed, what would happen next? Would Krampus thunder in, or would the villagers have to kill to survive?

As Gorven's sword angled down, ready to strike, the villagers braced for impact. At that exact instant, a shrill cry came from within the raiders' ranks. Another raider fell to his knees, screaming about something seizing him from behind, though nothing visible appeared. The others startled, stepping back. Gorven, enraged and confused, roared, "What trick is this?"

The villagers exchanged puzzled glances—this was not their doing. Could Krampus be acting invisibly, striking fear into raiders' hearts by unseen touches? If so, what price did they pay for divine intervention now? Would it deprive them of proving their own moral strength?

Gorven wavered, sword still raised, uncertain whether to attack or retreat. In the tense stillness, The Fatman clenched his jaw. This moment hung on a knife's edge. Bloodshed or retreat? Moral purity or pragmatic survival? If Krampus was intervening in unseen ways, would that scare the raiders enough to flee? Or would Gorven lash out in a frenzy?

The villagers held their ground, silent witnesses to a cosmic standoff. Krampus's invisible presence pressed closer, as if ready to materialize at full terrifying force if needed. The raiders shuddered, some muttering of curses and dark spirits. Gorven hissed at them to stand firm, but they looked rattled. The Fatman's heart ached, hoping no mortal blood must be shed. Branwynn watched from the bushes, sweat beading on her temple, wondering if she should release her smokes now.

Marta prayed silently that the raiders would break and run. Helgrid's knuckles whitened on her hammer. Jarlan, ledger clenched under his arm, balanced between horror and hope.

Then Gorven snarled, "Show yourself, cowardly demon! If you exist, come forward!" He swung his sword at empty air, challenging Krampus or any unseen force. The villagers' stomachs churned. This was madness. If Krampus appeared fully, what horror would unfold? Would he spare the villagers the trauma of witnessing a brutal punishment, or would his wrath be unleashed?

Before anyone could blink, a shape flickered at the tree line: a tall silhouette with horns and chains, barely visible in the dim light. It did not fully emerge, just a suggestion of nightmare form. The raiders saw it and gasped. One cried, "By all gods, it's real!" Another dropped his axe, stumbling backward. Even Gorven paled, eyes wide. His bravado faltered, hand trembling on his sword hilt.

The villagers stood transfixed. Krampus had given a glimpse of his reality. Not a full charge, not words, just a terrifying hint that these legends were flesh and blood. The raiders, faced with what they thought a myth, recoiled. Superstition gripped them. One man sobbed, "This place is cursed!"

Gorven tried to rally them, "It's a trick! They must have rigged something!" But a chain rattled again, and Krampus's eyes gleamed—amber sparks in the gloom—unmistakably alive. No trick of wood and iron could produce that silent malevolence.

As tension peaked, the villagers realized this was their moment. Jarlan stepped forward, voice calm but firm: "You see now that our code is not hollow. Leave us and never return. Harm no one. If you do, Krampus will find you, and The Fatman's mercy will not shield you. Go. Now."

The raiders wavered, torn between greed and terror. Gorven's knuckles turned white. He opened his mouth, perhaps to call their bluff again, but a muffled groan from behind him signaled another raider collapsing, clutching at invisible torment. It was too much. Panic rippled through the group. They stumbled back, muttering curses, shouting at each other to retreat. Gorven, eyes darting, slowly backed away, sword lowered. His gang followed, fear overpowering greed.

The villagers watched, hearts pounding, as the raiders retreated up the ridge, disappearing into the twilight forest. The Fatman stepped closer, breathing relief. They had avoided bloodshed. Krampus, or his partial manifestation, had turned the tide, preserving the village's moral purity and unity. Yet at what cost?

As the villagers lowered their staffs and exhaled shaky breaths, Branwynn emerged from the bushes, Helgrid and Marta embraced, Jarlan smiled tearfully. They had survived another test, relying partly on their code, partly on Krampus's terrifying aura. But as they sighed, exhaustion and gratitude mingling, something nagged at them: the raiders might spread fearsome rumors, but would that keep more violence away or invite darker challenges?

They turned to see if The Fatman was still there. He stood at the edge of the green, head bowed, as if burdened by what had just transpired. He raised his eyes to the villagers and opened his mouth to speak—

A scream cut through the village, high and desperate, from the direction of Teryn's room in the meeting hall. The villagers froze. Had one of the raiders circled around? Or was it something else? They rushed toward the sound, hearts plunging from relief to dread in a single heartbeat.

They pushed open the meeting hall door, lanterns swinging wildly. Inside Teryn's room, they found scattered blankets, a knocked-over chair, and no sign of Teryn. The window was open, curtains flapping. A single fresh splash of blood marred the windowsill. Shock washed over them. Had Teryn fled, injured, or been taken by someone lurking within their midst?

Marta knelt, touching the blood, eyes wide. Helgrid, breathing heavily, whispered, "But the raiders retreated... who took her?" Jarlan raised his lantern, scanning the shadows. Branwynn felt her stomach twist, remembering the entity and other horrors. The Fatman stepped in, face stricken. Krampus's distant chain rattled once, faint as a memory.

Outside, a shape darted into the woods—faster than any normal human could run. The villagers caught a glimpse through the open window: a silhouette not of a raider, but something else. Something lean, hunched, and silent. Horror clenched their hearts again. They had focused so hard on the raiders, on human cruelty, that they overlooked other lurking darkness. Could it be another monstrous presence awakened by their moral beacon?

Helgrid shouted for Edric and Takrin to pursue, but the shape vanished swiftly into thick undergrowth. The villagers clustered in shock around the empty room, dread returning tenfold. The Fatman's eyes filled with worry. They had just narrowly escaped a human threat, only to lose Teryn to something unknown and possibly more sinister.

Krampus's presence weighed heavily in their minds—would he assist against a new inhuman foe, or was this a separate trial testing their resolve again? Branwynn clutched her herbs, uncertain how to proceed. Marta wept softly, "We swore to protect the innocent. Teryn was a victim seeking refuge. Now she's gone!"

Jarlan's voice trembled, "We must find her. But how do we face a threat we know nothing about?"

Outside, the night deepened, wind whispering through pines as if mocking their ignorance. The Fatman stepped into the doorway, shadows cutting across his face. They needed answers, but the forest concealed its secrets. Could this new darkness be something old, awakened by their moral radiance or drawn by Krampus's ancient scent?

The villagers' hearts pounded, unity shaken. They had no choice but to follow the blood trail, to venture into a dark forest after a foe unseen and motives unknown. Fear coiled in their guts. They glanced at each other, at The Fatman's grave face, at the window's bloody sill, and then toward the night-shrouded forest where something monstrous lurked.

They gathered lanterns, staffs, herbs, and iron tokens, preparing to step beyond their safe perimeter into mystery and danger. The Fatman whispered, "Be strong," voice taut. The villagers nodded, each praying silently that their code and courage would suffice. Because now, they stood at the threshold of a darkness not born of petty greed or human cruelty, but something deeper, older, and hungry—something that might test their moral core like never before.

CHAPTER SIXTEEN

A hush gripped Sleetwood, not the comfortable hush of recent months, but a taut silence brimming with tension and dread. Inside the meeting hall, lanterns sputtered anxiously, their flames flickering over grim faces. The Fatman stood near the door, arms folded, eyes weighted with sorrow and concern. The villagers clustered around the bloodstained windowsill where Teryn had been taken only moments ago. Beyond that open window lay a moonless dark, a forest that had always harbored mysteries, now home to something far crueler than any cunning merchant or desperate raider.

Marta knelt beside the sill, fingers hovering over the smear of blood. It had not yet dried. Whatever seized Teryn acted swiftly and silently. Helgrid stood behind Marta, hammer in hand, her knuckles white. Jarlan gripped his ledger, though no ink touched its pages now. He stared out the window into starless gloom. Branwynn's heart pounded as she considered what manner of entity could snatch a person without being seen. After all their struggles—monstrous entities, cunning thieves, even attempts by raiders to test their code—this felt different. The raiders had been held at bay by fear and cunning illusions, but what if something less human cared nothing for moral warnings?

Edric and Takrin rushed in, having circled the building. They found no footprints in the mud, no sign of how Teryn's abductor approached or departed. Branwynn shook her head. "No tracks? That's… impossible. Something unnatural is at play." The Fatman stepped forward, placing a gentle hand on Branwynn's shoulder. She looked to him, seeking reassurance, but his eyes conveyed only grim resolve. They must act, not cower.

Marta stood, spine straightening. "We must go after Teryn. She sought refuge with us. We vowed to help the innocent. We cannot fail her now." There was no dissent. The villagers would not abandon their code because fear stalked their doorstep. They had learned too well: goodness and vigilance must prevail.

Helgrid nodded firmly. "We form search parties. Quiet and careful. Some remain behind to guard the village, others follow the faint clues we have. We'll carry lanterns, staffs, and herb smokes. If we face a foe not swayed by moral law, we must still defend ourselves." Her voice did not tremble. She remembered raiders and cunning merchants. Now was a different test: confronting what might be a genuine monster.

Jarlan took a trembling breath, "We must keep The Fatman and Krampus in our hearts. Our code must guide our actions. Even if we face something inhuman, we should not resort to cruelty without purpose. Protecting Teryn is paramount, but let's remember who we are."

Branwynn nodded, pouch of herbs rattling at her hip. She might concoct a powder to reveal hidden tracks or slow whatever took Teryn. Every skill was precious now. The Fatman inclined his head in approval as they organized into three search parties. One would stay to protect the children and elders, led by Marta, ensuring no second abduction occurred. Another, led by Helgrid and Jarlan, would circle the village perimeter. The main search party, including Branwynn, Edric, and Takrin, would follow any faint sign of disturbed foliage or scent on the wind, heading into the forest's deeper shadows.

The villagers readied quickly. They took iron tokens, not for commerce or show, but as moral anchors. The Fatman stood at the threshold as they filed out into the night. He whispered softly, "Be brave and true," and they carried his words like a lantern in their minds. Krampus remained unseen, but the hush of chains rattled faintly in their memory. If terror forced their hand, perhaps he would appear.

Outside, the world was ink-black, no moon, stars veiled by drifting clouds. The forest loomed as a wall of silhouettes and rustling leaves. Branwynn led Edric and Takrin toward the western edge of the village, where the intruders before had left faint signs. Maybe whoever took Teryn escaped in that direction. They moved slowly, lanterns hooded to avoid drawing too much attention, staffs in hand. Edric carried a short spear. Takrin a sturdy bow with a few arrows. None wished to kill lightly, but if forced, they would defend innocent life.

Leaves whispered underfoot as they ventured deeper. Branwynn sprinkled a pinch of crushed herbs every few steps—an old witch's trick said to sharpen senses. She closed her eyes occasionally, listening for breathing that wasn't theirs, sniffing for unnatural scents. Silence pressed down, broken only by distant owl calls. After a time, Takrin halted, pointing to a low bush. A thread of torn cloth, green and frayed, clung there. Teryn wore green when they found her. Branwynn's heart clenched. They were on the right track.

They followed a faint trail of snapped twigs and disturbed moss. Every so often, they found tiny hints—a drop of blood on a leaf, a shoeprint too large for Teryn's slender foot. Something dragged her, or carried her with ease. No grunt or growl announced its presence. It moved like a phantom. Edric shuddered at the thought of facing such a foe. He remembered their code: no matter what they confronted, they must retain their humanity. But how to reason with a creature that stole silently in the night?

Meanwhile, Helgrid and Jarlan's group patrolled the perimeter, ensuring no second creature infiltrated. They found nothing, but tension mounted. In the meeting hall, Marta comforted frightened children, telling them that their parents fought to save a life and protect their home. The Fatman passed by windows, leaving small tokens of encouragement—a sprig of lavender, a carved wooden flower—to calm restless hearts. Krampus's presence weighed heavily, invisible yet potent, reminding them that if moral compromise or terror overtook them, he would act.

Back in the forest, Branwynn's party pressed on. The ground sloped downward toward a hollow choked with old pines. The air turned colder. Branwynn's herbs picked up a strange scent—earthy, damp, tinged with something sour. She raised a hand, halting Edric and Takrin. They crouched, peering ahead. The lanterns revealed a slight clearing, where moonlight leaked through thinning clouds, illuminating a bizarre sight: a rough stone formation like a crude altar, moss-covered and ancient. On it lay something wrapped in tattered cloth—could it be Teryn?

Edric's pulse hammered. The shape was still. Takrin strained his ears, hearing no breathing, no movement. Was she alive? Why bring her here? Branwynn motioned them to move cautiously, no sudden noise. They crept closer, staffs and weapons ready.

As they neared the altar, Edric saw Teryn's form—her chest rose and fell faintly, she was alive but unconscious or restrained. A rope of twisted vine bound her wrists. Blood marked her forehead. Takrin suppressed a curse. Branwynn's heart twisted with sympathy and horror. What manner of being did this?

Suddenly, a dry rasping sound slid through the darkness—like bark scraping on bark, or claws on stone. The villagers froze, scanning shadows. Something moved behind the trunk of an ancient pine: tall, emaciated, skin pale as fungus, limbs too long. Edric's stomach churned. The creature stepped into the clearing's edge, half-lit by moonlight. It had hollow eyes, no lips, and teeth too sharp, arranged in a grim rictus.

They understood now: no human foe. A creature of old forests, perhaps awakened by changes in their valley or drawn by the aura of moral strength here. Maybe it fed on fear or blood. It hissed softly. Branwynn stifled a gasp. How do they respond?

With careful courage, Branwynn raised her staff, speaking in a low, steady voice: "We mean no harm. Release Teryn. This is our guest, under our protection. We don't want violence." Could this thing understand speech? She hoped so.

The creature's head tilted unnaturally, bones crackling. It emitted a low growl. Edric gripped his spear. Takrin drew an arrow, heart pounding. They prayed no killing blow would be needed. The Fatman's kindness and Krampus's caution urged them to try reasoning again.

Branwynn tried once more: "You gain nothing from harming her. We ask you to let her go. Our code forbids cruelty. You won't find easy prey here."

The creature hissed louder, stepping fully into view. It stood over seven feet tall, limbs crooked, nails long and black. A faint stench of rot and wet earth wafted from it. Takrin whispered, "This is no reasoning foe." Edric swallowed hard.

At that moment, Teryn stirred on the altar, moaning softly. The creature whipped its head toward her, hunger or malice gleaming in those hollow eyes. Branwynn had no choice. She must act. She tossed a pinch of her herb powder into the lantern flame, producing a sudden flare of bright, pungent smoke. The creature reeled, hissing and snarling, batting at the air as the flash disrupted its senses.

"Now!" Branwynn hissed. Edric and Takrin rushed forward, Edric lunging to cut the vines binding Teryn, Takrin positioning himself between the creature and their wounded friend. Branwynn circled wide, staff raised, ready to strike if needed.

The creature recovered quickly, snarling and lunging at Takrin. He raised his bow uselessly as a shield, arrow falling from his fingers. The beast's nails scraped wood, snapping the bow, forcing Takrin to stumble back. Edric tugged at the vines, finally freeing Teryn's wrists, blood pounding in his ears. Teryn's eyes fluttered, confusion and terror dawning. Branwynn swung her staff at the creature's flank, landing a blow that barely budged it. It turned its hollow gaze on her, hissing again.

Though frightened, Branwynn stood firm. She remembered their code: do not become cruel. But how to fight a monster that understands no reason? The Fatman had taught kindness, Krampus had taught the price of wrongdoing. This creature broke all rules. If forced, they must defend Teryn. Edric hoisted Teryn over his shoulder—she was weak and dazed. Takrin found a spare arrow in the grass, holding it like a dagger.

The beast lunged at Branwynn, claws aimed for her face. She ducked, staff parrying with a hollow thump. Sparks from the lantern flicked across their vision. Takrin tried to stab the creature's flank with his makeshift blade. The arrow's tip scratched its hide, drawing a thin line of blackish ichor. The beast shrieked, not in pain but rage. It swiped at Takrin, knocking him to the ground.

Edric retreated with Teryn, calling to Branwynn, "We must pull back! We can't kill it easily. Let's retreat and regroup!" Branwynn nodded grimly. This wasn't about destroying evil now, but saving a life and escaping a superior foe.

Takrin scrambled to his feet, blood on his lip. Helpless anger churned inside him—he wanted to protect Teryn, but what if their code demanded restraint? They must not descend into savagery. He backed away slowly, joining Edric and Teryn. Branwynn tossed another herb pouch into the lantern flame, causing a second flare of bright light and acrid smoke. The creature snarled, recoiling from the sudden brilliance.

Seizing this chance, the villagers retreated into the forest, carrying Teryn between them. They moved as quietly as possible, lanterns half-shuttered. The creature roared behind them, enraged. Twigs snapped under its pursuit. They had gained only a few moments' lead. They must outrun it or find another tactic.

Edric whispered through clenched teeth, "We can't outrun it forever. We must slow it down. Maybe lure it into a trap near the village." Takrin nodded, panting. Teryn moaned softly, barely conscious, whispering, "Don't leave me…" Branwynn patted her arm gently, "We won't."

They angled toward Sleetwood, weaving between trees, hoping to draw the beast closer to the perimeter where hidden alarm lines and chain rattles waited. If the creature hesitated at illusions before, maybe it would do so again. But this felt like something older and more vicious than the raiders. Would illusions of Krampus sway it?

Branches whipped their faces as they stumbled downhill. The beast pursued, growling louder now, crashing through undergrowth. Edric realized it moved more clumsily at speed, its lanky limbs less graceful. Maybe they could exploit this. He whispered a plan: when they neared a certain thicket, they'd turn suddenly and rattle chains, hoping to confuse it again. Branwynn agreed, gripping her staff tighter.

Behind them, the creature's snarls intensified. It gained ground. They smelled its foul breath. Takrin cursed under his breath. No time for careful illusions. They must try anything. As they reached the thicket, Branwynn pulled a chain hidden in the brush—placed earlier for raider deterrence—and a clank of iron echoed through the dark. The beast paused, hissing, uncertain. The villagers seized that second to slip behind a tree and pick another route.

But the creature wasn't fooled for long. It resumed chase, now more enraged by their tricks. Its snarls formed guttural half-sounds, as if trying to mimic speech. Could it learn? The thought chilled Branwynn. She prayed The Fatman watched and that Krampus would intervene if truly dire.

Back at the village edge, Helgrid and Jarlan's patrol saw distant lantern flickers and heard faint echoes of snarling. They prepared quickly —lighting more lanterns, arranging a line of villagers armed with staffs, chain rattles, and herb smokes. Marta, guarding the children, whispered calming words, though fear coursed through her veins. The Fatman stood by a fence, silent and tense, as if waiting for the right moment to show himself or call upon Krampus's wrath. But would that deny the villagers their growth?

Edric, Takrin, Branwynn, and Teryn stumbled into a small clearing not far from Sleetwood's boundary. Lantern light from the village glimmered faintly ahead. So close! If they reached home turf, they'd have reinforcements. Teryn moaned again, trying to stand on her own. She managed a few shaky steps. Edric supported her, relieved that she was regaining awareness.

The beast crashed into the clearing behind them, eyes gleaming with malice. Now it saw them clearly in faint light: four humans—three armed and determined, one wounded but defiant. It hissed, a sound like splintering bone. No words, no mercy, just hunger or cruelty.

Takrin met its gaze. He saw no hint of empathy, no space for negotiation. This wasn't like Lorad or Lirina, whose greed they could rebuff with moral strength. This creature respected no moral code, felt no fear of legends. Or did it? If Krampus appeared fully, would that terrify it? Or would they have to fight tooth and nail?

Branwynn spread her feet, raising her staff. "We are close to home. Don't falter," she urged them. Edric nodded, adjusting his grip on Teryn. Takrin hefted his broken bow's remains like a club. The creature circled them slowly, testing angles of attack. Without a word, it lunged at Branwynn, trying to knock her aside. She managed a half-block, staff connecting with its forearm, but the impact rattled her bones. It was strong, too strong to hold back forever.

Edric, desperate, shouted at the darkness: "We stand by our code! We harm no innocent, yield no ground to cruelty!" Maybe calling out their moral stance would summon Krampus's full fury or The Fatman's miracle. But silence answered.

The creature struck again, claws swiping at Takrin's shoulder, ripping fabric and drawing blood. Takrin bit back a scream. Pain flared, but he refused to yield. He jabbed at the creature's leg with the arrow-shiv, scoring another shallow wound. Black ichor oozed, the beast shrieking in anger. Now they knew it could bleed. Could they drive it away?

Teryn, though weak, refused to remain a helpless burden. She grabbed a fallen branch, swinging it wildly. "You won't take me again!" she cried, voice shaking. Her blow glanced off the creature's side, no real damage, but courage shown through. They fought as a team, each defending the other.

The beast howled, stepping back, stunned by their resistance. It expected easy prey—like Teryn alone. Now it faced four determined humans who, though frightened, would not fold. Yet it did not retreat. If anything, it seemed furious, compelled to break their spirit. Branwynn realized they must lure it closer to the village where illusions and traps waited.

"Fall back!" she shouted. "Toward the village!" They moved slowly, circling around the beast, trying to keep it at bay with staffs and feints. The creature lunged again at Takrin, perhaps seeing him as wounded. Takrin ducked, wincing at his bleeding shoulder. Edric swung a lantern, flaring light in the beast's eyes. Another hiss, another moment's hesitation.

They inched toward Sleetwood's boundary. The night crackled with tension. The Fatman, watching from a hidden spot near a fence, readied himself to rally the villagers if needed. Helgrid and Jarlan's patrol waited behind a grove, lanterns dark to remain hidden. The plan: once the beast came into range, they'd set off more chain rattles, flash powders, and if desperate, call Krampus aloud. But calling Krampus aloud risked horrifying escalation. Could they handle this without summoning that final terror?

The beast seemed suspicious as they retreated, as if it sensed a trap. It snarled, pacing sideways. Teryn coughed, struggling to remain upright. Time was running out; they couldn't stall forever. Branwynn reached into her herb pouch for her strongest mixture, a pungent powder that might burn its eyes if thrown directly. She'd prefer not to blind a living creature, but better that than let it slaughter them.

Just as they neared a thicket that concealed Helgrid's group, the beast lunged unexpectedly with terrifying speed. It ignored Branwynn's staff, swept aside Edric's lantern, and seized Takrin by the throat, lifting him off the ground. Takrin choked, dropping his arrow-shiv. Teryn screamed, and Edric swung desperately at the beast's arm, but it wouldn't let go. Branwynn flung her powder at its face. The beast recoiled, hissing, loosening grip just enough for Takrin to gasp a breath.

But the creature didn't drop him. Instead, enraged, it tightened its other hand into a claw-fist, preparing to strike Takrin's head. One lethal blow and Takrin might die. Horror seized Branwynn and Edric. Teryn sobbed, powerless. They had no time. If this thing was immune to fear and legend, what then?

A sudden flash of lantern light from behind the thicket—Helgrid and Jarlan's group emerged, rattling chains and shouting, trying to startle the creature. The beast froze, blinking at the sudden human chorus. That split second might be all Takrin had.

Helgrid's hammer whistled through the air. She didn't aim to kill, just break its hold. The hammer struck the creature's forearm with a dull crack. It howled in genuine pain this time, dropping Takrin to the ground. Takrin collapsed, wheezing. Jarlan and two others thrust staffs forward, herding the beast away from Takrin. Marta, from the perimeter, threw a small smoke bomb that hissed acrid fumes, obscuring vision.

The creature, surrounded now by more villagers than expected, screeched and lashed out blindly. Edric pulled Teryn back, shielding her. Branwynn and Helgrid coordinated moves—Helgrid feinted with her hammer from one side, Branwynn jabbed from another. The beast recoiled, uncertain. Its advantage of stealth and surprise was gone. It faced a cohesive group, their moral strength turned into strategic unity.

Yet as they pressed it back, a dilemma arose: could they let it retreat? Or must they ensure it never returns? Killing it felt wrong, a violation of their code that valued life, even monstrous life. But sparing it might let it abduct more innocents later. The Fatman, hidden in shadows, clenched his jaw, understanding their moral agony.

The beast, cornered by chain rattles and stern faces, hissed again and leapt upward, grabbing a low branch and pulling itself into the canopy. Villagers gasped—did it flee by climbing trees? They saw its glowing eyes peering down, waiting. They backed away, unsure how to fight a creature overhead in darkness.

Krampus's chains rattled faintly in their minds, a reminder that darkness would not yield easily. If the beast escaped, it might return smarter and angrier. Yet how do they stop it without murdering out of fear?

As they hesitated, the creature suddenly leapt to another tree, moving between branches with alarming agility. Helgrid cursed under her breath. Jarlan held his staff, knuckles white. Branwynn tried to track it with her lantern, but leaves and shadows swallowed its form. Edric guarded Teryn, who whispered, "Don't let it escape…it will hurt others."

That plea stung. Their code demanded protecting innocents, not letting evil roam free. But slaying a creature that might be part of nature's grim tapestry? They had never faced such a choice. The Fatman stepped out into partial view, face etched with sadness. If they killed to save future victims, was it justified? Krampus's presence implied wrongdoing must be punished, but was this beast's malice equal to human evil or just predatory instinct?

The villagers formed a circle beneath the trees, lanterns raised, staffs ready. Takrin recovered enough to stand, holding his bleeding shoulder. They waited, tension thick as tar. Silence prevailed—no sign of the beast. Did it flee entirely, or was it circling for another strike?

Then, a distant scream echoed from the village's eastern side. Another scream—this time, a child's voice. The villagers stiffened. Had the beast somehow doubled back, using cunning tactics to separate them? Fear and fury surged. They must defend everyone, but they were split between two threats now: one overhead and one far off.

Helgrid snarled, "We must not divide aimlessly. Half go check the village, half remain here." Edric hesitated, torn between Teryn's safety and the distant cry. Marta's group was still guarding children, right? Unless something else emerged. Could the beast be a lure for a second, unseen threat?

As they debated, the creature lunged again from above, claws raking down at Branwynn. She dodged barely, crying out as a nail grazed her arm. Villagers thrust staffs upward, hitting empty air. The beast retreated into darkness again, taunting them. The distant scream sounded again, more desperate now.

Panic welled. If they chased the beast here, children might die elsewhere. If they ran back, the beast might snatch Teryn once more. The Fatman stepped forward, mouth opening as if to advise—but he stopped himself, letting them choose. This was their moral crucible.

Jarlan's voice shook: "We must trust Marta's group can handle the village. Let's finish this here. If we drive the beast away for good or wound it enough, it might never return." He hated suggesting harm, but time pressed them cruelly.

Branwynn, arm bleeding slightly, nodded grimly. "We try to corner it against a tree trunk. Use chains to tangle its limbs. We need not kill if we can capture or scare it off definitively." Tears of frustration pricked her eyes. She never wanted to become a monster slayer. But innocence demanded action.

They formed a tighter ring, rattling chains, tossing herb powders. The creature shrieked, moving frantically between branches. Lantern light caught it momentarily—it looked panicked now, not just hungry. Perhaps it sensed that these humans were more formidable than expected, that Krampus's silent threat lay heavy in the night air. Yet it didn't flee far, as if compelled by hunger or dark instinct to stand its ground.

Edric and Takrin positioned themselves under a thick branch. If the creature landed there, they could yank a rope line to drop a curtain of rattling chains and herb smokes. Helgrid prepared to strike with measured force. Branwynn readied her last and strongest herb mix, a pungent powder that could blind even sturdy eyes.

Moments stretched into an eternity of tense waiting. Footsteps in the distance hinted that Marta's group might be handling another crisis back home. The Fatman hovered near the treeline, silent and torn, wishing he could guide them more openly but knowing they must claim moral agency. Krampus remained unseen, though the rustle of leaves and the faint chime of distant chains suggested he watched closely, judging every choice.

The creature hissed again, circling overhead. Then, in a sudden burst of fury, it dropped from the canopy, aiming to land among them and scatter their formation. The villagers gasped, raising staffs. The Fatman clenched his fists. Edric shouted, "Now!" Takrin pulled the rope line. A clamor of chains and smoke erupted beneath the beast's intended landing zone. Confused, it twisted midair, arms flailing.

Helgrid swung her hammer at the beast's descending form, aiming to strike a forelimb, not the head—hoping pain might drive it off without dealing a fatal blow. The hammer connected with a dull crunch. The creature shrieked hideously, black ichor splattering. Branwynn hurled her strongest powder, lantern light catching a puff of greenish smoke that enveloped the beast's face. It howled louder, thrashing blindly.

Takrin, gritting his teeth through pain, jabbed his improvised blade into a leg muscle. Not a killing strike, but enough to weaken it. Edric guarded Teryn at a safe distance, praying this assault would make the beast flee forever. The villagers pressed their advantage, jabbing staffs, rattling chains, chanting their moral code under their breath as if to ward off inner corruption.

The beast, wounded and blinded, lashed out wildly. One claw caught Helgrid's shoulder, drawing blood. She bit back a scream, refusing to yield. Branwynn smacked its head with her staff's end. The creature stumbled back, spitting ichor and hissed curses that sounded almost like words now—mocking, guttural attempts at speech. Could it learn their tongue? They shuddered at the thought.

It staggered, trying to retreat. Edric stepped forward, raising his voice: "Leave! Do not return!" His tone carried all the anger, fear, and moral conviction of their community. The Fatman's presence warmed the edge of the clearing, as if approving of their stance. Krampus's silent weight pressed down—evil would not triumph here.

The beast snarled, then turned, hobbling into the darkness. They heard it crashing through underbrush, leaving a trail of black droplets. They did not chase it. They wanted it gone, not cornered. Panting, wounded, they stood victorious yet shaken. No kill was made, but they inflicted pain. Was that acceptable? They defended life—Teryn's life—and drove away a threat. The Fatman sighed softly, relieved no villager died and no moral collapse occurred. Krampus, unseen, likely acknowledged their resolve. They had harmed a creature to protect an innocent. Morally complex, but necessary.

As they rushed to tend Teryn's wounds and calm Takrin's bleeding shoulder, distant screams from the village's east echoed again, louder and more frantic. Their hearts plummeted. They had succeeded here, but what now threatened the village? Another beast? Or had the raiders circled around after all, taking advantage of their distraction?

Helgrid wiped blood from her brow. "We must hurry back." Branwynn nodded, tears in her eyes—no rest for the righteous. Teryn clung to Edric, whispering apologies. She never wanted them to be in danger because of her. They hushed her gently. Saving the innocent was worth any risk.

They moved as swiftly as possible, supporting each other through pain and exhaustion. Every step crackled with tension. The Fatman followed at a distance, silent and grave. Would they return to find the village in flames? Or discover a new horror unleashed?

As they broke into a run, nearing the familiar scents of home, the screams rose again. Helgrid gripped her hammer despite pain, Jarlan stiffened his spine, Branwynn mustered her last herb pouch. Takrin, pale-faced, muttered a prayer. Edric steadied Teryn, eyes scanning for any sign of hope. The Fatman fell behind slightly, letting them confront what awaited. Krampus, too, remained hidden, a final card not yet played.

They emerged from the forest's edge onto the village perimeter, lanterns blazing. What they saw made their blood run cold—

CHAPTER SEVENTEEN

They emerged from the dense curtain of trees and stumbled into a scene of chaos on Sleetwood's eastern edge. The small clearing that once opened calmly onto the village's farmland was now awash in flickering light and terrified cries. Smoke curled above a thatched cottage, sparks dancing in the air, while villagers darted about in frantic attempts to contain the threat. Someone shouted for water. Another wept, calling a child's name. The acrid scent of burning straw assaulted their nostrils.

Helgrid, Jarlan, Branwynn, Edric, Takrin, and Teryn froze, hearts lurching. After all they had endured—rescuing Teryn from a monstrous forest creature and fleeing a deadly chase—they returned to find their haven beleaguered anew. The Fatman caught up behind them, chest heaving with worry. They had spent precious time fighting in the forest; what had happened here?

Marta rushed toward them, face streaked with soot and tears. She clutched a staff in one hand, her knuckles bone-white. "They came while we were focused on you," she gasped. "The raiders circled east, using the forest's darkness. They set fire to old Mori's cottage and tried to snatch children!"

Jarlan's blood ran cold. The raiders—Gorven's gang, presumably—had exploited their distraction with the beast. Now cruelty visited their doorstep. Edric eased Teryn to lean against Branwynn, who steadied the injured woman. Helgrid stepped forward, jaw clenched, fear and fury mingling in her eyes. "Is anyone taken? Are the children safe?"

Marta shook her head, voice quavering. "They threatened a few children, demanded we give supplies. When we refused, they torched the cottage. We managed to whisk the children away, but some villagers are wounded. The raiders vanished into the fields. We can't be sure they're gone for good."

The Fatman's sorrowful gaze drifted to the smoke. Sleetwood's code was tested again, this time by raw violence at their doorstep. Krampus remained unseen, but the tension thrummed with his silent warning. They had to face this threat directly. The beast in the forest had been instinctual, animalistic. These raiders were human, willful, malicious. Negotiations failed before. Would words suffice now?

Branwynn touched Teryn's shoulder gently. "We saved you, but at great risk. Now the raiders attack the village itself. We must act swiftly." Teryn nodded weakly, tears glazing her eyes. She understood the cost of her rescue—and that these raiders would not relent easily.

Helgrid barked out orders: "Form lines with staffs and chains. Alert everyone to keep children hidden, elders protected. We must not scatter. If the raiders test us again, we meet them as one. No cowardice, no cruelty—just resolve."

Marta helped direct villagers to form a defensive perimeter around the central lanes. Jarlan knelt to assist a wounded man—he had a shallow cut from a raider's blade. Edric and Takrin, though injured from the forest battle, stood guard grimly, refusing to rest. Teryn, still shaky, offered to help by carrying water to douse lingering embers in the cottage's remains. They thanked her, moved by her courage despite her ordeal.

The Fatman watched all this with heavy eyes. He saw no panic, no hysteria—only sadness and determination. They had learned so well. Yet how many tests must they pass? If only words could deter Gorven and his men. But these raiders seemed bent on proving that brute force outmatched moral principle.

Night pressed on. Lanterns and torches ringed the village center. Whispers spread among the villagers: Did the raiders truly leave? Or were they hiding in the fields, waiting to strike again when exhaustion took its toll?

Helgrid, wiping sweat from her brow, said quietly to Branwynn: "I think we must confront them. Letting them pick their moments gives them power. If we could track them and show them we won't be terrorized...but that risks open battle."

Branwynn's heart clenched. Sleetwood avoided murder or cruelty, always seeking a better path. But now, children were threatened and homes burned. Could they afford not to push back? The code demanded preserving innocence and justice. If these raiders wanted to break their morale, then standing idle invited further harm.

Jarlan listened, torn. "We must try one more time to talk. If we meet them in the fields at dawn, propose a truce or a parley. If they refuse and press violence, we have no choice but to defend ourselves with all we have."

Marta approached, overhearing. She nodded. "Yes, we should give them one last chance to leave in peace. If they attack again, we respond decisively but without cruelty. We can wound or disarm, not slaughter. This will be the hardest test of our code yet."

The Fatman stepped closer, voice low: "Your courage humbles me. Remember, balance: do not become what you despise. Use force only as needed. If you must harm, harm minimally. Keep The Fatman's mercy in your hearts and Krampus's sternness in your mind, neither overshadowing the other."

They agreed. At first light, a small party would attempt to find Gorven's men in the fields and demand they depart. If refused, they'd show no weakness. Branwynn prepared more herb smokes, not lethal but disorienting. Helgrid sharpened a few staves' ends. Edric and Takrin secured hidden rattles and chains at strategic points. Marta organized a system of signals so if raiders attacked from another angle, the villagers could regroup swiftly.

Throughout the remainder of the night, villagers took turns resting, though few truly slept. Wounds were dressed. Teryn dozed fitfully in the meeting hall, guarded by a kindly older woman who hummed lullabies. Children huddled quietly, frightened but trusting their parents. The Fatman passed among them, leaving small carved tokens: animals, flowers, tiny human figures. Gifts of comfort. Krampus's shadow weighed heavy but did not materialize. Perhaps Krampus waited for the crucial moment, letting humans face their destiny first.

Before dawn, Branwynn, Helgrid, Jarlan, Edric, and Takrin gathered again. They would form the negotiation party. Marta would remain behind with a strong defensive group, ensuring the village stayed safe. The Fatman watched them depart from the chapel ruins as they moved east, lanterns hooded low, staffs and chains at their belts, hearts pounding.

They chose the eastern fields—tussocked grass and patches of wildflowers not yet fully bloomed. The sky lightened to a bruise-purple hue. Birds muttered half-hearted morning calls. There, on a gentle rise, they spotted shapes moving—silhouettes against the slowly brightening horizon. Armed figures, no doubt Gorven's men.

Helgrid raised a staff high, calling out: "Gorven! We know you lurk here. Hear us. We come to speak plainly. Enough cowardly raids and cruelty. Face us openly."

A tense silence followed. Then a rough laugh drifted over the dew-kissed grass. Gorven and about seven raiders emerged from behind a thicket, weapons visible but not raised. They approached at a measured pace. The villagers stood firm, their resolve chiseling fear into a steely edge.

Gorven smirked. "You call this facing openly? A handful of you with sticks and chains against armed men? Brave, but foolish."

Jarlan stepped forward, ledger tucked away. "You tested us, threatened children, burned a home. We do not yield to violence. We offer you a final chance: leave now, unharmed. We want no bloodshed. But we will defend ourselves and our people."

A raider to Gorven's left spat. "We see no demons or horns. Your fabled punisher was a trick. The fire we set proves you cannot stop us." But another raider looked uneasy, recalling rumors of nightmares and the strange incidents in the forest.

Helgrid's hammer hung at her side. "We saved one of your former captives," she said, voice cold. "Her name is Teryn. We do not betray the innocent. If you think we are weak, think again."

Gorven's grin faded slightly at the mention of Teryn's rescue. He hid it with a sneer. "Rescue all you like, but now your supplies are ours for the taking. Your code is weakness. We demand you hand over half your stores and a few of your precious tokens. We'll sell them as curiosities. Refuse, and we burn more cottages—maybe worse."

Edric clenched his jaw. Takrin winced at his shoulder wound. Branwynn's pulse thundered. They had tried reason. Gorven's gang responded with naked greed and cruelty. Could words move them further? Likely not.

The Fatman watched from a safe distance, sorrowful. Krampus hovered in their minds—a last resort. The villagers shared a glance. They must show no weakness. Helgrid took a deep breath, "We refuse. No supplies, no tokens. You leave with nothing, or we fight. Your choice."

Gorven's lip curled. "Fight it is, then. We'll see how your code fares against steel." He lifted his sword, signaling his men. They spread out, forming a half-circle around the villagers. Seven armed raiders against five villagers—though skilled and morally sure, the villagers lacked lethal weaponry. Fear coursed through their veins.

Branwynn whispered to the others, "Remember: we use herb smokes, chain rattles, and careful strikes. No wanton killing." They nodded, bracing for the charge.

A moment's hush preceded the clash. In that hush, The Fatman's eyes glistened with tears. He could step in somehow, show a miracle, but that might undermine their independence. Krampus might erupt in terrifying violence. Would that scar the village's moral growth or save them from certain doom?

Gorven roared, swinging his blade. The raiders advanced, steel gleaming in the pale dawn. Helgrid raised her hammer, deflecting a sword aimed at Jarlan's chest. Sparks flew. Jarlan struck with his staff, knocking a raider's arm aside. Branwynn flung a powder pouch at two men, causing them to cough and stagger. Edric rattled chains and thrust a sharpened staff end toward a raider's leg, hoping to wound nonlethally. Takrin fought bravely despite pain, blocking a swing with a chain-wrapped staff.

The clash was fierce but not chaotic. The villagers fought with discipline, aiming to disable rather than kill. One raider lunged at Branwynn; she sidestepped and smacked his knee, sending him crumpling with a groan. Another raider slashed at Jarlan, nicking his forearm. Jarlan hissed, stepping back, maintaining composure. He must not let anger turn him cruel.

Gorven targeted Helgrid, seeing her hammer as a threat. He swung low, forcing her to jump back. She countered with a strike to his sword arm, barely missing his elbow as he parried. Sparks showered again. Gorven's grin had vanished, replaced by grim determination. He couldn't believe these villagers fought so well without descending into savagery. Their code truly guided them.

A raider tried to circle behind Edric and Takrin, aiming to backstab them. Teryn, watching from a slight distance—still weak but determined—picked up a fallen staff and whacked the raider's back. He yelped, turning, allowing Takrin a chance to disarm him with a swift strike to the wrist. The raider dropped his weapon, eyes wide at the wounded woman's courage.

The Fatman observed, heart pounding. They were holding their own, but the raiders still held lethal blades and more experience in raw combat. If the fight dragged on, someone might die. Could they afford to wait for Krampus's intervention, or must they summon him by name?

A raider feinted at Branwynn, drawing her attention, while another tried to strike her from the side. Branwynn caught the movement and dropped low, staff sweeping the raider's legs. He fell hard. But a third raider came at her from behind, sword raised high. She twisted desperately but wouldn't block in time.

In that split second, a chain rattled overhead—Krampus's ghostly presence? The raider hesitated, startled by the eerie sound. Edric took advantage, thrusting his staff tip at the raider's knee, buckling it and sending him down. The villagers thanked fate or legend silently. Perhaps Krampus aided from the shadows without fully materializing.

Helgrid and Gorven's duel intensified. Hammer and sword clashed repeatedly. Helgrid aimed to injure his sword arm or leg, not kill him, but Gorven fought viciously. He wanted blood. He lunged close, blade scraping Helgrid's ribs, drawing a sharp cry. She staggered, pain blooming hot. He sneered, "Your code won't save you now."

But Helgrid's eyes burned with conviction. She swung her hammer with controlled force, smashing into Gorven's off-hand, breaking a finger. He howled, reeling back. Helgrid seized the moment to reposition, staff rattles from Jarlan adding a confusing jangle. Gorven hissed, wounded pride fueling his rage. He eyed The Fatman lurking nearby—who was that figure? Another trick?

Takrin, bleeding from his shoulder and panting, managed to disarm another raider by looping a chain around the man's wrist and twisting. The raider cried out, dropping his sword. Edric kicked the sword away. With three raiders down, disarmed, or incapacitated by herbs and nonlethal strikes, only Gorven and two more stood armed and ready. But these three remained dangerous.

The Fatman saw a chance: the raiders were losing advantage. If they realized they could not win easily, they might retreat. The Fatman stepped into a slant of light, letting raiders see his calm, almost supernatural poise. He said nothing, but his kind gaze and fearless posture might unsettle them, hinting at greater powers not yet unleashed.

One raider faltered at The Fatman's silent presence. "Who is he?" he rasped. Another tried to ignore it, pressing forward at Branwynn again. Branwynn blocked, sweat stinging her eyes, pushing her herb-laced staff forward. The raider choked on the fumes and stumbled back, coughing violently.

Now only Gorven and one loyal raider remained fully armed and functional. The rest lay wounded, disarmed, or coughing up herbs. Gorven's eyes narrowed to slits. He could see he was outmatched by these villagers' unity and cunning. Yet pride and hatred burned in him. He wouldn't yield meekly. He snarled, "So you can fight. But can you kill? If I threaten one of your children again, will you slit my throat or let me do as I please?"

His words stabbed at their moral dilemma. Killing him would end his threat forever, but at what cost to their code? Branwynn's heart pounded. Helgrid, injured, raised her hammer shakily. Jarlan, arm bleeding, met Gorven's gaze, voice steady: "We need not become murderers to stop you. We've proven we can wound and disarm. If you persist, you will suffer more pain. Leave now, and never return."

Gorven barked a bitter laugh. "Pain is temporary. Fear rules forever. If I leave now, I leave empty-handed. No spoils, no victory. You think I'll crawl away like a whipped dog?" He spat blood, eyes flicking between Helgrid and Branwynn. His last loyal raider hovered behind him, blade trembling slightly—uncertain now. Maybe he'd had enough.

The Fatman stepped closer, arms spread, as if to embrace the tension. His silence spoke volumes: he offered mercy if they left. Krampus's silent threat lingered, rattling chains in their memories. Could Gorven's pride withstand this combination of moral fortitude and subtle supernatural menace?

Gorven's face twisted with indecision. He growled, "If I can't break your code, I'll at least scar it." He lunged unexpectedly, sword aimed straight at Teryn, who stood wounded and weaponless near Edric. Perhaps he reasoned that killing her would shake their morale. Edric, Takrin, and Branwynn reacted instantly, shouting warnings. Helgrid lunged forward, ignoring her rib pain. Jarlan hurled a lantern at Gorven's feet, hoping to distract him.

Gorven dodged the lantern, boots crunching glass. He swung, blade whistling toward Teryn's throat. Edric stepped between them, raising his staff to parry. A sickening clang rang out. The staff's tip split under the force, sending splinters flying. Edric stumbled, wrist jolted painfully.

Teryn screamed, trying to back away. Branwynn rushed in, thrusting her staff at Gorven's sword arm, hoping to deflect the fatal blow. She struck but not hard enough. The sword's angle shifted, still poised to slash Teryn's chest. Takrin roared in desperation, slamming a chain-laden staff into Gorven's side. Gorven grunted, losing perfect balance. The blade's deadly arc faltered, grazing Teryn's arm instead of piercing her heart. Blood welled from her arm, and she cried out, collapsing to her knees.

Rage lit Helgrid's eyes. This man would kill innocents without remorse. She reared back with her hammer. She knew killing him might stain her soul, but letting him slaughter Teryn would stain their code even more. Could she find a nonlethal strike? She aimed lower, at his leg. If she could shatter his kneecap, he'd be helpless. Painful but not fatal.

But Gorven sensed Helgrid's intent. He twisted, bringing his sword up to meet her hammer. Sparks flew. The raider behind Gorven, shaken by the villagers' stubborn resilience and these near misses, turned and fled, dropping his blade. Now Gorven stood alone. Surrounded, wounded in pride and body, he glared at them, hate etched in every line of his face.

Edric recovered, Takrin steadied Teryn, Branwynn positioned herself to block escape, and Jarlan circled wide, a staff raised. Helgrid breathed hard, rib burning, but hammer ready. The Fatman hovered at the clearing's edge, praying they would not have to kill. Krampus's silence pressed like a hand on their shoulders. They had the advantage—could they force Gorven to surrender without dealing a fatal blow?

Gorven spat blood, chuckling darkly. "You think you've won? I'll never kneel to your code. I'll find a way to break it, if not today, then another time. Let me go, and I'll return with more men. Kill me, and you stain those pretty morals."

A cruel ultimatum. If they released him, he promised future horror. If they killed him, they tainted their code. Branwynn's stomach twisted. The villagers exchanged anxious glances. Could they imprison him? But they had no jail, no chains strong enough to hold a determined criminal indefinitely. The orchard shed? Too flimsy. He'd escape eventually.

Jarlan's voice trembled: "We cannot kill without losing ourselves. We cannot free you without imperiling others. Is there no third path?" Despair tinged his words.

Gorven grinned with bloody teeth. "No third path. Morality means nothing if you can't enforce it with finality."

Helgrid clenched her hammer, tears gathering in her eyes. She stepped forward, heart heavy. She might have to cripple him severely, ensure he could never wield a sword again. A brutal act, but less final than killing. Could The Fatman or Krampus accept that? Would the villagers understand?

Teryn whimpered, clutching her wounded arm. The Fatman closed his eyes, as if silently urging them to hold fast. Krampus's presence grew heavier still. Branwynn sensed the tipping point—one wrong move and this would end in blood and regret.

Before anyone could move, a shrill whistle cut through the dawn air—someone from the village perimeter signaled. All heads turned. In that split instant of distraction, Gorven seized his chance. He feinted toward Branwynn, then pivoted and bolted into the undergrowth, a limping sprint. The villagers cursed, giving chase. They couldn't let him vanish again, free to plan new horrors.

They pursued him through tangled brush, lanterns bobbing wildly. The Fatman followed, desperate to see how this ended. Gorven hissed curses ahead, crashing through low branches. Edric, fastest despite injuries, gained on him. Helgrid pushed through pain, hammer raised. Branwynn readied another powder pouch. Takrin tried to flank him from the side. Teryn remained behind, safe with Jarlan now that Gorven fled.

As they burst into a small clearing beyond the orchard, Gorven turned, swinging wildly at Edric who was closest. Edric ducked, staff raised. Helgrid emerged at his flank, trying to strike Gorven's leg. Branwynn circled behind, hoping to corner him against a fallen log. The

Krampus

Fatman watched from the edge, powerless to intervene without shattering their autonomy. Krampus's silence roared in their minds.

Gorven panted, eyes darting. Surrounded again. But this time no raiders, no tricks. Just him and these indomitable villagers. He chose defiance. He raised his sword and charged Helgrid, aiming to force a gap and escape beyond. Helgrid swung her hammer horizontally. Metal met metal. Sparks and curses. Gorven's blade twisted in his grip, rattling his bones. He staggered.

Edric lunged low, thrusting his staff at Gorven's knee. Gorven hopped back, but Branwynn tossed her powder pouch, bursting bright dust into his face. He sputtered, half-blinded. Takrin swung a chain overhead, letting it clank menacingly. Gorven recoiled, blinking tears from his eyes, back pressed against a fallen log. No exit.

They had him. Panting, wounded, enraged, he glared. "Finish it," he snarled, daring them to kill him. They hesitated—was this a trap of their own morality?

Helgrid stepped forward, teeth gritted. She must make a choice. Crippling him might be the lesser evil. She raised her hammer, aiming for a disabling strike to his sword arm. Gorven watched her approach, chest heaving. The Fatman trembled inside, knowing once that blow fell, blood would flow and their code would gain a permanent scar, even if done in necessity.

A distant roar from behind made everyone freeze. The beast? The monstrous forest creature's roar echoed from the village direction. Had it recovered and come back to wreak havoc there, among the children and wounded? Fear spiked in the villagers' hearts. If they lingered here dealing with Gorven, that monstrosity might butcher innocents at home.

Gorven seized their moment of distraction again, throwing himself sideways, rolling over the log. Helgrid cursed, swinging too late, hammer hitting empty air. Edric and Takrin scrambled after him, but Gorven vanished into thick underbrush like a wounded wolf. Branwynn's heart sank. Their moral dilemma bought him time to escape.

Now two threats loomed simultaneously: Gorven lurking wounded and vengeful in the woods, and that monstrous creature possibly attacking the village. They must hurry back. But if they leave Gorven free, he might regroup. If they chase him, the beast might slaughter innocents.

Helgrid's decision was swift: "The village first! We must protect them. Gorven is wounded and alone. He's less immediate than that beast if it truly returned. Hurry!" They obeyed, rushing back toward the orchard and fields, hearts heavy with unfinished business.

As they neared the village outskirts, screams intensified. Lanterns bobbed in frantic patterns. Shadows danced wildly across cottage walls. The Fatman followed, dread knotting his stomach. Had the beast somehow circled around, or was it a new horror?

They rounded a bend and saw a nightmarish tableau: part of the village's east side lay in disarray. Tools scattered, a fence smashed. A group of villagers formed a desperate line facing the monstrous creature, which had indeed returned—or perhaps it never fully left, cunningly choosing a weaker point to strike. Marta and others held staffs and torches, trying to keep the beast from entering the central lane where children huddled in a safe house. Bloodstains marred the ground, suggesting some had already fallen wounded. The beast snarled, furious and confident now, despite its earlier injuries.

Branwynn's party sprinted forward, adrenaline surging anew. The creature noticed them, shifting its stance to face a two-front threat. The Fatman approached from the side, anguish in his eyes. He wanted to help, but how? Could he risk revealing powers or calling Krampus fully, robbing them of their moral independence?

Marta called out, "We must push it away from the children!" The villagers tried to herd it toward a corner of the village where reinforced barricades stood. The beast resisted, lunging at a young man, raking his shoulder. He screamed, collapsing. Another villager struck the creature's back with a torch, singing its pale skin. It shrieked in fury, lashing out blindly and knocking the torch aside.

Helgrid, Jarlan, Branwynn, Edric, and Takrin arrived, joining Marta's line. Teryn, still wounded, stayed behind at the orchard edge, sobbing in frustration, unable to help more. The Fatman hovered behind a broken fence, fists clenched.

Now they outnumbered the beast—at least a dozen villagers with staffs, hammers, chains, and powders. But it fought like a cornered demon, leaping from ground to a half-collapsed roof, then back, swiping at any who ventured close. Smoke from burning straw irritated its eyes, but also choked the defenders.

Branwynn readied her last special powder—stronger than before, laced with something that might sear the creature's senses more deeply. Helgrid and Edric coordinated hand signals, planning to trap it near a fence post. Takrin set chain rattles at a corner. Marta supported a wounded man, placing him behind a crate for safety.

As they prepared a final stand, the beast sprang into a furious charge, barreling straight at Marta and the wounded man. Marta gasped, pushing the man aside. She raised her staff to block. The beast's claws came down with brutal force. A heartbeat before impact, Helgrid flung her hammer like a missile, striking the beast's shoulder. It howled, momentum disrupted, claws grazing Marta's side instead of ripping her open. Marta stumbled back, groaning, but alive.

The villagers pressed advantage, flanking the beast with chains and staffs, trying to corner it against a shed. The Fatman trembled with worry—so close to deadly violence. Krampus's silence weighed again. Would the horned punisher appear at last, and what would that mean?

Edric swung a chain overhead, creating a whistling sound that disoriented the beast. Jarlan jabbed at its leg, forcing it to shift footing. Branwynn threw her potent powder at its face. The beast screeched, batting at its eyes as the greenish fumes stung. Helgrid recovered her hammer, stepping forward for a disabling blow to its spine or leg. They aimed to cripple it enough to drive it away forever or force a retreat. But it refused to yield, snapping its jaws and hissing curses that almost formed words now—unnatural mockeries of human speech.

Takrin circled wide, spotting a chance to loop a chain around a low branch behind the beast. If they could snare its limb and yank, toppling it, they might pin it down. He moved quietly, ignoring pain in his shoulder. The Fatman saw Takrin's maneuver and silently willed his success.

As Takrin set the chain, the beast sensed danger and lashed out wildly. Branwynn cried out as claws raked her calf, drawing blood. She struck back with her staff, tears in her eyes. Mercy and vigilance, but how much longer until mercy failed them if no one gave way?

The creature stumbled, blinking furiously, blinded by powders and smoke. Edric and Helgrid shouted, "Pull now!" Takrin yanked the chain line. The beast's ankle caught on the taut chain, and it crashed to its knees with a guttural roar. Villagers surged in, staffs jabbing at limbs, trying to pin it without landing a fatal blow. It thrashed, shrieking, black ichor dripping from earlier wounds.

For a moment, it seemed they might subdue the beast. The Fatman's eyes shone with relief—no need for mortal sins of killing.

Krampus's tension eased in their minds. But just as they began to hope, a distant shout rang out from the western side of the village: "Raiders! Raiders returning!" The alarm bells clanged, voices overlapping in panic.

Horror seized them. Gorven's men had regrouped, attacking now when they were locked in deadly struggle with the beast. Two dire threats at once. If they let the beast go to fight raiders, it might escape and return again. If they kill it now, they violate their code. If they hold it pinned, they cannot defend against raiders. A cruel triad of moral anguish.

Helgrid cursed, hammer shaking in her grip. Branwynn's face twisted with despair. Jarlan, gasping from wounds, tried to think of a solution. Edric and Takrin, bloodied and exhausted, looked to The Fatman for a sign. The Fatman stood frozen, tears in his eyes. Krampus's silent presence quivered.

The beast howled again, wrenching one arm free and slashing wildly at Helgrid. She dodged barely, panting, no strength left to hold this creature much longer. Marta cried from behind, "We must choose! We can't fight on two fronts!"

A second wave of screams confirmed the raiders' return at the west perimeter. Their cunning leader, Gorven, had chosen the perfect time to strike while they were tangled with the beast. The villagers' code demanded no killing if possible, but now they faced a crisis where sparing their enemy might cost innocent lives. Which enemy? The monstrous creature they nearly subdued, or the raiders who attacked again?

With hearts pounding, wounds bleeding, and minds racing, the villagers stood at a crossroads. The beast, pinned and shrieking, the raiders' screams drawing closer, children and elders screaming in terror as darkness threatened to engulf them from all sides. Branwynn, Helgrid, Jarlan, Edric, Takrin, and The Fatman realized the final moral test had come—no easy solutions, only painful choices.

The beast lunged upward suddenly, dislodging a staff pinning its arm. A flash of claws and a spray of black ichor. Helgrid cried out. Edric shouted a warning. Jarlan tried to strike again. The raiders' war cries grew louder from behind, blades clashing with whatever defenders Marta mustered. The Fatman watched helplessly as chaos closed in, not a neat test of morality but a raw struggle for survival on two fronts.

In a desperate decision, Branwynn raised her last powder—a lethal mix she never intended to use. She hesitated, tears streaming, knowing it might kill the beast. But if she didn't, how many villagers would die fighting both foes at once? Her hand shook. Edric shouted, "No! We can't—" but a raider's horn blast cut him off.

At that exact moment, as Branwynn's hand clenched around the lethal powder and the beast tore free another limb, as Helgrid swung her hammer, as Jarlan and Takrin braced for a final stand, and The Fatman's silent despair peaked, a massive crash sounded behind them, followed by the roar of triumphant rage. Gorven and several raiders burst into view, weapons raised, converging on their position while the wounded beast snarled, ready to leap—

Chapter Eighteen

Chaos thickened like choking smoke in the heart of Sleetwood. Lanterns swung madly, casting jittery shadows over bent saplings and crooked fences. The acrid tang of herb smoke and blood salted the air. Every cry, grunt, and clash of wood or metal fed a storm of panic. They had fought hard to maintain their code, their delicate moral order, but now they faced a monstrous creature and Gorven's raiders simultaneously. The villagers' breath came in ragged gasps.

Helgrid, ribs aching, hammer in hand, struggled to focus. Last she knew, they had cornered the beast, aiming to drive it away or subdue it without killing. Yet the raiders had returned like wolves circling wounded prey. Gorven's laughter—a bitter rasp—cut through the night as he and several raiders burst into the clearing. Sparks from a toppled torch danced in the gloom.

Branwynn's hand tightened around her last lethal powder pouch. She hadn't used it yet—she couldn't bring herself to cross that line. Edric and Takrin stood near her, bruised and bleeding, forming a line with Jarlan and a few others against both threats. The Fatman hovered at the outskirts, silent and grim, while Krampus's unseen influence weighed like a suppressed scream in their minds.

Krampus

The monstrous beast bared its teeth, black ichor trickling from wounds inflicted by the villagers' nonlethal strikes. It eyed the newcomers —the raiders—as if considering them fresh prey. The raiders fanned out, blades gleaming. One raider, eyes wide at the wounded beast, whispered, "What in all hells is that thing?" Another scoffed, "No matter. We'll kill it after we deal with these stubborn fools." Gorven smirked, "A perfect distraction. Let's see your code hold up now. Surrender, or we butcher everyone and feed them to that monster."

Teryn, still shaken, leaned against a broken fence post at the clearing's edge. She had tried to help before, but now her injuries left her dizzy. She saw helplessly how the villagers stood in a ring, backs to each other, facing two mortal enemies—human cruelty and bestial hunger. Could their code survive this crucible?

Marta and others, left guarding the village center, realized they must join or risk letting the raiders isolate the rescue party. Shouting signals, Marta led a small group of able-bodied villagers through the orchard, rattling chains, carrying torches, trying to reach the clearing. If all their strength combined, maybe they could force a standoff. But time was short. Every heartbeat risked tragedy.

Gorven stepped closer, raising his sword at Helgrid. "Hand over supplies and those tokens you hold so dear. And perhaps that wounded woman—Teryn, was it? We could ransom her somewhere. Do it, or we set your village aflame again, kill your children one by one." His voice dripped with malice, testing their moral boundaries like a blade on soft flesh.

Helgrid's hammer trembled in her grip. She refused to show fear. "We will never yield victims to you. We will never trade our code for safety." Her words cracked slightly, but her stance remained firm. Edric nodded, face pale but resolute. Takrin braced himself, favoring his wounded shoulder. Jarlan swallowed a lump of dread, recalling that they must not become murderers. Branwynn steadied her powder pouch, tears in her eyes—if forced, she would use it. But first, one last attempt at reason.

Branwynn called, "Gorven, you see our courage. We don't want to kill you or your men. Leave now, empty-handed, and no more will be harmed. This place doesn't bend to cruelty. You gain nothing by forcing us into bloodshed." Her voice rang through the clearing, carrying both plea and warning.

Gorven snarled a laugh. "Fine words. But words can't block steel." He gave a curt nod to his raiders. They advanced in a wedge formation, blades raised. The villagers tensed. Jarlan raised his staff, Helgrid steadied her hammer. The Fatman clenched his fists, wishing a miracle would solve this peacefully. Krampus's silence roared in their hearts—face evil or break.

The beast, startled by the raiders' approach, hissed and lunged at the nearest swordsman. With a shriek, that raider stumbled back, swinging wildly. The villagers realized with grim relief that the beast might attack the raiders as well, giving them a bizarre advantage. But the beast was unpredictable—it might turn on them any second.

A frenzied three-way struggle erupted. One raider swung at the beast's flank, the blade biting shallowly. The creature screamed, lashing out with claws, slashing a raider's arm deeply. The raider collapsed, shrieking. Another raider cursed, now wary of closing in. Gorven retreated two steps, reassessing the situation. The villagers saw an opening: with raiders distracted by the beast, they could push them back further.

Helgrid and Edric lunged at a pair of raiders who tried to flank the villagers. Edric jabbed a staff end into a raider's knee, dropping him. Helgrid struck another's blade aside, disarming him with a hammer blow to his wrist. The raider cried out, clutching his broken hand. No lethal strikes, just disabling blows. The villagers' code still held in the heat of battle.

Takrin moved to shield Teryn, dragging her behind a half-fallen fence beam for cover. Teryn thanked him weakly. He nodded, scanning the chaos, ready to jump in if needed. Jarlan assisted Branwynn, who prepared a powder pouch to toss if the beast or raiders charged again. The Fatman lingered at the clearing's perimeter, tears shining in his eyes as he witnessed mortals fighting to preserve goodness under impossible odds.

The beast roared, wounded and enraged. It turned on Gorven now, perhaps recognizing him as a greater threat. Gorven cursed, trying to dodge those lethal claws. He swung his sword desperately, scoring a shallow cut along the beast's neck. Black ichor splattered. The creature howled, staggering. For a moment, it looked weakened, trembling under wounds inflicted by both villagers and raiders.

Marta's group arrived, adding another half-dozen villagers to the fray. They rattled chains and thrust torches forward, forming a barricade of light and noise. The Fatman watched as this larger force slowly enclosed the clearing. The raiders, outnumbered and facing a monstrous foe as well, showed cracks in their resolve. One raider threw down his blade and fled into the underbrush, unwilling to die for Gorven's pride.

Gorven's face twisted with hate and frustration. He realized he might lose everything here. The beast panted heavily, glaring at Gorven and the villagers with equal malice. Branwynn stepped forward, staff raised, trying once more for peace: "Gorven, your men flee. The beast is beyond anyone's control. End this madness! Leave now, and we let you go!" She prayed he would listen, that he wouldn't force a final bloody conflict.

For a heartbeat, Gorven seemed to consider. His eyes darted to the beast, then to the ring of villagers, The Fatman's silent figure, and the trembling lantern lights. The moral power in this place was palpable. Could fear of the unknown—Krampus's rumored wrath—finally bend him?

Then the beast lunged at him again, claws aiming for his throat. Gorven shrieked, ducking low. The villagers, hoping to avoid a fatal blow, thrust staffs between them. Helgrid's hammer struck the beast's wrist, making it jerk back. Edric jabbed a sharpened staff end into the ground near Gorven's foot, forcing him to hop aside. The raiders who remained tried to help their leader, but two more panicked and ran off, leaving Gorven and maybe one loyal henchman behind.

Gorven, cornered now, cursed them as cowards. He raised his sword once more, attempting to deliver a killing strike to the beast. If he slew it, maybe he could intimidate the villagers again. But his arm shook with fatigue. He swung clumsily, blade skimming the beast's shoulder without a strong bite. The creature retaliated, slashing Gorven's leg. Gorven howled in pain, dropping to one knee.

This was the villagers' chance. They could let the beast finish Gorven, resolving one threat, but that would be an abdication of their moral duty—allowing a brutal creature to murder a human. Or they could intervene, saving Gorven's life only to let him attempt evil again later. They must uphold their code. Branwynn grit her teeth: better to save even a foe's life than to let the beast confirm cruelty's triumph.

Branwynn hurled her last powder pouch not at the beast's eyes this time, but directly at its mouth. The pouch burst, filling its maw with bitter, scorching powder. The creature gagged, thrashing, confused. Helgrid and

Edric seized the moment, hammer and staff striking the beast's legs, hoping to topple it. The creature fell to one knee, shrieking in agony and disorientation.

Jarlan and Marta rushed in with chains, trying to entangle the beast's limbs. The Fatman moved closer, heart pounding. If they subdue the beast without killing it, what then? Could they drive it away forever? The villagers wrestled with these questions in silence as they struggled to wrap chains around the creature's forearm. The beast flailed, claw tips scraping sparks off the chain links.

Gorven's last loyal henchman, seeing Gorven wounded and helpless, decided self-preservation mattered more than loyalty. He turned and fled into the darkness, leaving Gorven alone. The raider leader lay on the ground, clutching his bleeding leg, sword dropped. He stared at the villagers wrestling the beast, astonished by their courage and refusal to kill him even now. Shame and confusion warred in his heart.

With tremendous effort, Takrin and Edric managed to tighten the chains around the beast's leg and arm. Branwynn and Marta blocked its snarling jaws with a staff. Helgrid, gritting her teeth, delivered a precise hammer strike to the beast's side, aiming to dislocate a shoulder. The beast howled, movement faltering. Its strength waned under accumulated injuries.

But just as it seemed they might finally pin it down, the beast mustered a last surge of frenzy. It yanked its chained arm, flinging Edric backward. Edric landed hard, gasping. It twisted its body, snapping one chain link with impossible force, spraying sparks. The villagers recoiled in shock—this thing was stronger than they imagined.

The Fatman rushed forward, placing himself between the beast and Helgrid as she stumbled. His eyes locked with the creature's hollow gaze. He had never intervened physically before. Could his presence alone deter it? The creature snarled at The Fatman, uncertain, as if sensing an aura it couldn't comprehend. Just when it seemed the beast might lash out at The Fatman, a distant rattling of chains echoed—Krampus's phantom warning.

Under that spectral sound, the beast hesitated, trembling as if sensing an even darker predator lurking. This gave the villagers time to recover. Branwynn tried another tactic: she picked up a torch and moved it slowly before the beast's eyes, creating a flickering pattern of light and shadow. The beast hissed, mesmerized for a heartbeat. Marta and Helgrid

Krampus

seized that second to re-wrap chains around its ankle, Takrin and Jarlan grabbing a fallen staff to lever it off-balance.

The creature toppled onto its side, screaming, thrashing. The villagers piled on, forcing its limbs down. Helgrid struck its elbow once more, a brutal sound, causing it to drop its claw's tension. Not lethal, but crippling. The beast howled a mournful, eerie cry, black ichor pooling beneath it. The Fatman watched, heart heavy—this violence pained him deeply, but what choice was there?

As they pinned the beast, breathing hard, sweat stinging eyes, they faced the final moral crisis: What now? Can they keep it chained indefinitely? Release it to roam and kill elsewhere? Kill it to ensure safety, betraying their code?

Gorven watched from the ground, wounded, stunned. They had subdued the beast, something he and his men failed to do. They did it without killing him or the creature, at great cost. His contempt faltered, replaced by awe and confusion. Who were these people who fought so fiercely yet refused to embrace bloodlust?

The Fatman knelt by Edric, who wheezed from a hard fall but was conscious. Branwynn checked her powders—none left. Marta wiped tears. Helgrid's hammer shook in her trembling hand. Takrin held chains tight, arms burning with effort. Jarlan whispered, "We must decide now." The entire village's moral identity hung in the balance.

Before they could deliberate, a scream erupted from the village center. Another voice shouted, "Fires! The orchard's on fire!" The raiders, or what remained of them, must have done something spiteful while retreating. The villagers' hearts sank further. The orchard was vital for their future harvest.

They could not remain here, wrestling the beast forever. They had to secure the village. Yet leaving the beast chained and wounded might invite it to free itself eventually. Killing it felt like a horrible betrayal. If only Krampus or The Fatman would provide a sign. But this trial was theirs to solve, that much was clear.

The Fatman stood, tears in his eyes. He stepped forward to the beast's face, reaching out a hand as if to soothe it. The creature hissed, snapping at him, but the chain-held staff wedged in its jaw prevented a full bite. Helgrid and Branwynn watched in disbelief as The Fatman tried to communicate silently. The beast glared, uncomprehending, pain and fury clouding its hollow eyes. If it understood no reason, compassion might fail.

Gorven groaned, trying to crawl away quietly. Edric spotted him and blocked his path. Gorven glared up at Edric, snarling, "Let me go or kill me. Don't toy with me." Edric shook his head sadly, "We won't kill you. But we can't let you roam free to harm others. Maybe we must imprison you somehow." Gorven spat at his feet. "You have no prisons. You think kindness solves all?"

In that moment, The Fatman turned to the villagers, voice low but firm: "Your code must endure. Do not become murderers. Seek another way." Tears glistened on his cheeks. They knew this was agony for him. Krampus's rattling chains echoed in their memories—consequences must exist. Could they find a fate worse than death for these threats, a way to neutralize them without killing?

Suddenly, the beast convulsed, yanking fiercely on the chains. Branwynn and Takrin struggled to hold it down. Helgrid gasped, pain in her ribs flaring again. The creature's wounds bled dark ichor, weakening it, but not quelling its fight. It refused to die easily or submit.

In desperation, Jarlan shouted, "Krampus! If ever we needed your guiding hand—" He cut himself off, realizing calling Krampus by name might unleash a terror beyond their control. But what choice was left? The orchard burned, raiders lurked, the beast would not yield. Time drained away like blood in mud.

The Fatman's eyes widened. Calling Krampus might trigger a wrathful intervention. Would that mean killing the beast or torturing Gorven? That would scar the village's moral soul. Yet what if it was the only way to end this stalemate?

Helgrid, tears streaming, whisper-shouted: "No... we must handle this ourselves. We must find a path. Think—can we banish the beast by dragging it outside the valley, release it far away? And Gorven... we can break his weapons, strip him, send him wounded into the wild. He might die on his own, but we didn't kill him."

The Fatman nodded slightly, approving of this compromise— exiling threats rather than executing them. But first, they must survive this moment. Flames from the orchard lit the sky now, illuminating the clearing in a lurid glow. Screams echoed, villagers calling for buckets, trying to contain the blaze. If they wasted time here, the orchard might be lost, crippling their future food supply.

Branwynn clenched her jaw. "We must act now. Let's drag the beast, chained, away from the village, into the deeper forest, and leave it wounded enough that it fears returning. As for Gorven, we can disarm him completely, break his sword, strip him of gear, and send him limping off. Without supplies or men, he might never trouble us again." Grim solutions, but gentler than murder.

Jarlan and Edric agreed. Takrin swallowed hard, knowing it was risky. Gorven might survive and return. The beast might recover. But to slaughter them would erode their code. Mercy amid brutality defined them. They'd bet on these foes not returning or at least being diminished threats.

They prepared to drag the beast. Helgrid and Branwynn signaled some villagers to help. More arrived, shocked by the scene. Together, they wrapped chains tighter and tried to lift or drag the thrashing creature. It howled, but its energy waned. Wounds and blood loss sapped its strength.

As they strained to move it, Gorven seized the distraction. He lunged for a fallen sword. Edric spotted him too late. Gorven snatched the blade, face twisted in triumph. The Fatman gasped. Would Gorven strike Teryn or a wounded villager?

Edric rushed to intercept, but Gorven was closer to Teryn's hiding spot. He could reach her first. Takrin, half-lamed by wounds, tried to sprint. Too slow. Branwynn shouted a warning. Helgrid cursed, wishing she had no broken ribs.

Gorven laughed, a harsh bark in the smoky twilight. "If I die, I'll leave a scar on your perfect code!" He raised the blade, eyes fixed on Teryn, who struggled to stand, weaponless. The villagers cried out, too far to stop him in time. The Fatman paled, heart pounding. Krampus's distant chain rattles grew louder in their minds, tension rising to a breaking point.

The beast, half-dragged, convulsed again at the noise. It hissed weakly. The villagers knew they must choose: drop the beast and race to save Teryn, or trust someone else to act. Teryn screamed, voice cutting through the crackle of orchard flames. Gorven bared his teeth, blade descending toward her frail form.

In that impossible second, as Gorven's sword fell, something blurred at the edge of vision—an amber-eyed silhouette, horns catching the orchard's glow. The villagers gasped, minds reeling. Krampus's presence, at last, fully manifest?

They saw a towering, horned figure appear behind Gorven, chains rattling in a dreadful chorus. Gorven's face froze in shock. The Fatman shouted, "No!" But too late—the tension snapped.

Krampus's intervention might spare Teryn, but at what price? Would Krampus unleash a horror that stained them all?

Gorven turned his head just as a chain cracked through the air, targeting his sword arm. The villagers screamed warnings, the beast moaned, orchard flames crackled higher. Teryn cowered, tears in her eyes, as steel and chain met in a shower of sparks.

CHAPTER NINETEEN

A cacophony of flames, rattling chains, and frantic cries filled the orchard's smoky twilight. As Gorven's sword swung toward Teryn, a horned silhouette materialized behind him—Krampus, a shape of midnight fur and curling horns, chains glinting in the fire's glow. The villagers and raiders froze, hearts pounding. Here was no subtle suggestion, no half-glimpse. This was the full embodiment of their darkest legend, standing tall as if summoned by their moral crisis.

For a heartbeat, the entire scene hung suspended. Gorven, sword half-lowered, gaped at the towering figure behind him. Teryn cowered, pressing against a charred stump, tears on her cheeks. The villagers trembled between awe and terror. Even The Fatman stepped back, sorrow etched on his face. The orchard flames crackled, sparks drifting upward like dying stars. The monstrous beast, wounded and chained, hissed lowly, unsettled by the newcomer's presence.

Then Krampus moved with uncanny swiftness, a chain whipping around Gorven's sword arm before he could complete the killing strike. Gorven screamed, dropping the blade. Villagers gasped—Krampus had intervened without hesitation. But what now? Would Krampus dole out savage punishment, staining their code with brutality?

Helgrid tried to speak, voice cracking: "Krampus, we—" but her words caught in her throat. Krampus did not speak. He loomed over Gorven, who struggled and kicked, chains rattling. The raider leader cursed and spat, fear finally surfacing in his eyes. He had taunted their legends, and now faced them made flesh.

The Fatman, throat tight, dared a step forward. He had seldom approached his brother's darker aspect directly in such dire straits. If Krampus unleashed pure wrath, would it shatter what the villagers had built? The Fatman raised a hand, voice strained but calm: "Brother... remember their growth. They stand by their code. Let them choose mercy. Don't undo their progress."

Krampus turned his horned head slightly, amber eyes reflecting firelight. He did not release Gorven but seemed to pause, as if acknowledging The Fatman's plea. The villagers exhaled shakily. Had The Fatman's words softened this timeless enforcer of moral consequence?

But before anyone could breathe relief, the beast convulsed, struggling in its chains. The villagers holding it—Marta, Edric, Takrin, Branwynn, Jarlan—strained to keep it down. The creature's wounded limbs trembled with fury and pain. The orchard's flames intensified, wind fanning the fire, sending embers raining down. A branch overhead cracked, dropping sparks onto the beast's flank. It screeched, thrashing harder.

Distracted, the villagers faltered. Edric winced as the beast's tail-like limb battered his ribs. Marta cried out, losing her grip. Takrin tried to reinforce the chains, but the beast yanked its arm, slipping one loop free. Jarlan pushed forward with a staff, heart hammering—if the beast got loose now, with Krampus focused on Gorven, chaos would explode anew.

Branwynn gritted her teeth, wishing she had more powders. Her supply exhausted, she had only raw courage left. She jammed her staff under the beast's shoulder, leveraging its weight. The Fatman's eyes darted between Krampus and the beast, desperate for a way to end this madness without blood on their hands.

Gorven, chained by Krampus, spat curses. "You think a demon can scare me? Kill me then! Show your true nature!" He tried to provoke Krampus into delivering a fatal blow. Maybe if Krampus committed murder, it would corrupt the village's moral claim. But Krampus did not strike immediately. He held Gorven like a condemned man awaiting judgment.

Helgrid, ribs still aching, stepped closer to Krampus and Gorven. Fear prickled her skin at standing so near the horned enforcer. She raised her voice quietly: "Krampus, we do not want slaughter. We beg you—do not execute him. Let us handle this without becoming monsters." Her voice trembled with respect and fear.

Krampus's chains rattled softly, as if contemplating. The beast's snarls grew louder, distracting everyone. The Fatman urged, "We must subdue the beast fully, brother, help them save innocence." The Fatman's plea was gentle yet urgent. Time frayed at the edges. If Krampus remained fixated on Gorven alone, the beast might break free and rampage.

In a surprising move, Krampus released Gorven's arm, letting the raider slump to the ground. But as Gorven attempted to scramble away, Krampus grabbed his collar, dragging him to the side and pinning him against a half-burned apple tree. Gorven gasped, pinned but not yet killed. Krampus now had a hand free to act elsewhere if needed.

The villagers seized the moment, encouraged by Krampus's partial compliance with their moral desire. They refocused on the beast. With Krampus neutralizing Gorven, they could unite all efforts. "Chains tighter!" Marta shouted. Branwynn and Jarlan looped additional chain segments around the creature's legs. Edric and Takrin wedged staffs to keep its jaw pried open slightly, reducing its biting power. Helgrid forced her hammer's head against a joint, preventing it from thrashing one arm effectively.

The creature howled, black ichor dripping onto scorched grass. Its eyes flared with hateful intelligence, as if cursing their every virtue. But it weakened under their combined strength and injuries. The orchard flames crackled louder, and a fiery branch fell dangerously close to the group. They coughed on the smoke, eyes watering. They must end this soon or risk being trapped in a burning orchard with their enemies.

The Fatman circled behind the beast, searching for a sign of vulnerability. He dared not exert any supernatural force directly—this struggle defined the villagers' path. Yet his gaze fell upon a patch of ground where cool spring water seeped from a cracked irrigation channel. If they could drag the beast there, maybe quench its fury with cold water, shock it further, and give it reason to flee. It was a desperate idea, but better than killing it.

"Move it north!" The Fatman called, pointing. The villagers blinked—The Fatman rarely gave direct instructions, but they trusted him. They hauled the beast a few steps north, grunting with effort. The beast writhed, spitting foul drool. Gorven, pinned by Krampus, watched with twisted fascination. He now saw that The Fatman, too, was real and active, not a docile myth.

Inch by inch, they wrestled the beast toward the seep of water. Embers rained down, scorching shoulders and hair. The orchard's future withered in flames. Yet the villagers persevered. They would rebuild. Survival mattered more now.

The beast's claw scraped Branwynn's leg, tearing her tunic. She cried out, tears of pain and frustration. Jarlan steadied her, voice hoarse: "Hold on! Just a bit more!" Takrin gritted his teeth, drawing on reserves of strength he never knew he had. Edric focused on keeping the beast's jaws partially wedged. Marta helped secure another chain loop.

Krampus watched intently, still pinning Gorven. The raider leader tried to pry himself free, to no avail. Krampus's grip was iron. Gorven trembled—he had expected brutality, not this stoic restraint. Fear gnawed at him. Would Krampus torture him at any moment, or deliver him to the villagers for a more nuanced fate?

At last, the villagers succeeded in dragging the beast's lower body into the seep of cold water. The sudden chill against its wounds made it shriek and jerk violently. They tightened chains, holding firm despite splashes and mud. The shock of cold water and chains, combined with blood loss, began to break its spirit. It howled, more plaintive now, as if realizing it could not win here.

Helgrid, shoulders shaking, mustered courage: "We can let it go. If we pull the chains just enough to push it away into the deeper forest—maybe it will never return." Edric nodded, eyes fierce but compassionate. Killing it would be easy now, a mercy even, but would they become what they feared?

Jarlan agreed. "Release it, wounded and scared. It knows we're dangerous prey. It won't return lightly." Marta, tears mixing with sweat, whispered prayers of thanks. Branwynn bit her lip—this decision saved their souls. Takrin exhaled shakily, relieved that no final step into murder was taken.

Krampus

They prepared to loosen the chains strategically, guiding the beast's escape route. The Fatman nodded, approving their choice. Krampus remained silent, observing. Would the beast flee or lunge again? The villagers braced, ready to strike nonlethally if needed.

Carefully, they loosened a leg chain. The beast hissed, testing freedom. They unwrapped an arm chain, stepping back quickly. The creature staggered to its feet, trembling. Its eyes scanned them hatefully, but no longer saw easy victims. Behind them, orchard flames and rattling chains, before them fearless defenders. It coughed a wet snarl and backed away step by step, then turned and bolted into the smoking darkness, limping badly. The villagers watched it vanish, hoping the lesson stuck.

A collective sigh escaped their lungs. They had spared a life, even a monstrous one, preserving their moral code. But no time to celebrate—flames crackled still, and Gorven remained.

They turned to face Krampus and Gorven. The Fatman inched closer, hoping Krampus would yield Gorven's fate to the villagers. Helgrid limped toward them, hammer lowered. Branwynn, Edric, and others followed. Marta arrived with a few more villagers, coughing from the orchard smoke. Takrin guarded Teryn, who wept softly—relieved to be alive.

Krampus stood as a sentinel of doom, holding Gorven pinned. Gorven's breath came in ragged gasps. He had seen a monstrous beast bested by these "weak" villagers and a horned enforcer restrain him effortlessly. His arrogance cracked, replaced by dread. He realized no cunning words would free him now. They could kill him easily, or let Krampus tear him apart. The Fatman stepped closer, sadness in his eyes.

Jarlan, voice shaky but resolved: "Gorven, you have seen our truth. We outlasted your cruelty. We faced horrors without discarding our code. We do not kill wantonly. We spared even the beast. But you tried to slaughter innocents and burn our home. For your crimes, we must ensure you can't harm us again."

Gorven spat on the ground, but his defiance lacked vigor. "Do what you must," he muttered. He expected torture or a final blow. Instead, Helgrid approached. She raised her hammer not to his head, but to his belt and boots, smashing buckles and cutting away his gear. Edric and Takrin stripped him of any hidden blades. They removed armor pieces, leaving him in simple undergarments. He shivered in the cool night air.

Marta said softly, "We won't kill you. We will send you off, wounded and unarmed, into the wilderness. Survive if you can. Return here, and next time the outcome might not be so merciful." Her tone carried quiet steel.

Branwynn nodded. "This is your consequence. We do not relish it, but we must protect ourselves and others from you."

Gorven's eyes darted to Krampus, who still held him. He found no comfort there. The Fatman stood by, tears glistening again, relieved they chose mercy. Krampus's chains rattled slightly—was it approval, or an acknowledgment that a price was paid?

The orchard fire had spread, threatening more trees. Marta sent a few villagers to douse flames if possible. They grabbed buckets, wet cloths, anything to control the blaze. Smoke burned their throats. They must conclude this ordeal and save what they could. Time ticked on.

Krampus, sensing the verdict, released Gorven. The raider leader fell to his knees, shivering. He stared up at Krampus's horned form, amber eyes glowing with ancient judgment. Krampus stepped back, chains scraping ground. No words. Just a silent warning. The villagers parted to create a path leading out of the orchard, away from the village. Gorven understood—he must leave or face a worse fate.

Hunched and limping, Gorven stumbled toward the exit. He glared at them over his shoulder. "You think this is victory? You lost your orchard, bled for your code. One day… maybe not by my hand, but something worse will come." He coughed, grimacing in pain.

Helgrid shook her head. "If worse comes, we face it again. Go, Gorven. Pray you never cross our path again." Her hammer hung low, no threat now, just firm resolve.

Gorven spat again, then trudged away, disappearing into the smoky darkness. The villagers watched his figure vanish. Edric wondered if they should have crippled him further. But no, that would edge toward cruelty. Let fate decide if he survived wounded and alone.

Now came another battle: extinguish the orchard flames. The orchard represented their future harvest, hope for stable seasons. Losing it would be a blow. Marta and others rushed to form a bucket line from a nearby stream. Jarlan, arm bleeding, helped pass buckets. Branwynn, ankle throbbing, mixed a quick herb balm to ease pain, then joined efforts. Takrin and Edric supported Teryn and a few wounded to safer ground.

Krampus

The Fatman moved among them, offering silent encouragement. Krampus stood apart, watching. The villagers, battered and exhausted, fought the fire with the same determination they fought evil. Buckets of water splashed onto burning trunks, villagers beat down flames with wet cloaks. The orchard might not be fully saved, but perhaps they could contain the blaze.

In the struggle to douse flames, a sudden gust of wind scattered embers, setting another patch of trees alight. Cries of alarm rose. Teryn, leaning on a fence, watched helplessly. The Fatman flinched as a branch collapsed in a shower of sparks. Helgrid ground her teeth—just when peace seemed near, fate threw another challenge.

They formed new lines, adjusting strategy. Some villagers tried to dig a trench around the fire's perimeter, others climbed ladders to break flaming branches before they fell. Jarlan directed movements calmly despite his wound, proving their code extended to crisis management. Marta comforted a sobbing child who escaped just before the orchard caught fire, promising they'd replant trees if needed.

Krampus remained at the orchard's edge, silent. Had they passed his test? He intervened only to prevent murder. Now, as they wrestled with nature's fury, he neither helped nor hindered. Perhaps this final trial was theirs alone. The Fatman frowned—if Krampus chose not to vanish, maybe another danger lurked?

A muffled scream drew their attention—one villager stuck behind a burning log pile. Edric and Takrin rushed to rescue them, pushing through smoke and sparks. Branwynn coughed violently, tears streaming from smoke irritation. Helgrid tried to hoist a bucket of water but her ribs screamed in pain. She pressed on anyway.

The villagers displayed astonishing solidarity—no one fled, no one panicked. They handled each calamity with resolve. The Fatman marveled at their moral fortitude. Krampus watched silently. The orchard flames began to recede as their coordinated efforts took effect. Maybe they'd save a portion of it, enough to re-sprout life in spring. That hope fueled them.

As the flames dimmed, Marta and Jarlan surveyed damage. Half the orchard charred, a few trees still smoldering. Bodies of two raiders who dared the beast's wrath lay in the ashes, grotesque reminders of violence. The villagers avoided looking too closely, sorrowful that death occurred even if not by their hands.

The beast gone, Gorven banished, orchard mostly saved—peace at last? They could finally tend wounds and mourn losses. Teryn wept softly, apologizing again. Marta hushed her gently—Teryn did nothing wrong. The Fatman stepped forward, placing a carved token of a tree in Teryn's hand, a silent promise that new life would grow.

But as they began to breathe easier, a sudden rustle in the underbrush froze them. Helgrid raised her hammer, Branwynn gripped a staff. Could Gorven have returned? Unlikely—he was too wounded and weaponless. The beast? No, they'd driven it away, wounded and frightened. Another raider? Or something else?

The Fatman stepped toward the sound, heart thudding. Krampus's chain rattled softly. The villagers formed a defensive semicircle. Smoke and embers still floated in the air, giving the scene an eerie glow. Edric and Takrin readied staffs. Marta clutched an iron token. Jarlan stood by Branwynn, steeling himself.

From behind a charred thicket stepped a figure—hooded, slender, moving with quiet grace. Not a raider's ragged leathers, nor the beast's horrifying shape. This figure wore a cloak of dark fabric woven with strange runes. The villagers blinked in confusion. Another outsider? At this dark hour?

The figure halted a short distance away, head tilted. No weapon visible. Just a faint shimmer of something metallic at their belt. Helgrid narrowed her eyes: "Who are you?" Her voice was hoarse from smoke inhalation.

Silence from the hooded stranger. Wind rustled orchard ashes. The Fatman moved closer, intrigued. Krampus's presence intensified, chains rattling louder. Did this newcomer threaten their fragile moral victory?

Branwynn stepped forward, voice firm but cautious: "We just overcame horrors. If you bring harm, know we stand united. Speak your purpose." She expected threats or demands, but none came. The hooded figure remained silent, observing the aftermath—burned orchard, wounded villagers, The Fatman's sorrowful stance, Krampus's looming form.

Jarlan tried a gentler tone: "We have faced much tonight. Identify yourself, or leave peacefully. We crave no new conflict."

Still no response. The figure's hood turned slightly toward Krampus, as if studying him. The villagers tensed. Few outsiders would gaze at Krampus without terror. This one seemed curious. Could it be a wanderer drawn by rumors of their code? Or something darker, a herald of another trial?

Marta, holding a smoldering torch, took a step forward. "We mean it—state your intention. We cannot withstand more cruelty." Her words hung in smoky air.

The figure raised a hand slowly—a pale hand with long fingers—making a gesture, not threatening but cryptic. Then, in a soft, hollow voice: "You have chosen a hard path." The villagers shivered. The voice carried an odd resonance. The figure spoke their tongue but with an accent that felt ancient and distant.

Helgrid tightened her grip on the hammer. "Yes, we have. And we will stand by it. Who are you?" She insisted.

The figure lowered the hand, silence again. Then looked at The Fatman and Krampus in turn. The villagers realized this newcomer recognized their guardians. That knowledge raised new fears—someone who knew of these legends might have motives beyond trade or plunder.

Branwynn's heart pounded. "We've defended our code against men and monsters. If you test us further, we will not break." Her voice steadied, no empty bravado. Every villager nodded slightly, aligning behind her words.

The figure spoke again, voice low: "You spared a beast that would have slaughtered you. You cast out a raider who deserved worse. You fought flames to save your orchard, yet nature's fury scarred your home. Mercy prevails here—at what cost?"

Jarlan winced at the question—exactly their moral dilemma. Did mercy cost them dearly, leaving enemies alive to return or orchard half-burned? But he believed their code transcended cost.

"Cost or not," Marta said, "we stand by our code. Kindness tempered by vigilance. No matter what befalls us."

The figure nodded slowly. "Interesting." Then took a step closer, ignoring the tense stances of Helgrid and Edric. It halted near Krampus, who remained towering and silent, holding no one now. Gorven was gone. Wait—when had Gorven vanished? The villagers realized in their distraction with the orchard and newcomer, Gorven slipped away. Perhaps Krampus released him while they fought the beast, or in the confusion of the orchard fire. The raider leader escaped after all—an unsettling loose end.

This realization startled them. Jarlan cursed softly, scanning the shadows. No sign of Gorven. Did Krampus allow his escape intentionally? Or did Gorven slip free while Krampus focused on the newcomer?

The newcomer raised a hand toward Krampus, as if studying him. Krampus's chains rattled, a low warning. The villagers braced. Would this stranger dare confront their horned enforcer?

The Fatman stepped forward, placing himself between the figure and Krampus. "We do not seek more conflict," he said gently. "If you know our legends, respect our boundaries. We have endured enough tonight."

The hooded stranger regarded The Fatman. A faint chuckle escaped their lips. "You have guardians both bright and dark. A unique balance. I have seen places where kindness shatters into weakness or cruelty rules unchecked. Here, you attempt equilibrium. Admirable, if precarious."

Helgrid's eyes narrowed. Was this newcomer testing them philosophically, or planning another trick? The orchard smoldered behind them, wounded villagers moaned softly, and they stood in tense dialogue with a mysterious stranger at midnight.

Branwynn urged caution: "Your words suggest knowledge of distant lands. We care not for riddles. State your purpose or go. Our wounded need care, and our orchard smolders."

The figure inclined their head. "My purpose? To witness, perhaps. To see if mortals can uphold morality under dire strain. You exceeded expectations tonight—rescuing Teryn, sparing the beast, banishing raiders without mass slaughter. Yet cracks remain. You lost your orchard's bounty, let enemies escape. Will your mercy haunt you?"

A chill ran down their spines. This stranger sounded like a judge or observer from beyond. Edric's voice trembled: "We accept consequences of mercy. Better haunted by mercy than rotted by cruelty." His words came from deep conviction.

The figure seemed amused. "We shall see." Then it turned to The Fatman, "Your influence guided them well, gift-giver. And you," it addressed Krampus, "Your silent watch ensured consequence without wanton butchery. Fascinating."

Krampus

Krampus's chains rattled again, no answer in words. The villagers exchanged glances—this was beyond normal encounters. Were they meeting some wandering spirit, a herald of older powers?

Marta, aching and exhausted, dared ask: "Will you harm us or help us?" Simple, direct.

The figure paused, considering. "Harm? No. Help? That depends. You stand at a crossroads of fate. Your code holds so far, but new threats always lurk. I came to see if your balance is real or a passing dream. Finding it real is... comforting. Yet I will not shield you from future trials."

The Fatman exhaled softly. Another test, another watcher. The world teemed with forces observing their moral experiment. The villagers realized they had become a beacon, attracting curiosity and challenge. Would peace ever come?

Branwynn's patience thinned. "If you neither harm nor help, we ask you to leave us. We must tend wounds, rebuild what we can, and rest. We don't need more riddles tonight."

The figure tilted their head. "Very well. I will depart. But know that mercy radiates like a beacon, drawing not only foes but potential allies. One day, your code might inspire others. If you survive your scars." A warning and a hint of hope. The villagers said nothing, too weary for prolonged debate.

The figure turned away, melting into the smoky shadows as silently as it arrived. The Fatman watched them vanish, shoulders slumping in relief. Krampus stood rigid, chains still. Then, as if satisfied, Krampus stepped back into deeper darkness and faded from sight. The villagers understood: Krampus would not linger now. He intervened only when moral lines risked breaking. Tonight, they chose mercy again, proving worthy of his restraint.

With both mysterious stranger and Krampus gone, only the villagers, The Fatman, and their wounded orchard remained. They hurried to help the injured, extinguish last embers, and comfort children. Edric and Takrin collapsed against a half-burned trunk, breathing heavily. Branwynn sat beside them, tears of exhaustion on her cheeks. Marta checked wounds, distributing what few herbs remained.

Helgrid surveyed the orchard's ruin: half the trees charred, fruit lost, soil scorched. A hard blow for their future. But they lived, code intact. Teryn limped over, thanking them quietly, tears of gratitude. Jarlan wrote shaky notes in his ledger by lantern light—tonight they faced beast, raiders, fire, and strange enigmas, and still chose humanity over cruelty. Would future generations believe this?

The Fatman passed among them, distributing small carved tokens he still carried, each shaped like a sprout or seed. A silent promise that from ashes, new life could grow. The villagers accepted these tokens with trembling hands, touched by his gesture. Even now, The Fatman's kindness reassured them.

But where was Gorven now? He fled wounded into darkness. Could he return with vengeance or allies? The thought gnawed at them. And the beast, wounded and humiliated, might return too. They must remain vigilant. Yet tonight proved they could handle terror without shattering their morals.

As dawn approached, a faint blush colored the eastern sky. The villagers began sorting tasks: some would tend wounded, some salvage orchard saplings, some stand guard. They learned not to relax too soon. The Fatman offered no illusions: peace might be fleeting. Krampus's silence warned them never to grow complacent.

While pulling a fallen branch aside, Marta found a half-charred token once hung on a door. She showed it to Helgrid. The symbol partly melted, birch branch motif distorted. "A sign we must adapt," Marta murmured. They nodded, acknowledging that survival might demand new strategies, but never letting go of their moral compass.

Branwynn, bandaging her leg, watched smoke drift upward. Another hard-won dawn. They saved Teryn, spared the beast, banished Gorven, and survived the orchard's fire. Their code bent under weight but did not snap. If that strange hooded figure spoke truth, their mercy might attract allies or new challengers. They must be ready.

The Fatman lingered near Krampus's last known spot. Without speaking, he understood his brother's stance: Krampus allowed them to solve crises themselves, intervening minimally. This strengthened their moral backbone. The Fatman offered quiet thanks for not unleashing unchecked wrath. They emerged from the trial with moral purity intact.

Takrin and Edric helped gather buckets scattered during the chaos. Teryn joined them, limping but determined to assist. Together they whispered of repairing the orchard, planting new seeds, building a stronger village. They found hope in rebuilding. If enemies returned, they knew they could stand firm, maybe inspiring even those enemies to reconsider their ways.

Just as some relief settled in, a distant horn call shocked them. The villagers jolted upright, hearts racing. Another threat? After all this, who dared approach at dawn?

A figure rushed from the village perimeter, panting. "Strangers on the western ridge! Armed—and they carry banners!" Panic surged. Could it be more raiders? Another band lured by rumors of Sleetwood's code?

Helgrid groaned, body screaming for rest. Branwynn's eyes flared in alarm. Edric and Takrin exchanged resigned looks. Marta cursed softly, "Can we have no respite?"

The Fatman gritted his teeth, stepping toward the vantage point. Villagers readied their staffs again, exhausted but unwilling to give up. The orchard still smoldered, wounded moaned, Teryn barely stable. Another confrontation now felt cruelly unfair.

They gathered what strength they had and moved toward the village edge where the lookout stood. Jarlan tried to swallow fear and record details mentally. If their code demanded endurance, they must endure.

At the western ridge, a dozen silhouettes stood against the dawn glow. The villagers approached cautiously, lanterns lowered. As they drew closer, they saw these newcomers wore armor more organized than raiders, and carried tall spears and a banner emblazoned with an unfamiliar emblem. Not a ragtag band—it looked like a small contingent of soldiers or a disciplined war party.

Marta whispered, "We must show no fear. Let's greet them firmly." Helgrid nodded, though her hammer felt heavier than ever. Branwynn clenched her staff, Edric and Takrin grimacing in pain but standing tall. Teryn stayed behind, no strength to face another threat.

The Fatman stood at their side, face solemn. Krampus nowhere visible. Perhaps this new threat demanded political cunning rather than brute force. Or maybe this was the "ally" hinted by the hooded stranger?

As they neared hailing distance, a voice rang out—a woman's voice, authoritative: "Halt! Identify yourselves. We come seeking a village rumored to hold a special moral code. We wish to parley." No immediate hostility in her tone, but a sharp command. The villagers exchanged wary glances.

Branwynn mustered energy to respond: "We are from Sleetwood. We survived much this night. If you come seeking harm, know we stand firm." She tried not to sound too weary.

A pause, then the woman stepped forward, flanked by soldiers holding spears at rest. Dawn's first rays revealed her face—stern, lined with experience, but not cruel. Her armor bore strange runes. "Harm? Not if unnecessary. We heard tales of a place guided by mercy and consequence. We doubted. After traveling, we found evidence of recent battles—blood, footprints, ashes. We must see if your code truly stands, or if it's a lie."

Jarlan stiffened. More tests? More observers? Were they condemned to prove themselves indefinitely?

Marta raised her voice, tired but proud: "We uphold our code. Tonight we fought raiders and a monstrous beast without abandoning our morals. We stand battered but unbroken."

Helgrid lifted her hammer slightly, emphasizing their resilience. Edric and Takrin's injuries spoke volumes. The orchard's smoke drifted overhead, adding drama to their words. The Fatman watched silently, waiting to see if these newcomers would force another conflict. The villagers had no strength left for another brawl.

The woman studied them carefully. "Your orchard burns, your wounds bleed, yet you claim mercy guided you. Did you spare enemies who deserved death?"

"Yes," said Branwynn softly, "We spared them all. Even a monstrous beast that would have slain us. Even the cruel raider who tried to murder an innocent woman. We cast him out rather than spill his blood."

A ripple of reaction passed through the newcomers. Some frowned, perplexed. A few whispered doubts. The woman leader nodded slowly. "Then you are either fools or saints. We came to see if true moral balance can exist. It seems it can."

Marta sighed with relief. Maybe no fight. Maybe these newcomers respected virtue. But why come armed?

The woman lowered her spear. "We are from a distant principality that seeks allies who hold firm principles. We doubted rumors of a village protected by legends and codes. Now we find you scarred but steadfast. Impressive. Perhaps we can talk alliance, trade, mutual help. We lack your moral purity but admire it."

The villagers blinked in surprise. After so much violence, here was a chance at friendship. The Fatman smiled faintly. Maybe this was the "ally" hinted at. Maybe their code would attract not only threats but potential partners.

Helgrid stepped forward, hammer lowered in respect. "We welcome honest dialogue. We have lost much tonight—blood, orchard, peace—but we remain true to ourselves. If you come in good faith, we can share stories, learn from each other."

The woman leader nodded. "We shall. Let's lay down arms and speak—"

A shriek cut her off. All heads turned to see the monstrous beast's form—limping, battered—reemerge from behind a charred cluster of trees. Impossible! They sent it away wounded. How did it circle back? Did pain and rage drive it to one final desperate attack?

The villagers cried out in dismay. The newcomers raised spears, startled. The beast, eyes blazing with hate, lunged forward. It knew it was doomed but chose to die attacking rather than slink away. The Fatman gasped, stepping back. Krampus's influence flared—chains rattled in distant echoes.

With everyone distracted by potential alliance, the beast took advantage. It rushed toward Teryn, who stood vulnerable near the orchard's edge, trying to help a wounded villager. She screamed, too far for immediate rescue. Edric and Takrin ran, but too slowly. Branwynn and Marta shouted warnings, Helgrid swung her hammer but missed by yards. The newcomers readied spears, but they stood on the wrong side of the clearing.

The beast's jaws opened, ready to kill at last, defying all mercy shown to it. The Fatman cried out, "No!" rushing forward, arms spread as if to intercept. If Krampus did not act, would The Fatman? The villagers froze, horrified—if The Fatman tried to physically block the beast, might he be injured or killed? He was not meant for direct combat.

A thunderous chain rattle boomed in the smoky air. Krampus's silhouette reappeared, horned head low, charging with impossible speed. His chains whistled, lashing at the beast's flank. Sparks and black ichor flew. The beast screamed, twisting mid-lunge. Teryn tried to crawl away. The villagers prayed Krampus wouldn't just tear the beast apart, staining their code with monstrous brutality.

The newcomers watched, stunned by the horned figure's sudden intervention. Helgrid and Marta tried to call out, "Don't kill it!" but the roaring flames and beast's shrieks drowned them out. The Fatman struggled forward, reaching for Krampus's arm, hoping to restrain excessive violence. The orchard's dying glow cast grotesque shadows as beast and horned punisher clashed, chains rattling, claws scraping. The villagers could barely breathe.

The beast, cornered by death incarnate, lashed with frantic strength, forcing Krampus to adjust chains. If Krampus dealt a killing blow, would that betray the villagers' moral stance or affirm Krampus's role as ultimate enforcer? The Fatman wept silently, powerless to stop what might unfold.

Suddenly, a terrified scream of a child rang from the village center—some child wandered near the chaos. The villagers' hearts lurched: a child at risk again? They must secure the child. Branwynn and Jarlan turned toward the scream, torn between watching Krampus's deadly duel and protecting innocence. Marta followed, leaving Helgrid, Edric, Takrin, and The Fatman witnessing the brutal standoff.

The beast, bloody and cornered, tried a final desperate leap. Krampus swung a chain in a cruel arc, aiming to entangle its neck. If that chain tightened, it might snap the creature's spine. Helgrid shouted, "No, Krampus, don't—!" But her voice was lost in snarls and rattles.

As chain met flesh, sparks flared. The beast howled, twisting free at the last instant. The chain whipped the air, striking a burning tree trunk, shattering it. Ember and ash rained down. Krampus advanced relentlessly, forcing the beast against a half-collapsed fence.

The villagers and The Fatman closed in, hoping to influence Krampus's choice, to remind him they spare life even now. But Krampus's amber eyes glowed with ancient wrath. Perhaps he saw the beast's attempt on Teryn's life as final proof it deserved death. The villagers tried to recall their code: they overcame cunning foes without murder. Could they stop Krampus from executing the beast?

As they rushed closer, the newcomers with spears also approached, curious or eager to help. Confusion reigned. The orchard crackled, wind gusted, fanning lingering embers. In that swirling chaos, Gorven, half-limping, reappeared at the clearing's edge—had he circled around again? Unarmed, wounded, yet unwilling to vanish quietly.

Perhaps he sought one last vile act while everyone fixated on Krampus and the beast.

The Fatman spotted Gorven's silhouette slinking behind a charred trunk, eyes narrowed with malevolent cunning. Even now, Gorven refused to accept moral defeat. If Gorven seized a dropped blade or a wounded villager as a hostage, it could spark unspeakable violence. The Fatman gestured urgently to Helgrid and Edric, pointing to Gorven's shape. They nodded, changing course to intercept him before another atrocity occurred.

Meanwhile, Krampus and the beast clashed. The beast flailed, one arm broken, leg gashed, eyes wild with fear. Krampus pressed forward, chains spinning with lethal precision. A chain loop caught the beast's hind leg, yanking it off balance. The beast shrieked, falling sideways, pinned against a collapsed ladder. Krampus stepped closer, raising a chain-laden arm high, poised for a killing strike.

Marta and Branwynn, chasing the child's scream, realized they must trust The Fatman and others to handle Krampus. They found a child cornered by a small fire near a shed. Marta snatched the child up, comforting them. The crisis there resolved, they hurried back, hearts hammering. Every second counted.

Takrin, breathless, tried to shout at Krampus, "Don't kill it! We stopped before—don't break our code!" His voice cracked. The Fatman rushed forward too, arms raised, pleading silently. Helgrid and Edric raced toward Gorven, who crouched near a corpse of a raider, trying to scavenge a weapon. If they didn't stop him now, he might force their hand in lethal ways.

A scream from Teryn: "No more killing!" The villagers echoed her plea. The newcomers watched, astonished. The orchard's last flames sputtered, casting eerie shadows on Krampus's towering form.

Krampus paused, chain raised high, hearing their cries. The beast whimpered, pinned. Could it comprehend mercy at last? Or would it lash out if spared again? The villagers' moral law demanded no needless slaughter, but could they risk another chance?

In that charged silence, Gorven made his move. He snatched a half-burned spear shaft from a raider's corpse. Not a full blade, but sharpened enough to harm. Helgrid and Edric lunged to stop him, but he spun, hurling the spear shaft toward Teryn and a wounded villager nearby, hoping to kill at least one before he fell or fled. Teryn screamed, villagers shouted warnings. The Fatman turned sharply, eyes wide with horror.

At the same instant, the beast, sensing Krampus's hesitation, mustered a last savage effort. It twisted its head, snapping at a chain loop, teeth grinding metal. If it broke free now, it might tear into someone. Krampus growled low, preparing to strike if necessary.

Gorven's spear shaft flew through the smoky air, aiming at Teryn's heart. Helgrid and Edric, mid-run, too far to block. Branwynn too distant to intervene. The Fatman clenched his fists, powerless to stop a flying spear with bare hands. Marta, just returning with the saved child in her arms, saw it too late. Takrin, closer, tried to leap in front but stumbled on scorched debris.

The villagers gasped as death hurtled toward Teryn. She, battered and tear-streaked, raised an arm instinctively, eyes wide. Would their code be forever stained by losing an innocent now, after all this?

In that fraction of a second, a horned silhouette moved at impossible speed—not Krampus this time, but The Fatman. He stepped into the spear's path, cloak billowing, arms spread wide as if to shield Teryn with his own body. The villagers screamed, "No!" Krampus's chains rattled violently, and the beast shrieked at the sudden motion.

The Fatman's form blocked the spear. A sickening impact sounded —a dull thunk of wood on flesh. The Fatman staggered, gasping, taking the blow meant for Teryn. Horror exploded among the villagers. Helgrid and Edric cried out in anguish. Branwynn's heart nearly stopped. Marta pressed a hand to her mouth, child clutched in her other arm, tears streaming. The newcomers watched, stunned that the legendary gift-bringer would sacrifice himself.

The Fatman stumbled, knees buckling. The spear shaft protruded from his side, blood staining his cloak. He looked down, disbelief and pain twisting his features. Yet he did not fall. He turned his head slowly toward Krampus, who still held the beast pinned. The Fatman's eyes, filled with sorrow and apology, met his brother's amber gaze.

A collective wail of despair rose. Even Gorven, half-hidden, gaped in shock at what he had done. He had struck The Fatman, the symbol of kindness and hope. Would Krampus now unleash unimaginable fury? Would the villagers remain calm or succumb to vengeance?

The orchard's embers glowed dully, casting grotesque shadows. The beast snarled, trying to break free as Krampus's attention flickered between The Fatman's wound and the pinned creature. Krampus's chains rattled thunderously, a harsh metallic chorus that sang of wrath and heartbreak. The villagers quaked. If The Fatman died, how would they endure?

The Fatman coughed, blood on his lips, yet raised a trembling hand as if to calm them. He tried to speak but only a wet rasp emerged. Teryn sobbed uncontrollably, knowing he saved her life at a terrible cost. Helgrid and Edric rushed forward, desperate to support The Fatman, to remove the spear without killing him. Takrin stepped toward Gorven's hiding spot, fury in his eyes. Branwynn and Marta tried to hold composure, tears burning their cheeks.

Krampus snarled, torn between holding the beast and racing to The Fatman. The beast, sensing confusion, made another violent thrash. A chain snapped, and it freed a hind leg. Villagers cursed, torn in all directions: save The Fatman, recapture the beast, capture Gorven, who now attempted to flee again?

In a final catastrophic moment, everything unravelled: The beast yanked free another limb, roaring louder than ever. Krampus jerked his head, enraged, prepared to deliver a killing chain strike at last. The Fatman half-collapsed into Helgrid's arms, choking out a single whispered word. The villagers screamed for help, trying to maintain their code, their unity. Gorven, seizing chaos again, bolted for the orchard's far edge, limping but determined to escape.

The newcomers, startled and confused, raised their spears—unsure whom to help or fight. A child's cry rang out again from the village, adding fresh panic. Smoke thickened as a gust of wind stirred lingering embers, threatening a new flare-up in the orchard. Edric tried to pull the spear from The Fatman's side, uncertain if that would help or harm. Branwynn rummaged frantically for healing herbs she no longer had.

Krampus, maddened by The Fatman's injury and the beast's attempt to escape, swung his chains in a deadly arc at the creature's neck. The villagers shouted "No!" but too late—the chain whistled through heated air. The beast tried to dodge, but wounded and chained, it had little chance. Sparks flew as chain met flesh, a sickening crack echoed. Would Krampus deal a fatal blow, shattering their code?

At that instant, the beast's head jerked aside. The chain strike glanced off, drawing a spray of black ichor and a piercing shriek. Not a clean kill—yet the creature howled in unimaginable agony. In its pain frenzy, it lashed out blindly, one claw striking toward The Fatman and Helgrid. Helgrid threw herself over The Fatman's body, bracing for a lethal slash.

Branwynn screamed, Takrin lunged, Marta sobbed, Edric tried to block with a staff. Too many events collided: The beast's desperate thrash, Krampus's enraged chain strike, The Fatman's mortal wound, Gorven's escape, children crying in the distance, orchard embers flaring anew. The villagers could not handle all at once.

As the beast's claw descended, chain rattles boomed again. Krampus moved faster than thought, interposing himself between claw and The Fatman. A clash of claw on chain sparked greenish firelight. The Fatman gasped, Helgrid staggered, villagers stumbled backward.

In that chaotic second, the orchard flames kicked up one last gust, illuminating the scene in hellish brilliance: Krampus tangling with the beast, The Fatman gravely injured in Helgrid's arms, Gorven fleeing into smoky darkness, Branwynn and others powerless to stop him, newcomers with spears caught in confusion, Marta crying over wounded villagers, and a child's terrified scream echoing from the village's heart.

Then, a deafening roar shattered the night—whether from Krampus, the beast, or something else unseen, it was impossible to tell. The villagers froze, horror gripping their hearts as firelight danced on twisted silhouettes. The beast convulsed, Krampus's chains tightening. The Fatman moaned in pain, blood dripping onto scorched earth. Helgrid's hammer slipped from her numb fingers. Branwynn's staff fell as she raised her arms to protect her face from sparks. Edric and Takrin exchanged terrified looks. Marta clutched at a trembling newcomer soldier who looked ready to run.

In that flash of terror and agony, the final image seared their minds: Krampus poised to deliver a possibly fatal blow, The Fatman gravely wounded, Gorven escaping unseen, villagers paralyzed by moral dread, orchard embers flaring wildly, and the monstrous beast writhing in chain-bound fury. No one knew if mercy or wrath would win this last desperate moment.

CHAPTER TWENTY

Smoke clung to the charred remains of the orchard, curling around the villagers as they struggled to contain the chaos. Blood stained the ground, mingling with ash and mud. Gorven writhed, clutching his leg where Helgrid's hammer had finally struck true. His knee bent at an unnatural angle, his teeth clenched in a snarl. The sound of his scream echoed against the scorched trunks, but no one moved to comfort him.

The villagers stood panting, hands trembling, weapons gripped too tightly. Mercy had cost them nearly everything, yet Gorven's relentless malice had forced their hand. Even now, despite his injury, his glare burned with hatred, defiance written across his twisted features.

Helgrid let her hammer drop to her side, the weight of her action heavy in her heart. She didn't look at Gorven but instead glanced at

Branwynn, her voice barely above a whisper. "Is this what mercy costs us? Breaking a man's body?"

Branwynn's throat tightened, but she had no answer. The villagers knew they had reached a breaking point, their moral resolve tested beyond limits. Marta knelt beside Teryn, who had collapsed from exhaustion, trembling in fear. Nearby, Edric and Takrin wiped the blood from their bruised hands, silent but alive.

The Fatman still lay inside the meeting hall, his breathing shallow. Branwynn had stayed with him for a moment, his pale face etched in her memory, but the desperate cry from the orchard had pulled her back outside. Now she stood frozen, her staff hanging limp in her hand.

Beyond them, the masked stranger moved toward the orchard's edge, his staff glowing faintly as he murmured an incantation to restore the scorched earth. With each step, faint green shoots pushed through the ash, a hopeful whisper in the darkness. But even his magic felt like a fragile balm on a deep, festering wound.

The tension broke when Gorven spat blood onto the dirt, his voice rough and venomous. "You think you've won? Crippled me? Hah. You're weaker than I thought. You can't even kill a man to save yourselves. What do you think will happen when the next raiders come, when the next beast comes clawing at your gates?"

Helgrid spun toward him, her face a mask of fury and anguish. "Be silent!" she barked, her voice cracking. "We let you live—barely! Do not twist the knife after all we've endured."

Gorven laughed bitterly, his body trembling with pain but his resolve unbroken. "You think sparing me is mercy? It's cowardice, and you know it." He leaned forward, his bloodied hands gripping the dirt as he hissed, "The world doesn't care about your code. Mercy won't save you when it comes for your children next."

A gasp rippled through the crowd, low murmurs following. Gorven's words stung because they rang with half-truths, because they echoed the villagers' own doubts.

From the shadows at the far side of the clearing, a low, guttural growl cut through Gorven's speech. The villagers stiffened, their eyes snapping to the forest. The sound was not like the beast they had just driven away—it was deeper, wetter, and reverberated with an unsettling resonance.

"What now?" Edric muttered, tightening his grip on his staff. His knuckles whitened, and sweat slid down his temple. The air around them felt heavy, charged with a dark, primal energy that made their skin crawl.

Branwynn stepped forward, raising her staff as if the feeble gesture could pierce the thick underbrush. "Something watches us," she murmured, her voice trembling. "Something older than the beast."

Krampus's presence was notably absent. His chains had gone silent after the creature fled into the woods. Though the horned enforcer had lingered to stabilize The Fatman, his ominous figure had retreated into the smoky void. For the first time, the villagers truly felt alone.

The growl came again, closer now. A pair of faintly glowing eyes appeared between the trunks, low to the ground, moving like embers floating in the darkness. The creature's form was indistinct, cloaked in the forest's shadow, but its presence radiated malice.

"Everyone, fall back!" Helgrid ordered, her voice sharp, cutting through the rising panic. She gestured for the newcomers to form a defensive line, spears ready, while the villagers clustered around the meeting hall.

The masked stranger turned toward the threat, his expression unreadable beneath his ornate face covering. "Do not provoke it," he warned, his voice carrying an unnatural echo. "This is no mere predator—it is something called by the wounds of this land."

Branwynn's heart dropped. "Called? What do you mean?"

The stranger raised his staff slightly, the glowing runes along its length flickering. "The violence you've endured, the balance you've disrupted—it has awakened a guardian of the deep woods. This spirit does not distinguish between beast, man, or magic. It comes to reclaim what it believes is owed."

A gasp spread among the villagers. Teryn whimpered, clutching Marta's arm. "You mean... it wants the orchard? Us?"

The stranger nodded grimly. "It will not stop unless appeased."

The glowing eyes darted forward, the creature stepping into the light of the orchard's dying flames. The villagers sucked in their breaths—it was massive, its shoulders hunched and corded with muscle. Its body seemed fused with the forest itself, bark and moss growing along its limbs, and its antlers spread wide like branches dripping with sap. Its maw opened, revealing rows of jagged, splintered teeth. It was both beast and spirit, a living nightmare conjured by their fears.

Gorven cackled, even as he writhed in pain. "Perfect timing! Let's see your mercy save you now!"

Marta snapped, her voice shaking but firm. "Enough! Your poison won't sway us."

The creature reared back, a low bellow shaking the ground. The villagers braced, the stranger raising his staff in a defensive gesture. "It gives us one chance," he murmured. "One chance to make this right."

Branwynn swallowed hard. "What does it want?"

The stranger's eyes flicked to The Fatman's faintly glowing form inside the hall. "A life for a life. Blood for the orchard it guards."

The words sent a chill through them all. Teryn shook her head frantically, tears streaming down her face. "No! It can't have him! He saved me. He saved us."

Marta stepped forward, jaw set. "We will not trade lives—not his, not anyone's." Her voice grew louder. "We'll stand, and we'll fight, if we must."

The stranger's voice dropped, his words a warning. "If you choose to fight, know this—it cannot be killed by mortal hands."

The creature roared, charging forward. Its antlered head lowered, crashing through the orchard's remnants with terrifying speed. The ground trembled beneath its weight. The villagers shouted warnings, raising their weapons in a desperate attempt to hold their line.

Helgrid swung her hammer, catching the creature's shoulder. Sparks flew as metal clashed against bark-like flesh. The impact staggered it, but only for a moment. It lashed out with a massive, clawed limb, sending Helgrid sprawling. She hit the ground hard, coughing, but managed to crawl back to her feet.

Branwynn raised her staff, chanting under her breath. A faint circle of light formed around her feet, but before she could complete the spell, the creature lunged at her. Takrin and Edric shoved her out of the way, taking the brunt of the impact. They fell hard, gasping for breath.

The newcomers joined the fray, their spears jabbing at the creature's flanks. One spear lodged in its side, but the creature barely noticed, shaking it off like a splinter. Its antlers glowed faintly now, pulsing with an eerie green light.

Inside the hall, The Fatman stirred weakly, his eyes fluttering open. His voice, barely audible, carried through the air. "Brother…"

Krampus

As if summoned, a faint rattle echoed from the shadows. Chains clinked, growing louder with each step. The villagers felt a wave of cold dread and relief as Krampus emerged from the treeline, his towering form backlit by the flickering flames. His amber eyes locked onto the creature, his expression unreadable.

Krampus stepped forward, chains coiling around his arms like serpents. The villagers watched, hope mingling with fear. Would he intervene? Would he save them, or would his presence only escalate the carnage?

The creature snarled, lowering its head as it prepared to charge again. Krampus raised a hand, his chains snapping forward with a deafening crack. They wrapped around the creature's forelimbs, pulling it off balance. The ground shook as it struggled, roaring in fury.

But even as Krampus fought, the villagers noticed something strange—his movements were slower, his chains less precise. His earlier intervention had drained him, and now he seemed to strain against the creature's immense strength.

Branwynn's heart sank. "He can't hold it alone," she whispered.

The villagers rallied, stepping forward with renewed determination. Helgrid, her ribs aching, swung her hammer again, striking the creature's hind leg. Edric and Takrin looped a chain around its other leg, pulling with all their might. Marta and Branwynn focused their energy on supporting Krampus, their voices rising in unison as they chanted ancient protective spells.

The creature thrashed, its antlers glowing brighter. A sudden burst of energy sent the villagers sprawling, their weapons clattering to the ground. Krampus staggered but held his ground, his chains tightening around the creature's limbs.

Then, with a deafening roar, the creature broke free. Chains snapped, sending shards of metal flying through the air. Krampus fell to one knee, his amber eyes blazing with defiance even as exhaustion weighed him down.

The creature turned its gaze toward the meeting hall, where The Fatman lay vulnerable. The villagers scrambled to intercept it, but they were too slow. The creature surged forward, its massive body crashing through the remnants of the orchard.

Teryn screamed, standing in its path, her arms outstretched as if to shield The Fatman. "No!" she cried, her voice breaking.

Krampus rose slowly, his chains rattling weakly. He took one step forward, then another, his strength waning but his resolve unbroken. The villagers could only watch, frozen in terror, as the creature lunged toward the hall, its jaws wide and glowing with unearthly light.

And then, a blinding flash of green erupted from the masked stranger's staff. The creature halted mid-charge, its body writhing as if caught in an invisible net. The masked man stepped forward, his voice booming with ancient power.

"Enough!" he commanded. "You will not claim this place."

The creature roared, its body convulsing as the light from the stranger's staff grew brighter. But even as the villagers dared to hope, the masked man faltered, his staff dimming. The creature broke free of the spell, its eyes burning with renewed fury.

The villagers braced for the final blow, their breaths held as the creature lunged once more.

CHAPTER TWENTY-ONE

The air was a cauldron of tension, smoke curling from the scorched remnants of the orchard as villagers stood shoulder to shoulder, their eyes wide with terror and resolve. The antlered beast loomed larger now, its green-glowing eyes casting eerie light over the battlefield. Krampus, towering yet visibly strained, swung his chains with deliberate precision, the metallic clinking rising above the chaos. The villagers prayed his strength would hold; without him, they would surely fall.

The Fatman lay in the meeting hall, his breaths shallow but steady. Branwynn had hastily returned to his side after the initial strike from the monstrous spirit. Her trembling hands traced the faint glow of healing magic that lingered on his wound, a gift from the masked stranger. Yet even that light now seemed fragile, as if the land itself resisted their attempts to restore balance.

Outside, Helgrid barked orders to the villagers and newcomers. "Keep the line tight! If it breaches, we're done for!" Her hammer rested heavily on her shoulder, each swing slower than the last, but she refused to falter. Teryn stood beside her, the young woman pale but determined, holding a salvaged chain as though it were her last shield.

Edric and Takrin flanked the antlered beast, striking at its sides with coordinated swings of their staffs. Sparks flew as wood met the creature's bark-like hide, but their blows did little more than annoy it. The beast roared, swinging a massive claw that sent both men sprawling into the dirt.

"Regroup!" Helgrid shouted, her voice cutting through the panic. "Don't scatter!"

The masked stranger, still standing near the orchard's edge, raised his staff high. The runes along its length pulsed with a sickly green light that mirrored the glow in the beast's eyes. His chant, rhythmic and ancient, seemed to hold the creature in place for a fleeting moment. The beast snarled, its body twitching as if caught between obeying and resisting the stranger's will.

"It's bound to this land," the stranger called, his voice strained. "You must weaken it further before I can sever its ties!"

Krampus moved swiftly, his chains striking like serpents. He looped them around one of the beast's hind legs and yanked, pulling it off balance. The creature stumbled, its massive bulk crashing into a charred apple tree that splintered under its weight. The ground shook, and the villagers braced themselves against the tremors.

But the beast was far from defeated. It howled, twisting its body and snapping the chains that bound it. Krampus staggered backward, his claws digging into the earth to steady himself. His amber eyes burned with frustration, and for a moment, he glanced toward the meeting hall where The Fatman lay.

Marta caught his gaze and stepped forward, her voice desperate. "We're with you! Just tell us what to do!"

Krampus tilted his head, as though considering her words. Then, with a sudden motion, he pointed toward the beast's glowing antlers. The message was clear—strike at its source of power.

Helgrid understood instantly. "Take out those antlers!" she shouted, rallying the villagers. "That's our target!"

Edric and Takrin scrambled to their feet, nodding grimly. They repositioned themselves, staffs raised, while Helgrid motioned for the newcomers to circle the creature. The beast, sensing their intent, roared again, its breath hot and foul as it lashed out with renewed fury.

Branwynn emerged from the hall, her staff glowing faintly. She joined the fray, her voice rising in a chant that sent a ripple of energy through the air. The beast flinched, its movements momentarily slowed as the magic took hold.

"Now!" Helgrid cried, charging forward. She swung her hammer with all her strength, aiming for the base of the creature's left antler. The impact sent a jarring shockwave through her arms, but the antler cracked, a jagged fissure spreading along its length.

The beast shrieked, its glowing eyes dimming for a brief moment. Edric and Takrin seized the opportunity, striking at its right antler with their staffs. Each blow chipped away at the bark-like surface, sending fragments flying into the air.

The newcomers pressed the advantage, their spears finding purchase in the creature's exposed flanks. The villagers, though exhausted, fought with a ferocity born of desperation. Even Teryn joined the assault, swinging her chain like a whip and wrapping it around the beast's hind leg.

But the creature would not fall so easily. With a deafening roar, it reared up on its hind legs, shaking off its attackers. The force of its movements sent Helgrid sprawling, her hammer clattering to the ground. Edric and Takrin were thrown backward, landing hard amidst the ash and debris.

Branwynn stumbled, her chant faltering as the beast turned its glowing eyes on her. She raised her staff in a defensive gesture, but the creature lunged, its massive claws raking the ground where she stood. A flash of chains intercepted the blow—Krampus had moved between them, his form a shadow of defiance.

"Keep going!" Branwynn urged, her voice shaking. "We're close!"

The masked stranger advanced, his staff glowing brighter as he continued his chant. The runes along its length flared, casting a pale green light that bathed the battlefield. The beast roared again, its movements growing sluggish as the magic began to take hold.

Helgrid retrieved her hammer and staggered to her feet. Blood dripped from a gash on her forehead, but she ignored the pain, her focus locked on the beast's remaining antler. With a determined cry, she swung her hammer once more, striking the fissure with all her strength.

The antler shattered.

A brilliant burst of green light erupted from the beast's head, illuminating the orchard like a second sunrise. The creature howled, its body convulsing as the light consumed it. The villagers shielded their eyes, their breaths held as the beast writhed in agony.

And then, silence.

The light faded, and the beast collapsed, its massive form crumpling to the ground. Smoke rose from its body, mingling with the ash in the air. The villagers stood frozen, their weapons lowered, as they waited to see if it would rise again.

The masked stranger stepped forward, his staff still glowing faintly. He placed a hand on the beast's head, murmuring a final incantation. The creature's body dissolved into the earth, leaving behind only a faint outline burned into the ground.

"It is done," the stranger said, his voice heavy with exhaustion.

The villagers let out a collective sigh of relief, their bodies sagging with the weight of their ordeal. Helgrid dropped her hammer, leaning heavily on its handle as she tried to catch her breath. Branwynn knelt in the dirt, her staff resting beside her.

Krampus stood silently, his chains hanging limp at his sides. His amber eyes scanned the battlefield, lingering briefly on The Fatman's faintly glowing form inside the hall. Without a word, he turned and began to retreat into the shadows.

"Wait!" Marta called after him, her voice echoing in the stillness. "What happens now?"

Krampus paused, his silhouette framed by the smoldering remains of the orchard. He glanced back at the villagers, his expression inscrutable. Then, with a low growl, he disappeared into the darkness.

The villagers stood in silence, their eyes turning toward the meeting hall where The Fatman lay. They had won, but at what cost? The orchard was in ruins, their bodies battered, and their code tested to its limits.

And then, from the treeline, came a new sound—the distant thud of boots on the forest floor. The villagers tensed, their weapons raised once more as they turned to face this new threat.

Out of the shadows emerged a group of figures, their faces obscured by hoods. They moved with purpose, their weapons gleaming in the dim light. At their head was a tall figure clad in dark armor, a wicked grin spreading across his face.

"You've done well," the man said, his voice dripping with malice. "But the real fight has only just begun."

CHAPTER TWENTY-TWO

The acrid tang of smoke and burnt earth hung heavy over the village as the newcomers stepped forward, their presence sharp and disquieting against the aftermath of battle. The air seemed to thrum with a strange energy, neither hostile nor welcoming, as if the land itself were undecided about their arrival. The villagers tightened their circle around the meeting hall, weapons raised but trembling in tired hands.

At the forefront of the strangers stood a tall figure in dark armor, his face partially obscured by a hood that shadowed angular features. His smile was a weapon in itself—sharp, predatory, and unnervingly confident. In his right hand, he held a staff topped with a shard of jagged obsidian that caught the dim light and refracted it into a thousand shards.

Helgrid stepped forward, her hammer resting on her shoulder. Though she was battered and bloody, her voice carried the weight of leadership. "Who are you?" she demanded. "State your purpose."

The man's grin widened, but his words were measured, as though he relished the suspense. "I am called Drevon, a seeker of truths and keeper of forgotten bargains." He gestured to the villagers' weary faces, his tone mocking. "And I see I have arrived at a most opportune moment."

"Opportune for what?" Branwynn interjected, stepping up beside Helgrid. Her staff glowed faintly, a warning. "We've no patience for riddles."

Drevon tilted his head, examining Branwynn as though she were a curiosity. "For ensuring balance," he said smoothly. "The creature you vanquished was a guardian, bound to these lands by ancient rites. Its death, while necessary, has left a void that must be filled. I have come to offer... assistance."

Krampus's absence was palpable. The villagers exchanged wary glances, silently wishing for his looming presence to return. Without him, they felt exposed, vulnerable to whatever game this man intended to play.

"We don't need your help," Marta said, her voice trembling but resolute. "We've defended ourselves. We'll continue to do so."

Drevon's laugh was low, almost musical. "Oh, my dear, you misunderstand. This is not about need. It is about inevitability." He stepped closer, and his entourage fanned out behind him, their weapons glinting menacingly. "When one force is removed, another must rise to replace it. That is the way of the world. Nature abhors a vacuum."

Branwynn's heart sank. She could feel the truth in his words, a subtle shift in the energy of the land that echoed his claim. "And what do you propose?" she asked cautiously.

Drevon's smile faltered for the first time, replaced by something colder. "A pact," he said, his voice dropping to a whisper that carried through the stillness like a blade sliding from its sheath. "You will allow me to take the guardian's place, to bind myself and my followers to this land. In exchange, I will protect your precious village from all who would threaten it."

"No," Helgrid said immediately, her hammer raising slightly. "We don't trade one threat for another."

Drevon's grin returned, wider this time. "Ah, but I am not a threat, am I? I offer safety, stability, order. The Fatman is weak, your horned ally elusive. Can you truly afford to refuse me?"

Behind them, The Fatman stirred, his groan faint but audible. The sound was enough to bolster the villagers' resolve. Helgrid stepped forward, her hammer gleaming in the firelight. "We've faced worse than you," she said firmly. "Leave now, or you'll see how strong we really are."

Drevon's eyes narrowed, the flicker of amusement in them snuffed out. He raised his staff, and the obsidian shard atop it glowed with an unnatural light. His entourage followed suit, their weapons raised in unison.

"Very well," Drevon said, his voice icy. "If you will not accept my offer, then I shall take what I need by force."

The villagers braced themselves as Drevon slammed the base of his staff into the ground. The air shuddered, and a pulse of dark energy erupted from the obsidian shard, rippling outward like a shockwave. The villagers were thrown back, some tumbling to the ground while others staggered to keep their footing.

Branwynn gasped as the wave passed through her. It left no physical mark, but she felt a cold emptiness settle in her chest, as though the energy had stripped something vital from her. Around her, others clutched their heads or chests, their breaths coming in ragged gasps.

Helgrid was the first to recover, her hammer raised as she charged at Drevon. "Enough!" she roared, swinging with all her might. But before her blow could land, one of Drevon's followers stepped forward, intercepting the strike with a curved blade. Sparks flew as metal met metal, and Helgrid was forced to step back, her opponent's strength pushing her off balance.

The battle erupted in earnest. The villagers, though weary and outnumbered, fought with the desperation of those with nothing left to lose. Branwynn summoned what magic she could, her staff glowing brighter as she sent bursts of light toward the advancing enemies. Teryn, still clutching her chain, joined Helgrid in holding the line against the attackers.

Edric and Takrin flanked Drevon's entourage, their staffs striking with precision. The newcomers, though hesitant at first, rallied under Helgrid's leadership, their spears finding gaps in the enemy's armor. But for every foe they felled, another seemed to take their place, their ranks unyielding.

Drevon himself remained at the center of the chaos, his staff raised as he chanted in an ancient tongue. The ground beneath him began to crack, tendrils of dark energy snaking outward and lashing at the villagers. Branwynn narrowly avoided one, the tendril searing a blackened line into the ground where she had stood.

Inside the meeting hall, The Fatman's eyes fluttered open. He struggled to sit up, his body weak but his determination unbroken. "They... need me," he rasped, his voice barely audible.

Marta knelt beside him, tears streaming down her face. "You're not strong enough. Please, rest."

But The Fatman shook his head, his hand reaching for the sack of charms that lay beside him. "The village... cannot fall."

Outside, Krampus returned.

His arrival was heralded by the familiar clinking of chains, a sound that sent a ripple of relief through the villagers. He emerged from the shadows, his form towering and wreathed in a faint, otherworldly glow. His amber eyes locked onto Drevon, and for the first time, the stranger faltered.

"So, the horned one shows himself," Drevon said, his voice tight. "Come to join the losing side?"

Krampus didn't respond. He raised his chains, their metal links glowing red-hot, and sent them hurtling toward Drevon. The stranger raised his staff to block the attack, the obsidian shard pulsing as it absorbed the impact. But Krampus was relentless, his chains striking again and again, driving Drevon back.

The villagers took heart at Krampus's intervention, their attacks growing more coordinated. Branwynn and Helgrid focused on driving back Drevon's followers, while Edric and Takrin flanked the remaining enemies. Teryn and Marta worked together to protect The Fatman, who had managed to rise to his feet, his sack of charms clutched tightly.

But Drevon was far from defeated. He thrust his staff forward, sending a concentrated blast of dark energy toward Krampus. The enforcer grunted as the force struck him, but he held his ground, his chains snapping out to wrap around Drevon's wrist.

The two figures were locked in a deadly struggle, their powers colliding in a storm of light and shadow. The ground beneath them cracked and splintered, the air heavy with the scent of burning ozone.

And then, from the shadows, came another sound—a low growl that froze the blood in their veins. The villagers turned, their eyes widening as a new figure emerged from the treeline.

It was the beast.

But it was not the same creature they had fought before. This beast was larger, its antlers glowing with a blinding light that seared the darkness around it. Its body was wreathed in flames, its eyes burning with a fury that seemed to pierce through their very souls.

Drevon laughed, his voice triumphant. "You see? The balance demands a new guardian, and it has chosen me as its master."

The villagers stared in horror as the flaming beast roared, its massive form shaking the ground. It turned its gaze toward the meeting hall, where The Fatman stood, his weakened form illuminated by the creature's light.

"No," Branwynn whispered, her heart sinking.

The beast charged.

CHAPTER TWENTY-THREE

The flaming beast's roar shattered the fragile resolve of the villagers, its bellow cutting through the smoke and despair like a blade. Its antlers blazed with unholy fire, casting jagged shadows across the battlefield, and its glowing eyes fixed on the meeting hall where The Fatman stood, fragile but determined. The creature's massive claws tore at the earth as it charged, its raw power threatening to overwhelm everything in its path.

Helgrid shouted, her hammer raised high. "Hold the line!" Her voice cracked with desperation, but her feet did not falter as she threw herself into the beast's path. Beside her, Edric and Takrin moved in tandem, their staffs raised to strike as one.

Krampus's chains lashed out like angry serpents, wrapping around the creature's hind legs with a deafening crack. The beast stumbled, its charge faltering as it snarled in frustration. Yet, even with its movements slowed, the fiery guardian seemed unstoppable.

"Pull it down!" Branwynn screamed, her staff glowing as she chanted a spell. A burst of energy shot forth, striking the beast's chest and forcing it back a step. It howled in fury, the flames wreathing its body flaring brighter, hotter, as though feeding on the chaos around it.

The villagers rallied, their fear tempered by the sheer necessity of survival. Helgrid swung her hammer in a wide arc, striking the beast's shoulder with enough force to send sparks flying. Teryn darted in behind her, wielding a length of chain that she looped around one of the creature's antlers. With a cry, she pulled, attempting to wrench the fiery crown from its head.

But the beast was cunning. It twisted sharply, its claws swiping at Teryn. The young woman barely managed to throw herself backward, the chain slipping from her grasp as she hit the ground. The beast's claws tore deep furrows in the dirt where she had stood a moment before.

"Teryn!" Marta cried, rushing to her side. She knelt, her hands trembling as she checked for injuries. "Are you hurt?"

Teryn shook her head, her face pale but determined. "I'm fine," she gasped. "We can't let it reach the hall."

Inside the meeting hall, The Fatman stood with his sack of charms clutched tightly in his hands. His breaths came in shallow gasps, but his eyes burned with determination. He could hear the battle raging outside, the cries of his people fighting to protect one another.

"They need me," he whispered, his voice hoarse but resolute. "I must help."

Marta appeared in the doorway, her face etched with worry. "You're too weak. If you go out there—"

The Fatman cut her off with a wave of his hand. "If I stay here, they will die. We will all die." He reached into his sack, his fingers closing around a small wooden charm shaped like a star. The faint glow of magic pulsed through it. "This will give us a chance."

Branwynn, standing near the center of the battlefield, felt the shift in energy before she saw him. She turned, her eyes widening as The Fatman stepped out of the meeting hall, his weakened form silhouetted against the fiery glow of the beast.

"No!" she shouted, running toward him. "You can't—"

But The Fatman raised his hand, the charm in his grasp flaring with light. The beast froze mid-charge, its blazing antlers dimming for a fleeting moment. The villagers hesitated, their breaths held as the light grew brighter, enveloping the battlefield in a soothing glow.

The Fatman's voice rang out, steady and commanding despite his frailty. "This is not your place, guardian. Return to the shadows from which you came!"

For a moment, it seemed as though the creature might yield. Its massive form trembled, the flames around it flickering uncertainly. The villagers dared to hope.

But Drevon's laughter cut through the silence, sharp and mocking. "You think your trinkets can banish my guardian? Foolish old man."

The obsidian shard atop Drevon's staff flared with dark energy, its tendrils reaching toward the beast. The flames around the creature surged once more, its eyes blazing as it broke free of The Fatman's spell. It turned its gaze on him, its roar filled with a rage that shook the earth.

"No!" Branwynn screamed, throwing herself between The Fatman and the beast. She raised her staff, its light flaring in a desperate attempt to shield him. The beast struck, its claws raking against her magical barrier. Sparks flew as the barrier held, but Branwynn staggered under the force of the attack.

Krampus moved with inhuman speed, his chains lashing out to ensnare the beast's limbs once more. He snarled, his amber eyes blazing as he pulled with all his strength. The villagers joined him, looping chains and ropes around the creature's legs, their combined efforts bringing it to its knees.

"Now!" Helgrid shouted, her hammer raised. "Strike now!"

The villagers poured their strength into the attack. Edric and Takrin drove their staffs into the beast's exposed sides, while Teryn hurled a jagged piece of broken chain at its flaming antlers. Branwynn channeled her remaining energy into a burst of light that struck the creature's chest, sending it reeling.

But Drevon was not idle. He raised his staff high, the dark energy around him swirling like a storm. His voice rose in a chant, each word reverberating through the battlefield with ominous power.

Krampus turned toward him, his chains snapping in warning. He advanced, his movements deliberate and menacing, as though daring Drevon to make his move.

"Come, then," Drevon taunted, his grin returning. "Let us see if the old ways still hold sway."

The two forces collided in a clash of light and shadow. Krampus's chains struck with precision, their searing heat forcing Drevon back. But the dark energy emanating from the obsidian shard was relentless, pushing Krampus to his limits.

The villagers fought to hold the beast at bay, their attacks growing more desperate as its flames licked ever closer to the meeting hall. Helgrid swung her hammer with all her might, striking one of the creature's legs and forcing it to collapse. "It's weakening!" she cried, her voice hoarse. "Keep going!"

But just as victory seemed within reach, a deafening crack split the air. Drevon's staff struck the ground, sending a shockwave of dark energy rippling outward. The villagers were thrown back, their weapons scattered as the force of the blast knocked them off their feet.

Krampus fell to one knee, his chains slackening as the dark energy wrapped around him like a vice. He snarled, straining against the bonds, but even his immense strength seemed to falter.

The beast rose, its flames burning brighter than ever. It roared, a sound of pure rage and triumph, as it turned its attention back to the meeting hall. The villagers could only watch in horror as it charged, its blazing form hurtling toward The Fatman with unstoppable force.

"No!" Branwynn cried, scrambling to her feet. She raised her staff, summoning every ounce of magic she had left, but the spell faltered, her strength spent.

The Fatman stood his ground, his eyes locked on the creature. He raised his charm, its light flickering weakly. "You will not take them," he whispered, his voice steady despite the terror in his heart.

As the beast closed the distance, a deafening roar sounded from the forest. The ground trembled as a massive shadow emerged from the trees, its form wreathed in smoke and darkness. The villagers froze, their eyes widening as they recognized the figure.

It was the first beast, the guardian they had driven away.

But something was different. Its body was scarred, its movements slower, and its eyes no longer burned with malice. It charged toward the flaming beast, its roar filled not with fury, but with purpose.

The two creatures collided in a violent clash of fire and shadow, their roars shaking the earth as they grappled for dominance. The villagers watched in stunned silence, their breaths held as the battle unfolded before them.

Krampus broke free of Drevon's bonds, his chains snapping with renewed fury. He turned toward the stranger, his amber eyes blazing with a promise of vengeance.

But before he could strike, Drevon raised his staff, the obsidian shard glowing with an intensity that rivaled the sun. "You cannot stop what is already in motion," he snarled, his voice echoing with dark power.

And then, with a final, triumphant cry, he drove the shard into the earth.

The ground split open, a chasm of fire and darkness erupting between the battling beasts. The villagers screamed as the earth trembled beneath their feet, the world itself seeming to shatter around them.

And then, silence.

CHAPTER TWENTY-FOUR

The chasm split the battlefield with a jagged roar, spewing heat and smoke into the air like the breath of an angry god. Villagers scrambled to hold their footing as the ground trembled beneath them, the fissure snaking dangerously close to the meeting hall. Drevon stood at its edge, his obsidian staff still buried in the earth, a cruel smile etched on his shadowed face.

On one side of the divide, the flaming beast reeled back, its glowing antlers flickering with an eerie instability. On the other, the original guardian—scarred, limping, but resolute—lowered its head in defiance. Between them lay the abyss, a seething maw of fire and shadow that seemed to whisper ancient promises of destruction.

"Do you feel it now?" Drevon's voice carried across the battlefield, oily and triumphant. "The balance tipping, the old rules breaking? You thought you could deny me, but I am inevitable."

Krampus, standing amidst the chaos, bared his teeth in a low growl. His chains, still glowing faintly from his struggle, rattled ominously as he stepped toward Drevon. But even his formidable presence seemed diminished against the power radiating from the fissure.

"We must stop him!" Branwynn shouted, her staff glowing faintly as she struggled to summon her depleted magic. "If he widens that rift—"

She didn't need to finish. The villagers knew that whatever had been unleashed was not meant for their world. The fissure pulsed with dark energy, its tendrils spreading like roots through the earth, threatening to consume everything.

Helgrid, battered but unbroken, tightened her grip on her hammer. "If we can't seal it, we can still take him down," she growled. "Stay on the beasts—Branwynn, with me!"

The villagers divided, their movements frantic but purposeful. Helgrid and Branwynn charged toward Drevon, their weapons raised. Teryn, Edric, and Takrin turned their focus to the flaming beast, circling it warily as it regained its balance. The masked stranger, his staff still glowing faintly, stood near the edge of the chasm, his gaze fixed on the original guardian as though waiting for its next move.

The two beasts roared in unison, their cries reverberating like thunder. The flaming beast leapt across the fissure with terrifying agility, its claws slamming into the original guardian's scarred flank. The older creature howled in pain but retaliated with a ferocity born of desperation, its massive jaws snapping at the flaming beast's neck.

"Hold it back!" Edric shouted, raising his staff to strike. He and Takrin flanked the flaming beast, aiming for its vulnerable legs. Teryn darted in from behind, looping her chain around one of its hind limbs and yanking with all her strength.

The beast snarled, its fiery antlers flaring brighter as it twisted violently, sending Teryn sprawling. It reared up, its claws poised to strike, but a burst of light from Branwynn's staff forced it back. The flaming creature turned, its burning gaze locking onto the mage.

"You'll have to do better than that," Branwynn muttered, sweat pouring down her face as she readied another spell.

Meanwhile, Krampus advanced on Drevon, his chains whipping through the air with deadly precision. The stranger blocked the first strike with his staff, the obsidian shard absorbing the impact with a blinding flash of light. But Krampus was relentless, his next strike aimed at Drevon's legs.

"You cannot stop me, enforcer," Drevon sneered, sidestepping the attack. "This land is mine now."

Krampus snarled, his amber eyes blazing. His chains lashed out again, this time wrapping around Drevon's staff. He pulled sharply, wrenching the weapon from the man's grasp and sending it clattering to the ground.

But Drevon only laughed. "You think that will stop me?" He raised his hands, dark energy crackling at his fingertips. "I am the conduit. The power flows through me now."

With a roar, he unleashed a wave of energy that sent Krampus staggering back. The villagers braced against the force, their eyes wide with fear as the fissure widened further, spewing ash and fire into the air.

Inside the meeting hall, The Fatman clutched his sack of charms, his body trembling with exhaustion. He could hear the chaos outside, the roars of the beasts and the shouts of his people. He had always been their anchor, their source of hope. Now, weakened and vulnerable, he struggled to find the strength to stand.

Marta knelt beside him, her eyes glistening with tears. "You can't go out there," she whispered. "You've done enough."

The Fatman shook his head, his voice barely above a whisper. "It's never enough. Not when they still need me."

He reached into the sack, his fingers closing around a large, intricately carved charm. Its glow was faint, but steady—a reminder of the old magic that had always guided him. He closed his eyes, drawing a deep breath, and then rose to his feet.

Outside, Branwynn noticed the faint glow emanating from the hall and turned toward it, her heart skipping a beat. "He's coming," she murmured.

The villagers turned to see The Fatman stepping out of the hall, his frail form illuminated by the charm's light. He raised it high, the glow intensifying as he spoke.

"Enough."

The single word carried a weight that silenced the battlefield. Even the beasts paused, their roars fading to growls as they turned their attention to the glowing figure.

Drevon's grin faltered. "You cannot stop this, old man. You are but a relic, clinging to a world that no longer exists."

The Fatman met his gaze, his eyes filled with quiet defiance. "Perhaps. But even relics have their purpose."

He lowered the charm, its light spreading outward in a wave that washed over the battlefield. The villagers felt its warmth, a soothing balm against the chaos. The beasts hesitated, their movements sluggish as the light touched them.

But the fissure remained, its dark energy pulsing stronger than ever. Drevon sneered, raising his hands to summon another wave of power.

Krampus moved first.

With a roar, Krampus hurled his chains at Drevon, the metal links wrapping around the man's torso and pinning his arms to his sides. The enforcer's strength surged, his amber eyes glowing as he pulled Drevon toward the chasm.

"You wouldn't dare," Drevon hissed, struggling against the chains. "You'd destroy us all."

Krampus didn't respond. His grip tightened, his muscles straining as he dragged the man closer to the edge.

"No!" Branwynn shouted, running toward them. "If he falls in—"

Her words were drowned out by the roar of the fissure, its dark energy flaring as though it sensed its master's impending fate. The ground trembled violently, cracks spreading outward in all directions.

The villagers struggled to maintain their footing, their eyes darting between the battling beasts and the confrontation at the chasm's edge. The Fatman raised his charm again, its light pulsing urgently.

"Krampus!" he called, his voice filled with both command and desperation. "Do not sacrifice yourself!"

Krampus hesitated, his grip on the chains faltering for a moment. But Drevon took advantage of the pause, twisting sharply and breaking free. He raised his hands, dark energy surging as he prepared to strike.

Before he could, the original guardian roared, its massive form hurtling toward the fissure. It slammed into the flaming beast, driving it backward with such force that the ground shook. The two creatures tumbled toward the chasm, their claws locked in a deadly embrace.

Drevon's eyes widened. "No! The balance—"

The beasts plunged into the fissure, their roars echoing as they disappeared into the darkness. The ground trembled violently, the cracks spreading faster now as the chasm began to collapse inward.

Krampus turned toward Drevon, his chains snapping with lethal intent. But before he could strike, the fissure erupted, a column of fire and shadow shooting into the sky. The villagers shielded their eyes as the force of the explosion knocked them off their feet.

When the light faded, the battlefield was eerily silent. The fissure was gone, replaced by a smoldering scar in the earth. The beasts were nowhere to be seen.

But Drevon still stood.

His body was battered, his obsidian staff shattered at his feet, but his eyes burned with a defiance that chilled the air. "You think this is over?" he spat, blood trickling from his lips. "You've only delayed the inevitable."

He raised his hand, dark energy crackling at his fingertips. But before he could unleash it, Krampus struck. His chains wrapped around Drevon's throat, pulling him to his knees.

"Finish it!" Helgrid shouted, her hammer raised. "End this now!"

But Krampus hesitated, his amber eyes flickering with something unspoken. The Fatman stepped forward, his charm still glowing faintly. "No," he said softly. "Not like this."

Drevon laughed weakly, his voice rasping. "Mercy again? How predictable."

Krampus growled, his chains tightening.

And then, from the shadows, came a sound—a low, guttural growl that froze the battlefield. The villagers turned, their eyes widening as another figure stepped into the light.

It was a third beast.

Larger than the others, its body cloaked in darkness that seemed to swallow the light. Its eyes burned with a cold, calculating intelligence, and its presence sent a shiver through the earth.

Krampus released Drevon, his chains rattling as he turned to face this new threat. The villagers braced themselves, their breaths held as the beast stepped forward.

And then it spoke.

"Enough of this." Its voice was deep and resonant, filled with an authority that silenced even the wind. "The balance must be restored."

The villagers could only watch, their hearts pounding, as the creature fixed its gaze on The Fatman.

Chapter Twenty-Five

The battlefield was frozen in stunned silence, the deep, resonant voice of the third beast reverberating like thunder in the hearts of all who stood before it. Its form was cloaked in living shadow, its antlers jagged and sharp like broken obsidian, and its burning eyes pierced through the chaos, fixing on The Fatman. This was no mere creature. It radiated power—ancient, patient, and implacable.

Helgrid tightened her grip on her hammer, stepping protectively in front of The Fatman, though her knees threatened to buckle. "What… what are you?" she demanded, her voice trembling but defiant.

The beast's eyes flickered, almost with amusement. "I am what comes when balance is shattered," it rumbled. "When mortals play with forces they do not understand. You have unbound what was meant to remain tethered, and now I must restore what you have broken."

Krampus moved first, his chains rattling in warning as he stepped between the beast and the villagers. His amber eyes blazed with defiance, the shadows around him twisting and coiling like living things. The beast's gaze shifted to him, and for a moment, the two ancient forces seemed to size each other up.

Krampus

"You cannot challenge me, enforcer," the beast said, its voice low and calm. "Your strength is finite. Mine is eternal."

"Eternal doesn't mean invincible," Krampus growled, his chains snapping forward with terrifying speed.

The attack was met with a burst of shadow from the beast, a shockwave that rippled outward, forcing the villagers to shield their eyes. Krampus stumbled back, his chains recoiling as though burned. The beast didn't flinch.

Drevon, still kneeling where Krampus had subdued him, began to laugh. It was a rasping, broken sound, but his eyes gleamed with a twisted satisfaction. "You see now?" he croaked. "Your precious codes and rituals mean nothing. This is what true power looks like."

"Silence!" Branwynn snapped, her staff glowing as she leveled it at him. "Your ambition brought this upon us!"

Drevon's smile widened. "And yet it will be your undoing."

The villagers exchanged desperate glances. Their bodies were battered, their magic and strength all but depleted, and now they faced a creature unlike anything they had ever known. Even Krampus seemed hesitant, his chains curling protectively around him like a cocoon.

The Fatman stepped forward, his presence drawing every eye. He leaned heavily on his staff, his frailty stark against the enormity of the beast before him, but his voice carried a quiet authority that silenced even the shadows.

"Why do you come now, after all this time?" he asked, his tone steady but filled with sorrow. "We have fought to protect this land, to preserve the balance. Do you not see that we seek the same end?"

The beast tilted its head, considering him. "Your intentions are irrelevant," it said. "Balance is not an ideal; it is a law. And you have broken it."

Marta stepped forward, her voice trembling but brave. "We didn't break anything! It was him!" She pointed at Drevon, whose grin faltered under the weight of the accusation.

Drevon chuckled darkly. "And yet you unleashed the guardian. You drove it to madness, and now this is your penance."

The beast's gaze shifted back to The Fatman. "A life must be given to restore what has been lost," it said. "One who holds the balance within their grasp."

The villagers froze, the words hitting like a hammer. They understood immediately: the beast demanded The Fatman's life as payment for the chaos wrought upon the land.

"No!" Branwynn cried, stepping in front of him. "There must be another way!"

"There is none," the beast said, its tone final. "The Fatman's death will seal the rift and ensure no further corruption can take hold. This is the only path."

The villagers erupted in protests, their voices rising in a chaotic chorus of defiance. Helgrid raised her hammer. "You'll have to go through all of us to get to him!"

The beast's eyes narrowed, its shadowy form shifting as it took a deliberate step forward. "So be it."

The beast's first strike came like a thunderclap, its massive claw slamming into the ground and sending a shockwave that rippled through the earth. Villagers were thrown off their feet, their weapons clattering to the ground. Krampus lunged, his chains snapping toward the beast's exposed flank, but the shadows around it flared, deflecting the attack.

"Get up!" Helgrid shouted, scrambling to her feet. She swung her hammer at one of the beast's legs, the impact sending a jarring shock through her arms. The beast roared, kicking out and sending her flying into a nearby tree.

Branwynn chanted frantically, her staff glowing as she sent a bolt of light toward the creature's chest. The attack struck true, but the beast barely flinched. It turned its gaze on her, its antlers crackling with dark energy.

"Branwynn, move!" Edric shouted, tackling her just as a bolt of shadow energy shot past, narrowly missing them both.

Krampus circled the beast, his chains striking with relentless precision. Each attack forced the creature back a step, but it was clear he was struggling. His movements were slower, his strikes less forceful. The villagers realized with growing dread that even Krampus was nearing his limit.

The Fatman stood at the edge of the battlefield, his hands clutching his sack of charms. His eyes flickered with pain and determination as he watched his people fight. He knew what had to be done, but his heart ached at the thought of leaving them to face the world without him.

"Stay back!" Branwynn shouted, her voice cutting through the chaos. "We can handle this!"

But The Fatman shook his head. "No," he murmured. "This is my burden to bear."

As the battle raged on, Teryn and Takrin worked to set a trap, looping chains around the beast's legs and anchoring them to the ground with broken spears. The creature thrashed, its movements growing more erratic as the chains tightened. For a moment, it seemed as though they might succeed.

"We've got it!" Teryn shouted, her face lighting with hope.

But the beast roared, its shadowy form expanding outward in a wave of raw energy. The chains snapped, the spears splintering as the villagers were thrown back once more.

Drevon, watching from a safe distance, laughed. "You cannot win," he taunted. "Even your horned savior falters."

Krampus, blood dripping from a gash on his shoulder, turned his blazing eyes on Drevon. With a snarl, he hurled his chains at the man, the metal links wrapping around his waist and dragging him forward.

"You've caused enough pain," Krampus growled, his voice low and menacing.

Drevon struggled, his smirk finally faltering as he was forced to face the enraged enforcer. "You wouldn't dare," he hissed.

But Krampus didn't respond. He tightened the chains, lifting Drevon off the ground as the man's struggles grew frantic.

"Wait!" The Fatman's voice rang out, sharp and commanding. Krampus hesitated, his amber eyes flickering with uncertainty.

The Fatman stepped forward, his charm glowing faintly in his hand. "He is not our solution," he said firmly. "The balance must be restored another way."

The beast, watching the exchange, let out a low growl. "Enough delays," it rumbled. "The price must be paid."

Branwynn scrambled to her feet, her eyes wild with desperation. "There has to be another way!" she shouted, her voice cracking. "You said balance—does it have to be his life?"

The beast's gaze shifted to her, its antlers pulsing with light. "Only one who carries the weight of the balance can restore it. Do you volunteer, little mage?"

Branwynn froze, her staff trembling in her hands. She glanced at The Fatman, then at her friends, her mind racing.

"Don't," Helgrid said, her voice breaking. "There's got to be another way."

But the beast took a step forward, its claws raised. "Choose, or I will choose for you."

The ground trembled beneath its weight, the battlefield on the brink of collapse. The villagers braced themselves, their breaths held as the beast reared back for its final strike.

And then, from the shadows, came a familiar sound: the faint clinking of chains.

Krampus moved, his form a blur as he launched himself between the beast and The Fatman. His chains wrapped around the creature's limbs, his voice a low growl of defiance.

"You will not take him," Krampus said, his words like a promise etched in stone.

The beast roared, its shadows flaring as it struggled against Krampus's hold. The enforcer's grip tightened, his chains glowing red-hot as he pulled with all his strength.

"Seal the rift!" Krampus shouted, his voice carrying over the chaos. "Now!"

The Fatman hesitated, his charm glowing brightly in his hand. "But you—"

"Do it!" Krampus snarled, his amber eyes blazing. "Or all is lost!"

The villagers turned to The Fatman, their faces etched with fear and hope. The charm in his hand pulsed with light, its power waiting to be unleashed.

The Fatman closed his eyes, his voice a whisper. "I'm sorry."

And then, he slammed the charm into the earth.

The ground erupted in a blinding flash of light, the fissure sealing itself in a cascade of magic. The beast roared, its body writhing as the shadows around it dissolved. Krampus's chains glowed brighter, pulling the creature toward the closing rift.

The villagers watched in stunned silence as Krampus and the beast were consumed by the light, their forms disappearing into the earth.

When the light faded, the battlefield was silent. The fissure was gone, the shadows banished.

But so was Krampus.

CHAPTER TWENTY-SIX

The battlefield was eerily silent in the wake of the fissure's closure, the faint hum of magic dissipating into the cold night air. The villagers stood frozen, their weapons slack in their hands. Krampus's absence was a jagged wound in the landscape, the raw edges of his sacrifice leaving an emptiness that seemed to pull the breath from their lungs.

But the reprieve was short-lived.

Drevon, his charred and battered form still kneeling on the scorched ground, lifted his head. His grin, though cracked and bloodied, returned with cruel satisfaction. "You think this is over?" he rasped, his voice cutting through the silence like a blade. "Krampus was a fool to believe he could contain what has been unleashed."

Helgrid, still clutching her hammer, staggered forward. "You don't know when to stop, do you?" Her voice was sharp, but exhaustion weighed it down. "Your beasts are gone, your power spent. Yield."

Drevon's laughter was a hollow, broken sound. "Gone?" he echoed. "Oh no. You've merely given them a new vessel."

The ground beneath them trembled, faint at first but growing stronger with each passing moment. The villagers exchanged wary glances, their weapons rising again as instinct took hold. The sky above them darkened unnaturally, the stars winking out one by one until the battlefield was shrouded in a void-like blackness.

Branwynn raised her staff, its light flickering faintly. "What's happening?" she demanded, her voice trembling.

Drevon rose to his feet, his movements slow and deliberate. "You sealed the rift, yes," he said, brushing ash from his tattered robes. "But you left its essence behind. It needed a vessel, and I am more than willing to oblige."

The fissure's scar on the earth began to glow faintly, its edges pulsing with dark energy. From the depths of the land came a guttural, otherworldly growl. The villagers braced themselves as shadows poured from the ground, coalescing into a massive, shifting form.

Drevon stepped toward the growing shadow, his grin widening. "And now, we begin anew."

The shadow solidified, towering over the battlefield. Its form was monstrous, a twisted amalgamation of the beasts that had come before it. Antlers wreathed in fire crowned its head, while its limbs were cloaked in darkness that writhed like living snakes. Its eyes burned with cold fire, devoid of mercy or reason.

It let out a deafening roar, the sound reverberating through the village and shaking the very ground. The villagers recoiled, their faces pale with terror.

Helgrid was the first to recover. "Stand your ground!" she bellowed, raising her hammer. "We've come too far to fall now!"

Branwynn joined her, summoning every ounce of magic she had left. Her staff flared with light, sending a burst of energy toward the titan. The attack struck its chest, but the creature barely flinched.

"We need more power!" Branwynn shouted. "This thing isn't like the others!"

The villagers rallied, their movements coordinated despite their fear. Edric and Takrin struck at the titan's legs, their staffs glowing faintly as they aimed for its joints. Teryn darted in and out, her chain lashing at its limbs in an attempt to slow its movements.

The Fatman stepped forward, his charm glowing brightly in his hand. He raised it high, the light spreading across the battlefield and momentarily halting the titan's advance. But even his magic seemed to struggle against the overwhelming force of the shadow.

Drevon laughed, standing at the base of the titan. "Do you see now?" he taunted. "You cannot win. This power is beyond you."

Helgrid snarled, swinging her hammer with all her might. The blow connected with one of the titan's legs, sending a shockwave up her arms. The titan roared, its claws swiping at her, but she ducked just in time.

"We need a plan!" Teryn shouted, narrowly avoiding a blast of shadow energy. "We can't just keep hitting it!"

Branwynn's mind raced, her thoughts swirling in chaos. She turned to The Fatman, her voice urgent. "Do you have anything left? Any charm, any spell?"

The Fatman hesitated, his face etched with pain. "Only one," he said softly. "But it may cost me everything."

Before Branwynn could respond, the titan let out another roar, its antlers flaring with fire. It slammed its massive claws into the ground, sending shockwaves that knocked the villagers off their feet. Helgrid rolled to avoid a falling tree, her breath coming in ragged gasps.

Drevon raised his arms, his voice echoing with power. "Witness the dawn of a new age! An age of shadow and fire!"

Krampus's absence was a palpable void, the enforcer's strength sorely missed as the villagers fought to hold their ground. Branwynn glanced at the scarred earth where he had disappeared, her heart heavy with despair.

And then, faintly, she heard it—the clinking of chains.

The sound grew louder, cutting through the chaos like a beacon of hope. The shadows around the battlefield began to shift, their movements erratic. Drevon faltered, his grin slipping as he turned toward the sound.

From the treeline, Krampus emerged.

His form was altered, his fur singed and his horns cracked, but his presence was undeniable. His chains glowed with an intense, fiery light, their edges sparking as though charged with raw power. His amber eyes burned with a fierce determination, and the shadows around him seemed to retreat in fear.

"You should not have returned," Drevon hissed, his voice trembling with both anger and unease.

Krampus didn't respond. He raised his chains, their length extending unnaturally as they coiled around the titan's massive limbs. The creature roared, thrashing violently as it tried to free itself, but Krampus's grip held firm.

"Strike now!" Krampus growled, his voice low and commanding. "While I hold it!"

The villagers didn't hesitate. Branwynn raised her staff, her magic surging with renewed strength as she sent a blast of light toward the titan's chest. Helgrid swung her hammer, the impact sending cracks spidering through the creature's fiery antlers.

The Fatman stepped forward, his charm glowing brighter than ever. "This ends now," he said, his voice filled with quiet resolve.

He hurled the charm toward the titan, the glowing star embedding itself in the creature's chest. The light flared, spreading across its body like veins of fire. The titan roared, its form writhing as the magic took hold.

But Drevon wasn't finished. He raised his arms, drawing dark energy from the fissure's remnants. "You think you can banish me so easily?" he snarled. "I will not fall!"

Krampus turned toward him, his chains snapping with deadly precision. They wrapped around Drevon's torso, dragging him toward the collapsing titan.

"If you won't fall," Krampus growled, "then you'll go with it."

Drevon screamed, his voice filled with rage and terror as he was pulled into the titan's collapsing form. The ground shook violently, cracks spreading outward as the shadowy mass imploded on itself.

The villagers scrambled to escape the collapsing battlefield, their breaths coming in ragged gasps. Branwynn turned toward Krampus, her voice breaking. "You can't—"

But Krampus didn't move. His chains held firm, his gaze locked on the collapsing titan as it dragged him down.

The light flared brighter, consuming everything in its path.

And then, silence.

CHAPTER TWENTY-SEVEN

The battlefield was a smoldering ruin, the ground split by jagged cracks that glowed faintly with the remnants of dark magic.

Smoke rose from the earth like the breath of a sleeping beast, filling the air with the acrid stench of fire and decay. The villagers moved hesitantly through the wreckage, their breaths shallow, their eyes wide with disbelief.

Krampus was gone—dragged into the abyss alongside the titan and Drevon. For a moment, there was silence, a fragile and hollow stillness that settled like ash over the survivors. But the quiet was short-lived.

From deep within the fissure, a sound emerged. It was faint at first—a low, wet gurgling, as though something deep below was trying to find its voice. The villagers froze, their blood running cold as the noise grew louder, rising into a grotesque, bubbling snarl.

Helgrid raised her hammer, her voice sharp and urgent. "Stay together! Don't—"

The ground beneath her cracked with a sudden, deafening snap. A claw, skeletal and covered in blackened flesh, shot out of the earth, wrapping around her ankle. She screamed, swinging her hammer in a desperate attempt to free herself, but the claw pulled her down with terrifying force.

"Helgrid!" Branwynn cried, rushing toward her with her staff glowing. She sent a burst of light toward the claw, and it recoiled with a hiss, releasing its grip. Helgrid scrambled back, her face pale but determined.

"What was that?" Teryn whispered, her voice trembling as she clutched her chain.

The answer came in the form of another claw, this one larger, bursting from the ground only a few feet away. The villagers scattered as more claws emerged, tearing at the earth and pulling up grotesque, half-formed creatures. Their bodies were twisted and unnatural, their features warped by shadow and fire. They moved with jerking, insect-like motions, their glowing eyes fixed on the survivors.

Branwynn raised her staff, her voice trembling as she began to chant. "Stay behind me! I can—"

One of the creatures lunged at her, its claws swiping through the air with a sharp, hissing sound. She ducked just in time, the creature's strike missing her by inches. It let out a guttural screech, its misshapen jaw snapping open to reveal rows of needle-like teeth.

Edric and Takrin moved in tandem, their staffs striking the creature's legs and sending it sprawling. Teryn darted forward, looping her chain around its neck and pulling tight. The creature thrashed violently, its movements erratic and jerky, before it finally collapsed into the dirt, its body dissolving into ash.

"Don't let them touch you!" Edric shouted, his voice cracking with fear. "They're poisoned with that dark magic!"

But there was no time to regroup. More creatures clawed their way out of the ground, their grotesque forms skittering toward the villagers with unsettling speed. Branwynn struck one with a burst of light, her heart pounding as its shriek echoed through the battlefield.

From the fissure came a new sound—a low, rhythmic pounding, like the heartbeat of the earth itself. The villagers froze, their breaths caught in their throats as the sound grew louder.

Branwynn's eyes darted toward the fissure, her stomach twisting with dread. "Something else is coming."

The earth trembled beneath their feet, and then, with a deafening roar, a massive figure began to rise from the fissure. Its body was cloaked in writhing shadows, its eyes glowing with an unnatural light. It was humanoid in shape, but its features were grotesquely distorted—elongated limbs, jagged claws, and a face that seemed to shift and warp with every second.

The creature's gaze fixed on The Fatman, who stood at the edge of the battlefield, his charm still glowing faintly in his hand. It let out a guttural growl, its voice like the grinding of stone.

"You…" it hissed, its words dripping with malice. "You dared to defy the balance."

The Fatman didn't flinch. He stepped forward, his eyes steady despite the trembling in his hands. "I did what I had to do to protect these people."

The creature laughed, a sound that sent chills down the spines of everyone who heard it. "And now you will pay the price."

It lunged.

The Fatman barely managed to dodge the strike, the creature's claws slamming into the ground where he had stood. The impact sent a shockwave rippling outward, knocking the villagers off their feet. Branwynn scrambled to her feet, her heart racing as she raised her staff.

"Keep it away from him!" she shouted, sending a burst of light toward the creature. The attack struck its chest, but it only seemed to enrage it further. It turned its glowing eyes on her, its mouth twisting into a grotesque grin.

"You think your light can stop me, little mage?" it snarled, its voice filled with scorn. "I am the void. I am the end."

Helgrid charged forward, her hammer raised high. She brought it down with all her strength, striking the creature's leg and forcing it to stumble. "Keep hitting it!" she shouted. "Don't let it regain its balance!"

The villagers rallied, their attacks growing more coordinated. Edric and Takrin struck at the creature's limbs, while Teryn looped her chain around its arm, trying to pull it off balance. Branwynn focused her magic on its head, sending bursts of light to distract it.

But the creature was relentless. It swung its massive claws, sending Helgrid flying into a nearby tree. She groaned, struggling to stand as blood dripped from a gash on her forehead.

"Helgrid!" Branwynn cried, rushing to her side.

"I'm fine," Helgrid muttered, though her voice was weak. "Just… don't let it win."

The Fatman stepped forward again, his charm glowing brighter. He raised it high, his voice steady despite the chaos around him. "You will not take this place. I won't let you."

The creature snarled, its movements slowing as the charm's light washed over it. "Your magic is nothing compared to the void," it hissed. "You cannot stop me."

From the edge of the battlefield came a faint sound—the clinking of chains.

Branwynn froze, her eyes widening. "It can't be…"

The villagers turned toward the sound, their hearts leaping with hope. From the shadows, Krampus emerged.

His form was battered and scarred, his chains glowing with an intense, fiery light. His amber eyes burned with a fierce determination, and the air around him seemed to crackle with energy.

The creature froze, its glowing eyes narrowing as it turned to face him. "You," it hissed. "You dare return?"

Krampus didn't respond. He raised his chains, their length extending unnaturally as they snapped toward the creature. The impact sent a shockwave through the battlefield, the force knocking the creature back.

The villagers rallied, their attacks growing more coordinated as they fought alongside Krampus. The creature roared, its movements growing more erratic as it struggled against their combined efforts.

But even as they fought, the fissure began to tremble again, its edges glowing faintly. The villagers froze, their eyes widening as a new wave of shadows began to pour from the earth.

Branwynn's heart sank. "It's not over."

The ground beneath them split open, and from the depths came a deafening roar.

CHAPTER TWENTY-EIGHT

The fissure trembled violently, spewing ash and darkness into the air as if the earth itself was rejecting the horrors it had unleashed. The battlefield was cloaked in an unnatural stillness, the kind of silence that only comes before a storm. Krampus stood at its edge, his chains rattling ominously as his glowing amber eyes scanned the rising shadows.

Then the growl came.

It was low at first, barely audible over the rumble of the collapsing ground, but it grew louder, deeper, resonating in the chest of every villager. The sound carried with it an almost primal terror, one that clawed at their resolve and whispered of ancient, unforgiving things.

Branwynn's grip tightened on her staff as she stood beside The Fatman. Her voice was hoarse, her throat raw from chanting spells. "It's coming," she whispered, her words barely audible. "Whatever's down there... it's waking up."

Helgrid, bloodied but unbowed, spat into the dirt and hefted her hammer. "Then we kill it," she growled, though even her voice shook with uncertainty.

The villagers stood shoulder to shoulder, their weapons raised and their breaths shallow. Teryn, clutching her chain tightly, glanced toward the fissure, her wide eyes reflecting the faint, pulsing glow within. "Do you think it's—"

A scream tore through the battlefield.

The villagers whirled, their hearts leaping into their throats as one of their number—Edric—was dragged backward into the shadows. His staff fell from his hands, clattering against the rocks as he disappeared into the abyss. His screams echoed, sharp and desperate, before abruptly cutting off.

"Edric!" Teryn cried, rushing forward, but Branwynn caught her arm.

"Don't!" Branwynn snapped. "It's too late."

The shadows moved then—fast, too fast—skittering along the ground like living things. Figures emerged from the darkness, grotesque and half-formed. Their bodies were twisted, their limbs too long and their faces melting like wax. Their movements were jerky, insect-like, and they let out guttural, bone-chilling snarls as they advanced.

"Hold the line!" Helgrid roared, swinging her hammer at the first creature to lunge. The blow connected, shattering its chest with a sickening crack, but two more appeared in its place.

Teryn lashed out with her chain, looping it around one creature's neck and yanking hard. The thing let out a wheezing screech as it fell, its body dissolving into ash. But the victory was short-lived—another creature leapt at her, claws extended.

Branwynn raised her staff, a burst of light searing through the air and striking the creature mid-leap. It fell to the ground, writhing and shrieking as it burned, but more shadows poured from the fissure, their numbers growing with each passing moment.

The Fatman stepped forward, his charm glowing brightly in his hand. "We cannot fight them all," he said, his voice steady despite the chaos. "We must find the source and end it."

Krampus growled low in his throat, his chains snapping toward the creatures with deadly precision. "The source is beneath us," he said, his voice rough and edged with fury. "But it won't let us reach it easily."

The ground shook violently, and a deep, resonant voice echoed from the fissure. It was not a voice made for mortal ears—it was a guttural, otherworldly sound that seemed to resonate within the bones of all who heard it.

"You dare to defy me?" the voice boomed, filled with rage and malice. "You who cling to the scraps of old magic, who think yourselves worthy to challenge the void?"

Branwynn's heart sank. "What is that?"

Krampus's eyes burned brighter, his chains coiling tightly around his arms. "The shadow behind the beasts," he said grimly. "The thing that gave them power. It's been waiting, feeding on the chaos we've unleashed."

Helgrid's jaw tightened. "Then we take it down."

Krampus didn't respond. Instead, he stepped toward the fissure, his chains rattling as he prepared to descend. "Stay together," he said, his voice a low growl. "It will try to divide us."

The villagers exchanged nervous glances, but they followed him, their weapons raised as they approached the edge of the chasm. The shadows seemed to retreat as Krampus moved, as though wary of his presence, but the sense of dread only grew stronger.

As they descended into the fissure, the air grew colder, heavier, pressing against their chests like an invisible weight. The light from Branwynn's staff flickered uncertainly, barely holding back the encroaching darkness.

The silence was suffocating.

Then, without warning, a hand shot out from the shadows, grabbing Takrin by the shoulder. He screamed, struggling against the unseen force, but it yanked him into the darkness before anyone could react.

"Takrin!" Helgrid shouted, her voice echoing through the cavern. She charged after him, her hammer swinging wildly, but she found only empty air.

A faint whisper drifted through the darkness, low and mocking. "One by one, you will fall."

Branwynn shuddered, clutching her staff tightly. "It's toying with us," she said, her voice trembling. "Trying to break us."

Krampus growled low in his throat. "It will not succeed."

The ground beneath them shifted again, and the shadows surged forward, forming grotesque shapes that lunged at the group. Helgrid swung her hammer with practiced precision, shattering one creature's head, while Teryn lashed out with her chain, pulling another into the light where it dissolved with a hiss.

But the shadows kept coming, their movements erratic and unpredictable. Branwynn sent another burst of light into the darkness, illuminating a horrific sight: hundreds of clawed hands reaching toward them from the walls of the chasm, their fingers curling and grasping as if desperate to pull them into the void.

The Fatman raised his charm, its light cutting through the darkness and forcing the hands to retreat. "Keep moving!" he commanded, his voice steady despite the fear in his eyes. "We must reach the heart of this!"

The group pressed on, their movements cautious but determined. The path wound deeper into the earth, the air growing colder and heavier with every step. The shadows seemed to watch them, shifting and murmuring as though alive.

Then came the scream.

It was high-pitched, agonized, and chillingly familiar. Branwynn froze, her heart pounding as she recognized the voice. "Takrin…"

The scream echoed again, this time louder, closer. It came from ahead, from the direction they were heading. Helgrid tightened her grip on her hammer, her jaw clenched. "We keep going," she said firmly. "We can't leave him behind."

The tunnel opened into a massive chamber, its walls lined with writhing shadows that pulsed like living things. In the center of the room stood a towering figure, its body a shifting mass of darkness and fire. Its glowing eyes fixed on the group, and it smiled, revealing rows of jagged, needle-like teeth.

"Welcome," it said, its voice echoing like a thousand whispers. "You've come so far, only to fail."

Krampus stepped forward, his chains glowing brightly. "We'll see about that."

The figure laughed, a deep, resonant sound that shook the chamber. "You cannot defeat me, enforcer. You are but a relic, clinging to a world that no longer exists."

The shadows surged forward, forming grotesque shapes that lunged at the group. Branwynn raised her staff, sending a burst of light toward the nearest creature. Helgrid swung her hammer, shattering another, while Teryn lashed out with her chain.

The Fatman raised his charm, its light cutting through the darkness and forcing the creatures back. "We must destroy its core!" he shouted. "That's the only way to end this!"

The figure snarled, its glowing eyes narrowing. "You think you can stop me? I am the void! I am eternal!"

Krampus's chains snapped forward, wrapping around the figure's limbs and pulling tight. The figure roared, thrashing violently as it struggled against his hold. "Now!" Krampus growled. "Strike it now!"

The villagers surged forward, their weapons striking the figure with all their strength. Branwynn channeled her magic into her staff, sending a concentrated burst of light toward its chest. The Fatman raised his charm, its glow intensifying as he focused its power.

The figure let out a deafening roar, its body writhing as the light consumed it. The shadows around it dissolved, retreating into the walls of the chamber.

But just as the group dared to hope, the figure's form solidified again, its eyes burning brighter than ever. It laughed, a sound filled with rage and triumph.

"You cannot destroy me," it said. "You have only made me stronger."

The ground trembled violently, and the shadows surged forward once more, their movements more frenzied and erratic. The villagers braced themselves, their breaths coming in ragged gasps as the figure raised its clawed hand.

"Now," it snarled, "you will fall."

CHAPTER TWENTY-NINE

The chamber's oppressive darkness pressed against them, alive and smothering, a tangible weight that dragged at their bodies and minds. The shadowed figure loomed larger than before, its grotesque, shifting form pulsating with chaotic energy. Its blazing eyes fixed on Krampus, who stood at the forefront, his chains coiled tightly around his arms like living steel.

"You cannot win," the figure hissed, its voice echoing with a thousand whispers. "You cling to light, but here in the depths, the void is absolute."

Krampus snarled low in his throat, his amber eyes glowing fiercely. His chains snapped forward with blinding speed, aiming for the figure's chest, but the shadow absorbed the attack like water swallowing a stone. The creature didn't flinch, its jagged grin growing wider.

"Is this the best you have, enforcer?" it taunted. "Perhaps you have forgotten your place."

Branwynn raised her staff, its light flickering uncertainly as she struggled to summon her magic. Her voice was hoarse from chanting, and her hands trembled with exhaustion, but she stood her ground. "Keep it talking," she murmured to Helgrid, who gripped her hammer tightly beside her. "If it's distracted, we can—"

The figure moved suddenly, faster than anyone could react. Its clawed hand shot out, slamming into the ground and sending a shockwave that threw the group off their feet. Branwynn hit the ground hard, the impact knocking the breath from her lungs as her staff rolled out of reach.

Helgrid was the first to recover, her hammer swinging upward in a desperate arc. The blow connected with one of the figure's limbs, sending a spray of black ichor into the air. The creature roared, its form flickering like a dying flame, but it quickly reformed, its glowing eyes narrowing in fury.

"Fools," it spat, its voice dripping with malice. "You think your crude weapons can harm me?"

The ground beneath them began to shift, jagged cracks spreading outward as the chamber trembled. From the fissures rose twisted shapes—creatures made of shadow and fire, their forms writhing and incomplete. They moved with jerking, insect-like motions, their guttural screeches echoing through the chamber.

"We've got company!" Teryn shouted, lashing her chain at one of the creatures. The weapon struck true, slicing through its torso and causing it to dissolve into ash, but another took its place almost immediately.

Helgrid swung her hammer, shattering one creature's head before pivoting to strike another. "These things just keep coming!" she growled. "We need to stop them at the source!"

Krampus didn't respond. His focus remained on the shadowed figure, his chains striking again and again, each blow forcing the creature back a step. "You cannot hide forever," he growled, his voice a low rumble. "Your power has limits, even here."

The figure laughed, a sound that sent shivers down the spines of everyone who heard it. "Limits? Oh, enforcer, you misunderstand. This place is mine. You are the one out of your depth."

With a sweeping motion, the figure sent a wave of dark energy surging toward the group. Branwynn raised her hand instinctively, a shield of light forming around them just in time to absorb the impact. The force of the attack shattered the shield, sending shards of magical energy scattering across the chamber.

The Fatman staggered, his charm glowing faintly in his hand. "We cannot hold this forever," he said, his voice strained. "We must find the core of its power."

Branwynn scrambled to her feet, her eyes darting around the chamber. The writhing shadows on the walls seemed to pulse in time with the figure's movements, as though feeding it strength. Her heart sank as the realization hit her. "The chamber itself," she said, her voice shaking. "It's drawing power from the darkness around us."

Helgrid swung her hammer at another creature, her breath coming in ragged gasps. "Then we need to destroy the chamber."

Krampus turned his blazing eyes on Branwynn, his voice sharp. "Can you do it?"

Branwynn hesitated, her staff trembling in her hands. "If I can reach the center, I might be able to disrupt the flow of energy, but—"

"You'll have your opening," Krampus growled, his chains snapping toward the figure again. "Go!"

The villagers formed a protective circle around Branwynn as she moved toward the center of the chamber, her staff glowing brighter with each step. The shadow creatures surged forward, their claws raking the air as they attacked with relentless ferocity.

Helgrid stood at Branwynn's side, her hammer striking down any creature that came too close. Teryn and Takrin flanked them, their weapons a blur of motion as they fought to keep the shadows at bay. The Fatman moved behind them, his charm pulsing with light that seemed to weaken the creatures, causing them to recoil as they drew near.

But the shadowed figure was not idle. It let out a deafening roar, its form expanding outward as it sent tendrils of darkness snaking through the chamber. One of the tendrils wrapped around Teryn's leg, pulling her to the ground with a shriek.

"Help!" she cried, her chain falling from her grasp as she struggled against the suffocating grip.

Helgrid spun toward her, her hammer slicing through the tendril with a single, powerful strike. "Stay close!" she shouted, helping Teryn to her feet. "We can't afford to lose anyone!"

Branwynn reached the center of the chamber, her heart pounding as she raised her staff. The ground beneath her feet pulsed with dark energy, the shadows recoiling and writhing as though sensing her intent.

She closed her eyes, focusing every ounce of her strength on the spell she had been saving for this moment.

The light from her staff intensified, spreading outward in rippling waves. The shadows screamed as the light touched them, their forms dissolving into ash. The chamber trembled violently, the cracks in the ground spreading wider as the walls began to crumble.

The shadowed figure roared, its form flickering like a dying flame. "No!" it snarled, its voice filled with fury and desperation. "You cannot—"

Krampus's chains struck with blinding speed, wrapping around the figure's torso and pulling tight. The enforcer's amber eyes burned with fury as he dragged the creature toward the collapsing fissure. "You will not escape," he growled, his voice like thunder.

The figure thrashed violently, its claws raking at Krampus's chains, but the enforcer's grip held firm. The ground beneath them buckled, and the fissure began to widen once more, spewing fire and shadow into the air.

Branwynn's spell reached its peak, the light from her staff consuming the chamber in a blinding flash. The villagers shielded their eyes, their breaths held as the walls crumbled around them.

When the light faded, the shadowed figure was gone.

The chamber was silent, the oppressive darkness replaced by a faint, flickering glow from the remnants of Branwynn's spell. The villagers stood frozen, their weapons slack in their hands as they stared at the collapsed fissure.

But their relief was short-lived.

A deep, guttural growl echoed from the shadows, louder and more menacing than anything they had heard before. The ground trembled violently, and a massive clawed hand burst through the rubble, its jagged fingers stretching toward the group.

Branwynn's heart sank. "It's not over."

Chapter Thirty

The claw burst from the rubble like a harbinger of doom, its jagged edges gleaming with the glow of dark energy. It slammed into the ground, sending tremors that rattled the air and nearly threw the villagers off their feet. From the center of the chamber rose a new form, one that dwarfed even the shadowed figure they had just battled.

It was a titan of nightmares.

The creature's body was a grotesque fusion of shadow and flesh, its limbs elongated and twisted like roots of a poisoned tree. Fire burned in its core, visible through jagged cracks in its body, and its face was a horrifying amalgamation of the beasts they had fought before—antlers of fire, eyes like molten lava, and a mouth filled with shifting, jagged teeth.

Branwynn's voice was barely a whisper. "It's evolving."

Krampus stood at the forefront, his chains rattling with a low, ominous sound. His amber eyes locked on the titan, blazing with a fury that mirrored the fire in the creature's chest. "This is the source," he growled. "No more distractions. We end it here."

The titan roared, a sound so powerful it sent cracks rippling through the ground. It moved with terrifying speed, its massive claws swiping through the air toward the villagers. Helgrid pushed Branwynn out of the way just as one claw slammed into the ground, creating a deep crater where they had stood.

"Stay together!" Helgrid barked, her hammer raised as she charged. She brought it down with all her strength, the weapon striking one of the titan's legs and sending a shockwave up her arms. The blow forced the creature to stumble, but its massive size made it nearly impossible to topple.

Teryn and Takrin flanked the titan, their weapons a blur as they struck at its vulnerable joints. The creature howled, its movements jerky and unnatural as it swiped at them with its claws. Teryn managed to loop her chain around one of its arms, pulling with all her strength to hold it in place.

"Now, Branwynn!" she shouted. "Hit it!"

Branwynn raised her staff, her voice rising in a chant that sent waves of light cascading toward the titan. The magic struck its chest, searing through the cracks in its body and illuminating the darkness within. The creature roared, its movements growing more erratic as the light spread.

But the titan wasn't done.

With a guttural snarl, it slammed its claws into the ground, creating a shockwave that knocked the villagers off their feet. Shadows poured from its body, forming twisted, half-formed creatures that surged toward the group with terrifying speed.

The Fatman stepped forward, his charm glowing brightly in his hand. "Hold them back!" he commanded, his voice steady despite the chaos. "I need time!"

Krampus's chains lashed out, slicing through the shadow creatures with precision and fury. He moved like a force of nature, his strikes relentless as he cleared a path toward the titan. "Stay on the titan!" he growled. "Its creatures are distractions!"

The Fatman knelt, his hands trembling as he reached into his sack of charms. He pulled out a large, intricately carved star, its surface glowing with faint, pulsing light. "This is all I have left," he murmured, his voice filled with sorrow.

Helgrid staggered to her feet, her hammer resting heavily on her shoulder. "Whatever you're planning, do it fast," she said, her voice grim. "We can't keep this up."

The titan roared again, its antlers blazing with fire as it lunged toward The Fatman. Krampus intercepted the attack, his chains wrapping around the creature's arm and pulling it back. The strain was visible in his movements, but he held firm, his teeth bared in a snarl.

"Do it now!" Krampus shouted, his voice echoing through the chamber.

The Fatman closed his eyes, his grip tightening on the glowing charm. He began to chant, his words low and steady, filled with an ancient power that resonated through the air. The light from the charm grew brighter, spreading across the battlefield like a tide.

The titan howled, its body writhing as the light touched it. Cracks spread across its form, the fire within it flaring brighter as though struggling to escape. The shadow creatures dissolved into ash, their forms unable to withstand the power of the light.

But the titan wasn't finished.

With a final, desperate roar, it lunged forward, its claws slicing through the air toward The Fatman. The light from the charm faltered as the creature's massive form descended upon him.

"No!" Branwynn screamed, her staff glowing as she sent a burst of light toward the titan. The attack struck its chest, but it wasn't enough to stop its momentum.

And then Krampus moved.

He was a blur of shadow and fire, his chains snapping toward the titan with blinding speed. They wrapped around its neck and chest, pulling it back with a force that shook the ground. The titan roared, its claws swiping at Krampus, but he didn't let go.

"Finish it!" Krampus growled, his voice strained but unyielding. "Do it now!"

The Fatman raised the charm high, its light flaring brighter than ever. The chamber trembled as the power of the charm reached its peak, the air crackling with energy. The titan thrashed violently, its form beginning to dissolve as the light consumed it.

But in its final moments, the titan's glowing eyes locked on The Fatman. It let out a low, guttural laugh, its voice filled with malice. "You may destroy me," it said, its words echoing through the chamber. "But the balance will demand its price."

With a final, deafening roar, the titan exploded in a burst of fire and shadow, the force of its destruction shaking the entire chamber. The villagers were thrown to the ground, the light from the charm blinding them as it spread outward.

When the light faded, the titan was gone.

The chamber was silent, the oppressive darkness replaced by a faint, golden glow from the remnants of the charm. The villagers slowly rose to their feet, their bodies battered but alive. Branwynn helped Teryn to her feet, her hands trembling as she surveyed the destruction.

But Krampus was nowhere to be seen.

The Fatman staggered, his face pale and his body trembling. He clutched the remnants of the charm, his eyes filled with sorrow. "It's over," he said softly, his voice breaking. "The titan is gone."

But as the villagers began to regroup, a faint sound echoed through the chamber.

A low, rhythmic pounding.

Branwynn's heart sank, her eyes widening in horror. "No..."

The ground beneath them began to tremble again, the cracks in the earth glowing faintly with dark energy. From the depths of the fissure came a voice, low and guttural, filled with rage and despair.

"You cannot escape the void."

CHAPTER THIRTY-ONE

The tremors grew stronger, shaking the very bones of the chamber as cracks spread across the floor. From the jagged fissures, an eerie light began to pulse, its glow unnatural and malevolent. The villagers, battered and exhausted, stood frozen as a voice rose from the depths—a voice that reverberated in their skulls and hearts alike.

"You thought this was the end," it hissed, low and guttural. "You thought your light could snuff out the void."

Branwynn gripped her staff, its faint glow casting shaky shadows on the walls. "It can't still be alive," she whispered, though the fear in her voice betrayed her doubt.

The Fatman stumbled forward, the remnants of his charm crumbling in his hands. His face was pale, his eyes hollow. "This is something else," he said quietly. "Something far older."

From the fissure, a form began to rise.

It was no longer a beast of shadow and fire, nor even the titan they had just destroyed. This was pure darkness made manifest, its shifting form defying comprehension. Eyes, too many to count, blinked open across its body, each one burning with cold, unyielding light. Its voice, when it spoke, carried the weight of centuries.

"I am the First Void," it said, its tone calm yet filled with terrible authority. "I was before your gods. Before your balance. I will be after."

Helgrid stepped forward, her hammer raised. "I don't care how old you are," she growled. "You're not leaving this pit."

The Void's many eyes fixed on her, and it let out a laugh—low and mocking. "You are but embers, fading and insignificant. Do you truly believe you can stand against eternity?"

Before Helgrid could respond, one of its tendrils lashed out, striking her with brutal force. She flew across the chamber, slamming into the wall with a sickening crack. The hammer fell from her grasp as she crumpled to the ground, unmoving.

"Helgrid!" Branwynn screamed, rushing toward her, but another tendril shot out, blocking her path. It swiped at her, but Krampus's chains snapped forward, intercepting the attack.

Krampus emerged from the shadows, his form scarred and battered but unbroken. His amber eyes blazed as his chains rattled in warning. "You are not eternal," he growled, his voice like the grinding of stone. "You're just old."

The Void hissed, its form shifting as it turned to face him. "And you are just stubborn."

Krampus didn't respond. He lunged forward, his chains snapping toward the Void with ferocious speed. The metal links struck true, wrapping around one of its massive limbs and pulling tight. The Void roared, its many eyes narrowing as it lashed out with its tendrils.

The villagers rallied behind him. Branwynn raised her staff, her magic surging as she sent a burst of light toward the Void's core. Teryn and Takrin flanked it, their weapons slicing through its shifting form in a desperate attempt to weaken it.

The Void retaliated with terrifying precision. One tendril swept through the air, narrowly missing Branwynn but striking Teryn with enough force to knock her unconscious. Another tendril wrapped around Takrin's leg, dragging him toward the fissure.

"Hold on!" Branwynn shouted, sending a bolt of magic to sever the tendril. Takrin fell to the ground, gasping, but alive.

The Fatman stood at the edge of the battle, his body trembling as he clutched the remnants of his charm. "This won't be enough," he murmured, his voice filled with despair. "We need more."

Krampus turned toward him, his chains still holding the Void at bay. "There's no more time!" he snarled. "Do what you can!"

The Void laughed, its many eyes glowing brighter. "Do you feel it? The inevitability of my return?" It lunged forward, its form expanding as it consumed the light around it. "Your world belongs to me now."

The ground began to collapse, the fissure widening as the Void's presence grew stronger. The villagers fell back, their weapons barely slowing its advance. Branwynn stumbled, her staff dimming as her magic faltered.

"We can't stop it!" she cried, her voice breaking.

And then, The Fatman moved.

His steps were slow, deliberate, as he walked toward the Void. The remnants of his charm glowed faintly in his hands, their light flickering like the last embers of a dying fire.

"Old magic still has its place," he said softly, his voice steady despite the fear in his eyes. "Even against the void."

The Void paused, its many eyes turning to focus on him. "You think you can sacrifice yourself and stop me?" it hissed. "You are as foolish as the rest."

The Fatman smiled, a sad, weary smile. "Not just me."

Before the Void could react, The Fatman raised his charm high, its light flaring brighter than it had ever been. The ground trembled violently, the fissure sealing itself as the light spread outward, consuming everything in its path.

Krampus roared, his chains snapping as he lunged toward The Fatman. "What are you doing?!"

The Fatman turned to him, his eyes filled with sorrow and resolve. "I'm doing what must be done."

The light grew blinding, and in that moment, Branwynn understood. The Fatman wasn't just sacrificing himself—he was offering the last remnants of the old magic, the very essence of the balance, to seal the Void forever.

The Void let out a deafening roar, its form writhing and dissolving as the light consumed it. "This is not the end!" it howled, its many eyes blinking shut one by one. "The void is eternal!"

With a final, blinding flash, the chamber collapsed.

When the dust settled, the villagers found themselves standing in silence. The fissure was gone, the shadows banished, and the oppressive weight of the Void had lifted. The chamber was no longer a place of darkness but a quiet, empty space.

Krampus stood in the center, his chains slack at his sides. His amber eyes were fixed on the spot where The Fatman had stood, now empty. He didn't move, didn't speak.

Branwynn approached him slowly, her staff glowing faintly. "He... he saved us," she said softly, her voice trembling. "He saved everyone."

Krampus's claws tightened around his chains, his gaze unyielding. "At what cost?"

The villagers began to gather around them, their faces etched with exhaustion and grief. Helgrid, her injuries bandaged, placed a hand on Branwynn's shoulder. "We'll honor him," she said quietly. "The world will know what he did."

But as they began to make their way out of the chamber, a faint sound stopped them.

It was the soft, melodic tinkling of a bell.

Branwynn froze, her eyes widening. "It can't be..."

From the shadows stepped a figure. He was different now—taller, stronger, with a glow of light that seemed to radiate from within. His face was lined with age but filled with peace, and his eyes held a quiet warmth that made the villagers gasp.

It was The Fatman.

Or, rather, what he had become.

"I couldn't leave you," he said softly, his voice carrying a power that was both familiar and new. "Not entirely."

Krampus stepped forward, his chains rattling as he approached the glowing figure. "You're... different."

The Fatman smiled, his presence filling the chamber with a warmth they hadn't felt in days. "The balance needed a guardian," he said simply. "And I'm still here."

The villagers watched in stunned silence as Krampus extended a clawed hand. For a moment, The Fatman hesitated, then clasped it tightly.

"Together," Krampus said, his voice low but steady. "We'll keep it in balance."

And as they ascended from the depths of the fissure, the first snow of the season began to fall, blanketing the battlefield in a quiet, peaceful white.

The void was gone.
The balance was restored.
And a new legend was born.

Krampus

ABOUT THE AUTHOR

    Ladies and gentlemen, step right up to "Where the Magic Happens" - a literary circus that'll make your bookshelf do backflips! Meet Patti, the ringmaster of this wordy wonderland! She's not just an Executive Producer; she's a word-wrangling wizard, conjuring up an animated TV series based on "ELLIOT FINDS A HOME." It's the tail-wagging tale of a thumbs-up pup and his silent sidekick, proving that you don't need words when you've got opposable digits and a heart of gold!

Hold onto your bestseller lists, folks! This Polygon Entertainment superstar has hit the USA TODAY jackpot and Amazon's #1 spot more times than a cat has lives. With 7 dozen books under her belt, she's got more genres than a chameleon has colors. From Urban Fantasy to Horror, she's been spinning yarns longer than your grandma's knitting needles!

But wait, there's more! Patti's life is like a celebrity bingo card:

She rocked "Romper Room" at 4, probably making the other kids look like amateur rompers.

She rubbed elbows with Captain Kangaroo and Mr. Green Jeans. (No word on whether the jeans were actually green.)

She shared a train ride and a sandwich with Sidney Poitier. Talk about a meal ticket to stardom!

She high-fived President Nixon at the circus. Who knew the circus could get any more political?

She went to school with David Copperfield. We assume she didn't disappear during attendance.

She roller-skated with pre-famous John Travolta. Grease lightning, indeed!

She sipped cocoa with Abe Vigoda. Fish never tasted so sweet!

When she's not busy being a literary legend, Patti's juggling roles faster than a circus performer. Teacher, grandma, furparent - she does it all with a smile that could light up a haunted house.

Speaking of haunted houses, meet the "Queen of Halloween" herself! This Wiccan High Priestess is stirring up stories spookier than a skeleton's dance moves. Her books are flying off the shelves faster than witches on broomsticks, so follow her on social media or risk missing out on the hocus-pocus!

So, come one, come all, to Patti's phantasmagorical world of words! It's more exciting than a roller coaster, more magical than a rabbit in a hat, and more diverse than a box of assorted chocolates. Don't be shy - step into the spotlight and join the literary party where the pages turn themselves and the stories never end!

Patti Petrone Miller